Shannon—

Enjoy the journey!

RIPPLE

RIPPLE

THE RITE OF THE IVY SERIES

Heather Dunn

Copyright © 2016 by Heather Dunn.

Library of Congress Control Number: 2016910452
ISBN: Hardcover   978-1-5245-1304-7
             Softcover   978-1-5245-1303-0
             eBook   978-1-5245-1301-6

All rights reserved. No part of this book may be reproduced or transmitted in any form or by any means, electronic or mechanical, including photocopying, recording, or by any information storage and retrieval system, without permission in writing from the copyright owner.

This is a work of fiction. Names, characters, places and incidents either are the product of the author's imagination or are used fictitiously, and any resemblance to any actual persons, living or dead, events, or locales is entirely coincidental.

Any people depicted in stock imagery provided by Thinkstock are models, and such images are being used for illustrative purposes only.
Certain stock imagery © Thinkstock.

Print information available on the last page.

Rev. date: 07/21/2016

To order additional copies of this book, contact:
Xlibris
1-888-795-4274
www.Xlibris.com
Orders@Xlibris.com
739292

INTRODUCTION

I promise to keep this brief.

Thank you, first off, for giving this book a chance to come to life in your mind's eye. All I can ask is that you approach the world I have created with an open heart and a sense of humor. This story has very much written itself, the people, places, and things in it creations all my own, and I would like to think this is a compilation of all the voices in my head getting a chance to be heard.

I can only hope you will enjoy them and learn from them as they have certainly taught me how to view the world in a different light.

What I hope you will find among these pages is a story of love, hope, and inspiration to be something bigger than we all seem to think we can. As Gandhi so prophetically spoke, "Be the change you wish to see in the world"; that is the running theme in this book, and it will continue in the ones to follow.

Life in this world is full of daunting tasks and unbidden feelings that change courses already written to create new lines in an ever-tangled web. I named this book *RIPPLE* because at its center is one girl, and like a stone tossed into a pool of stagnant water, it all starts with *her*. It is through her that lives begin to change, hope is found and lost, and love springs up where it is least expected . . .

In a time that no one remembers, in a land that has never been, there lived a girl named Kiera Spero.

This is her world.

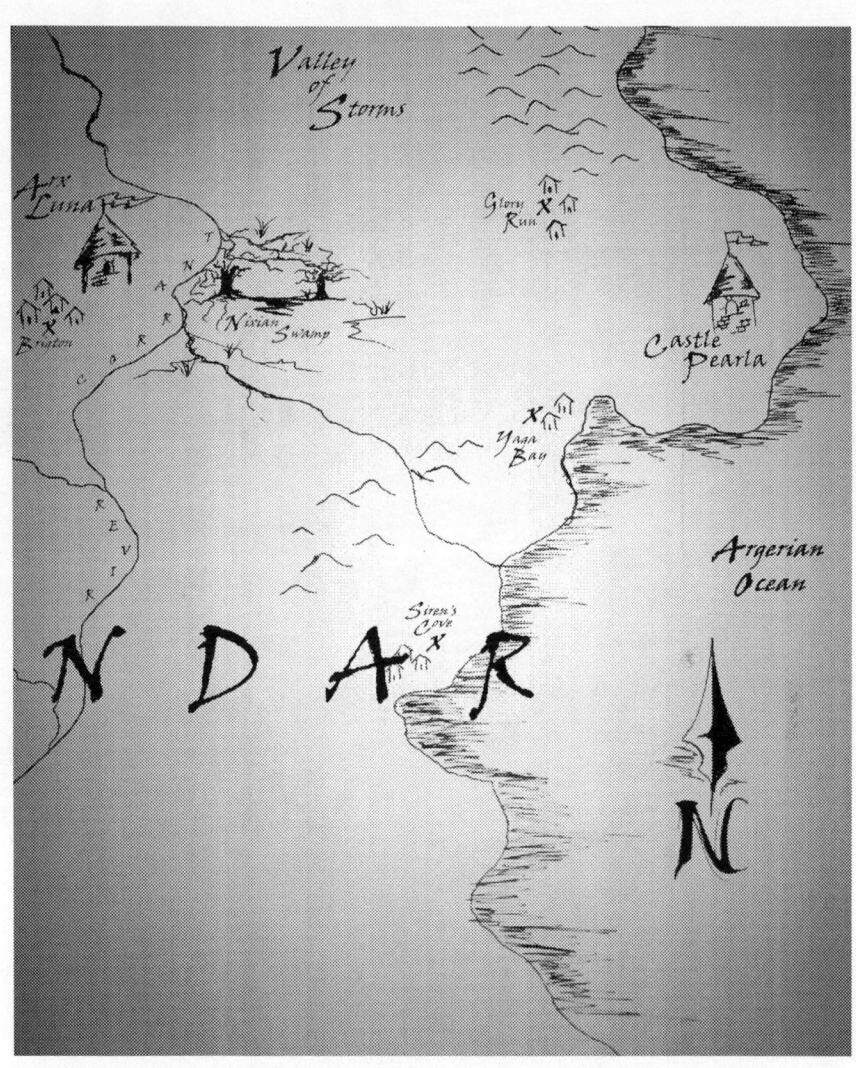

ONE

Where are you, Darian?

The thought snaked across her mind like the rivulet of sweat that was trickling its way down her back to further soak the hardened leather bodice under her long, green cotton tunic. She felt the muscles of her legs rebelling against the thigh straps that held the sheath for her dagger and the three throwing knives she carried on her right leg, but she didn't dare move.

Kiera crouched low in the shade of the underbrush, but under the excruciatingly hot afternoon sun that had wilted much of the forest, she only barely blended in with the foliage surrounding her. She couldn't help swaying slightly on the balls of her feet as dehydration set in and slowly sapped her energy, the subtle movement making her feel painfully visible. Kiera slowly reached her left hand out to steady herself and support her weight on the tips of her fingers, finding the ground hot to the touch.

She could smell the leaves as they baked in the sweltering summer heat, their clean, bright scent mingling with the tang of her own perspiration and the musk of the hot, wet leather clinging to her flesh. Dust covered her brown boots and left muddy smears across her forehead where she had swiped at the stinging sweat a few minutes ago, trying to keep it out of her green eyes. Her skin itched, her mouth was dry, and her hair felt too heavy even tied back into a long, glimmering line of white down her back.

Kiera breathed shallowly, her black glass dagger clutched so tightly in her right hand she could hear the leather on the hilt creak softly as she held the deadly curved ten-inch blade angled back against her wrist, resting in the well-worn groove of her thick hide bracer. She stayed down, motionless save for the flicker of her eyes, watching.

And waiting.

It's too damned hot under here, she thought, and Kiera knew she had to move. It was risky, but the sun was beating down too strongly to stay where she was, the foliage too sparse to shade her completely, and she was too exposed. She hadn't seen Darian in nearly an hour . . .

She took the chance and darted toward a nearby oak with sprawling branches and a thicker canopy.

It was the opportunity Darian had been waiting for.

She just barely heard the near-silent buffeting of air as the Aeroyn beat his wings only once behind her in the windless afternoon.

Kiera knew immediately that she was caught.

Almost, bird. Good try.

She heard Darian's surprised hiss as she simultaneously hit her knees and lay backward, her back flat against the ground, the soles of her boots digging into the backs of her thighs, his outstretched claws missing her by a hair's breadth as he swooped down on her from behind. Kiera used the momentum of her fall to swing her dagger back over her head like an inverted pendulum with a grace that was sure and skilled, and she felt the blade cut neatly through the heavy knot of fabric that held Darian's lightweight battlecloth to his hips.

She smiled to herself when he shrieked at his sudden nakedness, the long piece of silky gray fabric fluttering to the ground in his wake. Kiera sat up just enough to see Darian land a few feet away, wrapping his huge black wings forward protectively around himself, the dusky skin of his face flushing to a deep orange and his auburn braids falling over his hazel, almond-shaped eyes. Darian looked suspiciously like a woman caught undressing behind a screen.

"Damn it, Kiera! *Every* time we train . . . *Why* does something of mine get *ruined?*" Darian bellowed, sounding much more irritated than he really was.

Kiera quickly righted herself, sheathing her dagger securely under her tunic as she caught up the light piece of clothing that had been his only adornment other than the marred and ancient iron bracers that perpetually graced his wrists. She sauntered up to him, holding the cloth out by her fingertips, a smirk tugging dangerously at the corners of her mouth, her laughter barely contained.

"Is that really *my* fault? Maybe you should learn to wear more than just a *napkin* when we do this," Kiera quipped, a mischievous glint hiding in her eyes.

Darian narrowed his eyes at her as he reached out from between his feathered wings to grab the loincloth from her hand, but with one blindingly fast motion, he caught her wrist instead. Opening his wings, he pulled her against his naked chest, pinning Kiera's arms at her sides, the fabric in her hand suddenly forgotten. He glared down at her, a sadistic grin spreading across his face, his sharp white fangs gleaming against the dark gray of his lips. Darian was every bit the predator as his wings wrapped forward tightly around Kiera like a cocoon, trapping her against him.

There was no escape.

"Don't. You. *Dare!*" Kiera knew what was coming, and she breathed each word with a forceful malice she did not really feel though her eyes were wide with fearful anticipation. The sun was beating down on them, and Darian held her firmly in place in front of him, his naked body crushed against her on this too hot, too dry afternoon.

Kiera felt fresh sweat break out under her clothes. She was stuck, and he knew it. Darian bent his head as if to kiss her, and she cringed and squirmed, trying to pull away. His hot, sour breath assaulted her nostrils as he licked the side of her face with his tongue.

"Let me go, *beast!*" she shrieked, struggling harder. Kiera was trying to kick him, to break away, but his grip might as well have been made of stone.

She knew it was useless. She fought against him anyway.

Darian started shaking, his laughter flowing from deep within, and he knew how much she loathed him at that moment. He swept his tongue upward a second time, covering her chin to temple with slimy spit. His tongue caught some of her short, blunt bangs on the upstroke, his saliva making her hair stand straight up.

The Aeroyn was laughing so hard he was starting to feel weak. He released her mid-squirm so unexpectedly that Kiera stumbled back gracelessly and landed squarely on her backside, dust fleeing from underneath her as her rear made contact with the hard, dry dirt. Darian hugged himself, peals of laughter ringing through the trees, his nakedness completely forgotten as Kiera wiped furiously at her sweaty, muddy, spit-covered face with her sleeves and the hem of her soiled shirt.

She looked up at him dejectedly from the ground, her glorious white hair a mess of disheveled strays and half out of the tie, her bangs sticking up every which way. The kohl that usually so carefully lined her eyes had been smeared into large circles and streaked across her left temple, mixed now with dark lines of dirt on her fine pale skin.

Kiera looked absolutely tragic.

Darian couldn't stop laughing.

He was gasping for breath as he made his way clumsily toward the base of the large oak Kiera had been headed for, groping for the trunk with one hand and holding his stomach with the other. The Aeroyn leaned against the bark in the slightly cooler shade, his laughter bringing tears to his eyes, and he slowly sank into a sitting position as he slid helplessly down the ground.

When he finally quieted to short bursts of chuckling, Darian stretched his legs out in front of him, folding his arms behind his head and crossing his ankles, ignoring the battlecloth on the ground between them. He was enjoying the hot, dry air on his skin as he watched her, a wicked grin plastered to his face as his breathing returned to a rhythm closer to normal. He suppressed a giggle as he watched Kiera pick herself up off the ground, brushing at her robes and sneaking hateful glances at him.

Even a disheveled mess, Darian still found Kiera startlingly beautiful . . . for a human. Kiera wasn't *delicate* in any way, her features strong and striking, her body heavily framed but well proportioned. Her thick white tresses extended from a widow's peak that was usually hidden behind her bangs, the pearl-white strands melding seamlessly with her pore-less, almost too-pale skin. Her green eyes were large and fringed in black lashes and rimmed in kohl to cut the glare, and her eyebrows were dark as well, their angular shape almost mimicking her high cheekbones. The bridge of her nose bisected her face with a smooth, straight line and ended with the barest upturn. A pale, full-lipped mouth added to her striking beauty, forever warring with itself trying to hold a firm line and blot out the softness when she was angry or stern, her bottom lip one of Darian's favorite places to kiss.

Kiera was tall for a woman; she would have been considered tall even if she had been a man since she stood at nearly six feet. Her body was toned from years of heavy physical training in forest survival and self-defense, and she was well acquainted with a variety of weapons, her favorites her dagger, her throwing knives, and her bare hands. Kiera was strong, fast, and intelligent, and she had a tongue Darian sometimes thought had the past life as a rapier, it was so quick and sharp.

She was also the woman Darian had protected for six years and had loved passionately for the past two. For all intents and purposes, she was his *mate*, and he wasn't at all interested in finding a replacement.

Darian knew what Kiera was capable of, but he also understood her weaknesses, and he exploited them every time they took up training. Today he had waited her out repeatedly, watching her overheat as she sat close to the dry earth, roasting in that heavy leather armor under her light shirt, constantly trying to take her by surprise. Their game of hide-and-seek had started at dawn and almost nine miles west of where they found themselves at midday; they had taken turns tracking each other, creeping further and further from the ruined castle they called home, ending up deep in Baneswood with him naked and her dirty and ravaged with half the day behind them.

At that hour, Kiera was tired, hungry, and ready to head back soon.

Or at least Darian knew she would be, once she had recouped her *dignity*.

Grumbling and brushing angrily at her tunic, Kiera's thirst finally won out, and she stomped toward the brush she had been hiding under, ignoring Darian as she dropped to her knees and crawled partway underneath to retrieve her pack and the half-empty waterskin she had hidden there.

Kiera uncorked the pouch with her teeth and took a deep drink, which she promptly sprayed out of her mouth, sending Darian into a fresh fit of hysterics. The water had gotten too hot, even hidden in the shade, the animal skin lending a sweaty, mineral-heavy taste that caused an immediate rejection like soured milk.

Thoroughly angry and humiliated, Kiera wiped at her mouth hastily with the back of her hand and marched up to Darian, who was laughing helplessly under the tree. She dumped the rest of the foul-tasting water on him before he could move, throwing the bag at his chest once it was empty and glaring at him with her hands on her hips.

Darian shrieked, annoyed that he was suddenly soaking wet as water and tears ran down his face. Kiera knew how much he hated water. Then again, he knew how much she hated being laughed at, and he got his fair revenge when he started giggling again as he replayed that visceral reaction she'd had to the water that now beaded off his skin. Darian tried to climb to his feet, but the muscles of his stomach just didn't want to cooperate.

Kiera huffed in annoyance as she stalked away toward the river that waited just to the south of them and disappeared into the dense foliage. Darian tried to breathe slowly through the convulsive laughter; only when he had finally regained control of himself and could stand did he realize that his battlecloth, like Kiera, was gone.

Grinning like an idiot and chuckling softly, Darian started after her on foot, following the trail of her scent on every low branch he passed, his whole body still trembling too hard to even attempt to fly.

Two

Kiera gasped as the icy run off from the mountains of the north hit her face from her cupped hands, but she felt immediately cooler. She stripped off her tunic and dipped it into the cold water, wringing it out to release her sweat and clean off the dust. Her leather bodice of form-fitting armor that bound her breasts painfully was wretchedly hot, but Kiera knew that if she got it wet in the stream, it would swell and then she would chafe, and the last thing she wanted was blisters on her back. Better to leave the obnoxious piece of armor in place where the sweat had adhered it to her torso and peel it off like a thick fruit skin later.

She hung her shirt over a low tree branch alongside Darian's loincloth and sat down on a rock at the edge of the stream to remove her brown knee-high boots and the second dagger she kept hidden there. Kiera pulled her tight black leggings up to her knees and dipped her toes tentatively into the cold water, shivering slightly as her body rapidly cooled in the midday heat. She took the tie out of her long hair and let it flow freely, raking it smooth again with her fingers.

The soft rustle of dried grass behind her signaled Darian's arrival, and Kiera glanced over her shoulder to find him standing less than ten feet away, leaning against the tree that now bore their clothes, his powerful arms folded over his broad chest. Kiera couldn't help but stare at him. She thought he looked absolutely splendid in his nakedness.

So very human and yet so very . . . not.

It wasn't the first time that thought had surfaced in her mind. Without his wings, Darian would have closely resembled a human in face and limb, but with them, he became a dark angel, his fine features making him easy to openly gawk at. As an Aeroyn, he most closely resembled a gargoyle crossed with a seraphim, some of his more human features obscured by traits that were very obviously of a different origin entirely.

Darian stood nearly six and a half feet tall, about average for his race, and he was muscled similarly to a man, except his chest was broader and his hips a bit narrower, making him appear a little top-heavy. His bones were hollow like that of a bird, making him almost a hundred pounds lighter than he looked, and the decrease in weight meant there was less mass to move; Darian's reflexes reminded Kiera of lightning. His wings were enormous and were covered with beautiful black feathers that were silken to the touch and shimmered with an oily rainbow sheen to them as they shifted in the sun. The mottle of his skin created a subtle shading of tan to gray that helped him blend into the shadows, the gray seeming to accumulate in the creases and valleys of his skin, making his musculature look superimposed, almost painted on.

His skin was smooth and slightly downy, but the hair was fine and very short with uniformity similar to fur that thickened and thinned with the seasons. Darian kept his auburn hair rather long, usually to the middle of his shoulders; it peaked above his brows, arching back sharply away from his face and his slightly pointed ears, nearly always kept in tight braids with beads of bone and jet woven in at random. The skin of his face was smoother, devoid of hair save dark brows and lashes, leaving his hazel eyes, full mouth, wide nose, and strong jaw exposed.

A large black tribal tattoo covered his entire left shoulder, swirling from the base of his neck to the middle of his upper arm, wrapping forward to his chest, punctuated by a black-and-red braided leather band that circled his arm just above the bicep. The short talons that tipped his fingers and toes were dark gray, almost black, and were sharper than her glass dagger, which made touching each other a rather delicate affair.

Darian had seen almost three hundred summers pass by the time Kiera came into his world, and he was still considered quite young. The Aeroyn wasn't immortal, but he may as well have been: no human alive at the moment would ever live to see Darian die of old age. Several more generations would pass before he would be considered *old* by his people since approximately ten human years equated to just one for an Aeroyn. His elders had all been well over six hundred when he had last had contact with them, and there we many that had lived longer still. There were less than a thousand Aeroyn left Darian knew of, but there was always the possibility of rogues and small groups that hadn't ever tried to join the tribe. Not that it mattered to him anymore . . .

He's such a beautiful pain in the ass.

Kiera roamed Darian's body with her eyes, her gaze following the trail of dark *fur* that streaked the center of his abdomen to his pelvis, the hair that framed his heavy sex darker and coarser.

Kiera felt heat come into her face, and she quickly turned her attention back to the slow-moving current of the stream. She watched small silver fish darting about on the creek bed, no more than an inch or two beneath the surface.

"Feeling better, *Princess*?"

Kiera could hear the smile in his deep voice as Darian used the pet name he knew she loathed almost as much as his sticky face lickings. It had become a sort of twisted joke between them, and even after six years, it still made Kiera cringe.

"I would if you went *away*," Kiera answered curtly, not bothering to look at him as she leaned back on her elbows, closing her eyes, stretching her long body out on the rock and concentrating on the icy water nipping at her toes. Kiera's pale skin never held a tan as it was, and Darian usually teased her that he didn't understand why she liked to lie out when she just reflected the light, but she didn't care. The warmth of the sun always made her feel at peace.

She heard Darian approach her from behind with quiet careful steps, the grass rustling as he knelt down beside her. Her heart quickened as his shadow eclipsed the light; his chestnut hair mimicked a wreath of flames as the sun streaked through it when she barely opened her eyes.

"You're in my light, *beast*."

Darian didn't move, and she knew what he wanted, but she was going to make him work for it. Kiera would have been lying if she said she didn't want it too, the hunger for his touch and his roughness forever a delicious shock to her, but after the events of the day, she was tired and irritated. Her companion would have to tread carefully if he wanted her to play along.

"Shut up, *brat*," Darian laughed as he went to his knees and leaned over her, kissing Kiera gently, one hand holding the back of her head while the other searched out the lacing on the front of her leather armor. With a swift, sure stroke of his index finger, he reduced the lacing to shreds, and her bodice split like an overripe melon.

"Damn it, Darian . . ." Kiera smiled and laughed softly against his kiss. "*Every* time you want to make love to me, something of *mine* gets *ruined*!"

Three

"Don't move," the husky whisper commanded in the king's ear. "You have nothing to fear from me, but do not call your guards."

The man backed away quietly and bowed deeply.

"Sire, my name is Delámer, and I am the finest bounty hunter in this realm. Perhaps you've heard of me..." Delámer paused expectantly but was met with silence. Eryce couldn't help but wonder, *Why the production?* as he turned to face someone far bolder than bright, considering the king didn't need any assistance if he chose to snuff the life before him. The theatrics of appearing out of thin air and using a disguise felt a little over-the-top since Delámer could have just walked through the front gate of the castle and requested an audience instead of choosing to materialize like the ghost Eryce seemed to be chasing, but the pompous act the man was putting on almost made him smile.

"My king, I come in search of information regarding the woman you call Bane. If she lives, sire, *I* will find her."

"Oh, she *lives*, make no mistake about that. Neither my troops nor the Sukolai have ever seen her when they clean up the *mess* she leaves after each attack, but I *know* she lives. She haunts that damned forest and kills my men!" Eryce snarled, his temper getting the better of him at the mention of a name he had come to loathe.

The green eyes of the stranger standing near the King of Rhonendar flashed darkly from behind the half mask he wore, obviously on guard. Eryce was still trying to cover his surprise as he studied the man that had appeared from thin air, looking hi over as he decided how much he trusted the man to speak the truth. Taller than Eryce's six-foot frame by a good four or five inches, with short blond hair slicked back from his masked face, his well-muscled but slender frame clad from head to toe in expensive black . . .

While the king couldn't see any obvious weapons, he knew well enough that that meant nothing. The stranger certainly *looked* like he could be threatening, but Eryce was having a hard time judging if any of the possible *threat* was aimed at *him*.

As far as the promise of finding Bane, well, Eryce had heard too many men—who were bigger and stronger than this one, with a reputation to precede them—say those same words in the past six months, and they had all yet to make good upon a single vow. The problem was Bane hid too well when she wasn't killing the men who were unlucky enough to cross her path in the northeastern forests of his lands, and she continued to leave a trail of would-be hunters in her wake. The bounty for Bane had increased little by little after each recovered body made the King of Rhonendar more inclined to punish her as the months went by and no one showed with her in shackles. The reward had been doubled after the first of his Sukolai had been slaughtered three months before, and it had stayed high ever since.

In fact, every man who worked for Eryce had instructions to bring Bane in *alive, coherent, and untouched*, as he had plans for her when they finally did, but he wouldn't complain if they simply brought her in dead. Either way, Eryce wanted all five of his senses assaulted by her presence, and he wanted the culling of his troops to *stop*. That Bane had evaded him for so long was driving Eryce to distraction. He likened her to fine silver sand: always slipping through his tight grip. That thought irritated him, and Eryce grit his straight white teeth, struggling to keep his composure in front of his sudden *guest*, but he could feel his anger crawling up from the very pit of his stomach to leave a bitterness burning in the back of his throat. He had just returned from a long trek to the Southern Estates and Corengale, attending to business with both the Sukolai and a few of his councilmen, coming home to reports of a dozen losses, all bearing *her* signature.

She was still at large, plaguing the man she refused to bow before to no end.

Eryce turned his broad back to those eyes and the stranger they belonged to, resting his weight on his well-manicured hands as he leaned forward over the map of his kingdom in the castle library. Rhonendar incorporated the fallen kingdoms in its borders, edged with the Argerian Ocean to the east, the Montes Gelu range to the west, and the forbidding wastelands to the north and south that kept his lands protected and tough to breach. With Rhonendar's natural defenses, Eryce was prepared to take on threats from outside his borders; he just hadn't expected for one this annoying to pop up *inside* them.

It had taken him years to get the massive territory he ruled solidified under his name where it had once been divided under three, and Eryce was not about to let someone defy him like she did and live. He took Bane's attacks *personally*, each red marker a reminder that she was laughing at him from those goddess-forsaken woods on the edge of his lands; Baneswood belonged to *him*, and Eryce was frustrated that she was choosing to learn that the hard way. He felt fresh sweat break out under his clothes as his blood pressure rose higher, his anger making the stagnant air in the room turn from uncomfortable to sweltering.

His gaze roamed the uppermost corner of his lands as they were etched into the table before him, scanning for places where *she* could hide, looking for patterns that made sense from the little red pins that had been pushed into the wood to signify where each of her *presents* had been discovered. Party after party of troops and hunters had taken on this task in recent months, and Eryce's men had assured him they had her cornered at the end of last summer in the northern edge of Baneswood after the first few attacks had been reported . . .

Then she had popped up far south of them, leaving a trail of death in her wake as she took out sentries and riders trying to skirt the western edge of the woods, and they were forced to start all over. Eryce had had to keep from joining her endeavor of killing his men when *that* news had reached his ears.

He had been absolutely furious when the snow started to fall, and it had been too cold to send out more than one or two troops at a time to travel along Rhonendar's northern and eastern borders. Bane had seen fit to pick them off when they got too close to Baneswood, totally disrupting his communications with the northeastern portion of his vast kingdom until the snows melted and riders could head out in force again. He hadn't heard from his men in Grant's Perch for months by the time the river thawed enough that their bodies could be fished from the icy waters, and no one had since volunteered to take those empty positions even for better pay.

An entire year that little bitch has eluded me. "Bane" indeed! I will find you. Eryce narrowed his bi-colored eyes at the map, thinking, searching, planning . . .

The king's left eye was still the natural black brown that he had been born with, but the right was pale luminescent lavender. The aggravated expression he sported blighted some of the faint light emanating from his enchanted right eye that now saw more than he had ever wanted it to, but saw nonetheless when it should have been blind. Clean shaven with a wide jaw and subtle cleft in his chin, heavily framed, and broad shouldered, Eryce looked more like one of his own knights than the sovereign of the several thousand square miles that made up his kingdom.

Even on that hot day, Eryce wore clothing more suited for his staff than for himself; he was clad in a finer version of the uniform that was strewn throughout his kingdom on his troops, his emissaries, and the servants of the Arx Luna, the castle he called home and the last still standing in Rhonendar. The finely spun white cotton shirt with long, loose sleeves contrasted with the knee-length navy velvet tabard that bore his crest of a large golden lion's head clutching a globe in its jaws, while fitted black cotton pants and polished black boots completing the ensemble. His tabard was cinched with a gold plate belt at his hips, and he wore just one piece of jewelry: his simple gold wedding band.

Intelligent, bold, and reasonable to a point, Eryce was certainly capable of running a kingdom and taking on the challenges that came with it. Holding the title of *king* was what he had been born, bred, and raised to do, and he came from a long lineage of nobility that would continue on if he ever named an heir. He had been destined for one throne and had ended up claiming three, uniting the kingdoms of Ohnasta, Andar, and Falyyn under his crest and crown through cunning, perseverance, and the bold use of hired mercenaries.

He reigned through cunning tactics and fear, and his subjects were well aware that the relative *peace* they lived in was fragile. Missteps would cost them dearly.

The King of Rhonendar usually showed a calm façade to the rest of the world, but those who knew him well were not unaccustomed to his fits of rage, and he wasn't afraid to make those who stood in his way bend to his will by threat of death. Those who couldn't be bent were broken, sometimes with their entire family at their side as a reminder to the rest of his world that he would not tolerate the presence of any that would work against him. It was rare that subjects felt justified in challenging that particular king and rarer still that they lived through it.

Eryce wasn't *liked*, but his powerful reach was respected, and *that* was what he was after. He personally believed that the only person who should *like* him was his wife. Everyone else was could fear him just as long as they did what he wanted.

Eryce liked it better that way.

He had been a king for nearly fifteen years and the sovereign of Rhonendar for almost six, but Eryce still hated donning a crown, finding it both cumbersome and pompous. His people *knew* who he was, and with the amount of travelling he did through Rhonendar, Eryce felt that if he needed a crown to be recognized by anyone in his kingdom, then he wasn't doing a very good job of being the ruler he wanted to be remembered as.

Though his travels took him far and wide, returning home was usually a welcome idea, but when he had returned *this* time, Eryce had been confronted with news he had *not* wanted to hear. There were other, more pressing matters to attend to, especially those concerning the rumor of a coup among his councilmen to cause a civil war and oust Eryce that had cropped up during his absence, but he couldn't even concentrate. The Sukolai, his personal group of mercenaries, still needed his consent for new recruits. Taxes needed to be levied. The menu for his forty-third birthday celebration needed his approval.

He had been back at the Arx for less than two days, and he was already too caught up in trying to find *her*.

His gaze roamed the map he had seen just about every corner of, the little red markers spattered across its northeastern corner like cancerous sores where *she* had left the bodies of those unlucky enough to cross her path over the past twelve months alone incredibly infuriating. Eryce hated each and every one of the crimson-tipped pins that lined all three borders of Baneswood and filtered into the Glenfolds, the expanse of open plains between his castle and the forest she had usurped. He hated even more that those pins had *multiplied* while he was away for three weeks, the newest ones clustered along the edge of the Oriens River and the southeastern corner of the woods themselves.

Bane had been bolder as of late, and her attacks had become more aggressive since Eryce had been sending hunters into Baneswood with greater frequency in recent months specifically to find *her*. Men from all over the kingdom had lined up to take on the quest of the mysterious threat in those dark woods, and Eryce had stopped counting two months ago when the numbers of those who had not returned reached into the high twenties and continued to climb. Once those numbers included the death of one of his Sukolai, he had given up keeping track. It didn't seem to matter who they were or if they went alone or in a group of ten.

No one ever came back.

Not able bodied and breathing, anyway.

The mangled corpses were always found the same way: strung high in a tree and stripped naked, the legs and feet and most of the lower torso missing where the black wolves had been able to tear the meat off the poor bastard while he still lived, his last screams etched on his face. Panic and pain would stop their heart before they bled to death . . . if they were lucky. Eryce didn't know exactly how many men had been removed from service at her hand, but he knew *who* many of them were; somewhere on his desk was a list of names he refused to look at.

She had certainly made *that* part simple enough. The bodies were easy to identify since they were left with a note that was usually found either clutched in the hand of the dead man or nailed to the tree from which an empty rope swung freely. The name of the unfortunate soul was always written in what Eryce assumed was the victim's own handwriting because no two were alike, the mean and arrogant tactic one for which he secretly liked her. He kept a small wooden box of those scraps of parchment on the edge of the table; Eryce referred to them as *love notes*, and he hated when anyone brought him any to add to the collection.

Especially because they almost never brought him just *one*.

Even now he found he was *waiting* on a few since three of his best field scouts were unaccounted for and hadn't been seen for nearly a month. Rumors had reached him that bets were being placed among his men as to where those particular carcasses would be found, and Eryce had immediately put a stop to *that* nonsense by deeming it punishable by banishment to the damned woods themselves if anyone was caught gambling on the lives of their comrades. *She* was already laughing at him. He didn't need his troops to join her.

What irritated Eryce more than the loss of men was *who* she chose to leave for those beasts of the forests, and it baffled him that *they* had died and *she* plagued him still. Several had been excellent hunters and skilled killers, men he had wanted to recruit for the Sukolai or his legion, but she had removed them from service before the transfer could be made. That he could blame a *female* for those losses made him irate.

A woman should never be this big of a nuisance . . .

It hadn't been until the beginning of the summer and two days after the festival of the equinox that Eryce had discovered he was chasing a woman; he, and everyone who had intimate knowledge of the multiple deaths, had always assumed it was a band of men. That idea had come to a screeching halt when a terrified horse had run through the city surrounding the Arx Luna burdened with a bloody sack made from familiar blue fur. Bane had been kind enough to send the *whole* man directly to him that time, albeit in pieces and gift-wrapped in the pelt of his own dog, and had given Eryce a name to curse under his breath every time he glanced at the map in his library.

Eryce still had the sweet little note she had pinned to the saddle of the first of the two Sukolai she had managed to slay to date, the handwriting distinctly feminine:

> *Great King,*
> *Thank you for the gift.*
> *Regretfully, I must return it to you.*
> *It seems to be broken.*
>
> *~Bane~*

Eryce had laughed when he read it after one of his knights had handed it to him with shaking hands. At first, her clever words made him wish she was working *for* instead of *against* him, but with *two* Sukolai having been delivered this way, the second showing up at the gate just two weeks ago, made him wish he could return the favor. *Slowly.*

He still couldn't figure out how she had pierced the hide of those iron-coated hounds, much less how she was able to bring down the man himself when more vicious foe had failed to leave behind a slight scar here or a bite mark there. Rumor had it that she didn't travel alone; by the way the bodies were discovered, some suspected she had an Aeroyn at her side, but they were rumors Eryce hadn't been able to solidly confirm. He was *very* interested to find out if that was true.

This man, this *Delámer*, had gone to a lot of trouble to show he was willing and able to track her down, and Eryce found he was mildly hopeful this particular hunter might stand a chance at success. It was rare that he ever met the men chasing down the bounty in Baneswood; they were directed to speak to ether one of the Sukolai or the captain of the guard of the Arx since most were *unfit* to be announced in the hall or stand before the king, but this man had ignored protocol completely, entering the castle undetected in the middle of the day. Polite, well groomed, and a little arrogant, Delámer played on Eryce's curiosity, and the King of Rhonendar was already considering using him for other work *if* he proved himself useful.

The king was more than willing to pay the man he was studying thoughtfully from the corner of his eye, but he doubted he would ever see Delámer alive again once he took to the mission. Eryce didn't care if the man died. He just didn't want to be disappointed *again*.

Eryce set his mouth in a lipless line as he debated his level of trust for this man, the muscles of his mouth pulling the scars that ran down into his cheekbone painfully taut, the old, dull ache only adding to his malicious thoughts and fueling his anger. He took a deep breath as he raked his fingers back through his thick black hair, now riddled with gray, pulling it roughly as he dragged his nails across his scalp and the action sending pleasurable chills down his spine.

"Gather what you can, and report back. I want to know where she hides, what she does, how she kills. You have until the double full moon, Delámer. *Find* her. Bring her *here* if you can manage that. And take care: there's rumor of an Aeroyn following her, and I'll add to the reward if you bring it down . . ."

. . . should you survive, of course. Eryce kept that thought to himself as he finally turned to Delámer, folding his arms across his powerful chest, regarding the masked man with a grim expression.

"Force doesn't seem to work, so I might suggest trying something else. Gain her trust if you can find no other way, but bring her to me alive and in good condition. If *anyone* is going to cause her pain, it's going to be *me*. If you do not show up with her by the time the Lunar Festival is upon us, I will have that goddess-forsaken forest overrun with soldiers and burnt to the ground. Then all she will have to hide behind is *ashes*."

Eryce glanced back at the map, studying the pattern of death markers that studded the top right corner of his kingdom yet again.

"The Glenfolds. She circles them, always coming back to them. Start—" The king turned back to his guest and was struck speechless when he found he was talking to an empty room. Eryce stared at the spot where the man had stood, his lips still slightly parted as though he meant to continue speaking. He finally closed his mouth, an icy smile forcing its way onto his face, the scars tightening painfully.

Delámer certainly held *promise*.

I hope you are ready, my dear. You have had your fun, but your expenses are high, Eryce thought as he stole one last glance at the map before striding out of the room, the heels of his hard-soled boots echoing loudly down the empty stone hall, the velvet tabard rustling softly, the links of his gold plate belt tinkling with each step.

He didn't hear any of this over the thoughts running rampant in his head, fantasies of his hands around a soft throat and the look of fear in her eyes, the life slowly being choked out of her . . .

Bane, your time is at an end!

Four

Her shrill scream cut through the sweltering stagnant air so forcefully that an enormous flock of startled birds took to wing within a half-mile radius.

Kiera rose up onto her hands and knees, retching violently, the smell of burnt flesh still clinging to her memories seeming to drift into reality, making her gag. A thin stream of sour yellow liquid dribbled from her mouth onto the dirt, the screams still lingering in the back of her throat, trying to force past the bile that fought its way up from her nearly empty stomach. Fresh tears coursed down her face in a new torrent, diverting from the path laid by the ones that had been seeping from between her closed eyes as she slept under the warm grove of evergreens beside Darian.

They had lain down naked in the shade upon the long cloak Kiera perpetually carried in her pack, trying to escape the midday sun. While Darian seemed to be rather immune to the high temperature, Kiera would have chafed and become further dehydrated in the still heat that seemed to emanate not just from above but also from the earth itself, liquid waves floating upward as if reaching for the cloudless sky high above them. It was cooler beneath the branches, out of the sun's view, but not by much.

It seemed as though all living things had been oppressed into slumber by the stifling afternoon heat. No birds had been singing in the trees, no small animals had scurried through the underbrush, and the world around them had dozed quietly . . .

But Kiera's violent screams had torn the world around her from its heat-induced nap, reminding the inhabitants of the forest that it was midday and sleep should be reserved for after dark.

Darian was crouched over her, his hand on her back as the retching turned to sobs. Kiera, spent from the heat, the exertion and her terrible nightmares, collapsed on her side, covering her face with her arms as she wept on top of the cloak, her whole body shaking as if wracked with pain. Darian sighed, watching her for several minutes until the sobs eventually melted into hiccups and her breathing slowed to a more reasonable rate. It wasn't until the shaking finally stopped that he felt she would even hear him if he spoke.

"They're getting worse, aren't they?" Darian's deep voice was roughened by both interrupted sleep and his own emotional reaction of watching that terrible pain he couldn't help her through. Kiera didn't answer as she stared past him at nothing, trying to slow her racing heart and her wild thoughts, desperate to quell her panic.

She didn't need to.

He already knew the answer was *yes*.

The Aeroyn was well aware what those dreams entailed, and he always found himself guiltily thankful that they weren't his. They were of her family and her last few minutes with them as the Sukolai had slaughtered nearly everyone in the castle and set it ablaze. Kiera had survived thanks to her mother, who had been carried away into the night by a dark rider that still haunted her dreams. Darian had known that story for a long time, but it had only been during the past year or so that she had started to dream again and again about that awful night.

More than once, Kiera had woken up screaming. Her nightmare was like a living, breathing demon that haunted her, and it always ended the same way: with her mother being ripped away from her, leaving her alone in the cold moonless night just outside the castle walls. Every single time, Kiera tried to scream after her, and a handful of times, that scream had come through to the world outside her dreams.

Darian was always there to hold her, letting her cry against his chest with his arms enfolding her, protecting her, stroking her hair. He was gentlest with her then, cradling her silently as the bitterness and the anger and the fright came forth in her sobs. Kiera usually felt so drained afterward that she would fall into a dreamless sleep for several hours, her mind and body shutting down completely. On rare occasion, she would stay awake for several days, unable to sleep, until her body gave out and she was too tired to dream at all. If she was really lucky, the dream would stay out of her head for almost a month.

That day had not been one of the lucky ones.

Five

The first thing Kiera noticed when she finally awoke in Darian's arms was that it was already dark. That thought was followed by the realization that she was still naked, though she was thankful to be wrapped in her cloak even if the wool blended with cotton was itchy on her exposed skin. Darian had built a small fire, more for light than for warmth, and stayed near her lest she need him, holding her as he waited for her to come around.

Kiera had blacked out shortly after waking up to her own screams, and she hadn't responded when Darian had called her name repeatedly and shook her or when he picked her up and moved her away from the river to the small clearing where she found herself when she opened her eyes. Now that she was awake, Kiera snuggled against him, thankful to be safe and warm until she looked up at him and saw that Darian was staring sleepily at the fire.

If he's falling asleep during the night hours, then he needs to feed, she thought, suddenly trying to push away from him, but he held her still.

"No. Stay. I'm fine," Darian whispered into her hair as he kissed the top of her head, pulling her protectively against his chest. "I'll go shortly. Just *stay*."

He knew what Kiera was thinking, and she was right to be concerned but not for several more hours. An Aeroyn needed blood to survive, and the night was when they liked to hunt, using their senses and their nocturnal vision to seek out anything warm-blooded that moved. Left too long and his kind would turn aggressive even to those they recognized as friend, but that took days; he would simply be weak and tired if he didn't feed soon, and with Kiera to protect, he didn't want to risk that. He knew he would have to leave soon enough, but in that moment Darian was far more concerned about her well-being than his own.

It was his hunting that kept the black wolves well away from them most of the time, the pack of twenty strong only rarely crossing their path anymore. There was a long-standing unspoken truce that Darian hunted, and the wolves followed; he could smell them on the wind, waiting outside their camp for him to take flight. They happily feasted on the half dead animals he left in his wake *and* the men he left strung up in the trees when they were unlucky enough to be in his way. Bandits, mercenaries, thieves, soldiers . . . Anyone who could be a threat to Kiera was fair game, and Darian had lost count of the bodies he had left hanging like morbid ornaments from the branches of the ladder pines in the forest over the past few years. Eryce only ever found the ones Kiera wanted him to, leaving them strung along the border of Baneswood, warning both the king and his men to stay *out*. The rest were bound low enough that their remains were never discovered.

It had been Kiera's idea to start attacking Eryce's men at all, and it was because of her dreams that they had relentlessly pursued them over the past year, slowly taking pawns from the king in ways that hurt. It all started when Kiera had spotted a Sukolai on the other side of the Oriens River the previous summer; Darian could still remember the horrified look on her face when she had crouched high up in a tree, studying the huge blue dog and the man in the cobalt robes on horseback who had stopped to drink from the Oriens, and how she had fought with him when she had wanted to follow the Sukolai to find out why the man was even there.

The dream had surfaced that same night, and Kiera was so ill from that first nightmare Darian wouldn't let her out of his sight for nearly an entire day, delaying their pursuit of the lone mercenary. She had been furious, and Darian had been silently relieved that the man and his hound were already gone by the time they reached Grant's Perch a few days later.

When they finally got to the Perch and Kiera was able to tear down a notice that the Sukolai were recruiting, she had laughed darkly, the circles forming under her eyes from a few nights of fitful sleep making her look a little mad. She had only wanted to kill thieves and poachers up to that point, avoiding the king's men since they rarely came through the woods anyway, but the appearance of the Sukolai had changed her mind on leaving Eryce's men alone.

Once the dreams had started, none of them were safe; she wanted to go after *anyone* who set foot in her woods, and Darian certainly didn't mind making sure threats to either of them felt as much pain as possible. Aeroyn were naturally aggressive toward outsiders as it was, and Kiera was the only human Darian had never hurt with the intention to kill. He knew his elders would have been more than upset with him if they ever found out about her, or that he protected her.

Or the fact that I share my blood with her. They would kill me for that. Darian frowned as he thought about his people and their incredible resilience, their lust for life itself that he loved, and their warrior ways that had kept them safe in the mountains for nearly a millennia. But his most recent memories also included an odd, defeated depression that had caused their numbers to dwindle over the past hundred years or so, and there had been several reasons for it. Humans had begun taking up more and more space, encroaching on *their* mountains, and the Elves barely respected the boundary on the other side; the loss of their hunting grounds, privacy, and even some of their members had affected the Aeroyn in awful ways as they tried to keep the outside world at bay. More recently, some of the younglings had been stolen...

But those are no longer my concern. Darian had thought about his tribe often over the past six summers since he had met Kiera, but it was always briefly and never with regret. Kiera had become his lover, his companion, and his sole friend since leaving his people, the current summer marking the passing of the thirteenth since he had last seen the land he hailed from. She was the one human Darian couldn't despise, and Kiera held his monstrous heart in her warm strong hands.

What bothered Darian most was that he knew Kiera would pass into oblivion someday, and she would age where he would not. That thought always sat uncomfortably in the back of his mind. With him, she would never bear children, and her once-royal blood would be wasted as she grew old and became barren.

I would never wish to bring a child into this world as it stands, even if she could...
Darian shook his head as if to clear his thoughts, turning his focus back to the woman resting in his arms. He needed to feed, but as he held her close, breathing her in, feeling her weight and her warmth against him, he didn't care.

I'll wait all night if I have to.
But Kiera had relaxed in his arms, her hand and cheek pressed against his naked chest, her eyes focused on the fire. Darian, hungry but patient, had waited for her to settle so he could leave her to hunt from the trees far enough away that the wolves wouldn't come after *her*. He shifted under her, and she sat up to look at him.

"Time?" Kiera knew it was an unnecessary question before the word ever left her mouth, but she asked anyway. His face looked drawn in the low light of the fire, and she knew he needed to leave her. She moved away from Darian and stood, pain shooting down her back from being in the same position for several hours as she slept against his chest.

"Damn this hard ground! Reminds me why we sleep in trees when we're out here," Kiera groaned as she stretched out her tired body, feeling fresh shoots of pain in her shoulders and her hips as she forced stiff muscles to move, looking around for her clothes. Darian chuckled softly as he stood up, brushing the dust from his velvety skin and stretching his wings, distracting Kiera from the pile of cloth and leather that sat next to her pack by the fire.

Kiera had always been fascinated by his body and the way he moved, the way the fire glinted off his fur and his feathers and turned his eyes a deep brown as they adjusted to the light in the night. Darian was so distracting that some days she found herself mesmerized by him, and he usually caught her and teased her about it. Kiera could see him out of the corner of her eye as she shed the cloak in favor of her simple tunic, black leggings, and boots. Once she was dressed, she buckled her knives to her thigh, a little irritated that she had to ignore her leather bodice since she didn't have any lacing to fix the one Darian had shredded.

Pain in the ass . . . I guess I should be used to this shit by now. She smiled faintly as she rolled up the armor that needed replacing soon anyway and stuffed it into her pack. Darian had a funny way of feeling both familiar and new every time she focused on him, and Kiera felt the deep ache of love in her chest as she watched him now, the sudden impulse to kiss his soft mouth, strong and vibrant. She knew that was a bad idea when Darian was hungry, and there had been times where she had actually felt fear of him, like when she had first stumbled upon him, the rain pouring down . . .

"Watching me again, *Princess*?" he teased.

Kiera blinked, her face reddening when she realized she had been staring openly at him as she adjusted her bracers. Darian smirked, stretching and flexing in ridiculous poses, and Kiera couldn't help but laugh. He was chuckling as he pulled her against him, kissing her lightly on the mouth, but Kiera wasn't in the mood to fool around; she pushed against his chest, smiling up at him as she backed out of his embrace.

"Go *feed*, beast." Kiera smacked him in the arm as she turned her back on him and rummaged through her pack, pulling out a red apple and biting into it, letting the sweet juice run down her chin.

She felt the rush of air that always accompanied his takeoff from the ground, the dust swirling around her feet and dampening the fire for a moment or two. She heard the soft flap of his wings receding as he gained height, the quietude punctuated only by the chirping of the crickets surrounding their little camp as he flew off into the night.

Six

Kiera shivered slightly as the evening air seeped through her cloak, making her skin prickle with gooseflesh. The nights were getting cooler now that the seasons were changing and the summer beginning to wane. The day had been wretchedly hot, but she was glad now that she had brought her cloak as she pulled it tighter around her shoulders.

The skies were clear and well lit, both nearly full moons high above her making the world outside the light of her fire glow a soft, ghostly blue. In the dark, Kiera was having a hard time pinpointing where she even *was* in Baneswood, the small clearing she stood in unfamiliar to her. It was rare that she was in the woods at night, and the combination of the moonlight and the surrounding darkness made the world around her seem alien. It didn't help that Darian had moved her when she was unconscious either.

From her position on the ground, Kiera was surrounded by tall trees and couldn't see the lay of the forest or the valley around her, but she planned to rectify that with a quick climb into the branches of the large ladder-pine she was leaning against as she devoured her apple.

She chewed the last bite as she tossed the core into their little blaze and wiped her hands on her leggings before turning her gaze upward, scanning for the nearest branch. With a powerful leap, Kiera caught and pulled herself up onto the one she wanted and started her journey into the treetops. She climbed swiftly, loving the thrill of her aching muscles as they obeyed her commands and began to warm, the night no longer so chilly as the blood pumped through her limbs. When she came to a height where the branches only barely supported her weight, Kiera looked out over the dense foliage and across the moonlit valley.

We're farther than I thought. She recognized the crumbling old relic of her castle, several miles away to the southwest as it loomed big and black in the night, perched on its ledge high above the village of Grant's Perch. Now that she had a good idea where she was, Kiera surveyed the surrounding forest that edged the valley, the lake at its heart ringed on one side with the houses of the fishermen and woodsmen and their families that called Breach Lake home. The Breach was four or five miles long and nearly a mile wide, the light from above turning the water into a flat black mirror that reflected both the white and smaller red moons in their shroud of stars.

Kiera inhaled deeply, taking in and deciphering the earthy aroma all around her: the scent of the trees and dry dirt that were still warm to the touch, the sweet smell of water from the nearby stream that rushed along in the darkness, the smoke from the campfire below only lightly tingeing the cool breeze as it blew to the south. A gentle gust rustled through the branches, and she suddenly caught the sound of what she thought were voices and running feet not far from her little camp, intermittently carried away by the wind.

She strained to hear the low, deep sounds that were unfamiliar to her. She couldn't quite make out their words, but eventually, she could distinguish three distinct voices, knowing that what she heard wasn't necessarily indicative of the approaching party's true size. Two small torches were headed in her direction, their dying flames flickering like fireflies as they were blotted out by the foliage that separated her from them.

They were still a ways off to the northeast, but they were getting closer as the minutes ticked by, and Kiera waited impatiently for them to approach so she could assess how much of a fight she would need to put up to get *rid* of them.

Kiera was silently thankful that she downwind from them, but even if they could catch her scent, they wouldn't know where to even begin looking, and she wasn't terribly worried about them finding her immediately. They were, however, getting louder, and she could guess there were at least four of them together, talking minimally in hushed tones as they moved cautiously toward the fire blazing in the middle of the woods.

"Well, we can only hope they're friendly. We don't have many other options, you know," a voice chided below her, and Kiera scrambled down the tree as quickly and quietly as possible, perching on a large limb near the base of the ladder-pine a little more than ten feet up. The voices suddenly halted as the small party came to the edge of the clearing, their wariness and confusion almost palpable as they approached the unattended fire and the leather pack she had left behind on the ground.

Kiera cringed and silently cursed herself, knowing full well she had been careless. A random fire was one thing; it could have been built by faeries that wanted to help, or goblins that were trying to lure men into their encampment to rob them of any gold they possessed. But her personal belongings left in the open were another matter entirely. She was getting much too comfortable in those woods.

"Hello? Is anyone *here*?" a male voice rang out.

Kiera didn't answer the call as she watched them with intense curiosity. The party of four moved about the small clearing; all were male, but only three looked human. They split up and wandered around the fire, looking for signs of friend or foe as the two torches were added to the fire, throwing sparks into the air as the new wood disturbed the embers.

"I hate being lost in these woods. Its shit like this that makes me miss four walls and a *real* bed," the being directly below her whispered. The quiet words floated up to her as he wandered close and complained only to himself. Kiera let out a breath she had been holding as he headed back toward his companions without spotting her.

Kiera gritted her teeth when she realized that one of them had picked up her bag from the dust and was busy pulling out its contents. She hadn't noticed at first because the man had his back to her, and Kiera contemplated sending one of her throwing knives into the heavily muscled shoulders that were turned her way as he stood up. In the glow of the fire, Kiera could tell he had a good bit of height to him with broad squared shoulders under his sleeveless black shirt, his waist belted with brown leather that held an ornate sword and the scrollwork down the center of the blade glittering in the firelight. He turned sideways, and Kiera figured him to be in his early twenties with loose, curly brown hair that fell to his shoulders, but she couldn't quite determine the color of his eyes…

Kiera winced when he turned toward her to toss an apple from her pack to one of his companions and she caught sight of the brilliant threesome of scars that ripped down the right side of his face. The remnants of violence started just outside his eye and ran all the way to his upper lip, marring his features and dividing his short beard with three thick, ragged lines.

"Here, Tance. If they're not going to show themselves, at least they can share." The man's arrogant and goading words only lifted one side of his mouth, the muscles of the right side of his face deadened by claws that had left their mark, but he didn't seem to notice, and neither did his companions. He threw the apple to the closest of the other three, a dark-blond young man with narrow features and a wiry stature whom Kiera guessed to be in his midteens.

The slender youth was clad in a shirt that was almost the same color as the crimson apple tossed in his direction and tan pants and brown boots that looked like they might be too big for him. Tance smiled, the fire glinting off his hair, his hazel eyes, and the hilt of the dagger that peeked over the top of his high brown boot. The scarred man and the boy looked similar enough that they were probably related though the older of the two was a few inches taller, and he certainly filled his clothing out far better than his younger relation.

The other two males moved closer to the fire and into better light, and Kiera tried in vain to watch them all and study each in turn. The third man was short, closer to five feet tall, and a little on the pudgy side. His features were obscured by a long black beard, and his dark-brown clothing and a brimless cap fit him in a way that reminded Kiera of a small bear; the image of the man-bear was completed with bushy eyebrows over brown eyes, a broad nose, and ears that stuck out slightly. He carried a pack with a pan dangling from the side and a short crossbow, neither of which left his shoulders as he crouched to add wood to the blaze.

The last was clean shaven, slender, and much taller than the other three, with long raven black hair, narrow, almost feminine features, and blue eyes. He was clad in a belted knee-length robe and pants made of what looked like tan buckskin and dark burgundy boots that made no noise as he walked slowly around the fire, still wary of impending company. A longbow and a quiver full of magnificent arrows were his weapon of choice, the light wood of both glowing in the light of the moons as he turned his back on the fire and continued to scan the trees.

Kiera scrutinized the one with the bow since he seemed to be the most wary and seemed to pose the most immediate threat. He had an arrow set loosely against the string, turning his head left and right, searching out whoever might have started this fire in the middle of the woods. She caught the hint of pointed ears poking through the dark hair, his skin shimmering slightly in the moonlight.

What in the name of Tirath is an elf doing with these men?

Kiera knew the Elves were in and beyond the neighboring mountains, but they rarely spoke with men, much less socialized with them. She hadn't seen any in the last six years, so this one was a bit of a surprise. He was an obvious part of this tight-knit group, which was also out of the ordinary; like the Aeroyn, the Elves were a secretive, reclusive race, tending to stay away from populated areas unless they had something to trade, and they had a history of killing outsiders rather than accepting their presence.

From what she understood, the Elves had been banished from the surrounding lands by Eryce once he had taken total control, but this one moved easily with the other three, a part of the whole and showing no fear. Kiera found that she was immensely curious about him, hoping he wouldn't have time to shoot her if and when she decided to show herself.

The elf scanned the trees. He could feel someone watching them; he just couldn't sense *where*.

"*Relax*, Jaçon. There's no one here," the bearded man said quietly as he rested his hand on the elf's elbow, trying to get him to put the arrow away. "They're probably long gone by now-"

"Shut up, damn you!" Jaçon responded with an aggravated whisper as he shook the hand off, wary and irritated. "I can't hear over your prattling. This fire certainly didn't start itself. There's someone here. I can *smell* them." Jaçon sniffed the air cautiously, his voice suddenly full of surprise. "I think it's a *woman*!"

Well, well. At least one of you is paying attention, Kiera thought, fingering the hilt of the knife on her thigh.

"Isn't . . . Isn't there supposed to be one that *lives* in these woods?" Tance squeaked, his voice cracking. He cleared his throat, glancing around nervously as though he was expecting someone to suddenly appear. "I heard she's seven feet tall and has even killed a Sukolai. I mean, I'm certainly not *scared* of her, but the men at Raven's Roost said to stay out of here, and if she's *real*—"

"*Hush*, boy," the short man whispered loudly. He closed his eyes, and Kiera suddenly felt her skin prickle weirdly. His eyes popped open, and the sensation vanished. "I can *feel* her. She's close… and she's *not* happy."

They were immediately on guard, and Kiera smiled as they grouped together, trying to decide their next move against an invisible adversary. Darian would probably still be gone for a while, and she wasn't going to pass up an opportunity to strengthen her hold on Baneswood even though she knew four was a bit of a stretch for her abilities. However, they didn't strike her as particularly threatening, and with an elf in tow, they probably didn't work under Eryce, so she wasn't going to try kill them *just* yet.

"Hello?" the one with the scars called into the woods again in the exact opposite direction from her.

Kiera snorted a soft laugh, and the elf's head jerked her way. With Jaçon now equipped with a general direction to look for her, it wasn't going to be long before he aimed an arrow up into the trees if he spotted her. If she wanted to keep the oods in her favor, Kiera was going to have to show herself.

There was no getting out of it now.

"Didn't your mothers ever tell you not to go traipsing through the woods at night? You never know what lurks in them." Kiera's voice came steadily from the tree, but she knew she was just high enough that her words came from a general direction without giving her away completely, and she could have been higher or lower than she really was.

All four men turned toward the sound of her voice with wide eyes, their weapons suddenly drawn in response to her veiled threat as they searched the branches, trying to locate its source. She was provoking them, and she knew it.

"Apparently we don't *listen* very well." The sarcastic remark from the elf made her raise an eyebrow, and Kiera smiled when the little man-bear smacked him in the arm.

"Be serious! If it *is* her, you're going to be the first one strung up in a tree!" His loud whisper made Kiera shake with silent laughter. She had to take a deep breath before saying anything else, trying to keep the smile out of her voice.

They're sort of fun. Maybe I'll spare them after all.

"Promise not to shoot, and I will show myself. I have no desire to harm any of you. You would do well to remember that. Don't make me *defend* myself."

The foursome was quiet for a moment, staring into the trees, still trying to spot her, all of them frozen in edgy silence.

"You have my word that no harm will come to you by way of me or these men. Show us no ill temper, and we will leave you in peace," the scarred one responded, his voice carrying easily on the breeze.

So he's the leader. Kiera studied him intently as he scanned the trees. The firelight glinted off his brown curls, and his skin took on a warm glow, the muscles of his arms and the curve of his cheekbones highlighted in the flickering light.

If it weren't for those scars, he would be beautiful. She felt an unexpected heat come to her face at that thought, the blush surprising her. Kiera smiled a little in spite of herself. *Well, now or never.*

Kiera dropped to the ground, landing in a crouch. She locked eyes with each of them in turn, ending with the scarred man, holding his gaze as she unfolded her body to her full height, her hood up and her cloak shrouding her. All of them regarded her warily, but to her silent relief, none moved to attack.

"Are you out here *alone*?" the brown-haired man asked cautiously, his expression thoughtful as he watched her from across the fire as the light from it danced over her face.

Kiera's cloak gapped as she folded her arms over her chest and concealed the dagger she had pulled from her boot as she stood, the blade glinting momentarily, but if he saw it, he didn't seem to feel threatened; he still had his sword drawn, but the tip was pointed toward the ground.

"Does it *matter* if I *am*?" Her retort seemed to catch him off guard, and Kiera felt her mouth twitch as she fought not to smirk at his surprise.

"A woman shouldn't be out in these woods on her own especially at night. I've heard the wolves, and I know troll trails when I see them. Isn't . . . Isn't there someone *protecting* you?" He cocked his head to the side, focused entirely on her, his companions silent and wary as they watched the exchange.

"Why? Because I'm missing the parts that would make me a *man*? These are *my* woods. Tread carefully, *sir*, or it won't be *me* that needs *protecting*." Kiera frowned and shifted her weight, lifting her chin haughtily toward him. She narrowed her eyes at him, daring him to challenge her, but it was the boy who took the bait.

"*Seven feet tall,* my ass! She's just a *girl!*" Tance sneered, stepping forward, his dagger still in his hand. "How *dare* you speak to us that way! I think this *bitch* wants to *fight!*"

Kiera may not have lived up to the hype, but she still stood a good four inches taller than the youngest of the quartet, yet he seemed determined to show that he was not afraid of her.

She caught the annoyance that registered on the faces of the men and the elf rolling his eyes, so she completely ignored the others as she trusted them to stay out of it. She watched him openly, waiting for him to make the first move, knowing he was in for a terrible surprise when he did.

You're going to regret this, little boy. You have no idea what you're up against. Kiera could see the mean glint in his eye, the young man stalking toward her as though she were a threat *he* could do anything about. She laughed softly, more to herself than at him, but she knew what she was doing; it was meant to provoke the boy enough to take a shot. Kiera had grown tired of waiting, and when Tance finally lunged at her, his dagger steady in his right hand, she reacted so quickly he yelped in surprise and nearly dropped it on his own.

She stepped toward him, batting his weapon to the side easily with her right hand to grab his wrist. She twisted his arm painfully and made him cry out in pain while his dagger bounced harmlessly as it hit the ground. She brought up her left hand, boxing the right side of his head with the butt of her own blade, knocking him away from her.

Tance stumbled and failed to keep his balance, blood already pouring from his ear before he hit the ground. He landed on his side, clutching his head, whimpering, but stubbornly refusing to cry.

"Do you want to try that *again*, or was once enough?" Kiera turned her back on his friends, trusting them again to stay themselves as she regarded the brave but stupid boy at her feet.

"Bitch!" he yelled back, but when Kiera took a threatening step toward him, he panicked and tried to scramble away.

That's what I thought. She smirked as she crouched to pick up his knife and slip it into her boot, backing away from the boy and allowing him to get up on his own once his head cleared enough for him to see straight. Humiliated and now unarmed, the boy slunk away from her, taking refuge beside the little bearded man, blood oozing between his fingers. He watched her hatefully, but she felt no further threat left in him especially now that she held his weapon.

"Anyone *else* care to give it a shot?" Kiera eyed the other three, her arms crossed defensively, green eyes blazing from under her hood. She had made it clear she wasn't going to kill them, but she wouldn't stand for aggression toward her either. She knew she couldn't kill them all on her own especially if the elf joined the fray, but she would make sure they never forgot their run-in with her if they tried anything more.

I'll add to those scars if you survive long enough to heal, she thought as she tucked her own blade under her bracer, the metal cold against the back of her forearm. When no one volunteered, Kiera focused completely on the man with the scars, addressing him alone.

"May I have my pack, please?" Kiera extended her hand toward him, palm up, and waited.

"Will you disarm me as well?" He stood his ground, his words full and clear even with the lack of movement from half of his mouth. Kiera was suddenly aware that his sword was still drawn.

"Only if you give me a good *reason*," she fired back. "I would have killed *that one*, but I have a rule about taking the lives of those who still need to *learn*." Kiera locked eyes with the boy and smiled sweetly.

Tance glared back with malice.

The man with the scars looked irritated until he caught the younger man's expression and suddenly laughed, the unexpected sound startling the entire group including Kiera. He replaced his sword into its scabbard and picked up her pack where he had dropped it at his feet when he had unsheathed his weapon. With long, even strides, he came around the fire that separated them and held out her pack to her.

Kiera moved to snatch it from him, but he suddenly dropped it and caught her hand. She reacted instinctively by trying to jerk away, but he held her firm and drew close enough to bring her hand to his lips, kissing it softly. She was so surprised she didn't even react, the warmth of his fingers new and weird to her, the smell of him flooding her senses now that he was so close.

"Alyk, at your service, Lady . . . ?" Alyk said softly as half his mouth twisted up into a smile, waiting for a name and still holding her hand.

It had been a very long time since anyone had regarded Kiera with anything other than fear, and she found herself at a loss for words. Her eyes were wide with surprise, and Kiera found herself fighting the urge to smile genuinely back at him. She bit the inside of her lip and debated on giving him anything at all to call her by, but that thought was derailed when a familiar sound caught her attention and his.

"What the *hell*?" Alyk's eyes left hers, and he turned them instead to the skies. The rustling of branches and the sound of loud flapping from above caused Alyk to drop her hand in favor of the hilt of his sword, but Kiera grabbed his wrist, keeping the sword in place. Jaçon drew his arrow back to his shoulder, also scanning for the origin of the unfamiliar sound, the man-bear glancing almost nonchalantly up at the stars that were being blotted out by a large form.

Darian dropped from the sky and into their midst, landing across the fire from Kiera, standing tall and spreading his huge wings until they almost touched the branches a dozen feet above the ground. Alyk moved to shield Kiera, Jaçon holding the shot ready, and the blonde boy scrambled away from Darian, seeking refuge behind the elf.

Only the bearded little man-bear didn't move, and he watched Darian with marked interest.

"Don't even try it. You'll only make him angry," Kiera whispered as she held Alyk's wrist steadily, focusing at Darian over the flames. She had already decided not to kill them; now she had to get her *bird* to go along with the idea too.

"I take it this means you're *not* alone." Alyk glanced at the hand gripping his wrist, but Kiera wasn't looking at him when he turned his attention back on her. She shook her head, a slow smile spreading across her face as she watched the upset look on Darian's face shift to one of confusion as he focused on her.

"What in the name of Tirath is going on here?" Darian roared, but Kiera could tell he was just incredibly worried, and very annoyed. She could hear the hint of guilt in his voice, and she knew he was upset with himself for letting her be found, but that part was over and done with. She had been discovered, and *he* hadn't been there to protect *her*.

Now Kiera needed to decide if *she* would protect *them*.

"Okay, everyone calm *down*!" she barked as she dropped Alyk's wrist and stepped away from him, taking command before the fight even had a chance to begin. "Put away your weapons. He means you no harm, *right*, Darian?"

Kiera regarded the confused Aeroyn seriously from across the fire, willing him not to kill them. Darian grunted and looked exasperated, but when she crossed her arms over her chest and glared at him, he knew that she had made up her mind and that it wasn't going to change. He suddenly sniffed the air and caught a whiff of foreign blood; homing in on the source, he noticed the blonde boy was bleeding still from his ear, large red smears running across his cheek where he had wiped at the blood.

"You're lucky she didn't kill you, *boy*. You would do well to avoid trying to finish whatever you must have started. She usually *wins*." Darian directed a bemused look at Tance, and the boy made a face in response. The Aeroyn smiled back threateningly, showing those vicious fangs. Tance paled and hid completely behind Jaçon, who immediately stepped away from him, offering him up to the bigger being.

"Now then, *who* are you?" Darian demanded, suddenly serious. "And *what* are you doing with my *mate*?"

Seven

Mate? This is certainly a night of surprises, Alyk mused to himself. The idea that the girl was protected by this *thing* wasn't such a weird idea, but the thought of them *together*...

Kiera pushed back her hood, and his thought process came to a screeching halt when he was hit with an immediate sense of déjà vu.

I know her! Why do I know her? Alyk didn't have time to think about it as one of his companions stepped forward and introduced himself to break the tension. The bearded Man-bear touched his right fist to his left shoulder and bowed low to Darian, showing profound respect.

"Henelce, Shephard of the Southern Woods." Henelce had a gruff but pleasant voice, one that seemed to bear no wariness toward this monstrous being. He seemed, in fact, to be very trusting of Darian as though he were familiar with him.

"It has been a long time since I have seen anyone from *those* woods, much less a Shephard. You are a long way from home, *friend*," Darian said as he bowed back. Kiera wasn't the only one confused by the exchange, but neither seemed inclined to elaborate further as Henelce kept talking like he and Darian were in the middle of a conversation and no one else was standing there.

"It may be longer yet! Not many of us left with the old magic," Henelce chirped, smiling brightly as he turned to Kiera. "We're a bit lost, I think. It's a good thing we ran into you when we did, or we might have had to keep ahead of those wolves that ran us out of our last camp! These damned woods are *beastly* for navigating through!"

The Shephard dropped his pack on the ground, his rear following suit. Henelce started pulling items at random from his pack, settling himself next to the fire without asking; *he* was obviously staying whether or not he'd been *invited*. Alyk looked slightly embarrassed, but Jaçon just shook his head, trying not to laugh, used to the Shephard's antics. The elf stood straight, shouldering his bow and replacing the arrow in his quiver as he took the opportunity to introduce himself, too.

"Jaçon of Haven's Fall. Bowman of Sorveign's Royal Guard. I am familiar with your kind, Darian, and I hope you find me peaceful in your presence," Jaçon nodded to the beast and then to Kiera. "My lady."

As Kiera nodded back, she caught the glint of red on his right hand, the signet ring she knew would be on his middle finger flashing for an instant in the firelight. She had seen those rings before on the many occasions when Sorveign and a dozen of his men had come to Corengale to speak to her father, and that particular detail told her he spoke truth.

That said much for a member of a race not always known for their honesty. Elves were no longer welcome in Rhonendar, and most cities and towns had banned their presence completely because the man who sat on the throne *disliked* the lot of them. Sorveign, however, was an elf Kiera remembered well from her earlier years and she was not surprised to hear that Sorveign still ruled supreme in his kingdom on the other side of the Montes Gelu; he had been on his throne for almost forty years when she had last seen him, and he would likely rule for at least that much longer.

"Alyk. Just . . . Alyk." The man with the scars didn't give his surname when Kiera cast a curious glance in his direction, a nagging feeling telling him it wasn't a good idea. Alyk turned his head and raised his chin to indicate the blonde boy. "And this is my little brother, Tance. We're from Corengale . . . or what was left of it anyway."

Alyk eyed Tance, telling him silently to keep his mouth *shut* with his raised eyebrows, still trying to remember where he had seen this particular woman. Only when Tance had bowed slightly and mutely regarded his brother sourly did Alyk follow suit. When he righted himself, he found Darian looking past him, watching Kiera. She didn't even notice, her hard gaze locked on *him*, and Alyk felt the hairs rise on the back of his neck as he fought to take an instinctive step backwards.

"You . . . *you* are from Corengale?" Her mouth was slightly open, her green eyes wide, and Alyk nodded, looking terribly confused. Kiera closed her eyes for a moment, thinking . . .

I swear I know her . . . Why is she so familiar?

There was something about her.

Something *important*.

It wouldn't surface—not until she opened those bright eyes again and reached up to touch the scars on his face.

"Did *they* do this to you? Or was it one of their *dogs*?" Her voice had an edge to it, hardened by an old, deep anger.

Alyk reflexively tried to shy away from her as she touched his skin lightly, his face thrilling under her fingertips. The image of a dark-haired girl suddenly came back to him, a girl in a castle, the castle he had spent part of his young life in and around . . .

It was her white hair that was throwing off his memory. He saw Castle Corengale in his mind, the fortress that was burnt until it was a husk of blackened and crumbling stone, King Garegan the Second hanging from the tree outside the front gates, his body full of arrows like a morbid pincushion.

Alyk remembered the sweet laugh of that girl, the pretty young princess.

He remembered her green eyes—so very green.

He stared into those same brilliant pupils and immediately knew who she was.

"You . . ." Alyk felt his heart begin to pound. "You're . . ."

It can't be. You're dead!

Kiera gave him a dismissive nod and cut him off, trying desperately not to panic after the look of recognition had crossed his face. She glanced at Darian, and as she turned to regard the other three, she forced her mouth into a smile, trying to think fast and keep her cover intact.

"I'm afraid I have become something of a *legend* in these woods, and while I am *not* seven feet tall, nor do I breathe fire or have the claws of a lion or whatever other *ridiculous* tales you've heard outside these woods, I *do* rule them. If I thought you worked for Eryce, know that you would already be dead. *Most* people know better than to tread here, and you're either brave or stupid to do so at night.

"But can't take it back now, I suppose. Gentlemen, I am pleased to make your acquaintance. You may call me *Bane*, and I welcome you to my woods . . . however reluctantly."

Kiera bowed low, trying to breathe normally and slow her racing thoughts. Darian she knew would never betray her, but this man, this one from her home, from all those years ago . . .

She didn't know if she could trust *him*.

Not yet.

Kiera righted herself and grabbed Alyk's wrist before he could move away from her, addressing him quietly before he could move away from her and settle next to the fire.

"We will speak but not now. *Understood?*"

Her whisper wasn't a question, but only Alyk nodded, content with just being confirmed in his suspicions, leaving the others wondering as they started to set up camp for the night.

This is a disaster! If he found me by chance and recognizes me, then so will they. Kiera looked at Darian helplessly as she turned her back on them, knowing he could almost read her mind from the expression on her face. *I'm as good as dead.*

* * *

Alyk knew he wouldn't be able to sleep well, if at all, so he volunteered for first watch as everyone settled in for the evening. As the hour grew later and his companions bedded down for the night, Alyk stared at the fire, trying to remember *her* more clearly, but his mind was a mess from coming face to face with her, and the memories wouldn't surface. Bane had retreated up into the trees with her *companion*, leaving the foursome alone on the ground and Alyk to his musings about a girl he used to watch from the castle yards.

Sighing dejectedly, Alyk turned his attention to stoking the flames, adding another log before taking his place next to Tance, who was already sound asleep and snoring lightly.

Henelce and Jaçon were laying on their backs, having a tête-à-tête while staring at the night skies through the trees, as was their custom every night that one of them didn't have first watch. They were such an odd pair, these close friends of such different origins, but Alyk reminded himself that the Shephard had been with the Elves of the East on his last assignment, and the little man genuinely *liked* the race. Henelce could even speak several different Elvin dialects, which was sometimes annoying as he and Jaçon had a tendency to converse in them without realizing that no one else understood.

Alyk pursed his lips grimly and went back to his thoughts about Bane, which faded into images of Corengale. He recalled the flash of yellow eyes, the heat of brilliant green flames, the screams . . .

And the morning after with bodies strewn about like morbid dolls thrown haphazardly from a children's toy chest.

His hand went to his face almost absently as his scars began to throb, her image dancing through his mind once more.

How in the name of Tirath did she get all the way out here?

Eight

Dawn broke over the horizon, and Kiera woke high in a tree, thankful that the dream hadn't reared its ugly head for a second night in a row. Darian's arms held her safely cradled against his chest as he slept with his back to the trunk of the ladder-pine she had climbed the night before. The foursome below were already awake and were moving about quietly, the smell of cooking meat wafting up into the trees, making Kiera's mouth water and her stomach respond noisily.

"I *heard* that," Darian grumbled but didn't open his eyes. Instead he pulled her closer, tightening his arms around her waist as she lay against him, keeping her firmly in place. Kiera sighed, wanting to stay, but the smell from the fire was reminding her that she hadn't eaten much the day before, and her hunger was winning out. She leaned her head back against his shoulder, nudging his chin with her nose, and when he grumpily opened one eye, she kissed his jaw and nudged him again.

"Don't make me lick you like a puppy. Let me go so I can eat and stop bothering you," Kiera whispered as she looked up at him through her dark lashes, willing him to relent.

Darian responded by holding her closer and burying his face into her exposed neck. She felt her skin react to his kisses on her throat, but when the brush of his lips was followed by the subtle scrape of his teeth on her flesh, she froze. Kiera knew better than to move suddenly when his fangs were out.

"If *you* get to have breakfast, can *I*?" Darian breathed against her neck touched his teeth to the vulnerable spot again, but he didn't break the skin.

He wouldn't!

She knew he wouldn't.

Kiera trusted that he would stop . . .

Her heart beat faster anyways, and the adrenaline surged through her as his arms wound tighter, trapping her against his chest. His lips suddenly covered his teeth as he sucked lightly at her skin, sending shivers down her back. Darian touched those sharp points to her neck once more, pressing a little harder this time, and Kiera felt the skin resisting his bite, but it wouldn't for much longer.

"Darian, that is *enough*! Let me *go*!" Kiera tried to keep her voice both steady and quiet, but the fear came through, and Darian stiffened when he realized he was scaring her.

He was instantly sorry as he relaxed his arms, and Kiera moved away from him as quickly as the branch would allow. She stared at him with confused and slightly frightened eyes, one hand steadying her as she sat on the swaying branch, the other checking for wounds on her neck. Her hand came away a little shaky with only the moisture from his lips, but her heart was still racing, and she felt a heated indignation flood through her.

How dare you! Kiera shrieked in her head as she frowned angrily at him. She swung backward off the branch when he tried to reach for her, catching the one below and easily tumbling from limb to limb as she fell gracefully to the ground beneath them. She hit the dry, dusty earth and glared up at him from twenty feet below, hurt and anger radiating from her as she broke eye contact and stalked off.

Darian stared at the spot where Kiera had been standing only moments before, wondering what his problem was. He had been deliberately dominant over her, and she hadn't deserved it. Even if she did want to eat with *them*.

Darian didn't eat their food, and he had no interest in watching others eat, and she was a human and was *hungry* on top of that. He had acted like she was purposely defying him for no good reason when she had simply asked that they be allowed live.

But it wasn't that simple, and he suspected she knew it too. No one had ever survived long enough to pique her interest. Something had changed, and Darian knew it had to do with the brown-haired man with the scars, but she hadn't said much the night before so he wasn't sure what was going on in her head. The man was no match for the Aeroyn physically, and he would simply kill this *Alyk* if he tried anything stupid...

Darian sighed and let the jealous thoughts go, deciding instead that he would find Kiera later and talk with her in private, apologize, and maybe make love to her, but he refused to think she would choose a man over *him*.

He refused to give it any more thoughts as he stood on the branch, lazily stretching his wings and contemplating an early morning hunt for a snack. For now, it was probably a better idea to let her be anyway, and after the look she had given him, Kiera was likely going to ignore him for a day or so until she cooled down or the intruders were gone.

Darian sprung out of the tree and took to the air, leaving the braches dancing in his wake. He left Kiera behind with her new *companions* that she so obviously *trusted*, figuring it was where she would be safest for the time being, but he needed to think. He needed to be away from her and let his head clear.

She'll understand.

NINE

If Kiera heard Darian leave the tree she gave no indication. She didn't even glance in the direction of the rustling branches, though three of her new companions did. Everyone except Alyk watched the Aeroyn take off because he was busy studying *her* as she deliberately ignored Darian's noisy departure.

That's interesting. I wonder what that was all about, he thought as he slowly chewed on a tough piece of bread.

Kiera sensed eyes upon her and looked up to meet his gaze, smiling wryly and shaking her head as she went back to picking at the portion of meat they had given her from the three hares Jaçon had caught and cooked before the sun was even up. She had sliced the remaining apples she had with her in half and shared some of the bread that would have gone bad in another day or two anyway.

This is so weird. I can't even remember the last time I ate with people. *It must have been in Corengale.*

She realized then just how lonely she had been for her own kind, and she felt the idea like a lump in her throat. Even with Darian's constant company and with no real want for a life outside her trees, she wondered why it hadn't dawned on her before now that she might actually *miss* this. That thought was accompanied with a pang of self reproach, and Kiera wondered again if she should have just killed them to begin with.

"Forgive my curiosity, but how did you end up in the company of an Aeroyn? They're not exactly *friendly* creatures," Jaçon asked quietly, pulling her out of her confused and guilty thought pattern. The elf had been watching her as he sat cross-legged on the ground to her left, his plate of bones and half an apple core resting in his lap.

In the light of day, Kiera could see that his flesh wasn't ivory but tinged with the faintest blue while his hair was very truly black and was striking in its contrast. His eyes were actually lavender, not the blue she thought she had seen in the firelight. He was wiping his hands on a bit of cloth from his own pack that he had moistened with water, fastidiously removing bits of food from his pale skin as his question hung in the air.

So very human yet so very . . . not. Kiera suddenly realized that she was studying Jaçon as she might study Darian: in simple wonder and plain curiosity of a being that was so unlike herself. That thought made her heart sink; as upset as she was, Kiera missed Darian already. She tried to cover her hurt and surprise by keeping them to herself when she opened her mouth.

"I found him, and my mother said I could keep him," she quipped. Jaçon stared at her blankly for a moment, confused, but Henelce laughed loudly, realizing her joke. Kiera smiled weakly before she sighed and went on.

"I really *did* find him, almost six years ago. I was fourteen, and I had run away from a home I couldn't go back to." She glanced at Alyk, silently telling him to keep his mouth *shut*, but he just nodded for her to continue. Kiera turned her gaze to the remains of her breakfast as she thought back to her first encounter with her friend and companion.

He certainly didn't start out that way...

"I think I had been gone at least a week, but time gets funny when you have nowhere to go, so it could have been longer," she began, pausing to search her memory.

"I don't really remember now. It was raining, and *that* part is pretty hard to forget because I was thoroughly soaked and was so cold I was having a hard time moving. It was one of those spring storms that started out of nowhere, and I had no place to hide. It had been raining for quite a while when I stumbled upon a hunting lodge with a small barn hidden in the trees Tirath knows how many miles from my home.

"Smoke was coming from the chimney, and I could smell food, but I was too afraid to go near the lodge and strange men, so I headed for the stable. I can still clearly remember taking off my cloak and draping it on a nail that stuck out of the wall and the smell of the horse blanket that I traded it for. I always thought it was weird that those two details stick with me . . .

"Anyway, there were at least five horses in the barn. They wanted nothing to do with me, but they made the place feel warm, and that was all I cared about. I was tired, dirty and was just looking around for a place to settle for the night when I heard someone moving around above me in the hayloft. I thought that I would be caught and almost ran back outside, but then I heard coughing, like someone was sick. I found the ladder and climbed it very slowly, trying to be as quiet as possible as I went to investigate.

"I was *not* prepared for what I found. I had never seen anything like him. I always thought the Aeroyn were a myth, but Darian was right in front of me in the hayloft with chains locked to his wrists and ankles and his wings bound with leather straps. He looked so pathetically thin, all miserable and weak, and he must have smelled me before he saw me because he tried to grab me as I came up the ladder, but the chains stopped him short. I shrieked, and he jumped, covering his ears with his hands.

"We stared at each other for a moment, and I thought one of the horses below was wheezing until I realized it was coming from *him*. It wasn't until he started coughing that I saw the collar around his neck, and the tension was keeping him from breathing very well. He started coughing hard, and his eyes rolled back in his head just before he fell onto his side, and his entire body went limp. At first, I thought he was faking, but when he didn't move after a few minutes, I-I couldn't leave him like that."

Kiera paused, seeing Darian in that miserable state in her head bringing an ache into her chest. She hadn't thought about that day in quite a while, and remembering how hurt Darian had been made her miss him all the more.

"I don't remember going the rest of the way up the ladder and moving to help him, but I was suddenly there, trying to loosen the collar. He woke up while I was trying to get it off, and Darian lay still while I worked the leather until it gave. I thought the collar would have left a scar because the dark-red ring circling his neck was so deep, but his breathing improved dramatically within seconds of it coming off, and the skin began to heal.

"Then he started *jabbering* at me, and I couldn't understand him at *all*. I put my hand over his mouth to shut him up, and he tried to bite me, so I did what any woman would do—I slapped him as hard as I could. I think it was the last thing he expected and was sort of stunned, and I didn't really think about it when I put my hands on the sides of his face and made him look at me. Neither of us knew what the hell we were saying with our mouths, but we somehow connected in that moment. I tried to be gentle, to be calm, and he settled a bit but I could tell he still didn't quite trust me when I stood to move behind him and touched his wings.

"I could see they were swollen under the feathers from his straining against the straps that held them closed. He was watching me over his shoulder, and when I saw the straps were just buckled like belts, I was able to remove them fairly easily, but he moaned through the whole process, clawing at the rough wooden floor, leaving deep scars in the boards supporting us a dozen feet off the ground. That scared the hell out of me, and I remember wondering if I was releasing a monster."

Kiera felt eyes on her skin and suddenly stopped talking, and she glanced away from Jaçon to the others in the group; they had all stopped eating and were hanging on her every word. Kiera flushed, not used to this much attention, and she fixed her gaze back on Jaçon, who sat just as rapt and attentive as the others, waiting for Kiera to continue her story.

"Uh . . . so . . . Once his wings were free, Darian started to cry. He told me later he had never been in that much pain, and I have never seen him shed a tear since. The throbbing in his back was making him feel hot and feverish, but his breathing was easier, and his color was getting better, so I let him be since I had no key to free him completely. We were both exhausted, and I ended up asleep in a pile of hay a few feet from him, just beyond his reach. I trusted him not to bite me when I was awake and able to get away and he was stuck to the floor in his shackles, but not when I had no idea what he would do if I slept.

"I tried to stay up and watch him, but I must have drifted off because it was close to dark when door to the barn opened, and quiet voices woke me. Darian was already alert and looking at me, making all sorts of silly hand movements to tell me to hide. I ignored him and crawled quietly to the edge of the loft, peeking over to find the boys who had come in to feed the horses looking at the cloak I had left below. Darian must have felt my fear of being discovered because he suddenly whistled shrilly and fell over on his side to get their attention, sending up a huge cloud of dust and startling the horses while I scrambled to hide in the hay I had been sleeping on.

"I heard 'He better not be dead!' and the ladder creaking as they climbed it to get a look at Darian. Those stupid boys approached him fearlessly with a club and a pitchfork, missing me completely. Darian just lay there, barely breathing, and he waited until both were hovering over him, neither of them noticing the leather straps on the floor around him.

"When they were close enough, Darian grabbed the ankle of the boy furthest from him, letting the first stumble backward and fall over the other. I know you haven't seen him catch prey, but he moves like a damned *spider* and he had them by the throats in less than a second. He bit into the neck of the first one, and both he and the boy went quiet, but the other one struggled harder, trying to scream. The second boy was turning blue by the time Darian had drained the first. He killed them both like that, and they were so pale when he was done with them they looked like they might be made of wax.

"Once he had *fed*, he started to change. I remember being totally fascinated as his wings smoothed and the feathers were suddenly glossy while his face and limbs filled out a bit. Darian tried to come toward me but was stopped short by his chains, and he did one of the scariest things I have ever seen him do—he started to laugh as though he had gone mad and ripped the chains that held him from the hooks on the floor.

"I almost bolted. Darian was free, and I was *terrified*. The horses below us must have sensed my fear because they started to panic too, making awful screaming noises and trying to get out of their stalls. I was frozen in the pile of hay as he crouched down in front of me, resting his elbows on his knees with those enormous wings of his folded behind him. I squealed when picked me up out of the straw like I was nothing, and I thought he was going to kill me too, but he nuzzled his face to mine and licked me, which was *disgusting*, but he let me go. I was still trying to get his spit off my face when he jumped down and left the barn."

The others were quietly laughing, and Kiera would have been too if her mind wasn't already racing ahead in the story. The next part had a tendency to turn her stomach when she thought about it, but she had never actually *talked* about what happened shortly after being left behind in the barn.

What he did to those men . . . Kiera swallowed hard, staring at the elf sitting next to her. She shifted her focus on the fire, licking her lips nervously before she continued.

"What Darian did next is a testament to how ruthless an Aeroyn can really be when they're mad. He went straight for that hunting lodge, ripped open the door, and roared so loudly I almost fell off the ladder as I was climbing down. There must have been ten men in that hunting party, and I can only imagine that they scattered like rats, but Darian was ready for a hunt. He caught every single one of them, drank them unconscious, and dragged them outside.

"The drinking of blood doesn't bother me. I have seen worse ways to die, and that—at least—*looks* fairly painless. But Darian left them *alive.* Alive enough that they all recovered within an hour or so, only to find themselves stripped of all their clothing and tied by their hands among the trees, facing each other in a big ring. They all began to scream and yell, but they were exhausted, and I remember thanking Tirath when it didn't last long.

"They were fairly quiet until it got dark, and the wolves came. *Then* they started screaming and yelling much, *much* louder."

Kiera had to keep herself from cringing, hating the memories of those terrified voices echoing through the woods and the howling of the wolves as they feasted, but she still felt that those men had deserved their fate. Darian had done it so many times since, but they *always* left before the wolves came.

She made *damned* sure of *that*.

Her voice dropped to almost a whisper, her focus on the sunlight filtering through their campfire smoke as she finished her story.

"Darian had strung those men just high enough that the wolves had to jump to catch their legs, pulling and ripping the flesh from them, eventually either pulling the man's arms from his body or breaking the ropes—whichever gave first. There was nothing but *pieces* hanging from those trees the next morning, and Darian still does that to intruders in these woods when they come to cause harm—especially to *me*."

Kiera looked at all of them in turn, letting it sink in that Darian would perform that *ritual* on them too if they weren't well behaved. Jaçon had become impossibly pale even for his faintly iridescent blue skin, and Tance looked like he might throw up, but Alyk only nodded when she locked eyes with him.

"I spent that entire time in the lodge sitting by the fire, eating food from their table, happy to be dry in the clothes left by the boys, and trying to ignore the screams of the men outside. Looking back, I don't think I really cared then what was happening, and the screams didn't go on long. Darian found me curled up on the rug in front of the fire, sound asleep. He watched over me until I finally woke up to the sun setting the next day.

"That was over six years ago, and I have been with him ever since."

Kiera abruptly stopped talking, the fire little more than embers. Without another word, she stood up, brushed the dust from her clothes almost absently, and turned away from the group, seeking the solace of the creek and its cold water and its total absence of sentient beings as she headed away from the camp.

No one tried to follow.

At that moment, Kiera wanted nothing more than to be alone, and without Darian nearby, she felt keenly aware of just how alone she really was.

TEN

Kiera hadn't had to tell that story before. She hadn't intended to end it so awkwardly, but she couldn't really think of anything else to add. Everything that had happened since included teaching Darian Man Tongue - since she couldn't even come close to mimicking his language - and her training and the *hunting* of threats in her woods.

And our sex life . . . which is absolutely none *of their business.*

Kiera sat on a large flat boulder overlooking the stream she and Darian had ended up at less than twenty-four hours before, her knees drawn up to her chest and her chin resting on top of them, her arms wrapped protectively around her legs.

Was that really only yesterday? She suddenly felt like Darian had been gone for more than a few hours. Kiera was still hurt he had even shown his fangs to her in a way that seemed domineering, but she had never seen him act jealously.

Then again, she had never wanted to let anyone live, much less actually *talk* with them. He had also never seen anyone else kiss her, hand or otherwise, and she was silently thankful he hadn't observed Alyk's display of manners. That had been a normal custom for her at one point, and it was oddly comforting to have someone remind Kiera she was a human and a *woman* and to show her a sort of reverence for that simple fact alone, but it wasn't any cause for him to show *dominance* over her.

He knows as well as I do that I love him, she mused as she watched tiny fish dart about in the stream. *It's not like I'm planning to leave...*

"If you're thinking what I *think* you're thinking, stop it. I'm sorry."

Kiera had been so caught up in her thoughts she hadn't heard the Aeroyn approach, but that was easy enough to dismiss since she was next to a source of noise in the running water and Darian had approached from downwind. His wings kicked up dust as he settled, and Darian knelt beside her as close as he dared, waiting for a sign that she would let him touch her.

Kiera kept her frame compact and protected, wrapping her arms tighter around her legs. She wasn't ready to give in just yet. A simple apology wasn't what she wanted. Kiera wanted to know *why*. She glanced at him, but Darian was staring past her at the water as it sparkled in the late morning sun.

"It . . . *changed*." Darian's simple explanation just made her frown. He could be talking about anything since his senses were so much sharper than hers. Kiera waited until he found the words to tell her what she really needed to hear.

"*You. You* changed, Kiera. Your breathing, your heart rate, your *smell* . . . *everything* changed. You caught sight of *him*, and *you* changed. *Before* you found out that he knows who you are. When you let him touch you."

His last words were quiet but accusatory, and her anger flared. The only way he would have known that was if he had been nearby and *watching* instead of hunting like she thought he had been. She waited several heartbeats, but Darian still wouldn't look at her.

"And *what happened*, Darian? I suddenly stopped *loving* you? I stopped *wanting* what we have? So *what* if he *touched* me—"

"Kiera, *stop*. Calm down. I know this isn't about you and I but that you instinctively want your own kind. I can't say I wouldn't want to be with a female like myself, but I don't *seek* it."

Kiera opened her mouth to rebuke him, but he held up his hand to stop her.

"I *know*. You didn't *seek* this, you didn't ask for this, but you didn't feel inclined to *stop* it either. I don't even think you could. But I'm being honest, and *you* need to be honest with *yourself*." Darian raised his eyebrows at her as she stared mutely back at him. They both knew he was right, but he knew her well enough that she wasn't going to admit it.

"I apologize for acting on the jealousy, but that doesn't mean I don't still feel it. Kiera, I love you, but maybe I was naive to think this would never change. You meant something to many people once. You *could* do that again—"

Kiera shook her head, not interested in heading down that conversational path. She already relived one horrible night of her past in her dreams; she didn't need to seek out setting herself up for such a thing to happen again. Her whole family had been ruthlessly obliterated, including her friends and the people who loved her even if she didn't always love them back.

"Darian, don't try to dangle a carrot in front of me to see if I'll take the bait. You *know* I can't go back. Corengale is beyond my reach, and the borders of Andar don't even exist anymore. I just want to protect my woods—*our* woods. *Our* life. Does that make me naive too? I want *this* world, not the one that is long gone because that ended with my family ripped apart. *Literally*."

Kiera stared hard at him, but Darian's expression said he was still questioning not only her loyalty to him but also how realistic she was being. He sighed and looked away.

Kiera was having trouble staying calm.

"*No one* in their right mind wants me as their queen, Darian! I'm too *damaged*. I don't do diplomacy, I don't ask nicely, and I don't accept *no* as an answer. I would make a *terrible* ruler especially to a kingdom that I don't *want* to govern and that doesn't even *exist* anymore. Eryce made damned sure of *that* when his greed swallowed my father's lands and all those around it without a second thought.

"You weren't there. You couldn't know... Corengale could have been a stronghold, but we didn't even *know* they were coming—" There were few times that Kiera could muster tears, much less let them fall, but they crept down her face at that moment, her memories replaying in her mind's eye. She could see *them*.

"*Ten* men with *ten* dogs, and Corengale died in *one night*. That was *all* it took, and we couldn't even fight back. I see them when I close my eyes and even when I'm awake. I will *never* let them hunt me down or give them another opportunity to take away those that I love. I only wish to rid this world of the Sukolai because I want nothing to do with the one they have created, and I would *love* to pay them back for the lives they have destroyed.

"Those were *my* people, and I know that's why the dreams haunt me now. I will *continue* to make it my mission to send those *men* back to the hell that let them loose when they set foot in this forest because I will *not* let them spoil it for either of us."

Kiera was more than a little upset at having to defend herself to the one being with whom she could even freely talk about these things, but she needed to let it out, or it would consume her. The destructive anger was an old companion, and she wanted to quell it any way she could even if it meant burdening Darian with it. She suddenly reached out and caressed Darian's hand, her soft touch startling him out of his staring contest with the stream. Their eyes met, and he felt his heart quicken under her intense gaze.

"You are my *home*, Darian. *This*"—she swept her hand out to indicate the forest—"is my *world*, and I would rather die *protecting* you both."

Eleven

Walking back to the impromptu camp gave Kiera a few precious minutes to think about how she wanted to approach Alyk; she needed to know she could trust him to leave her company and live. Just knowing he was from Corengale was reassurance enough that he didn't answer willingly to Eryce and probably never would. Kiera didn't want to kill him, but Alyk knew *who* she was and now knew *where* she was, and that information could get her—or Darian—killed.

Or captured, which was the most recent command she had seen upon rifling through the last bounty-hunter's pack. Those little notes used to just specify "bring back her head," but now Kiera was to be taken alive and unhurt. She dreaded to know *why*, but she was hell-bent on finding out.

She could still feel the ghost of the pressure from Darian's mouth on hers. The kiss had been ardent and intense, her body distracted by his passion, her mind trying to rip away long enough to complete her task so she could rejoin him. Kiera had agreed to meet her Aeroyn back at the river before the sun reached its peak to give him time to hunt nearby, and she promised to leave after speaking to the little band of travelers and sending them on their way.

Then they would head *home*.

Her unexpected guests were already packed and ready to leave when Kiera strode into the clearing, the fire extinguished and the sun getting higher overhead. They stopped talking and nodded in greeting—all except Tance, but she ignored his glacial stare and ugly frown by focusing on his brother immediately.

Alyk stood across the dampened fire from Tance and noted the look on his brother's face, half of his mouth forming a grim line of irritation. Henelce saw it too and smacked the back of Tance's head.

"Ow! What was *that* for? I didn't say *anything*!"

"You didn't *need* to, *boy*. Now, get your disrespectful butt *moving*!" Henelce pointed to the path that led east and out of the woods, waiting until Tance was almost out of sight before winking at Kiera and saying his goodbyes.

"Thank you for sharing your fire and your company, Bane. Maybe one day we will cross paths again. Light's grace, my dear." His touched right fist to his left shoulder and bowed slightly, the old custom not lost on her; she suddenly wondered if *he* knew who she was as well. Kiera nodded her own farewell as Henelce hefted his pack and his crossbow and started after Tance.

"Light's grace, Shephard," she whispered, wishing she could talk to him. Kiera turned to Jaçon as he readied to follow the Shephard, pulling the strap to his quiver over his head and settling it into place across his chest before threading his bow over his shoulder. "Elf, safe travels, be they in these or your own lands. Tread lightly beyond these trees, for your kind is no longer welcome here."

"So I have been told. Light's grace, Lady Bane. May Tirath bless you and these woods." Jaçon gave her a curt nod and turned to leave, pausing to look quizzically at Alyk who was fumbling with the attachments of his scabbard. The man glanced up just long enough to nod to his Elvin companion, and Jaçon left without another word, his noiseless footsteps carrying him along the path and out of sight.

Kiera and Alyk were left totally alone.

He immediately stopped fidgeting with the buckle and started to scan the treetops warily, obviously looking for Darian. Kiera took advantage of that moment of carelessness to grab the front of his shirt and slam him against the closest tree, pinning him there with her forearm crushing his collarbone, her face inches from his and her free hand on the hilt of the glass dagger strapped to her thigh.

"*Listen* to me, and listen *well*, for I will *not* repeat myself. I will *not* tolerate your living on this earth if you intend to be a threat to me or my *mate*. Spare me the trouble of tracking you down and feeding you slowly to the wolves if I should just kill you *now*." Kiera's eyes were narrowed, her words laced with venom, and Alyk stared back at her with a mix of understanding and a healthy amount of fear.

"How can I betray someone who is already *dead*?" His response was quiet, devoid of malice. Her secret would be guarded, but the thought that someone had recognized her still set her on edge. For the most part, Alyk was right; she had died in the raid six years ago.

Princess Kiera Spero no longer *existed*.

But someone who still answered to that name did, even if the title and the kingdom no longer survived. To let this man walk away with that confirmed suspicion left a bitter taste in her mouth. Kiera begrudgingly let go of Alyk's shirt and stepped back so that they were no longer touching, but she stayed close enough to hinder him if he tried to draw his sword.

"I know for a fact that you've heard of the *ghost* in these woods, but I wonder if you know that it slays those loyal to evil men. One in particular hopes to capture it. Do you know *why*?" Kiera was just paranoid enough to guard her words, slowly pulling the dagger from its sheath and holding it low at her side, silently telling him to watch what he said, or it would cost him dearly.

One never knew *what* lurked in the woods.

Alyk absently rubbed at his neck and chest, hoping the bruises he could already feel forming would be hidden under his shirt. He stared hard at her for a moment, body and ego both slightly damaged, before he let out a defeated breath as he looked away.

"If you mean King *Eryce*, he searches for a *woman*, not a ghost. I do not know *why* he wants her alive, but rumor has it she is to be brought to him *untouched*. The bounty is very, *very* high for her, and were I foolish enough to think I could take her on I might try to collect it myself." His words hung in the air, making her raise an eyebrow. Alyk jumped involuntarily when she snorted a laugh.

"That arrogant *king* is in for a surprise if he thinks he'll ever get her *untouched*. I'm sure she'll find a way to arrive dead *if* she arrives *at all*."

And it sure as hell wouldn't be you dragging me in! Kiera pivoted and took a few steps, warily trusting him to see her back and not try anything stupid as she sheathed her dagger. She had already admitted she didn't want to kill him if she didn't have to, and something said he felt the same; Alyk would only defend himself if Kiera gave him no other choice.

She bristled when she heard Alyk take a tentative step toward her, hoping that turning away hadn't been taken as a sign of weakness to be exploited, or there would be *consequences*. Kiera would make sure the pretty side of his face matched the damaged half.

Alyk cleared his throat, and Kiera looked back at him over her shoulder. His brown eyes caught hers with that look of recognition—of knowing exactly who he was talking to—but there was something else there she couldn't decipher.

Admiration, maybe? Her emotional wall slammed into place, those rich brown eyes piquing interests she didn't want to acknowledge. But something was nagging at Kiera as she studied Alyk, turning bodily toward him to get the full view of his face. She had known so many people in and around her home, but there were so many more whom she didn't.

He knows me. *Why don't I know him at all?* Kiera was close enough to see individual hairs in the rim of dark lashes around his eyes and the minute detail of the subtle blonde hairs in his short beard. The scars that traced his jaw and ruined his mouth on the right side were pale pink and glossy, long ago healed and probably no longer painful. His scent was musky and strong—leather and fire and sweat and forest dust almost masking the smell of *him*, which reminded Kiera a bit of maple trees warmed by the sun. That scent burrowed its way into the back of her brain, lodging into her unconscious memory, never to be forgotten . . .

Kiera hadn't realized she was reaching up to touch his scars until Alyk spoke and turned his face away from her hand. She hadn't even felt her feet moving, but there were definite footprints in the dust behind her. Her proximity to him was a little unsettling.

Kiera dropped her hand, but she didn't back away.

"I doubt you remember me, Bane. I was a squire when Corengale burned, and our paths didn't cross in ways you would have noticed. But to answer your question—one of the dogs did this to me as the Sukolai fled from the castle, burning everything in their path with dragon's fire," he said quietly, focused on the hilt of the sword that rested on his hip, trying to ignore her presence so very close to him.

"They dragged your fath . . . Garegan behind them, bound to one of the saddles by a long rope while the dogs tore through everything that moved and even some things that didn't. The knight I served, Deidric, banded with several others to try to defend the villagers and kill the Sukolai if they could, but even with nearly fifty men, those *demons* and their dogs cut a path like they were slaying children.

"I lost my family and my home that night too. I was not originally from Corengale, but I loved it and felt like I *belonged* there. My parents and my sister were staying in the castle itself while Tance and I were in the barracks. If it had not been for that and Henelce, Tance and I would not have survived...."

Alyk was staring at the ground, lost in his memory. Kiera wondered if she looked that forlorn when she got caught up in her own.

"Most of us fled to the south that night until the Sukolai stopped giving chase, and when the dawn broke, they were gone. We would have tried to rebuild, but most of Corengale was in cinders, and the damage was too great. We gave up fairly quickly once the dead were buried. There was simply too much sorrow ruining the soil for any of us to want to stay.

"The people of Corengale have found new homes now, either in other villages or in the ground, and I have not been back since. I headed to the northern territories with my brother and that Shephard, but one can only run from their destiny and their obligations for so long. Tance keeps pushing me to go *home,* but I still feel like I'm not ready, nor do I really belong there. It's not home to me anymore. Not like Corengale was."

He shifted his gaze back up to meet her brilliant stare and reached out to gently squeeze her elbow, trying to be reassuring, but he dropped it back to his side when Kiera stiffened under his touch. Alyk sighed, feeling a bit defeated. It wasn't going to matter what he said or did; she wasn't going to soften toward him, and he would be foolish to try.

"Looking at me like that, trying to see if you know me, well, that won't help you. We never met or spoke though I saw *you* on more occasions than I can count. I wouldn't have approached you anyway without permission, but *I* remember *you*. I have *many* memories of you, and I know you better than you probably think, but . . . as I leave you now, you will stay with me as a memory, if that is all you wish to be."

Kiera cocked her head curiously at his words. Her soft mouth formed a rigid line, and something shifted in her expression when she realized she *wanted* to have something in common with this man, but a wave of guilt reminded her of her words to Darian. She crossed her arms defensively and took a step to the side; no longer able to look Alyk in the eye, she studied the path behind him instead.

"No matter what you think you remember about me, I would ask that you forget me entirely. Unlike you, *I* have a *home*. I have a place I *belong*, and I do not wish to change that." Kiera could feel his gaze as he studied her, his energy changing too as he put his own defenses back into place. They stood in awkward silence for a moment, both waiting for the other to make a move, and Kiera finally broke the spell by deciding to end the conversation the only way she felt would keep her safe and leave him breathing.

I hope I don't regret this.

"I wish you well in your travels." She extended her hand to shake his, and he grasped it firmly. Kiera squeezed hard enough to make him wince, but Alyk didn't try to pull away.

"Just remember this the next time you come traipsing through my forest—these are *my* woods, and I won't be this lenient twice. We part now because I will not allow you to stay, and while I am not your enemy, we are *not* friends. The girl you think you knew is *gone*, and you will *not* like the woman that stands in her place if you don't heed my words.

"Get out and *stay out* of Baneswood."

Kiera dropped his hand coldly and walked away from him without another word. Alyk watched after her until he could no longer glimpse her white hair, and the low brush and branches stopped dancing in her wake.

"One day, *Kiera*, you may regret those words," Alyk whispered out loud. He glanced around once more, but only the trees and the birds were listening.

Alyk turned and took off at a run up the path, away from a forgotten woman he wasn't sure he wanted to let stay that way.

Two Weeks Later

Twelve

The King of Rhonendar paced in front of the enormous fire as the sun set outside the stained glass windows that punctuated the library wall of his castle. It was just one of many in the Arx Luna, the pattern spattering the ceiling and the opposite wall as the orb outside began to vanish. The evenings had begun to take on a chill as the summer finally started to fade and the fall months approached, but the crisp air was welcome after the brutal heat of the day.

Eryce found himself thirsty and exhausted after the long hours of dealing with his men, his wife, his staff, and the damned heat. He had drained two goblets of cold water as soon as he had entered his *sanctuary* and slammed the door, and a third was already half gone, the beads of sweat on the outside of the metal cup leaving rings on the table like wet footprints when he picked it up and set it back down at random while reflecting on his day.

He hadn't wanted to go to Brigton to preside over the hanging of the man accused of raping someone's daughter; he knew the poor young man had been an overzealous suitor, and the father was having none of it. The eye had warned him that the accusations were false, but Eryce needed that particular family to continue to contribute to his coffers willingly, and the peasant was worth sacrificing to keep the other man happy. It wasn't the first time he had made a decision based on money, and it wouldn't be the last, no matter how much he might wish it.

But other matters had irked him as the day progressed and time strode doggedly on. He hadn't wanted to give his new cook instruction as to how he wanted his venison prepared that evening, or to dine in the main hall when he would rather have been couped up in his office, hiding from his kingdoms demands.

And those of his wife: he hadn't wanted to explain why he would be absent from his wife's bed *again*, the fight an old and tired one. He had expected Serra to accuse him of satisfying himself with the pretty blond chambermaid in his tower while leaving her alone in her own section of the castle, hoping to bear another child for them, but he had waved her off, not interested in a conversation he could not win.

But when she had brought it up again at dinner after several glasses of wine, Eryce had had enough. *I certainly hadn't planned on confirming those lies just to get her away from me until the words were out of my mouth. Tirath help us both...* Eryce cringed at the thought. He sighed as he leaned against the table and pinched the bridge of his nose with his fingertips, feeling tired every time he thought of Serra and her desperate desire for a family to replace the one she had lost. His wife had been pregnant several times in the last three years, but the fetus never survived, and he wished she could just be happy with the two that *had* survived. Serra wanted a daughter so terribly, and Eryce knew she was fearful that her age wouldn't allow them another screaming baby. The death of her favorite haunted her still, and she desperately wanted a girl in the castle. Eryce, who thought four-year-old twin boys were quite enough, wasn't so sure he wanted to oblige.

He didn't understand her sense of loss either since the daughter she missed had been illegitimate anyway.

It's not like that bastard girl could have ruled a kingdom, anyway... Eryce shook his head, trying to push away the annoyance and the headache he felt building at the base of his skull so he could focus on more pressing matters that weren't so near at hand. It had been a *very* long day, and he was ready to put it behind him as he glanced at the map of his kingdom and went back to pacing to and fro along the table's edge.

Two weeks had passed since he had heard from Delámer, and Eryce was curious as to the hunter's supposed progress. A short letter had been delivered earlier that day, bearing a strange wax seal and sharply penned handwriting that promised a report by the end of the moon cycle, which was still three days away. The note still sat on his desk on the other side of the room, and Eryce felt like three days might be too long with recent events as they were.

In the past two weeks alone, pieces of two of the three missing field scouts had been found along the border of Baneswood, and the third had been dragged from a tavern and branded as a deserter. Moreover, one of the Sukolai's female breeder hounds had gone missing in that time, and he had raised hell to get her back. The bitch's carcass was eventually recovered a few days later—without its fur—many, many miles from where she had been "abducted" from her master's watch. Her red collar had still been wrapped around her hairless neck, and her muscles were left nearly white from the loss of blood. The beast had been tied hanging upside down along the border of Baneswood, both her tongue and her womb torn out, the whole ghastly body covered in flies.

The litter of expected pups was never found, and neither was her cobalt pelt, though Eryce had a sneaking suspicion he might see it again one day. Bane was creative, if nothing else, and he could only imagine what she might do with a hide like that...

Eryce stopped pacing and leaned over the map yet again drumming his fingers on the table and focused on the newest pin that had been pushed into the wooden surface. The Sukolai had simply ordered the disgusting body burned, but the loss of at least two trainable hounds made Eryce rage inside; breeding pairs were hard to come by as it was, and females didn't survive into adulthood unless the whole litter was devoid of males because the mother would kill any female pups to give the males a better chance at survival. Trying to get *any* of the pups away from the mother was impossible until she was ready to wean them, and raising them to adulthood was a challenge left to a highly skilled trainer and some very expendable stableboys. Very few females were ever allowed to run with the Sukolai as companions, but her handler had refused to leave her behind on his last patrol.

Which was an unfortunate mistake. One that won't be repeated in the future, Eryce thought as he continued his trek to exactly nowhere.

Cobalt hounds were ludicrously expensive to keep once the female was pregnant, and this one had proven to be a waste of money, her due date only a week or two away after a three-month gestation. The females were slow and vulnerable when they bred, making them an easy target, and the handler was just as much to blame; rather, he *had* been when he was still alive. Carik's services had *ended* when both Eryce *and* his commander found out that the young mercenary had been hiding in a tree when the hound had gone into labor and turned on him before taking off into the woods to give birth.

Damned coward, he huffed in his mind as he picked up his goblet again and took a deep swallow of water, briefly considering switching over to wine once the cup was empty. He set the cup back on the surface of the table and continued his slow back and forth, taking a deep breath of the cool air as the last light of day faded and left much of the library in shadow.

The pacing was finally beginning to soothe his burning nerves, and the glow in his blinded right eye was cooling to a softer iridescent light as his blood pressure slowly decreased. His breath came more steadily as the advancing night cooled the room, and the area of palpable warmth was reduced to just outside the hearth. Eryce slowed his pacing and stopped in front of the fire, folding his arms across his chest, letting the hot embers and the flames swirl in his vision as his right hand absently played with his lower lip...

"I sense deep thoughts. Should I offer a penny for them?" Delámer whispered; he stood less than a foot behind the king, and this time, appearing out of thin air sparked a reaction as Eryce stiffened and grunted in surprise. But he quickly relaxed into a more easy posture when he turned and realized who was invading his personal space.

"Must you always appear like a *ghost*?" As irritated as he was at the sudden intrusion, Eryce was actually glad to see the man before him that meant his current bout of waiting had ceased. Delámer grinned, his cheeks lifting his mask ever so slightly off his nose as he stepped back from Eryce and walked noiselessly toward the table in the center of the room.

"Now, now, great *king*, if I stopped being unpredictable, you would lose interest with me, and I happened to like all parts of me exactly where they are." Delámer picked up Eryce's goblet, and instead of drinking from it, he simply moved it to the far corner of the large map carved into the wooden surface.

"Pity, I was hoping this was wine. No matter. I bring you news of this creature you call Bane: I have seen her, and lived to tell about it. *Here*, your Highness. She's *here*."

Delámer lifted the glass so it left a ring around a spot along the Oriens River that extended from Breach Lake to the Corrant, nearly a hundred miles and almost directly west of the castle where they now stood.

"And the Aeroyn?" Eryce asked cautiously.

"Gray with black wings, and *very* protective of her, or so the townsfolk of Grant's Perch would have me believe, though I only saw him at a distance. Rumor has it that she shares the ruined fortress above the Breach with her *bird*, and several townsfolk in Grant's Perch have confirmed a woman with white hair and green eyes comes into the village at dusk on rare occasion to purchase goods and speak to the weapons smith. They swear her name is Bane."

Eryce leaned forward with his hands on the table, studying a part of his kingdom he had only been to on few occasions. Grant's Perch, the fishing town where she had been spotted, was just on the edge of his lands. It was a long trek through some rather forbidding forest no matter which side of the Oriens River one chose to travel westward on. Even without her presence, Baneswood was not a place even the Sukolai would willingly go without good reason, and it was terrifyingly easy to get lost under the sunless canopy and tangled underbrush if you didn't know the paths, not to mention the fauna of the area, much of which would readily kill a man and pick its teeth with the bones. That Bane had chosen such a place wasn't surprising; that she had survived it for so long certainly was.

Eryce's eyes wandered the map, the little red dots of the previous attacks on his men making more sense as they were congregated directly between his castle and hers. The bodies were always found close to the Baneswood border, and that meant she actually left her trees on rare occasion. The Glenfolds may have been a healthy distance from his castle and bordered her plot of living lumber, but with the help of an Aeroyn, distance was probably not much of an issue for her.

She could probably travel all the way to Corengale in less than a week, he mused, focused on the decrepit relic of a fortress that had been ruined well before his father had taken power some sixty or so years before. *Interesting...*

"I see you have quite the challenge in retrieving this one, assuming, that is, that she—or that *thing*—doesn't kill you first." Eryce stood and crossed his arms, thoughtfully planning as he studied the map.

"Your time limit stands as before, but use it wisely because my forces *will* be unleashed into those trees, and you will *not* want to be caught in the crossfire. What do I owe you for this bit of information?"

Silence greeted him, and Eryce was suddenly aware the pouch of gold he was reaching for on his belt was gone. He glanced around almost disinterestedly, knowing the room was devoid of Delámer. It took a moment longer for it to register that his hunting knife with the large amethyst on the hilt was also missing; gold was one thing, but that knife had been a gift from his wife, and he was less than thrilled that it was suddenly gone. Anger flared in his enchanted eye for a moment, but dark, deep laughter crept up the back of Eryce's throat, and he let the walls ring with it as he imagined green eyes filled with an intense fear, the likes of which they had never known.

The thought of her neck being crushed under his hand flipped a switch in his brain. Eryce felt powerful heat rage through his body, his cock growing hard with lust and hunger, and he suddenly had the urge to *visit* that pretty chambermaid.

No one would even bat an eye if they found her naked and ruined.

Not that she would live through it anyway.

Like a wolf on the hunt, Eryce headed up three floors toward his rooms, knowing this was about the time she would be making up the fire there.

I'm coming for you, little bitch.

He turned the corner in the hall and slammed his chamber door open, startling the petite blonde who was dusting the soot from her apron and was about to leave the room. Eryce smiled at her with all of his teeth, and the enchanted eye burned in the socket, ready to be fed with another extinguished life. The young woman stood stock-still like a frightened deer, and Eryce closed the door behind him slowly without taking his eyes off her, growling low as he turned the key, leaving her with nowhere to go.

This is going to be fun.

Thirteen

The waterfall thundered against the rocks thirty feet below her, the late morning sunlight creating a rainbow that stretched from one side of the falls to the other and followed her as she moved along the precipice. A fine, cool mist rose from the pool at the bottom as she peered over the edge, checking the water level before backing carefully away from the wet, slippery rocks.

Kiera removed her boots, her weapons, her tunic, and her armor, leaving her brown leggings and sweaty linen top in place. She shoved her clothes into her pack, hid it under some brush, and padded back to the rushing water with bare feet. Her toes curled over the edge of the rocks as she felt the wind from the falls lift her loose hair back from her face.

She breathed deeply, closing her eyes, letting the world evaporate around her.

Spreading her arms wide, she jumped.

* * *

Kiera broke the surface of the water, gulping in a lungful of air and quickly disappeared again. She swam quietly toward the shore, resurfacing when she could stand and wade her way out of the pool. She ran her hands through her thick locks as she emerged from the pool, squeezing out some of the clinging droplets before letting it fall long and straight down the middle of her back. Her sleeveless linen shirt and thin leggings clung to her body as she climbed onto the sandy shoreline, leaving nothing to the imagination as she emerged from the river and headed to one of her favorite sunning spots. The sun was bright overhead, and Kiera savored every ray as she stretched out face up on the warm sand.

She knew she would only get to do this a few more times this year as the summer days were fading fast. In a few short weeks the weather that was already starting to cool would turn chilly, and diving into this pool would have to wait for another winter to pass before she could *fly* again.

Kiera envied Darian's wings and his natural ability to leave the ground and soar, and this was the closest thing she had to doing it on her own. Those few short seconds before the water rushed up to greet her were precious, private moments and were the only time she felt truly *free*. Darian didn't particularly care for water, and she often ended up at the river alone anyway, but the cliffs, the pool . . .

That was her private sanctuary.

Kiera sat up suddenly, her eyes searching for the source of the rustling she could just barely hear over the waterfall when a twig snapped on the other side of the river; she felt the unnerving sensation of eyes upon her, and she froze in the middle of reaching for the knife in her boot as it dawned on her that she was totally unarmed. Kiera may have been weaponless, but her fighting skills were honed enough that she didn't really need one.

It just made her feel better to be the one with a pointy object.

She heard the arrow before she saw it, but she didn't react quite fast enough to dodge it completely as she scrambled backward. It pierced the front of her calf, narrowly missing the bones but puncturing straight through the muscle and digging into the sand. Kiera reached out instinctively to pull at the offending object, but the angle was too steep, and she couldn't stand. She gritted her teeth, refusing to scream even with her leg burning, her blood pooling under her slowly. The pain in her leg was excruciating, nearing unbearable, and the urge to scream for Darian was winning the race against all other thoughts in her head. The lodged arrow seemed to be keeping the bleeding to a minimum, but that thought wasn't comforting considering she was now trapped.

"Fuck!" she seethed, still searching the opposite shore.

The glint of metal caught her attention as another arrow whizzed past Kiera's head, barely missing her face as she tried to dodge to the left. It, too, dove deep into the sand, and a green ribbon that kept a small note attached to the shaft fluttered directly in front of her face when she opened her eyes. The arrows had come from across the river directly in front of her, and she felt stupid for allowing the illusion of safety to cloud her judgment. Just because she kept her woods *clean* didn't mean she was safe from the other shore.

Kiera felt her panic rising as she scanned the rocks above the falls, but she saw no one.

She hadn't really expected to.

Finally, Kiera screamed for Darian. Over and over, his name fleeing her lips almost convulsively, the shrill cries startling the nearby birds; they rose in a cloud as they fled the offending noise. Kiera didn't care as she watched the other side of the river and kept pressure on her leg as best she could. The blood loss was slow, but the pain was starting to wear at her; the pounding of her heart in her ears drowned out the thundering of the falls, and unconsciousness was getting harder to keep at bay.

The tails of the ribbon danced in the wind, distracting her enough to tear the arrow out of the sand and rip the piece of paper away from the shaft with her bloodied hand. Her vision was starting to blur, but Kiera made out the dark words scrawled on the bit of parchment.

Next time, I will not be so lenient either.

"Darian . . ." Her last cry came out as a whisper as darkness rushed up the meet her, and blissful painless unconsciousness left the forest quiet once again.

Fourteen

The fire popped, and Kiera sat straight up.
Her heart was racing, and her head hurt.
But she was *alive*.
She was *home*.

She was also naked, sandwiched between two skins to keep her covered, but even with the warm afternoon and the fire blazing away, she felt chilled. Kiera reached down and touched her calf where the arrow had pierced her flesh; the spot was a little tender, but the wound was totally gone. She sighed and flopped back, the furs barely cushioning her from the hard stone floor, but she didn't care just then.

Kiera was just happy to be breathing.

Something pointy poked at her through the hide that covered her, and Kiera turned to see Darian watching her, the firelight making his features waver in and out of the shadows. He looked exhausted, worried, and mildly horrified. In one hand, he held a small scrap of paper, and the "stick" was half of the arrow it had been attached to.

"Glad to see you're awake. You've been out cold for two days." Darian sounded anything but *glad*. He was angry—very, scarily, seriously angry. Kiera could actually smell him, and that was rare. Normally the Aeroyn didn't have much of an odor, but stress made him smell like ozone before a thunderstorm; he was gripping the arrow so hard it was creaking.

"Darian, *calm down*. I'm *fine*," Kiera chided with a trembling voice as she threw her arm over her face, trying to hide her relieved tears, but soon she was shaking so hard that he reached under the fur and pulled her up and onto his lap. Darian held her tightly, his warmth seeping into her, letting Kiera cry uncontrollably. He watched the flames and waited, resting his cheek on the top of her head.

So many tears lately . . .

Her sobs finally abated to sniffling, and she wiped at her eyes and nose with the back of her hand. Kiera started to hiccup, and she held her breath to quiet her spasming diaphragm as she turned her head to watch the fire too, grateful for Darian's familiar form.

"You are going to have to face this at some point, you know." Darian's voice rumbled in his chest, resonating like a deep purr. "The world seems to be very keen on getting your attention, and I cannot keep you safe, Kiera. This tells me that you aren't going to be hiding much longer, no matter how hard you try, because you have already been found."

He pushed her away enough to bring the scrap of paper up to her face. Kiera read those haunting words again, wondering what could have possessed *him* to do this. She hadn't thought he was a threat when he had walked away, and that idea still seemed wrong.

"My last words to Alyk." Kiera whispered as she took the note from Darian and brought it closer to the fire, reading the words through the paper. "I told him I would not be lenient if he crossed the borders of Baneswood again. It seems I should have made sure he never left them to begin with."

Alyk had been gone for at least two weeks, and Kiera hadn't even thought of him more than once or twice since he had walked out of the forest. The man had been in their life for less than a day, and she had begrudgingly trusted him to keep her secret.

She tossed the offending bit of trash at the fire, but it landed just outside the reach of the flames. As the parchment warmed, the room took on a peculiar odor. She caught the sweet perfume of old books, the slightly bitter scent of the dried ink, and something else . . .

Something black and oily and a little like sulfur. Her brain screamed *danger* as her body remembered that smell—her muscles were tensing, her heart was racing, and her mouth was watering as she recalled the pungent odor of burning flesh as she stared at the curling parchment, tempted to reach for it . . .

"*What*, Kiera?" Darian asked hurriedly, sensing her panic. He held her closer and inhaled her scent. "*You* smell wrong."

"I *know* that *smell*." Kiera's gaze was fixed on the scrap of paper, the bile fighting its way up her throat and her heart hammering in her ears.

"What smell? All I smell is *you*," Darian said, thoroughly confused.

"Dragonsfire," she whispered. "Darian, *Alyk* didn't do this. I-I think that's from *Eryce*."

Fifteen

"*What the hell are you doing?*"

Tance's head whipped around, his hazel eyes showing no guilt and glinting meanly, his hand still under the skirt of the unconscious girl he was crouched over as his brother rushed him from behind.

Alyk grabbed Tance by the scruff of his shirt before he could react and dragged him from the barn, Tance's feet kicking at nothing and his hands clawing at his brother's unbreakable grip. Alyk threw his little brother against the outer wall and backhanded him.

"*This* is how you repay their kindness? How could you do this to her? What is *wrong* with you?" Alyk hit him again, and Tance's nose started to bleed. He grabbed Tance by the front of his shirt, slamming his head against the wall, making his body go limp. Alyk's face was an angry red, his scars standing out a vivid white against the flush of his cheek, his mind registering nothing but fury as he pressed his forearm against his little brother's throat, keeping him from answering *and* breathing.

"*Hey! Alyk? Stop!*"

He barely heard the Shephard yelling behind him as Henelce came running from the other side of the stables, his eyes bright with panic, Elbert, the horse breeder that had given them a place to stay on their trek south, not far behind.

They had originally intended to only stay a night, but Alyk had enjoyed helping with the chores, and they had already been there for nearly two weeks. Finding his brother molesting the man's young daughter was the last thing he had expected, and it was taking what little sanity he had cowering in the back of his mind to keep him from simply ending Tance's life then and there.

Henelce's strong grip wrapped around Alyk's elbow and pulled him away from Tance, whose lips were turning blue while tears and blood streamed down his face. Alyk finally let go, and his brother crumpled to the ground, the boy suddenly on his hands and knees and gulping ragged lungful after lungful of air, coughing uncontrollably. Clenching his fists, his stare boring holes into Tance's back, Alyk fought the urge to kick his sibling in the ribs as he forced out words through his clenched teeth.

"In the barn. I found him in the barn . . ." Alyk looked at the kind man who had given them a place to stay. His anger thawed a bit, pity breaking through as he locked eyes with the breeder. ". . . with Alysan."

Elbert's eyes went wide, and he ran into the barn, calling her name. Alyk turned his attention back to Tance, who was still coughing and bleeding and now trying to stand, leaving bloody handprints on the side of the barn as he reached out to steady himself.

"What's the matter, *brother*?" Tance laughed contemptuously as he shakily wiped at his face. "Did I *beat you to it*?"

Henelce pushed Alyk aside and punched Tance so hard the young man spun and fell against the barn with a loud bang, his body falling limply to the ground. The role reversal of Alyk suddenly struggling to hold Henelce back didn't strike him as ironic until much later.

"She's *ten*, you arrogant bastard!" Henelce screamed at Tance's unconscious form.

Alyk wasn't blind to Tance's mean streak, but he hadn't thought his own *blood* capable of *this*, and he really didn't want to imagine what would have happened had he not needed Tance to help him haul water. Just knowing the boy had it in him to take it as far as he had was nauseating.

Elbert's face was ashen as he emerged from the barn, his daughter cradled against his chest, her arms and legs dangling limply. He turned to the three of them, his eyes hard and cold. Alyk felt responsible, and he wanted to make it right, but Elbert cut him off before he could even open his mouth.

"If you want him to live, get him out of Chirk. *Now*." The breeder turned away and walked a few paces, stopping to adjust his hold but refusing to turn toward them. "I don't care *who* you are—if I ever see you here again, I'll kill you all."

Sixteen

The sun was already setting by the time Tance regained consciousness. The pouch full of cold water was rather helpful in rousing him from his "well-earned nap" as it was dumped unceremoniously over his head.

Tance sputtered awake and cried out, the cold water shocking his system and soaking his bloodied clothes. Alyk didn't even look up from the fire as Henelce threw the waterskin aside, glaring at the bedraggled and bloodied young man at his feet, his barely contained magic prickling Tance's skin like thousands of pins and needles all over his body like every inch of his skin had gone to sleep.

"You listen to me, *boy*," Henelce growled as he reached down and grabbed Tance by the front of his shirt, bringing his face so close Tance instinctively struggled to back away. "The *only* reason you're still breathing is because your *brother*"—Henelce pointed angrily over his shoulder—"doesn't have the heart to *kill* you even though he probably should have. You cost us the roof over our heads and the trust of good people. I hesitate to ask if you have *anything* to say for yourself that I even want to hear."

He threw Tance roughly back on the ground, and Tance stared hatefully at Henelce, his mouth firmly closed and his jaw too painful to even try to speak. Henelce's eyes flashed dangerously, the irises sparkling with little dots of white light, daring Tance to give him a reason to end him.

"Let him go, Henelce. It's not worth it." Alyk's quiet words were full of defeat as he poked at the fire, trying not to look at his brother. The Shephard sneered at Tance as he backed away and took a seat next to Alyk, positioning himself between the two of them as though he would protect one from the other.

They had set up camp in a clearing in Blightwood, about a mile directly west of Chirk. Alyk already missed the small settlement where they had taken up residence in on the other side of the Oriens not long after leaving Bane behind, wishing he could return and make things right. They had separated from Jaçon shortly thereafter, the elf deciding to return to his own kingdom instead of risking his neck by continuing to escort the other travelers once they were out of Baneswood.

It had been just the three of them ever since.

Henelce found himself wishing Jaçon was there; the elf was the only one who could really keep Tance in check because Tance knew—they *all* knew—that Jaçon would kill the young man if he got the chance. Only respect for the Shephard and a begrudging acceptance of Alyk had kept him at bay, but it was a thin line and one that kept Tance in better behavior. It had been that way since they had met the elf, and this was just the sort of thing that would have more than justified him notching an arrow and sending it through the boy's heart.

Tance sat there for a few minutes, watching the fire and trying to ignore Henelce's icy glare before finally deciding it was time to assess the damage. He touched his jaw tenderly, the pain making him wince, and when he swallowed, he tasted blood. His head was pounding, and he was starting to shiver as the cold water on his skin mixed with the cool breeze in the evening air, lowering his core temperature, his thin frame doing nothing to help keep him warm.

Finally, Tance could take the chill no more and stood shakily to move to the opposite side of the fire, his entire body resisting any and every voluntary movement. He sat down gingerly, hugging his knees to his chest and resting his forehead on them, muffling his words.

"All this over some *stupid twat*," Tance whispered to himself.

"That's it!" Henelce tried to stand up, and Tance panicked, scrambling away from the angry Shephard, but Alyk caught the back of Henelce's pants and dragged him back down.

"*I said* let it *go!*" Alyk barked. He studied Tance like he was a stranger, which he was surprised to find wasn't all that hard since he suddenly felt that he didn't know his brother anymore. Gone was the shy, brooding boy who took life too seriously and looked up to his older brother for advice and support; in his place sat a disgusting, wriggling worm of a young man who was quickly becoming harder and harder to look at.

Tance showed no remorse, and that made the decision his brother was about to make that much easier to stomach.

"Justance Fairaday, I disown you," Alyk addressed his brother like a judge sentencing a criminal. Tance made a face at Alyk, wincing at the pain in his jaw from the effort. Alyk ignored him as he went on.

"You, little brother, have betrayed me, betrayed Henelce, and betrayed the trust of people that were willing to help us. I cannot even fathom where you learned that bullshit behavior from, but the thin ice you've been walking on lately finally cracked. You have *dishonored* our family name, and I won't let that go.

"Tomorrow, Henelce and I will head north toward the Runes of Obilio. *You*," Alyk's voice was grave, "will head in whichever direction gets you the farthest away from us. If you show your face in Chirk again, Elbert will kill you. I spared your life at my own hand because I had the faintest hope that you would see your error, but that seems to be beyond you. I let you live now because I won't be there to help you anymore, and to me, that's as good as killing you because we all know you won't survive more than a week without our help."

Alyk glanced down at the bag he had packed with Tance's few belongings and a little food. He tossed it toward the ungrateful youth, who let it hit the ground next to him and slide a few feet away.

"Oh, and don't bother trying to go *home*. I have already sent word that you are not to be trusted, and you are no longer welcome in my house. You are well and truly on your *own*, little brother. You may share the fire tonight, but in the morning, if you are still here . . ."

Alyk's brown eyes sparkled threateningly over the flames. He took a deep breath and spoke his next words slowly, every one of them resonating to his very soul.

"If you're still *here*, I will kill you *myself*."

Seventeen

Dark-green eyes were attentive to the flickering firelight in the window of the crumbling old castle directly across the lake from them. Those eyes had seen the Aeroyn take *her* unconscious body into the ancient fortress shortly after he had returned to Grant's Perch two days before, and she had yet to leave, though the *bird* had shown his face since. The man behind those eyes smiled to himself, knowing he had more than enough time and money to wait an entire month for her to come back out of her rabbit hole.

White Rabbit. That's a much better name than Bane. What the hell kind of name is that, anyway? It's so . . . unoriginal. Delámer leaned against the railing of the dock outside the Inn-land Starfish, a temporary residence with its own *terrible* name, his mind on the woman he was supposed to retrieve.

From what he had already seen, this *Bane* was quite the prize. She had been hard enough to track, he would certainly give her that, but now that he had a very good idea of where and how to find her, it was only a matter of time before she saw the inside of the Arx Luna and became Eryce's problem. He could imagine the King of Rhonendar being more than mildly interested in the girl when that he finally laid eyes on her.

Bane may have started piquing Eryce's interest and inviting his wrath by killing his men and a few of those disgusting dogs, but Delámer was sure that when Eryce actually had Bane within his grasp, he would be glad he had decided to spare her life.

And those breasts . . . Delámer smirked as he thought back to the first time he laid eyes on her. Bane had taken him by surprise a week or so ago when he was first scouting the area, appearing high above him at the waterfall. He had followed the river on the Blightwood side, looking for places Bane might frequent, careful to avoid stepping foot into *her* territory until he knew what he was really up against. Her track record said she wasn't overly tolerant of outsiders in her woods, though now that he was able to put a face to the name, he couldn't help but wonder if this Bane was really as ruthless as Eryce—and everyone in the village—seemed to think she was.

He could barely hear the scratch of his pencil against the parchment as he added to the map in his journal, leaning against a large rock set back from the small beach. It was already midafternoon, and the heat was only tolerable when he stood completely still in the shade. He had been walking since dawn, leaving his horse behind in Grant's Perch, and he figured he was at least ten or twelve miles east of town when he had happened upon the secluded falls and the welcome break in the day's heat.

The moisture in the air from the falls and a gentle breeze made the area a good twenty degrees cooler, and Delámer had decided to spend the rest of the day right where he was, this woman he was tracking be damned. The shade and the underbrush had hid him nicely without obscuring his view as he sketched in his journal, and he was just readying to leave his spot when he had caught movement out of the corner of his eye.

That has to be her, Delámer thought as he fought the urge to let out a low whistle. He had expected someone older, maybe more tattered and possibly missing a limb or covered in warrior's gear... He had known only that he was looking for a woman, just not one that looked like that. The white hair was something he had been prepared to find, but he hadn't expected to like it.

He hadn't expected her to be beautiful.

Bane stood a good thirty feet above him at the edge of the cliff, her white hair dancing in the breeze. She wore only a short shift of cream-colored material that had been cut off just above her knees, and it rippled in the wind while the moisture from the spray of the falls gave her exposed arms and legs a soft sheen as she stepped forward into the light and looked over the edge of the cliffs. Creamy skin, curves that were intermittently defined as the breeze pressed the fabric of her shift against her frame, and vivid green eyes that he could see from where he stood almost a hundred yards away were making him second guess if she was even *real* or if the heat was finally getting to him.

'*Why are all the pretty one's spoken for?*' Delámer thought, almost disappointed that she had been deemed marked prey as he watched Bane intently from the shade below, waiting for her to sit at the edge of the cliff, silently thanking Tirath that luck was on his side. He moved a little closer, trying to get a better view of her, and when she looked his way, he froze, waiting quietly and hoping he hadn't been spotted.

"No one here but us squirrels, beautiful," he whispered to himself. Bane's appearance had made his job so much easier, and he was studying her carefully, memorizing her features from his lower vantage point, wishing he could sketch her without having to move.

Bane was still looking his way when she stepped back from the edge cautiously, and Delámer swore under his breath when she left his view altogether, figuring she had seen him and was now getting her gear with the intent to either find him and beat the hell out of him or simply leave.

Either way, she was gone.

"Well, so much for that," he sighed as he picked up his own pack from the ground and shoved his journal deep inside, shouldering the bag and readying to leave, glancing up at the top of the fall one last time.

Delámer almost called out to her when Bane suddenly ran toward the edge and jumped off, arms spread wide like she had wings of her own. He actually envied her at *that moment as he watched her fall gracefully, bringing her arms together into a smooth dive as the thirty feet of open air ended and the water rushed up to greet her.*

She looked so free, and he hadn't felt that way in a long, long time . . .

He absently caressed the edge of his glass with his thumb as he imagined her body when Bane had emerged from the water on the other side of the river to lie in the sun. Every inch of her had been visible through that wet shift even at a distance, and he felt almost like he was cheating at a game the other person had no idea they were even playing; he was looking forward to raising the stakes and seeing her up close.

Delámer took a deep breath of the mountain air that blew over the Breach, his green eyes no longer interested in the derelict castle but focused on the moons chasing each other across the sky overhead. The larger white moon was on its third day of waxing toward full in its twenty-eight-day rotation, while the smaller red moon was nearer to whole, only five days left in its seventeen-day-cycle until it reached full.

So much to do . . . His thoughts turned to other tasks he had piled upon himself, the list getting longer as his available time grew shorter. The double full moon were approaching fast, their cycles set to coincide in forty days, right around the beginning of October. If Delámer played his cards right, he would be able to kill a few birds with one stone: collect this Bane and drag her back to Eryce before his deadline, retrieve the crystal he had paid one of the maids to hide in the library at the Arx so he could surprise the arrogant king whenever he felt it necessary, and move on with his life.

Delámer needed to have all five of his crystals in hand to recharge them with the power of the double full moon, and he could get to three of them easily enough plus the one he had in his room at the Starfish, but he hadn't been able to use the fifth in almost a year. While he knew *exactly* where it was, the thought of collecting the damned thing made him mildly irritated because he would have to actually *travel* into the mountains to retrieve it, and that sounded tedious.

And *dangerous.* It wasn't a task Delámer was looking forward to, but if he wanted his set to continue to work, he would have to have them all. Getting *to* the Runes of Obilio to perform the ritual wasn't an issue because one of the crystals he needed was already hidden near there, but getting home was another story. He had done the ritual enough times that he knew he could look forward to a few days of riding to the nearest river port then the four-day boat ride *home* to start all over again.

This will be my first year going alone— Delámer cut that thought off midstream as he ran his hand back through his short, sandy blond locks, silently hating how much had been sheared. *That's the* last *time I let Peter cut my hair. He did this on purpose!*

It would grow back, but he liked to let it fall roguishly over his eyes when flirting with the girls. He had a certain *look* he liked to sport, and the current change in his appearance made him feel *boring*. He loathed the word, and he would rather it not pertain to *him*, no matter what someone else thought would look good on him.

Delámer knew he needed every advantage he could get, especially now, and his clothing was just as important, his current outfit carefully chosen to highlight every aspect of the body Tirath had graced him with. His long-sleeved black linen shirt was loose and the neck left untied, the cool breeze making the fabric flutter around his arms and intermittently expose his smooth chest. His black leather pants and boots were more for aesthetic than comfort, fitting to his muscular legs like a second skin. But if any woman was immune to the clothes on that sleek body, they were never safe from his smile with his bright white teeth and beautifully formed mouth or the way his eyes crinkled at the edges when his smile was genuine—though he couldn't pinpoint the last time that was.

His half mask was gone, hidden in the pack in his room, but his eyes remained dramatically lined with the kohl he wore beneath it that he would have to remove before the morning. He actually liked the stuff, even if it was a pain to scrub off, especially when women told him it made him look *mysterious*. Or *dangerous*. Or whatever word made them like the idea of playing along.

Delámer *knew* what he looked like, but being deviously aware of how to exploit his looks wasn't really the same as being as vain as Narcissus, and he considered his features a useful tool. The goddess had been generous when she had made him, and several past *assignments* had enjoyed teasing him, calling him "as gorgeous as he was arrogant" and "Tirath's personal plaything." Delámer had always thought that second one was rather funny, especially when most of them never got to find out if that was actually *true* since he only acted the part of the playboy when it suited his needs, which rarely ended in the bedroom. *Usually* it ended with a woman trusting him; that was how he got most of his information, and information was his business. *People* were his business. Only when an assignment required extra *effort* did Delámer sweet-talk a woman out of her clothes and even then, it was boring only because it was too easy, but at least he was well paid.

Money isn't everything though it certainly helps. That thought made him smile when he put it into context with this particular retrieval. The bounty would be a nice bonus, but this *Bane*—*his* White Rabbit—she was going to be a dangerous, albeit well paid, challenge, and that interested him in ways he hadn't been in years. Most women were chatty and excited by his attention, and more often than not, there were dozens of people who knew the *ladies* he was assigned to. Delámer was accustomed to sources from which he could get background and dirty little secrets and pinpoint ways to get under powdered skin to the fullest effect.

He was *used* to having at least some sort of guidance, but with Bane, he was flying blind, and he found that both annoying and a little exciting. At the moment, Delámer knew where she was and what she looked like, but there were no available sources to tell him *who* she was, and that intrigued him most of all. No one in Grant's Perch knew where she had come from, only that she had shown up somewhere between five and six summers ago, white hair and Aeroyn pieces of the puzzle from the very beginning. They described her as quiet, to the point, and told him not to cross her because she had her own *rules* when it came to who she let in and out of the forest.

So far he had heeded their warnings and stuck to the other side of the Oriens as the river that served as the dividing line between Baneswood to the north and the slightly safer Blightwood to the south. But his mission was about to change, and Delámer's goal now wasn't just to get Bane to let him *into* the forest since he could simply find her, grab her, and drag her directly to Eryce. He cringed at the thought of doing something so *expected*.

He was aiming for something he found *much* more... *interesting*. Bane presented the chance at a good game where the rules were uncertain, and there was a very real danger of getting on the wrong side of a creature known to dismember first and ask questions later, not to mention the Aeroyn, but he wasn't about to let that stop him. Personal accomplishment was on the line, and Delámer wanted to truly test if he was as good as he liked to think he was.

I either win or die. Those seem like fun odds. Delámer smirked as he picked up his rum from the railing and sipped it, the warmth trickling down the back of his throat as he watched the slivers of the double moons slowly chase each other across the sky, relishing in the wind on his exposed face. He would have to don another mask soon, but it was going to take a while to paint it fully; he needed to see how Bane responded to him first *if* he even got the chance to open his pretty mouth before she tried to kill him. That was always a real possibility, and he would have to tread carefully.

Tomorrow. I will find out tomorrow. Knocking back the rest of his rum, Delámer tossed the glass over the railing into the lake, the small splash creating ripples that fled in all directions as they hurried to reach the far shore. He took one last look at the castle, impishly blowing it a kiss, and turned to head back through the door and up to his room. He needed to rest before dawn showed its glorious head over the forest and made him get his ass in gear.

Delámer hoped it would be an interesting day, and if he was disappointed...

Well, he would just have to show up at her door.

Then it would be interesting whether he liked it or not.

Eighteen

The dawn found Kiera awake and wrapped in a long, amber-colored robe of a soft woollen fabric that pooled on the floor. She stood at the half-broken window of the ballroom that faced to the east, her arms crossed over her chest as she reminisced about all the times her ever faithful Aeroyn had saved her as she surveyed the land that spread out a hundred feet below.

The lake and the small valley were slowly being brought to life by the morning sun, the cool breeze that filtered in through the shattered panes bringing with it the soft scent of pine and the distant sound of men already working on the docks. The summer was fading into fall, the trees already tinged with red and gold along their uppermost branches. The heat from the summer sun would stick around for another week or two at most, and then the crisp air would take over especially as the days continued to get shorter and shorter.

Kiera inhaled deeply, savoring the familiar smells she had grown to love as they carried to her on the gentle current of mountain air that stirred the dust at her feet.

If Eryce comes after me, we will have to leave. I cannot put us, or these people, in danger.

She hated the thought of deserting a place she had found so much comfort in, the village below full of people Kiera knew respected her authority in the woods that cut them all off from the outside world, while the ruined castle had become a home she always felt to be a slightly ironic residence for her. Her own stone fortress had been decimated, and sometimes she felt as though she had gravitated here out of sheer need to still feel in control of something long lost.

You meant something to many people once. You could do that again...

Kiera sighed as Darian's words trickled through her mind and she shifted uncomfortably at the thought, wincing reflexively though her leg had been thoroughly healed thanks to Darian's blood, but she still felt wary of putting her full weight on it just yet. She replayed his words from the night before, and she knew Darian was right in that he wouldn't be able to shield her anymore. She had made herself too well-known to be considered anything other than a threat to a king she would rather see in the ground than bow to especially after what he had done to her family.

Then again, she wouldn't be able to save anyone caught in the crossfire if Eryce did what *she* would do if faced with this particular situation: Kiera was just *waiting* for him to send in an overwhelming force and flush out the prey like a pack of hunting dogs after a fox.

It would be Corengale all over again.

Kiera pushed that web of thoughts away to focus on her Aeroyn instead, the one she had left sleeping soundly on the other side of the stone wall, replaying those memories of their first encounter and the ones that followed and the ways they had changed each other. She had saved him once, and he had repaid the favor countless times since. Kiera felt it was her turn to look out for both of them.

No matter if Darian *was* the more ruthless hunter of the two of them, Eryce wouldn't send men into Baneswood after *Darian*.

They would be coming after *her*.

For six years, he has watched over me. Mate or not, he's the closest thing to family I have.

Kiera had been fourteen when she had stumbled upon her Aeroyn, and it had taken almost two years for it to dawn on her that he was *male*. While many girls in her own kingdom were being married off at an even younger age, Kiera had been mildly oblivious to the opposite sex, *human* or not. She had been too busy acting like a boy to be really interested in them, the men in her life never piquing any interest in her as she wandered the castle, the river, and the fields without so much as a guardian.

Kiera had already grown into a pretty young woman by that time, with clear, pale skin and dark, straight hair down to her waist, her green eyes a little too big but a strikingly bright emerald hue that always garnered compliments. Kiera took after her mother, looking like an exaggerated version of Serra, but she had inherited Garegan's height; she was already taller than the queen at five feet seven, and she was still growing. She certainly turned the heads of most of the village boys, but she was still a little awkward at that age, learning how to balance her increasing height with her increasing bust and ever elongating legs.

Her father, her brother and man of the men in the court had loved her and doted on her, and their stable master, Gavin, had treated her like she was one of his own, but men held little interest. The knights had bowed to her, the squires were terrified of her, and the hired help went about their days without so much as a second glance until she was named heir; then they were pestersome. Otherwise, she rarely crossed paths with men on any regular basis other than the guests to the household and whoever might be in the stable when she went to get her horse, and even if they did try to flirt with her, she simply didn't know what to say. Most of the time, she had thought they were just being *nice*.

That didn't mean she had been completely naive. Even at fourteen, Kiera had known that she was running out of time to do as she pleased, that her days of freedom coming to an end with her ever-impending wedding and assuming the responsibilities of truly running the small kingdom her family had presided over for centuries. But her father kept deciding that she was still too young to give thought to marrying her off even though he had betrothed her years before, and Kiera kept her focus on her studies and her riding, putting the day she would be joined to a total stranger out of her mind.

Not that the subject wasn't even brought up in the household. If her mother had gotten her way, Kiera would have been married and have been gone from the castle the previous summer, but Garegan wouldn't budge. He just kept pushing the date back until *both* were ready, which annoyed her mother and made Kiera wonder if she would be *old* by the time she finally met the man she was intended for.

Kiera had been betrothed for two years by the time she was fourteen, but it was when she had turned ten that she had been named heir of Corengale by her father, much to the dismay of her mother and half of the council. Kiera was headstrong and bright, where her brother was shy and a bit of a pushover, and Garegan had made his decision without consulting *anyone*, not even *her*. But Kiera had taken it in stride, and once she had been named heir and regent, she had spent two days a week reading, writing, and learning to sew with her mother, and the rest of the time entirely under her father's tutelage regarding the kingdom and their people. The hours of poring over current decrees, laws, and rites with Garegan and the tedious *domesticated* talents she hated made the days when she could escape the confines of the castle all that much more precious.

Kiera could still remember the patterns of the stained glass windows that lined the library on two sides and the way they had washed her father in colorful light when he sat at his desk. She could still recall the way he had always smelled earthy and clean like freshly cut hay to her. Her heart ached when she thought of his warm smile, the way he would hug her before sending her off to bed, and how he would laugh when she surprised him by what came out of her mouth. Garegan had been a fair and passionate man, and Kiera smiled to herself when she thought about the arguments they used to get into when he was trying to teach her about their kingdom and all she wanted to do was go outside.

I miss him most of all . . .

Garegan had seen her interest in the world around her, and instead of trying to browbeat her into a submissive role like her mother wanted, he decided to give Kiera some of the freedoms her younger brother enjoyed by granting her permission to wear cast-off pants and tunics for afternoon riding in the forest that edged their small castle or go swimming in the river, catching crayfish and turtles and coming home soaking wet to her father's laughter and her mother's complete dismay. He was only strict when it came to her studies, carefully watching what she read and correcting her when her ideas swayed too far outside the ways he wanted her to think. Garegan wanted her to move forward and to use his approach as her sole example, warning her away from the old rulers and their histories, changing the subject when she had asked why, and sending her from the room when she persisted.

Only once had she ever felt her father's indignation when Garegan found her high up on a ladder one day, searching out old texts regarding the Spero family, a lineage she still knew very little about . . .

"What do you think you're doing?" Garegan bellowed fro where he stood at the bottom of the ladder, his hands on the frame and his face red with anger. "I have told you to stay away from those books! Get down here now!"

"I just—"

"No, Kiera. Put them back!"

Kiera had never seen her father so upset, especially with her, *and she was suddenly scared to come down. Garegan must have sensed her fear because he backed away from the base of the ladder and let her climb slowly to the floor, her shaking hands making her decent feel uncoordinated.*

Garegan pulled Kiera off the ladder as soon as she was only two rungs from the ground, setting her down roughly and yanking the ladder away from the wall, letting it crash to the floor behind him as he rounded on her. Kiera had never seen him so furious.

"There is nothing *in those books that will do anything but harm, and I forbid you to follow in old footsteps! If I* ever *catch you up there again, Kiera, you will lose you privileges and that horse until you are* married! Do not *defy me again, girl, or you will be sorry for it!"*

Kiera felt her heart hammering in her chest, the room full of the scent of rotting vegetation that threatened to make her sick as she backed away from him and ran from the room.

Garegan sought her out in her bedroom less than an hour later, finding her sitting by the window and furiously picking at the stitches of an old piece of mangled embroidery she had never finished, angrier at herself than at her father's reaction.

Garegan took the piece of cloth from her hands and hugged her close.

"I want you to be a good, fair, and just ruler, Kiera. I will give you what I can, but those old tales will only bring trouble. One day, you will sit in my place, and I would have you remembered as a ruler willingly served, not as a tyrant..."

I never got to ask him what he meant. That was one of the last memories she had of her father. Less than a week later, she had been forced to run from the burning castle only to end up in the care of a monstrous being. Darian had taken her with him, and she couldn't even argue; when he had taken her east and far away from Corengale, she hadn't wanted to.

In fact, Kiera hadn't spoken for two days after the slaughter of the men in the hunting lodge though Darian wouldn't leave her alone with his incessant chatter that she couldn't understand. He had shaken her roughly when he'd had enough of her silence, and Kiera had slapped him, screaming savagely as the palm of her hand collided with the tough skin of his jaw. The outburst of anger had startled Darian completely, and he had shoved her roughly away from him, her head slamming into a tree trunk, knocking her unconscious.

When Kiera finally came to almost a day and a half later, she found Darian cradling her, and he had hugged her tightly against him when she opened her eyes, only to hiss in pain as the light made her head erupt with sharp pain. It was then that the exchanges started: Darian had bitten his tongue and closed his mouth over hers, forcing his blood between her lips. The action so surprised Kiera that she simply allowed it. She had only ever kissed her family, and the sudden intimacy was startling, but the throbbing in her head was immediately lessened, and she realized he was trying to help her. Kiera kept her mouth still and her body rigid, hurriedly pulling away from him when her head stopped aching and the pain was dulled.

That became their ritual every time she was hurt, and she rarely experienced pain for more than a few minutes, the semi-regular exchanges seeming to change her in subtle and not-so-subtle ways. She grew another four inches that first year, her skin didn't tan, she healed faster on her own, her senses were sharper, and she didn't *bleed*—a change Kiera was silently happy about. Having to deal with menstruating around a blood-drinking creature could have made things very awkward, but it seemed to have stopped after the first mouthful of his blood. She certainly didn't miss the mess or the pain.

Kiera counted backward . . .

Nineteen

Time goes by so fast. I can't believe it was only two years ago. I was halfway through my eighteenth year when the blood kisses evolved into something else entirely. I would do it all again the same way even if I knew then what I would be facing now.

Kiera reflected back to that fateful afternoon, the one that changed their relationship from unlikely companions to lovers. Up until that day, Darian had only ever given her blood when she was hurt, and the kisses were always quick, usually only lasting a moment or two, and he had never seemed interested in them becoming anything else. Kiera had grown in that four-year span from an awkward teen into a somewhat hardened young woman, her constant training with weapons and forest survival leaving her well muscled and graceful, but she was cold and wary when she encountered other humans. After the trauma of Corengale and being trained under Darian's watchful eye, she certainly liked it better that way.

They had been in the crumbling old castle for three and a half years by that point, and the only time she saw the villagers was when she needed food or weapons she couldn't steal or make herself; she had gotten good at bartering meat and furs and flora of the forest that were otherwise hard to come by. The townsfolk had called her the Ghost of Baneswood during that first winter because of her white hair and her tendency to appear out of nowhere after dark, but she finally adopted the moniker Bane because it was simply easier than giving her real name or accepting the title of *ghost*. Besides the few people she dealt with in Grant's Perch on a random basis, the only other *people* she encountered were considered intruders, and *they* rarely lived long enough to plead for their lives if her Aeroyn caught them first.

They had both been training for over three years at that point; Darian had finally mastered Common Tongue, and Kiera was busy honing her skills in close combat with a weapon. Darian's talons alone were more than ample to cleave flesh from bone, and his tough skin could deflect most armaments, making him the perfect sparring partner. They trained nearly every day, and Kiera was proud of the scars that faintly laced her arms and legs from previous battles with the Aeroyn.

Darian, however, always tried to be careful when he trained with her, keeping his enthusiasm for battle in check, but he didn't avoid getting into a true match when she was ready for it or if she caught him off guard. During one particularly spirited training session in the spring of her first adult year, Darian had gashed her side by chance, a long dark welt of blood seeping out from under her shredded leather armor where his claws had ripped clean through to her flesh . . .

Kiera hissed through her teeth as two of Darian's talons sliced through both her bodice and the skin over her ribs. She reflexively brought her elbow up to catch the side of his face with much more momentum than either of them had expected; she slammed hard into his jaw, his fangs drawing blood as his lower lip smashed against them, and she knocked him off balance. Kiera grabbed his wrist as Darian tried to absorb the blow by twisting his body and spinning away, and she ducked his wing as he brought it around to defend himself.

The adrenaline in Kiera's blood made her faster than Darian had anticipated, and she fought harder that day than she ever had before. Pushing upward with all her strength, Kiera pinned his wrist between his shoulder blades and effectively immobilized both his arm and his wing. She immediately snaked her free arm around Darian's neck from behind, the edge of her knife tucked between his throat and her thick bracer, pulling his trapped hand upward painfully while kicking at the back of his knee to break his stability and make him bend backward. It was a move that would have broken or dislocated a human male's extremity, but it only frustrated the Aeroyn when he realized that Kiera had better leverage. Darian dug the claws of his free hand into her forearm as he tried to keep his balance, drawing more blood from her already scarred flesh.

"Yield, beast!" Kiera yelled in his ear, holding on tightly despite the pain. He was silently proud of her, but Darian could already smell that there was too much of her blood on the ground as he fought to level out. He was breathing hard as he struggled further, but Kiera wasn't letting go, and he open-hand slapped her bleeding arm twice in surrender.

"I yield, youngling!" he bellowed. "Let up!"

Kiera released him and dropped into a defensive crouch, breathing hard and bleeding heavily, a wicked smile plastered to her face. Up to that point, she had only won a handful of times, and though Kiera couldn't effectively kill or even seriously wound Darian without the help of a flame, even a stalemate was a triumph if he gave out first. Her head swam giddily from the rush of adrenaline that coursed through her veins, immensely pleased with of the victory she had fought so hard for.

Darian stood a few feet away from her, eyeing her warily as he rubbed his bruised but already healing wrist, his serious expression making his handsome features seem brooding and dark as he openly studied her wounds. When his expression morphed to show concern and he took a tentative step toward her, Kiera finally looked down at her shredded arm; Darian had clawed her so deeply there were probably marks on the bone. The wounds were short but very deep, and the blood was flowing quite freely, and seeing that much red liquid pouring out of her was making Kiera feel a little light-headed as her smile wavered and retreated fully as a sudden panic gripped her. She stood too quickly and stumbled forward, trying to fight both gravity and the swoon that overtook her, losing miserably to both at the same instant when she lost consciousness and fell.

Darian rushed forward and caught her, her bloodied arm pressed against his chest leaving large wet smears across his velvety gray skin. He chided himself for losing his composure during the match, getting caught up in the thrill of battle as the adrenaline surged through his body when Kiera had caught him off guard and he found himself having to truly fight back. Darian hadn't meant to hurt her, and the result of matching her ferocity meant the loss of blood was startling.

He laid her down on the sweet-smelling spring grass at their feet and bit his tongue, letting the stream of blood flow onto the wounds on her arm, watching in mild fascination as her own blood stopped flowing and the muscles and veins repaired themselves, leaving a small but very red scar in the place of each deep cut. He then turned his attention to the gash on her side.

Without hesitating, Darian sliced through the lacing on the front of her leather armor and stripped it away, leaving Kiera naked from the waist up as he examined her flayed skin. The tight bodice had kept pressure around the wounds, making them look superficial, but as he removed the piece of thick hide, the blood rushed to the surface, and the injuries widened, revealing the white gleam of two of her ribs. He bit his wrist this time, directing his blood into the wounds and watching calmly as the skin and muscle closed over the bones, her breathing becoming more regular as his blood flooded her veins and repaired the ruptured cells.

But when Kiera didn't regain consciousness after several minutes once the wound had fully closed and his constant repeating of her name, Darian bit his tongue once more and brought his mouth down to hers, forcing the blood between her lips. She came around suddenly, coughing and sputtering, blood spraying his face as he pulled away to give her room. Kiera rolled onto her undamaged side, coughing hard, the newly formed scars on her ribs causing her obvious pain as her hand crept up to cover them while she tried to breathe.

Darian left her side and retrieved the water skin that was hanging from a nearby tree limb, offering it to her as her coughing diminished, but Kiera pushed it away and remained panting at his feet with her brows knit and her eyes closed. He knelt in the grass next to her and poured some of the cold water over her bloodied arm, rubbing away the garish red smears so he could make sure she was thoroughly healed. She gasped when he pried her hand away from her sore side and poured the icy liquid over the thin red scars, but she let him clean the blood from her skin and examine her without argument.

"You need to take more from me, Kiera. Your recovery will be very slow if you do not."

She finally opened her eyes, rolling slowly onto her back with a groan. Darian put his hand under her shoulders and helped her into a sitting position, and Kiera winced as the muscles and skin over her ribs pulled against the newly repaired flesh, sending a searing pain up her side.

The Aeroyn bit his tongue hard and let his mouth fill this time, and Kiera bent her head back to receive his kiss, the blood flowing slowly down her throat, seeking out the damaged cells and ceasing the pain. He had never given her so much, but she had never lost so much either, and the kiss turned long and intimate. His tongue eventually healed, but the kiss continued, and Kiera found herself lost in his arms and an unfamiliar hunger for his touch as his blood coursed through her like white fire.

Kiera wound her arms around his neck and kissed him passionately, cutting her lip on his sharp incisor, and the tiny amount of her blood that seeped into the kiss threatened to drive him over the edge. In all the time she had known him, Darian had cleaned her wounds and used his own blood to heal her, but he had never tasted hers, always choosing to wash it away.

He licked lightly at the cut on her lip, wanting more...

Darian realized what he was doing and quickly broke contact. He was breathing heavily, questions and unspoken desires warring in his eyes as he looked at her, trying to gauge what she would allow.

It took Kiera a moment to realize he wanted permission to touch her. She kissed him deeply, forcing her tongue into his mouth, and he let go completely any inhibitions that held him at bay. Darian crushed her against him and ran his hands down her naked back, careful not to let his claws dig into her. He silently reminded himself that Kiera wasn't like one of the females of his kind, and her skin wouldn't withstand the punishment of the brutal act of mating he would have relished in with one of his own.

Darian pushed her back on the grass, the sweet smell of the broken plants beneath her mingling with the strong scent of her blood all over him, and as he kissed her neck, he tasted it again.

He sat up with a start. Her breasts and stomach were covered with blood, the wet smears on his own chest having transferred to her pale skin. Darian lapped at her neck and moved downward, licking her skin clean in long, slow strokes. Kiera gasped and arched her back when his tongue touched her nipples, sending a rippling pleasure through her that she had never expected and now thoroughly craved. Darian moved down to her stomach, catching the last of the mineral-rich red droplets that lingered. His hand found the hem of her heavy cotton skirts, and his mouth found her nipples again as he slid his palm up her inner thigh.

When his fingers brushed her wet sex, Kiera dug her nails into his shoulder, her back arching and her breath coming on short, heavy gasps. His own hardness was almost painful as he pressed the palm of his hand against her, and she moaned through clenched teeth, pulling at his arms, his shoulders, his hair, silently begging him to cover her with his weight. She may not have realized what she was asking for, but her body certainly knew what it wanted.

Darian pulled away from her and sat up, resting back on his heels, leaving her panting and aching and half naked on the grass. He undid the knot of the long, silvery-white battlecloth he always wore, letting it fall away from his hips and his heavy sex, and he waited for her to come to him. Kiera looked up at him from the grass, her white hair splayed beneath her head, her pale skin and hair contrasting beautifully with the verdant green all around her.

"I won't take you, Kiera. If you want this, you have to come to me."

It was all the challenge Kiera needed for her to scramble to her knees and wrap her arms around his shoulders, pressing her naked breasts against his chest, his claws ripping her skirt as he pulled it up over her hips. Darian picked her up by the back of her thighs, and she wrapped her legs around him, her wet sex rubbing against him as she moaned against their ardent kisses.

He lifted her and slid slowly inside her, pulling her hips down against his, holding her tightly against him as her body stiffened and her head fell back, her brows knit as she hissed in pain. Everything up to that point had felt incredibly good; she hadn't expected that part to hurt. *Darian could smell fresh blood mingling with the scent of* her, *and he grappled for control of himself as he lifted her gently, slowly, pulling completely out of her to let her decide if she had already had enough.*

"Please tell me this gets better." Kiera looked at him warily, trying to catch her breath as unfamiliar pain throbbed through her.

"Oh, Kiera," Darian laughed quietly at his sudden loss for words, barely able to think straight. He nuzzled against her breasts, his hands letting her down enough that the head of his cock rubbed against her soft, wet flesh, making her squirm. "It gets addicting, and when it's with one you love, *it's like breathing. You can't live without it."*

Kiera was quiet as she held his gaze, biting her bottom lip, debating if this was such a good idea after all. Darian broke eye contact so he could gently kiss her neck and breasts, silently willing her to let him finish what they had started. With a female of his kind, there would have been no question, no hesitation, and both of them would have already been covered in blood, but with Kiera's human softness, he had to throw that thinking away.

"I want this, Kiera, but if you are not ready, I will wait," he breathed against her chest. Kiera was getting swept up in the sensation of his mouth on her skin, the earlier pain subsiding enough that she pressed herself against him, wanting him to enter her again. She dug her nails into his shoulders, wrapping her arms around his neck as she kissed him, forcing her tongue into his mouth and deliberately scraping it against his sharp teeth to make the blood flow.

Darian was surprised by the bold move on her part, and he crushed her in his arms, pulling her down hard. Kiera felt the pain again though not as intensely this time. He was slow with her after that, the ache subsiding into a cresting pleasure, his thick sex filling her again and again as he drank from her. Her skin prickled with gooseflesh as she felt herself become incredibly tight as though her body was suddenly forbidding him entry, her heart hammering in her ears. Darian was impossibly hard inside her, impaling her over and over, their tight embrace, the smell of her all over him, and her blood in his mouth all threatening to push him past the point of conscious thought.

The Aeroyn nearly stopped breathing as he came, his pulsating climax bringing the girl in his arms to her own, her head falling back, her skin flushing a deep red, the white-hot pleasure making her heart skip and her entire body go rigid. She was gasping for breath in his tight embrace, feeling lightheaded and a little unstable as the waves of the orgasm subsided and her brain was finally able to think *again.*

Darian finally loosened his grip and simply held her to him, letting what had just happened catch up to him too. He had watched her through the entire winter, that very idea running rampant in his mind on several occasions when they had been in close quarters for hours at a time and boredom had let his mind wander to places he knew it shouldn't. It had snowed heavily, and they had sought refuge in the castle like they had in years past, but something had changed in him as Kiera let go of her childhood and came into being a woman. Her scent had changed, her body had changed, and she had become so like him *that he sometimes had to remind himself that she didn't possess his wings or his fast healing skin.* Kiera hadn't known he watched her while she slept, usually curled up against him with her head on his chest. Up until that point, he had been content as her protector and her teacher, the idea of taking a human lover seeming almost absurd, but it had manifested still, and the curiosity had gotten the better of him.

Apparently, it had been on her mind too, and he felt no shame, no regret. It had been far better than he had ever imagined, and if she gave him the chance, he would do it again...

"I think that's enough training for one day," he whispered against her lips, his heart beating fast, his hands still supporting her hips. Darian loosened his grip to let her go, but Kiera clung to him, not wanting to be separated just yet. She squirmed against him, wincing as his hands clamped against her thighs so tight she would probably bruise.

"I beg to differ, Darian," she purred. "I'm just learning to breathe, and I desperately need air."

"I know what *you* are thinking about," Darian whispered in her ear as he brushed the hair off her shoulder and ran his tongue up the side of her neck, wrapping his arms around her waist. Kiera shivered when he sucked at her earlobe. She hadn't heard him approach her from behind, too caught up in her memories to notice the quiet padding of bare feet on the cold stone floor.

"*Princess*, you dream about me *entirely* too much," he growled.

"And *how* did you know I was thinking about *you*?" Kiera giggled, leaning back against him, her hands finding his and intertwining their fingers. Darian pushed his nose into her hair and inhaled deeply. He let go of her hands and bent to pick her up behind her knees, cradling her against his chest.

"I *know*." He chuckled quietly as he looked past her, out the window, and over the lake and forest to the sun peaking over the distant hills. "And I also know it's too early to be *awake*."

Darian acted like he was going to drop her, and Kiera threw her arms around his neck, laughing at his playfulness, grateful for the much-needed break in the serious mood of the past few days. He held her close and kissed her, nuzzling his nose against hers.

"But since you insist on being *up*," he grinned wickedly at her, "I guess I'll just have to keep you in that room until I'm ready to leave it too."

Kiera threw her head back and laughed as he carried her away from the window, through the derelict ballroom, and into the chambers they had claimed for themselves at the heart of the old castle.

The sun would be getting high overhead before either of them saw it again if Darian had anything to say about it.

Twenty

Alyk breathed a sigh of relief when he woke to find that Tance was nowhere to be seen. As angry and hurt as he was, he wasn't sure he could have stomached seeing that wiry form still sitting there at the fire's edge, welcoming his brother's wrath. Henelce was still awake from his turn at watch, frying eggs in his trusty pan. Alyk glanced around, noting the horses tied to the line and their packs still in place next to the tree.

At least Tance hadn't tried anything stupid.

"He left after you fell asleep." Henelce glanced at Alyk, his eyes weary but still shining with anger. "I had half a mind to chase him off into the dark and let the forest beasties have their way with him, but he beat me to it and walked off not long after you fell asleep."

The Shephard slid the eggs onto a metal plate and handed them to Alyk with a hunk of bread and some smoked meat.

"Eat. We've got a long day ahead of us." Henelce cracked two more eggs into the pan for himself, poking at them with his greasy wooden spatula.

Alyk dipped the bread into the runny yolks and chewed thoughtfully, the eggs rich and delicious on his tongue until a guilty little voice started whispering in the back of his mind, making his mouth go dry. He had to take a long drink of water to get the food down, swallowing hard. The bite of eggs and bread hit his stomach like a rock and threatened to reappear, but he stubbornly kept it where it was.

"Was this . . ." Alyk choked on the words as he felt the blood drain from his face. "Henelce, was this *my* fault? He's been my charge since he was nine. Did I *let* this happen?"

"*What?*" Henelce turned a deep shade of purple and threw his spatula at Alyk with a loud yell, barely missing his head. "You get *that* idea out of your fool head! That boy was always on the cusp of making an ass of himself, and he *chose* to ignore the good example of a human being in front of him. You *know* why Jaçon told you to drown him, and he *wasn't* wrong. I felt that thread of evil in him too, and I know for a fact that you saw it on more than one occasion over the past year. This was only the beginning, and who knows what that cocky little son of a bitch is capable of."

Henelce took a deep breath, trying to calm himself, his anger at Tance making him volatile, and Alyk was *not* the one he wanted to direct his wrath toward. He snatched up a stick and went back to poking at his eggs as they burned over the fire.

"My friend, if you are to blame for anything, it's for being too ready to hope that he could be good. I understand loyalty to family, but had Tance been *my* brother, he would have been tied to a tree, smothered in blood, and left for the wolves a *long* time ago."

Alyk sighed and pushed his food away, no longer hungry. He couldn't discount Henelce's words, and he knew he had been hiding behind the hope that Tance would come around. They were blood, and that had partially blinded Alyk, allowing him to rationalize and forgive Tance's bad behavior for a long, long time. His hand found his sword on the ground next to him, and he fingered the grip, comforted by the familiar twisted metal of the hilt and the ornate carvings of the blade that had been passed to him by their father.

Tance had always looked like Charles, and maybe that was why Alyk had made so many allowances; he simply missed the man and was trying to keep his memory fresh. But Tance was a poor replacement for the father who had raised them, seeming to have picked up only the bad qualities of Charles's stubbornness and his sharp tongue while leaving behind the kind and honorable nature Alyk remembered.

Alyk knew how the night of the fires in Corengale had affected himself, but he had never really considered what they might have done to Tance, and the years of turmoil had obviously taken their toll. Being six years older had given Alyk an emotional buffer and the ability to cope with his losses in ways Tance just hadn't been capable of, and Alyk's training as a squire had given him structure and discipline Tance hadn't ever really had access to, nor had he been interested in learning. He sat wondering if his actions could have changed Tance for the better, but somehow he doubted it. His brother had been kicking dogs and biting other children since he was two, and that was probably a good indicator of the man he was going to grow into, but seeing what Tance was capable of firsthand wasn't something Alyk had been prepared for.

Now his brother was gone, and it made him uneasy to think of the boy without supervision.

Alyk finally let out the breath he hadn't realized he had been holding, the sound of a throat clearing making him blink and look around. Henelce stood a few feet away holding his bedroll and his pack, ready to get his horse saddled and on their way. Alyk hadn't even heard him gathering his things or covering the fire or taking away the plate of unfinished food. He looked at

Henelce guiltily, silently chiding himself for letting his friend clean up their camp by himself.

"When you're done trying to levitate that rock with your mind," Henelce pointed to the fist sized stone Alyk had inadvertently focused his gaze upon, "I'm ready to get this show on the road."

Twenty-One

Kiera stared at her reflection in the dusty old mirror, absently playing with a strand of her pearl-colored hair. She had never really gotten used to seeing that shock of white where the hair had been as dark and glossy as Darian's sleek black feathers, even though it had changed over six years earlier.

Run, you fool!

She could hear her panting, terrified breathing in her ears as her feet carried her in a mindless sprint toward the forest that had swallowed her life from that day forward. Every footfall rang through her body like the concussion of a cannon, her bare feet senseless to the stones and soggy mud of the field as she fled toward apparent safety with the long black cloak flying behind her.

"Kiera! Come on! I thought you were hungry!" Darian's voice rang against the stone walls as he called to her from across the ballroom, startling her out of her thoughts.

She hastily pulled her hair back out of her face, finished tying her bracers, and smoothed her dark-brown tunic over her leather bodice and tan leggings and readied to leave. Kiera barely heard her well-worn knee-high boots whisper softly against the stone floor as she reached for her pack, shouldering it as she took one last look at the cracked and dirty mirror, not sure she really knew the woman staring back at her.

"Kiera…?"

"Okay, okay," she mumbled under her breath as she left the room, closing the heavy oak door on the mirror and the thoughts that threatened to drag her back into her memories.

Kiera knew they would both be there when she got back, waiting impatiently for her return.

Twenty-Two

Crouching on a tree limb wasn't the most comfortable position in the world, and holding still while her legs burned trying to balance on the branch for twenty minutes was not making it any better.

But if Kiera was going to take down the boar, she had to be careful, especially since it probably outweighed Darian and would kill Kiera in seconds if it got the chance. The large black swine with six-inch tusks hadn't sensed her presence yet, and she was waiting impatiently for the beast to turn just the right way. She had already spent the better portion of an hour tracking the damned thing, and now it wasn't cooperating at all.

"Come on, come on," Kiera whispered quietly as she pressed the edge of her throwing knife into the tip of her thumb, trying to concentrate on hitting the artery in its neck. The boar stubbornly kept its back to her, rooting obliviously in the dirt. Kiera focused hard on the pig, watching its head go up and down as it shoveled earth out of the way, silently willing it to move *just a little more*.

The big animal suddenly froze, letting out a grunt and a short squeal before falling heavily on its side. Dust and leaves formed a cloud around the beast, briefly obscuring the large black arrow with white fletching protruding from its ribs.

"What the—hey!" Kiera scanned the forest in the direction the arrow had come from, but she saw no one.

She stood shakily on the branch, letting the blood flow back into her legs before jumping down and angrily yanking the arrow out of the still quivering pig. It grunted as the weapon left a void in its body, finally lying still, but she barely noticed as she studied the blood-covered projectile, noting the red bands of sinew that held the fletching and the barbed iron tip.

"You may keep the arrow if you need a souvenir, but I'm afraid the boar belongs to *me*."

Kiera looked up in surprise at the man leaning casually against the tree directly in front of her, his black longbow in one hand and a quiver of matching arrows strapped across his back. She hadn't even heard him approach.

"*Funny*. Last I checked, *I* control these woods. I don't remember giving *you* permission to hunt." Kiera, barked, eyeing him warily.

The man flashed a sly smile as he held up his hands in surrender.

"I'm not one to argue with a woman, but I was told by several *men* in Grant's Perch that I could hunt here. I wouldn't even *be* in this area if it weren't for rumors of good sport. I see they weren't lying when they said the game was . . . *remarkable*."

Kiera lifted an eyebrow and gripped the arrow so hard she could hear it creak under the pressure. Sending strangers into her woods to hunt was already one strike against them; sending in a man to try and catch a glimpse of *her* like Kiera was some rare animal was downright absurd.

I'm going to have to make a trip into the tavern and lay down some rules. Someone is going to have to fix a broken nose later.

"*You* may hunt on the other side of the river"—Kiera kept her words flat and dismissive as she pointed southward—"but Baneswood is *my* territory, and I won't have hunters in it without my knowledge or permission. The boar stays with *me*."

The man folded his arms over his chest and leaned against the tree at his back, giving her a haughty look, not bothering to respond. She chose to ignore him, waiting for him to leave, feeling him watching her as she debated how she wanted to kill him if he decided to be an *issue* while she focused instead on the large creature at her feet.

She suddenly smirked as she drew her glass blade, and with a quick jab under the sternum and a long slice, she opened the beast all the way down to the testicles with her sharp knife, letting the blood and offal spatter the ground.

Damn it, now I need Darian. Kiera cursed herself for the hundredth time, her forgetfulness leaving her alone at a very inopportune moment. He had gone back to the castle four or five miles east of her current position for the rope Kiera had left behind. The smell of the gutted boar would direct him to her location, and she hoped he came soon because it was also going to bring the wolves if they weren't careful; it was already midday, and the pack would be on the hunt once the afternoon light started to wane. She wasn't at all interested in still being there if and when they showed.

Kiera was unsure when the Aeroyn would return to help string up the kill, but the blonde man standing just far enough away to be able to shoot her made her wish her *mate* was at her side. It was rare that she took on threats alone, and this particular one made her a little nervous. Taller than her, outweighing her, and armed for distance and probably close combat by the way the smooth leather on his boot bulged on the right side . . .

Kiera didn't like the uncomfortable feeling in the pit of her stomach that she was getting from the man in the black leather pants and dark-blue sleeveless shirt he had belted low on his waist. Nor did she particularly care for the way he was studying her openly as she watched him out of the corner of her eye.

She certainly wasn't a fan of the *flirting*.

"You know, I can *help* you with that."

She could hear the smile in his voice.

Oh, go away! Kiera stood and threw one of her knives deftly, directing it at his head, purposely missing but not by much. The blade sank deep into the tree, an inch or so away from his ear.

"Or *not*." His bravado—and his smile—faltered.

"Are you *deaf*? Or just *stupid*? I told you to *leave*!" Kiera stared threateningly at him, unconsciously taking in the dark-green eyes, the sandy-blond hair, the well-defined arms with smooth tanned skin . . .

Whoa. She quickly turned back to the boar again, letting her hair hang down to cover the redness of her face. *Tirath help me. Gorgeous or not, he's already annoying.*

Kiera momentarily paused in her excavation of the animal's underbelly, confused by that thought. She tried to concentrate on what she was doing as she thrust her hands into the steaming pile of organs and intestines at her feet, separating out the liver and the kidneys and the heart, throwing the lungs and the ropy entrails well away from the carcass. She was so absorbed in her task she had almost forgotten he was still standing there until she heard him laugh.

"I like a girl that can get her hands *dirty*."

That does it! Kiera suddenly didn't care *what* weapons he might have on him as she stood and stalked the few paces toward him, reaching out with her bloodied hand to catch the front of his shirt and jerk his face toward hers. It made her realize just how much taller than her he really was and brought the scent of the fresh mint in his mouth right into her nose.

"Look, I don't know *who* you are, but this is *my* land, and I want you off it. *Now*."

"Or *what*? You'll *make* me? You better be careful. I might actually *like* that." He raised his eyebrows at her, but he didn't move to defend himself as he grinned, stifling a laugh.

Kiera genuinely surprised him: she hit him so hard he stumbled back and fell directly on his ass, losing his grip on his bow as he tried to catch his fall and the arrows in his quiver scattering around him. She didn't hesitate as she followed him to the ground, straddling his hips to pin him in the dirt, her dagger suddenly drawn and at his throat.

His green eyes no longer held any laughter, but they didn't hold any fear either. He simply looked at her, gauging her actual level of threat to him, and Kiera could see him choosing his next words carefully.

"I'm not here to hurt you, Bane. I came to offer my *help*."

Kiera sat up a little, her eyes first wide with surprise then narrowing quickly in suspicion. She didn't remove the blade, just let up enough that he could swallow without the threat of a close shave.

"I knew something didn't *smell* right about you," Kiera hissed as she studied his features, and he watched her passively, submissively, trying to show her he wasn't lying.

"Well, I certainly hope it wasn't my *breath*." His mouth twisted into a self-deprecating lopsided smile. He caught the side of her mouth tug upward, and he felt her relax just slightly.

Big mistake, woman. With strength and reflexes Kiera wasn't anticipating, he grabbed her wrists and rolled her under him, pinning her hands above her head. Anger and panic flared through her, and Kiera squeezed her legs around his hips painfully, trying to give him as little maneuverability as possible. She wasn't going to give up easily even if he had the upper hand.

"Drop the knife, and I'll let you up." He brought his face close to hers, the scent of mint flooding her senses, those dark-green eyes refusing to give her a reason not to believe the words coming out of his mouth. "I *mean* it when I say I won't cause you any harm."

Kiera knit her brows, her mouth set in a firm line of determination, not willing to give in and admit defeat. But after a minute or two of struggling and getting nowhere, she let out a growl of frustration and relaxed her hands, letting the blade fall to the ground.

"Good girl." He smiled brightly down at her before planting a light kiss on her nose that she wasn't expecting and didn't know how to react to. Kiera was still a little stunned when he pressed himself flat against her to reach for the knife and toss it out of both their reach. He momentarily hesitated with his face just above hers until Kiera recovered and tried to bite him, but he pulled back too fast, and her teeth only caught the air between them.

"Now, now! *That* is a very poor display of hospitality!" He laughed as he tried to lift himself up, but Kiera wasn't going to let him go, her legs still wrapped tightly around him. He had let go of her wrists and she tried to bring her arms close to her chest so she could get into a better position to cause damage, but he saw what was coming and quickly lowered himself back down, laying all his weight on her, his face suddenly in hers.

"*Don't*, Bane. I really don't want to have to hurt you, and while I have to admit this might be a fun position without the inconvenience of clothing, you're going to have to let me go if you want me to get off"—he glanced down at her chest and then back at her face, a wicked glint in his eye—"of you."

Kiera narrowed her eyes and hesitantly relaxed her legs. He rolled off her and stood in one fluid motion, taking a few quick steps away from her while she slowly climbed to her feet. She was watching him warily, debating if she could catch up the knife that lay on the ground to her left since he was too close for one of her throwing knives to be very effective.

Then she heard it.

Kiera suddenly smirked, and the man took a reflexive step backward.

Dust flew as Darian dropped from the sky between them and immediately pinned Delámer against the nearest tree.

"Where the *hell* have *you* been?" Kiera said almost nonchalantly as she started dusting herself off, briefly taking her focus off the Aeroyn and his newfound quarry as she retrieved her knife from the ground and settled it back into the strap on her thigh.

"Care to *introduce* us?" Darian growled into Delámer's face, his wings spread wide and his claws ripping through the finely spun navy cotton of the shirt wadded in his fist.

Delámer was trying to stay calm, the Aeroyn in his face a far riskier threat to him than the white-haired woman he had been tracking. He had seen that look of curiosity hiding in *her* eyes; all the Aeroyn's expression held was barely contained fury and the threat of death.

"*Hold*, Darian!"

Both males were surprised by the words that came out of her mouth, and Darian turned sharply when her hand was suddenly on his back and she ducked under his wing.

"Let's say, for a moment, that I actually *believe* that this one isn't here to cause me harm. If that proves true, then it looks like I have a new *pet*." Kiera stared at Delámer over Darian's tattooed shoulder for a moment before she cocked her head to the side and smiled sweetly. "I think I'll call him . . . *Dirtbag.*"

Darian felt his indignation rise; Kiera's refusing to kill an intruder for the second time making him wonder exactly what had been said between them.

Delámer simply felt relieved. She could call him anything she wanted, as long as it kept him alive. He wouldn't even bother to try to correct her.

Yet.

Twenty-Three

This had better be worth it. I just bought these! Blood dripped onto the ground and all over his expensive new boots, making Delámer sigh grumpily. The boar's head with its shiny white tusks was lying at his feet, dead eyes staring up at him accusingly. The bow and arrows he had been carrying were now a useless pile of black sticks at his feet. Darian had snapped every piece.

At least she let me keep my knife . . .

* * *

"What happened?"

They may have been out of earshot, but the Aeroyn still kept his words low; had she been able to understand him, he would have used a different language entirely. The annoyed Aeroyn stood with his arms folded across his chest, focused on the man but directing his question to the woman at his side whom he knew was studying *Dirtbag* too. Darian grit his teeth as he watched Delámer quarter the boar into more manageable pieces and hang each limb from a tree, hoping Kiera hadn't suddenly gone soft.

"I didn't hear him, didn't smell him, didn't even *see* him until he *wanted* me to see him. He shot the boar I was stalking and then acted like he was just some innocent hunter. Considering how he's dressed, that's obviously a lie. I think he's here for *me*."

Kiera's words were muffled as she spoke around the tip of her thumb in her mouth, pulling at the nail she had broken in their little scuffle with her teeth. She hesitated before opening her mouth again, knowing Darian was already trying to justify killing the man without her permission.

"He . . . he knew my *name*."

Darian turned his head sharply at that bit of information, and Kiera could feel that thunderstorm of rage he was trying to hide building.

"*Bane*. He knew I was called Bane," Kiera corrected quickly as she worried at the thumbnail, trying to get it smooth. "That's not exactly a *secret*, Darian, but I'll bet he works for Eryce—"

"And you want to *keep* him?" Darian huffed, not liking that idea in the slightest. "What do you suggest we *do* with him, *exactly*? Get him a collar and a bowl of water and let him pee on the rug? You realize he'll probably try to escape the very first chance he gets."

She shrugged, not really sure how to answer. *Dirtbag* had said he was there to help her, but he hadn't had much of a chance to tell her why or how.

"I don't know about that, Darian. He said he wanted to *help* me, whatever that means. I'm hoping he'll either tell me *why* he's here or give me a reason to string him up next to that pig, and if he tries anything stupid, I'll let you do as you please."

She studied her nail as she spoke, feeling it with her index finger and trying to decide if she wanted to continue or if she had tasted enough blood and dirt for one day. Kiera knew she was acting far more nonchalant about the whole thing than she really felt, not terribly keen to show Darian that she was actually *curious* about this man. Chewing on her thumbnail kept Kiera from staring at *him* for too long, which would only aggravate the winged being at her side, and she was trying not to give Darian a reason to lash out at the man she wanted to protect until she knew what she was up against.

"I can't allow him to go back to the village. It's bad enough I probably have to go into town and set someone straight." Kiera glanced up at Darian, but he was still focused on the man butchering the pig twenty feet away. "For now, I guess we'll just have to take our chances that he has been properly housetrained. Don't kill him."

Darian sighed as she left him standing there to go wash the blood off her hands, knowing her answer was final.

"Oh. *Goody* . . ."

* * *

"Hey, *Dirtbag!* Are you done with that meat yet?"

Oh, so many ways to answer that, he thought with a smirk as a string of obnoxious answers flit across his mind.

"Almost." Delámer wasn't facing her, so Kiera couldn't see him smile, but she could hear it in his voice as she shook the water from her hands. He had been ignoring the Aeroyn that watched over him, the icy stare directed at his back almost palpable. Delámer was fairly certain the *bird* was plotting his demise, but he wasn't about to let that keep him from enjoying this task.

Keep it together. Don't give them a reason to end this before it begins. He didn't elaborate as he continued to clean away the fat and skin and sinew with the knife he had so brazenly stolen off Eryce, though the thoughts running rampant in his brain were making it difficult to keep from laughing outright.

"I *do* have a *name*," he muttered under his breath.

"I *know*. I already *gave* you one," came the arrogant reply.

Delámer paused in his task, her voice much closer than he had anticipated when she answered his quiet quip, suddenly very aware that Bane was scrutinizing him. He smiled to himself and decided to up the ante by stabbing the knife into the boar's thigh and taking a moment to remove his shirt, using it to clean his hands before tossing it aside. Delámer *knew* what he looked like, and he was letting her get a good, long view of his muscular back and seamless tan.

He glanced over his shoulder as he yanked the knife back out, cocking an eyebrow at her.

"What's the *rush*?" Delámer laughed quietly when she colored and huffed in annoyance, hastily retreating back to her Aeroyn.

This is going to be interesting, all right. He started whistling a little tune, very much in the mood for *interesting* as he went back to his task. *Let the games begin!*

* * *

"Darian, I want to talk to him. He hasn't tried anything so far with you around, but I want to know why he's even *here*. I don't like him either, but I want to see if he knows *why* Eryce wants me alive. I need to know just how much of a threat I pose to that arrogant king and if we need to find a new place to call home.

"Eryce can't be happy with me after that last Sukolai, and if *he* is here—" Kiera lifted her chin to indicate the man whose bared back was to them, "—then Eryce can't be too far behind."

"But why *this* one, Kiera? What makes *him* different?"

His gaze shifted uncomfortably from Kiera to the half-naked *Dirtbag* and back again when she still didn't answer him. Darian didn't like the idea of leaving her alone with this man, much less giving him the opportunity to open his mouth. Kiera was only able to hide so much, and Darian could sense the hesitation in her to kill this particular *threat*.

He could sense a lot more than that, and he didn't like it.

Not one bit.

I should just hang him from that limb and be done with it. Darian weighed his options, but it would be Kiera who stopped him. It was always her. Her reasoning was sound enough, but her motives weren't so clear anymore.

"Can't I just torture him until he tells you want you want to know?" Darian was more than keen to flay that tanned flesh. He didn't trust the man and didn't want to. Kiera's only response was a hard stare as she willed him to back off, irritated that he was acting so defensively. Kiera's mouth formed a thin line as she leveled her attention fully in Darian, annoyed that he was questioning her judgment.

"I mean it, Darian. *If* Eryce is planning to move against me, I want to know when and how. I think this idiot may have an answer or at least some idea. I want to be ready even if it means we need to abandon these woods. Let me do this. I need to know where I stand."

Kiera felt her heart sink as the thought of leaving hit her full force. She loved Baneswood, and she certainly didn't want to leave, but Eryce was breathing down her neck more heavily as of late. If they were in danger of bringing the wrath of the king down upon themselves and he sent in more than a few hirelings, she wasn't interested in trying to keep them at bay.

The king could have the woods.

She wanted to stay *alive*.

Darian wasn't so concerned. He just wanted this stranger dealt with and Kiera to stop being so lenient on intruders. The look on her face said she had made her decision, whether or not he liked it, and it wasn't going to change. Those bright green eyes were unnerving when she was determined, and Darian knew a losing battle when he fought one.

"*Fine*," he sighed. "But if I'm going to leave you here alone with *that*, we're going to do this *my* way."

Kiera cocked her head to the side.

"What, *exactly*, did you have in mind?"

Twenty-Four

I am going to pluck every single feather from that damned bird if I live through this. Delámer was glowering, and for someone used to wearing a smirk, that particular expression felt entirely unnatural. He wasn't angry because his hands were bound behind him around a small tree in the late afternoon heat.

Oh no. He had submitted to *that* willingly enough.

Delámer was royally upset because there were *ants* infesting that particular tree, something he was convinced that both Darian *and* Bane had been well aware of when they had tied him to it, and now the obnoxious little insects were all over him. The tiny bastards didn't bite or sting, but they ran in aimless patterns all over his naked chest, back, and arms, making him itch like crazy. Every time he shifted to scrape his skin against the bark, it sent the ants into a panic and made Bane howl with laughter.

Why couldn't she have lived in a city *like a civilized being?* Delámer was really starting to rethink ever taking this assignment on at all.

"Poor *Dirtbag*. Does the big bad *man* not like the itty bitty *bugs*?" Kiera pouted at him playfully from a few steps away, trying to control her giggles.

Yup, she knew. Pretty and *mean. Great.*

"Oh, I am *so* glad you're *enjoying* this, *Princess*," Delámer hissed as he struggled against the ropes, trying to knock the ants off any way he could, shaking the whole tree and making leaves shower down. "Nice to know you're human after all and that you find *something* humorous. I was starting to wo—"

Her hand made contact with his face out of nowhere, the hard slap cutting him off. Bane stood directly in front of him, breathing hard, her green eyes flashing vividly.

"Don't *ever* call me that *again*," she snapped, forcing the words out through clenched teeth.

"Whoa! Okay! Apologies, o' crazy lady of the forest!" Delámer stopped squirming, the side of his face stinging, the ants still running rampant on his skin suddenly forgotten as he focused on her in stunned indignation. "Do you do this to *all* the men you meet? Or only the *attractive* ones that are unlucky enough to wander into *your* forest and offer you their *help*?"

Her face flushed bright red, and she took a tentative step back, suddenly feeling too close to him as she crossed her arms and shifted her weight, intently focused on the forest floor.

So she is human. And here he had thought maybe she wasn't interested.

"Oh ho! So the *truth* comes *out*," Delámer smirked and raised his eyebrows at her suggestively as Kiera turned her annoyed attention back to him. "Does that *Aeroyn* know you have an appreciation for the finer specimens of your *own kind*?"

His emphasis made her go pale. There was something in the expression on her face that made him cock his head to the side, trying to read her. Some of the threat had subsided in her eyes, and another emotion was struggling to surface, but she was doing a good job of hiding it. Bane kept up her defensive pose, looking at anything but him.

Then it clicked.

"*Oh.* Oh, now *that* just makes me *sad.*" Delámer shook his head, his voice full of sympathy. "You've never been with a man, have you?"

Kiera didn't respond or even look at him, but he could see the red crawling back up her neck. He was just about to open his mouth again when he realized she had opened hers.

"I don't see how that's any business of *yours.*" Her response was quiet, and Delámer knew he had struck a vein.

"I didn't say it was. What you choose to *play with* is entirely your decision, but that doesn't mean I can't have an opinion on the matter." Knowing what he did about the *thing* she kept as company, he wondered how much of that particular choice had been *hers.*

This is too easy. Delámer leaned back against the tree, looking up into the leaves, smiling inwardly. The ants suddenly seemed worth it.

"Is that why you live out here? You must know you are missing out on so much especially being away from your own *race.*" That was an outright lie on his end; Delámer couldn't think of a damned thing he wanted out of the rest of the human populace except money. Bane probably had the right idea being away from the complications of society, but it seemed like a good chisel to use for this particular armor.

His posturing was intentionally vulnerable, his words quiet and empathetic. Sometimes a softer approach was necessary.

"People *lie* . . ." *He must think I'm stupid.* ". . . like *you* just did," she countered flatly.

Damn.

"Okay, you caught me. Life with *people* doesn't really interest me either, but I would venture to guess it's for a very different reason than yours."

Really stupid. Kiera didn't take the bait; instead she regarded him thoughtfully, studying his features. He was silent until her eyes started to wander down his body *then* his face lit up with a wicked smile. Kiera fought to keep from laughing and taking a step toward him.

"I have a *question*." His voice was smooth and controlled, and Kiera felt her heart pick up unexpectedly as he smirked. *She's going to slap me again, I just know it.*

"*Why* do I get the feeling I'm going to *regret* asking what it is?" Kiera asked quietly, trying not to return the energetic smile he was focusing on her.

Delámer laughed brightly, excited that she was finally starting to play along. *Maybe there's a chink in that armor after all.*

He stared brazenly at her crotch, then her white hair, then back at her crotch.

"Does the rug match the drapes? Inquiring minds want to know." He waggled his eyebrows comically, just *waiting* for her to take the step forward and let her hand collide with the side of his face once more.

"*What?*" Kiera was too surprised by the question to do more than sputter and laugh. Delámer could tell she was somewhere between amused and exasperated, but by the way she shifted her weight, he could also see the tension was starting to dissipate from her body.

Her guard was coming down.

Thank Tirath.

"There is something *seriously* wrong with you. It's no *wonder* you sought me out. Leave it to me to spare an *idiot*." Kiera covered her eyes as she giggled, the absurd question replaying in her head and making it hard to even look at him without feeling the blush crawl up her neck.

Delámer decided it was time to cut the charm and just said what came to mind.

"*That's* what I wanted. Did you know your eyes *sparkle* when you laugh?" Those words were genuine, which surprised even *him*.

Careful . . .

And there was that lovely deep red again.

"Okay, *Dirtbag*—"

"Connor."

"—that's about eno— *What?*"

"I *told* you—I *have* a *name*. Please stop calling me *Dirtbag*. I probably deserve a worse pet name, but my name is Connor." *Where the hell did that come from? When was the last time I had even answered to that name? When I was eight? Real names are bad, genius.* Connor mentally smacked himself, his expression suddenly grim.

"I think I liked *Dirtbag* better." A smile tugged at the side of her mouth as she watched him thoughtfully.

"Okay, *Connor*," Bane put dramatic emphasis on his name, and he suddenly regretted opening his mouth. The way she said it made him feel a little exposed.

Bane took a step closer, looking up at him. ". . . explain. *Why* are you here to 'help' me?"

"Oh. Right. *That.*" Connor leaned back, looking to the leaves for ways around this question that didn't send her back to calling him *Dirtbag* or make her want to use him as a target for those throwing knives on her thigh. *Get her to trust you if you have no other way.* Eryce's words rang in his head, and he suddenly didn't like the idea of following through with his original plan.

"What if . . . I said you wouldn't like my answer?" Connor closed his eyes, trying to think. He caught a faint whiff of honey in the air, and he inhaled reflexively, trying to determine if his mind was playing tricks on him. In that moment, Connor noticed that the ants were back; he could feel them congregate just above his hip, suddenly very irritating, but when he tried to shift and knock them off, he brought his side into contact with something solid.

He froze and opened his eyes.

It wasn't ants but *her* fingertips.

Bane was right in front of him.

He hadn't expected her to be so close.

Bane was touching him, just barely, but she wasn't looking at his face as she traced one of the faint scars on his abdomen. Connor's mind raced, trying to remember where that particular set had come from, failing miserably as her touch began to travel over his bare skin and became all he could really focus on. Her hand was warm, her light caress making his skin tingle, the rich scent of honey coming from *her* flipping a switch in his brain that he was trying desperately to keep in the *off* position.

He was mostly succeeding until she scraped a fingernail along one of the thin white lines, causing his skin prickle with gooseflesh and him to suck in an involuntary breath. *So much for that!*

"Oh, that is *not* fair. Go ahead. *Touch away,*" he dared, his voice deeper, huskier, his breathing getting shallower. Connor let his head fall forward, silently cursing his shorter than normal hair as he looked at her through his lashes instead of his bangs. "I'm not complaining, but keep in mind that I won't always be bound, and I touch *back.*"

"Darian will kill you." Her reply was flippant, almost reflexive, but Kiera didn't move her hand or look up. She was fascinated with his skin, unsure of what she was even doing. Kiera had never been exposed to so much naked flesh except for Darian's, and this felt totally different. Where Darian's body hair had a distinct knap to it, Connor's skin was smooth in contrast, the hair fine and blond.

It felt an awful lot like *hers.*

Her pale hand stood out against his bronzed body, and Kiera was getting lost in the sensation of the contact between the two. She closed her eyes and inhaled deeply, breathing him in; Connor smelled like mint and faintly of cedar. She pressed her hand flat on his stomach, running it lightly and slowly up to his chest, her fingers following the grooves of hard muscle under soft skin, reading him like Braille.

Connor felt incredibly natural and incredibly *good* to her. It didn't even cross her mind that she should probably feel incredibly guilty too.

"Woman, *you* are going to *kill* me if you keep *that* up," he breathed in her ear.

Startled, Kiera's eyes popped open as she dropped her hand and looked up at him defiantly.

"*Why* are you *here*?" She searched his face, looking for a lie, a truth, a reason, anything. Connor laughed softly. He could have kissed her; they were so close.

"I'm beginning to wonder that myself."

* * *

Darian hadn't gone far. He watched from high up, and he bristled when he saw Kiera reach out to touch *Dirtbag*. He could feel the change in her even from almost twenty yards away. He couldn't hear their words, but he could certainly *see* the way their conversation was going.

For the second time in as many weeks, Darian questioned whether Kiera was being honest with herself...

He was a little surprised when he felt guilt creep into his mind. Kiera was acting on instincts while Darian's motivation had been far more selfish, and somehow, in tying this half-naked man up directly in front of her, he had made the issue *worse*.

He suddenly couldn't watch.

He didn't want to know.

Darian jumped and spread his wings, casting his silhouette over the humans below as he took off. He needed to get away from ugly truths for a short while. If Kiera wanted to play with her new *pet*, then Darian wasn't about to stand in her way, and she could find out just how hard it was to survive without *him* there to protect her.

Twenty-Five

The large shadow passing overhead made them both look up, breaking the spell.

"Darian . . . *no!*" Kiera's whisper sounded horrified as she watched him disappear, heading east and away from the castle they shared. And *her*.

"Good to know he trusts you enough to spy on you, considering I'm not exactly a threat at the moment." Connor's voice was so close to her ear it made her jump. Kiera stepped back, suddenly very aware that Darian had seen what she had been doing. Something was drawing her to the man in front of her, and she was rapidly becoming confused by him.

Connor recognized that frightened animal look in her eyes and started straining toward her, his hands still bound behind him around the tree.

"Hey! No, no, no! Bane? Bane, *listen* to me. *Don't* run. Please, *please*, don't run."

Kiera took another step back, her eyes narrowed, watching him accusingly, and her heart hammering in her chest. Panic began to spread through her limbs, adrenaline and fear leaving her brain a jumbled mess. *Darian is gone! I have to go after him! Run!*

"Bane?" Connor was trying desperately to stay calm. If she left him, there was no telling when—or if—she would come back. He felt exceptionally stupid for agreeing to being bound in the first place, but if she took off, there was a very real chance he wasn't going to survive the night. The boar meat was still hanging from a nearby tree with blood and offal all over the ground, and *he* was trussed up like a lamb being sent to slaughter with bits of pig all over his boots.

Wolf buffet was *not* on Connor's list of how he wanted to leave his world.

"Bane, *listen* to my voice," he whispered as he lowered his tone, trying to breathe slowly and keep his own rising panic at bay. Connor stared at her, trying to keep her focused, forcing his way through her fear.

"I cannot get out of here if you leave me. I am here to *help* you, not hurt you"—he swallowed before saying the next words, a little unnerved that he had to force them out of his mouth—"or your Aeroyn. *Listen* to what I'm telling you. *I will die* if you leave me here. I need your *help*."

Now, there *are words I never thought I would say.*

Kiera was breathing shallowly, trying to listen and trying to stay level. She fought against the panic, struggling to shove it back down, but it was rapidly slipping out of control.

Darian was her protector, her mentor, her lover . . . If he left her, she would be lost.

Without Darian, I will be alone*!*

"Hey! Stay with me, Bane. Darian's not gone. He's just upset. He'll come back. And if he doesn't, I'll help you find him." It caught Connor off guard when he realized that the words coming out of his mouth might as well have been vomit. The *last* thing he wanted was to trek through these damned woods to find some jealous *bird* that was probably going to kill him when he had the chance.

It hit him then that Connor didn't *want* her to find the Aeroyn at all.

Keep her calm. Tell her what she wants to hear.

"I *promise*, Bane. I promise I will help you go after him." He let out a ragged, defeated breath, inwardly cringing when he realized he was actually *pleading*. "But *please*, Bane . . . please don't leave me *here*."

Twenty-Six

"We're not going to get very far if you refuse to get on that horse, Alyk," Henelce teased as he kept pace on his palomino.

"*You* saw how she was. I even *try* to get next to her, and she bites at me. This is easier, and honestly, I'd rather walk. It's helping to keep me from *killing* something," he retorted as he stared hard at the big black horse in tow. Alyk was trudging along beside his mount, not overly interested in being thrown again.

"Don't take your anger at Tance out on that poor beast. She didn't do anything wrong, and she's probably just reacting to your inability to stay *calm*." Henelce was still livid too, but he had his own agenda to worry about, and Tance was not on the forefront of his mind anymore. "Well, we have time to kill, I suppose. Just don't *walk* all the way to the Runes, okay?"

Alyk snorted a laugh.

"Henelce, I'll be lucky if I don't end up strung from a tree if Bane catches me back here. She's already made her intentions *quite* clear." He scanned the trees to the west, the path they followed along the rolling foothills snaking through the Glenfolds and along the edge of the denser woods. "We may not be *in* Baneswood, but skirting it is probably just as risky."

"Maybe if she knew who you were . . ." Henelce raised his eyebrows at his companion as he glanced down at Alyk from his higher perch. Alyk's expression darkened, and he stopped walking, glaring up at the Shephard he called friend.

"*No*, Henelce, and *if* we ever see her again, you're going to keep your mouth shut too."

Twenty-Seven

"Woman, slow *down*! You're going to wear us both out if we keep this pace up in this heat!"

Kiera was stalking through the forest at a rapid clip, annoyed that Connor was still following her and now complaining about it.

Not that she had given him much choice.

"I could always *kill* you if you would rather stop *walking*. Tirath knows I would be better off *without* you in tow," she replied arrogantly as she glanced over her shoulder at him. *You wanted to find me. Now you're going to have to suffer for it, Dirtbag.*

"*I* would rather settle somewhere for the night and let Darian find *you* when he's got his thick skull on straight instead of traipsing through these goddess-forsaken woods! I'm fairly certain that neither of us will do well once it gets *dark*, Bane, no matter how good with a knife you think you are."

They hadn't gotten far from the tree Connor had been tied to, maybe eight or nine miles, following the eastward path just north of the Oriens, searching for wherever Darian had taken off to when the Aeroyn still didn't return after an hour of waiting. Kiera had spent nearly the entire time sitting in a tree, angrily tearing leaves apart and letting the pieces rain down like confetti while searching the sky for Darian and wishing Connor would simply *leave*.

But when Darian didn't come back, she had jumped down from the limb and started after her bird, and Connor had followed suit. They had been marching along the path ever since. Now that the day was starting to wane, Connor wanted to collect firewood while they could still see, and Kiera was hearing none of it.

"Seriously, Bane, we should stop and build a fire while we've got daylight on our side—"

Kiera suddenly pivoted and laid her hand flat on his chest, holding him up.

"We will stop when I *say*, got it?" she said flatly.

Connor just stared back at her, his mouth firmly closed. Kiera didn't move her hand at first, the warmth of his skin filtering through the cool linen of his shirt. She could feel his heartbeat under her fingers.

She dropped her hand and turned away, picking her pace right back up where she left off. Connor sighed and started after her.

I wonder if she realizes how weird *she really is . . . or that she keeps touching me.* He could still feel the warm spot where her hand had just been, and Connor felt a smile trying to form. There was something innocent about it, like she had no control and didn't realize it was wrong.

Is it so wrong? She is only human, after all. She had already admitted that she had never been with a *man*, and Connor suddenly wondered what made the Aeroyn so interesting. He had known she was in the company of one, but it had been a bit of a surprise to find out they were more than just *companions.*

It's not like she could bear children with him...

Connor hurriedly pushed that thought away, the idea of the two of them together too bizarre even for him. *We should have just headed back to the castle. Staying out here is a bad idea.*

He had wanted to go back to Grant's Perch and get the rest of his gear, but Bane had flatly refused. At present, all Connor had with him was a pack with a fresh shirt and a few things that would allow him to stay out in the forest: a cloak, flint and tinder, and some odds and ends . . . just enough gear to get by on for a night or two at the most, but not much else. Connor felt a little naked without a weapon since Bane had taken his knife and Darian had turned his bow and arrows into kindling hours earlier, and he watched the amethyst glint erratically as he followed her, the hilt of Eryce's hunting knife peeking out of her left boot catching the light as she picked her way through the brush.

He found himself quietly debating if he was good enough to get it back.

Kiera had her own bag with her cloak and some apples, bread, and a few folded sheets of heavy brown paper for some of the better meat, but she had expected to go back *home* with Darian; she wasn't at all thrilled to be stuck out here with *Dirtbag*, and she wasn't about to take him back to the castle with her either.

Each of them had taken some of the boar meat, but most of the dead animal was left hanging from the tree.

At least it will keep the damned wolves busy for a night. Out here, we may as well have painted ourselves in blood and run around naked and yelling so they could find us more easily.

Connor had finally had enough of marching through the underbrush when Bane let go of a branch and it smacked him right in the face, startling him out of his grumpy thoughts.

"Okay, *that's* it! Kill me if you want, but I'm *not* going any farther, Bane!" Connor's annoyance came through loud and clear as his voice rang out more loudly than he had intended.

Kiera stifled a laugh, trying to keep her face serious as she turned around and crossed her arms over her chest, shifting her weight and giving him a haughty expression that belied her relief of not being in the forest alone.

"Fine, *Dirtbag*, we can stop. But *you* can gather the firewood since this is *your* idea."

Don't argue. Don't open your mouth.

"On one condition." Connor removed a familiar brown paper parcel from his pack before he dropped his bag in the dirt at his feet. Kiera raised an eyebrow at him. He smirked, the little voice in his head overruled in favor of annoying her just as much as she was annoying him as he tossed the wrapped pieces of pork directly at her chest, forcing her to react and catch it. "Be a good *woman* and *cook*, will you?"

Kiera turned a shade of purple as Connor turned his back on her and started picking up twigs and branches, ignoring her glacial stare.

I'm going to get you for that, Dirtbag.

Twenty-Eight

Eryce lay awake as the light of day began to fade, listening to his wife breathing softly as she slept next to him. He was watching her, studying her, still loving the curve of her neck, the high, rounded breasts, and her soft, pale skin . . .

In her sleep, Serra still looked like the girl he had fallen in love with so long ago.

It wasn't the body he was starting to question but the mind that controlled it. Something in her was slipping, and Serra wasn't quite the same woman he had been so enamored with nearly two decades earlier though he had loved her since she was born. Some of those subtle reminders were still there on occasion—the softness in her eyes when she looked at their boys, the warmth of her genuine smile . . .

But he couldn't help but notice that those things were fading too. Eryce couldn't remember the last time he had made her laugh or even held a civil conversation with her. Serra still came when he called, showed up in court when asked, and even invited him into her bed, but her words seemed hollow, her stare sometimes vacant. Her skin was still soft and pliant, but the wrinkles around her eyes and the dark circles that threatened underneath sometimes made her look weary and *old*.

Eryce hated to think of her in those terms.

Serra had aged so much from stress and worry, the repeated pregnancies and miscarriages of the past few years leaving her a little frail. She spent much of her time quietly reading and sewing, only rarely joining him for dinner anymore. When she wasn't sequestered in her rooms, Serra was usually tucked away somewhere with their twins though she had been doing that less and less of late, choosing instead to simply be alone.

Sometimes he wouldn't see her for a week or more, but today he had chosen *not* to let her be. Eryce had come to her room late that afternoon out of sheer need to be near her, still loving her the way he had when he was young and Serra was barely a woman in his eyes. The unexpected visit had surprised her, and when he had kissed her, he could taste the wine on her breath.

But the passion still surfaced easily enough, and Serra had *wanted* him to touch her, to push her dress of her shoulders and cover her with his weight.

Halfway through, she had started to weep, telling him to leave. Eryce had refused. He simply held her against him and let her cry herself to sleep.

She seems so damaged inside . . . Eryce caught himself wondering if he should just put both of them out of her misery as he brushed strands of her raven hair away from her face, quickly pushing that thought away. Not too far away but far enough that he wasn't going to dwell on it. A servant girl here and there was easy enough to get rid of, but his wife would be *noticed* if she went missing.

Look at her, Eryce. She is so peaceful. You could say she died in her sleep. Let her go, great king, his right eye whispered in his head, shifting and starting to warm expectantly.

Eryce shook his head and sighed.

Shut up. I can't do it. Not to her.

He kissed Serra lightly on the forehead and crawled out of her bed, the floor chilly under his bare feet. He picked up his heavy robe from the footboard, suddenly needing the solitude of his own chambers, the fading light of day filtering through the row of windows that lined the south side of the hall that bridged their separate apartments lighting his way.

But the eye was throbbing, wanting to be fed, and Eryce had little choice in the matter.

The King of Rhonendar pulled the thin rope to call for his valet once he was through his own door. He gave the man instructions to send one of the maids to build up the fire in his wife's room and to send someone in to tend to his *needs*.

The valet simply nodded and retreated to fulfill his sovereign's commands. He knew better than to ask questions lest he become the expendable *someone* his master wanted.

Orders given and command heeded, Eryce settled into the plush chair in front of his own empty grate and waited.

Twenty-Nine

"*B*ane? Bane! Wake up! You're dreaming!"

Kiera's eyes snapped open to someone shaking her shoulders in the dark. She tried to sit up, but strong hands held her down, and she instinctively fought back. She didn't even think as she brought her arms to her chest, sweeping outward and breaking the hold as she pulled her knees up and against the chest of whoever was trying to pin her. Kiera grasped the bare forearms as she kicked up, sending the assailant bodily over her head, releasing her grip as they went flying and landed with a loud *oof* several feet away. Kiera jumped up, steady on her feet and armed in less than a second, ready for a fight.

"Ow! Okay, Crazy Lady of the Forest... I'm getting *really* tired of being hit by you!"

She suddenly recognized the male voice directly ahead in the blinding darkness that surrounded her. His black clothing helped him blend in too well with the inky darkness, and the dirt of the forest floor was too void of debris to rustle under his boots. She heard him get up, but after a few seconds all she heard was *nothing*. No wildlife hooted or cried in the night, no wind blew . . .

Kiera felt like her ears were stuffed with cotton.

"*Connor*? Connor . . . Where are you?" she whispered.

Kiera backed up a little, the silence eerie and foreboding, and she had no idea where Connor was. The moons were still low in the sky, only the quarter-full white one partially visible through the trees, its light too weak to illuminate her surroundings. A noise behind her made Kiera pivot and take a step backward, right into Connor's chest, and his fingers quickly but gently wrapped around her wrists before she could react and hurt one or both of them.

"*Okay*. Okay. It's just *me*." Connor's voice was soft and calm, his breath warm in her ear, making her skin break out in gooseflesh. Kiera shivered, her whole body shaky and cold, and he took the knife from her, tossing it on the ground. She shook him off and covered her face with her hands, just trying to breathe normally.

Kiera froze when Connor pulled her back against his chest, rubbing her arms, trying to get her warm.

"It was just a dream. I'm sorry if I scared you," Connor whispered into her hair. He didn't even think about it as he kissed the top of her head and wrapped his arms around her.

Why does it feel like I've done this before?

"It wasn't *just a dream, Dirtbag*. Let me go." Her words were muffled by her hands as Connor hesitated to comply.

He forced his arms to relax as Kiera stepped out of his embrace and let out a ragged breath, running her hands back through her hair and kept her back to him.

Do your job, idiot.

"Do you want to talk about it?"

Silence.

"Okay, point taken." Connor moved cautiously toward the embers that were still glowing from their earlier fire, the dry wood he had collected burning too fast to stay lit very long. Connor groped for a log and a stick to coax small flames into life, granting them both heat and light and chasing some of the inky darkness away.

How the hell did I fall asleep too? It has to be close to midnight by now. Bane had fought with him when he said he could take first watch, and she had taken up into defensive position with her arms around her knees, watching the fire defiantly as the day faded. An hour later, she had been curled up on the ground, and Connor had moved closer to her, leaning back against a boulder, waiting for the sound of flapping wings and the Aeroyn that refused to show. Hours later, Kiera had rolled over in her sleep and jarred his leg, waking him to her whimpering cries. He had never heard anything so heartbreaking. His expression said as much when Connor looked up as Bane knelt down next to him.

Kiera pulled her cloak around herself, mostly eclipsing her face, trying to simultaneously get warm and hide from those attentive green eyes. The last thing Kiera wanted was his pity, and his earlier threat of *touching back* still made her a little wary of him, even if she found his annoying presence reassuring.

He's not the only one to blame, silly girl. You *started it.* She couldn't help but replay the feeling of his exposed skin under her hand in her mind, the texture, the color, the smell . . . Kiera could still smell him now, even so close to the fire, that combination of mint and cedar clean and a little comforting. At least she wasn't alone, and she would have been if he hadn't gotten through to her, gotten her to cut him free from the sapling.

Connor would still be there now, covered with ants and swearing up a storm. Kiera felt her mouth try to twist up as she imagined him squirming and cursing . . .

"Care to share what's going on behind those pretty eyes?" Connor was openly watching her, and he found himself reaching up to push her hood gently away from her face, absently tucking a strand of hair behind her ear.

Kiera was so startled by the gesture that she didn't move at first as she stared blankly at the fire, not sure how to respond. Eventually she shifted so that she almost faced him, sitting back on her heels, putting most of her body just out of arm's reach.

"What are you *doing* here, Connor? What are you *really* after? Just tell me the *truth*." Kiera searched his face, and Connor inwardly debated what he could let out and still hold the advantage. He was going to have to tell her sooner or later.

Without the threat of Darian around to hear and probably arrange his limbs in a new order, he took a chance.

"There is a very high bounty to be paid for you. I'm sure you're aware of that."

Connor locked eyes with her, watching her expression carefully, ready to defend himself if she decided to attack. Bane might have been armed, but he had already bested her once.

Connor was willing to bet he could do it again.

"Yes, and I am also *aware* that I'm supposed to be taken alive and *untouched*," she sneered. "I hope *you* have heard of those who have perished in that futile quest. I don't know what Eryce wants with me other than to take vengeance on my hide for the lives of his expensive Sukolai, but I have *no* intention of going *easily*." She held his gaze, calm on the outside, but her muscles were wound tightly, ready to spring and run if she needed to.

"Eryce sent you, *didn't* he?" It wasn't a question. Kiera shook her head when he didn't immediately respond. "I should have just let Darian torture you. I knew you felt *wrong*."

"I *told* you earlier that you wouldn't like my answer, Bane."

I knew it! Kiera suddenly reached for one of the knives on her thigh and tried to stand, but Connor caught her wrist through her cloak, pulling her off balance and making her sit rather ungracefully next to him. Kiera found that she was fighting against both him *and* her clothing, the cloak tangling with her limbs, keeping her knives out of her reach.

She growled in frustration when Connor caught her other wrist and she fought harder.

"Bane. *Stop*!" The command caught Kiera off guard enough that she hesitated, surprising them both. Connor let go of her wrists and caught her face in his hands, forcing her to look at him and trusting her not to put a blade between his ribs.

Kiera immediately thought of the first time she had met Darian, the knife in her hand suddenly forgotten. *There is no way I'm going to trust you!*

"*Listen* to me, Bane. I have no intention of giving you up to Eryce. I told you I was here to help you, and I *am*."

You better not really mean that, idiot.

Kiera tried to pull away, but Connor held her firm. Those dark-green eyes would not be ignored. Connor held her that way for another few moments, watching her carefully before opening his mouth again.

"I should have just left you to yourself and let some other money-hungry idiot take my place . . ." *Stop talking. Stop talking. Stop talking!* ". . . but whatever *happened* between us, whatever I felt when I was tied to that damned tree makes me want to—"

Damn it! You're letting this get personal! Connor's mouth finally agreed with his brain, and he abruptly closed it, knowing he was going to regret his words if he kept going without a filter. He let her go and sat back, but Kiera didn't move, silently studying him as something between disbelief and curiosity flickered across her face. Connor ran his hand back through his short hair, trying to think fast and cover his mistake. He was digging a hole he was going to get stuck in if he wasn't careful.

One rule, moron: Don't get sucked in. He let out a frustrated breath. *Change the approach.*

"Bane, I am not, by any means, an honorable man."

That felt oddly good to admit. Connor paused, letting that realization sink in before opening his mouth once more.

"I lie, I cheat, and I do things for money that my mother would disown me for if she ever felt inclined to acknowledge me. Eryce didn't send me—I *volunteered*, thinking I could find you relatively easily, and I wasn't wrong."

That much was totally true. Connor glanced at her, struck again by those green eyes as he reached up tentatively to push the hair out of her face, his fingertips lightly tracing her brow, his thumb touching her cheek. It felt strange to him to be even semi-genuine, but the words felt right in this particular instance.

I guess I'm going to have to suck it up and be as honest as I can if I want her to trust me. He just wasn't sure he trusted himself when he realized he *wanted* to touch her.

Then again, she was *letting* him.

The words he needed to say next were *not* the ones that came out of Connor's mouth.

"I would *never* have taken this on if I had met you *first*."

Shut up, idiot! What the hell are you doing? Connor tuned out the little voice in his head as his hand went under her hair, his fingers gently encircling the back of her neck, and he pulled Bane toward him. He was a little surprised when she didn't resist, and Connor could feel her racing heartbeat under his hand. His fingertips traced a raised mark on the back of her neck, its shape faintly familiar, but that information was kicked roughly to the back of his mind; he was too focused on drawing her near.

They were so close Connor could feel her breath on his mouth, and he licked his lips, still waiting for her to pull away. Kiera surprised him when she closed the gap and covered his mouth with hers; Connor closed his eyes, letting out a breath through his nose that he had been holding as he kissed her back.

Good job, idiot. This *is going to be bad*. For a few short seconds, Connor didn't care. But somewhere between pushing his tongue into her mouth and pulling her on top of him, the shape of the mark on the back of her neck manifested itself in his brain, and his eyes popped open.

Oh.

Shit.

Thirty

Shit. Shit. Shit! She's royalty? He hadn't seen that coming, and Connor doubted Eryce even knew what he was chasing. *Dear goddess Tirath, thank you for answering my prayers and making my life more complicated. Much appreciated. This game has to change—and fast.*

Bane was kissing him deeply, and Connor's heart was starting to race; he was having a hard time concentrating on anything but *her*. She was every bit as delicious as he had thought she would be under that sour exterior, and the last thing he wanted was to stop.

But Connor put his hands on the sides of her face, breaking the kiss and pushing her gently away. Bane looked confused and a little hurt, and he could feel her heartbeat pattering rapidly against his skin as he tried to catch his breath.

"Bane, wait—"

"*Why?*" She demanded, still trying to kiss him.

"What's the *rush?*" He covered his surprise with a smirk and a cocked eyebrow.

"Don't kiss me like *that* then make me feel like an idiot! If you're going to try to seduce me, at least have the decency to let me *enjoy* it." Kiera sounded annoyed and looked offended until he laughed, and she smacked his chest. Connor's smile faded, and he looked at her more seriously, trying to gauge where her head was really at. Bane smelled like honey, but it masked that she was like playing with fire; the mark on the back of her neck confirmed that if nothing else. Connor was uncomfortable with how much he wanted her and how good she felt to him, and in his current position, there was certainly no denying it.

Even if he tried, his pants weren't loose enough to play it off, and now that Bane was straddling him, the friction was making the *problem* so much worse. Connor wasn't excited about the next few uncomfortable hours, but following through was not a good idea this early in the game; if he didn't stop now, he was going to end up a red stain at the base of a cliff somewhere once the Aeroyn found out. He wasn't about to risk his life trying to get her to trust him even if it felt this good.

Self-preservation, idiot. Self-preservation. Connor finally took his own advice as he inhaled a deep breath and said the only thing that was going to save him from himself.

"What about *Darian*? How do you think *he* would feel to find us like this?"

Cue the look of horror.

Cue backing away and looking at me accusingly.

Cue self-reprimanding curses for being so stupid and forgetting her loyalties to someone else.

He had run this same scenario enough times to know the responses, though usually it was to his benefit for the other half of the equation to react badly. Connor waited for Bane to get off him, to start crying, to maybe slap him . . .

None of that happened, leaving Connor totally confused when Kiera simply cocked her head and looked at him.

Darian wasn't forgotten, just put aside for the moment, as though he didn't really exist. That was easier to do than she really wanted to admit, and she couldn't just blame the man atop whom she was willingly sitting.

"Connor, I cannot even begin to describe how *strange* you feel to me."

"Well, I—*what?*" Her response left him further perplexed. Connor had been called a *lot* of things, but *strange* was not one of them, and those were certainly *not* the words he had imagined would come out of her mouth. He also wasn't expecting Bane to pick up his hand and ran her thumb over the end of his index finger, the intimate gesture fueling a fire Connor was now trying to put out, but that was exactly what she was doing just then.

He didn't feel entirely inclined to stop her either.

"No fangs, no claws, no wings—none of what I'm used to," she mused, playing with his fingers. "You asked me if I had been with a man, and the answer is no, I haven't. I haven't been around men, or *people*, in a long time, and that wasn't always true. I'm starting to wonder if you weren't right when you lied to me—maybe I *am* missing out on something."

She smiled bitterly, knowing Darian would never let that be a real option. Kiera looked away, contemplating as she continued, trying to put her jumbled thoughts into words.

"This forest is where I have found peace and escape from a world that didn't want me in it, and *Darian* has been the one constant in all that time. He is my protector, my friend and is as gentle as he can be with me, not always because he *wants* to be but because he *has* to be. He told me once that my body wouldn't withstand what mating with a female like *him* could, and I can always feel the restraint.

"Sometimes I wonder if he wants to let go and do what comes naturally. No thought, just instinct. There are times when I want that—no limitations, no worries, just . . . I can't even find the words for it."

The thought of her naked with a welcome vision, but the idea of her naked with the *Aeroyn* was a mental image Connor could certainly do *without*. He studied her before saying anything, trying to tread carefully. Kissing her had already been a bad idea.

"Is that what this is? Curiosity to know what that feels like? Because that's *not* what this is for me." Connor pulled his hand away and rested it on his chest, trying to untie his own tongue as his brain attempted to work with less blood flow than it was normally accustomed. "I don't even *know* what *this* is, Bane. Not for me, anyway. I can, however, promise that I am *not* the safer choice even if I'm a more *conventional* one."

Connor found he hated that those words were so honest. As much worldly experience as he had, he hadn't the faintest idea how to be *real* with anyone, much less even consider that this weird girl in a far-off forest was capable of making him *feel*, whether or not she knew it. This was the closest he had come to being genuine in at least a decade, and it felt like a badly tailored coat that was never going to fit well or feel quite right unless he made some adjustments, and that was going to come at a high cost.

Connor wasn't convinced he was ready to pay up just yet.

Kiera wasn't watching him anymore as she ran her fingers over his wrist where the ropes had abraded the skin, leaving semicircular marks on him that would take a few days, not a few minutes, to fade.

How long has it been since I've had to deal with even minimal pain like that? It suddenly struck her that she *wanted* to be more like Connor, to *feel* like he did. The emotional walls she had been able to keep in place with Alyk were far weaker against the man under her, and Kiera was keenly aware that they weren't going to hold up if he pushed hard enough. She didn't know that she wanted to give him the chance, but she didn't really want to discount that possibility just yet, either.

"Honestly, Connor, you scare me more than my *mate* does. I *know* Darian can hurt me"—Kiera locked eyes with him, and Connor suddenly felt like he couldn't breathe—"but underneath it all, *you* are just as vulnerable as I am."

Kiera held his gaze for a moment before she got up and moved just out of his reach, sitting back down next to the fire. She hid her red face behind her hair as she started rummaging through her pack like nothing had happened, but her heart was still beating rapidly, and the taste of him lingered on her mouth.

Connor stared up at the stars overhead, trying to calm his racing thoughts. Bane was going to be a far bigger challenge than he had ever imagined. He felt himself swallow when he realized the mission was going to have to change.

Eryce was *not* going to be happy.

Shit.

Thirty-One

The smell of a campfire caught Darian's attention, taking his focus away from the buck he had been following for the past few minutes. He had been gliding from tree to tree in its wake as he hunted quietly in the early morning stillness, but he suddenly settled to sniff at the acrid smoke, debating if he should investigate or if he should just let whoever it was pass. He was coming to the border of Baneswood, just before the territory he and Kiera defended turned into the Glenfolds and the forest became less dense. Darian was at least thirty miles southeast from where he had left Kiera and *Dirtbag*, and he was just trying not to think about them.

Maybe it's better to let them be for now. He sat back against the trunk of the tree, tired, sore, and still unsure if he was doing the right thing as the buck trotted off, never knowing the peril it had been in only moments before. The sun started to warm the air around him as it peeked through the branches, rousing the birds and the squirrels and bringing the forest alive with sound, Darian's prey gone and forgotten.

The unexpected scent of leather and bacon floated up from the ground, carrying with it an oddly familiar voice.

"Don't make me shoot you down from up there, *bird*!"

Darian looked down in surprise to find Henelce standing at the base of the tree twenty feet below, his fists on his hips like a scolding mother and his crossbow slung over one shoulder. The Aeroyn couldn't help laughing despite his bad mood.

He had been concentrating on picking apart the needles of the pine bough above him and hadn't heard Henelce approach. That part of the forest had a smoother carpet from the conifers, making walking quietly that much easier, but a Shephard didn't really need the help.

You only heard them when they wanted you to.

"How long have you been standing there, Shephard?"

"Long enough to know sulking when I see it! Get down here so I don't have to yell!"

"You could always come up." Henelce blanched at the suggestion. Darian rolled his eyes and swung easily off the branch, dropping quietly to the ground.

"Thank you." Henelce patted as high up on Darian's arm as he could, and considering he only barely came up to the Aeroyn's chest, almost touching the shoulder was an accomplishment. "It's too beautiful a morning to be pouting. Walk with me." Henelce started back toward his camp with the Aeroyn in tow as he looked around expectantly. "Tell me, where is that pretty mate of yours?"

"She's not my *mate*. I'm not really sure *what* she is," Darian grunted, annoyed. "Not *lately*, anyway."

"If you ever find a female that doesn't make you wonder, let me know. I'm pretty well convinced they're all designed to make our heads spin, and I've been dealing with them for a good deal longer than you have," Henelce chuckled. "You two are an *interesting* match but a good one, I thought. What changed?"

"She realized she's *human*," Darian sighed, sounding bitter.

The Shephard pondered that quietly for a moment.

"*She* did,"—Henelce glanced sideways at Darian—"or *you* did?"

"What are you getting at, *Shephard*?" Darian bristled and stopped walking, the scent of ozone filtering into the air. Henelce rounded on Darian and stood staring up fearlessly at the irritated being that towered a foot and half over him.

"Humans are funny creatures, Darian. They're fickle. They doubt. They're curious. And they have a lot less time to figure out life than you and I do, my friend. Their decisions aren't always made with a clear head but with an emotional heart . . . which is something I hadn't seen an *Aeroyn* do until I met *you*." Henelce poked the bigger being in the chest, raising his eyebrows, and Darian frowned down at the stubby finger pressed against his sternum.

"I know your kind almost *too* well, and Bane must be a pretty strong woman to have such an influence on you. Most of the Aeroyn I have met are stubborn, closed-minded, proud, uncompromising—"

"*Careful*, Shephard," Darian cut him off and brushed Henelce's hand aside. "Those points are true to some degree, but my people aren't as aloof as you would make us out to be."

"*Really*?" Henelce pulled at his beard. "Then tell me, Darian, why is it that all of the other races have found a way to coexist, but *your* people have yet to join the rest of the world as it moves forward?"

Darian stared hard at the Shephard, but they both knew he didn't have an answer for that.

"Now back up and explain—what do you mean 'she realized she's human'?"

"It started with your *friend*," Darian growled low.

"*Oh*. You mean Bane realized that she's a *woman*!" Henelce laughed loudly, the idea that Darian was even remotely surprised by this notion striking him as terribly funny. "You can't hide someone like *that* away forever! Bane's a beauty, all right, but she's also young, and there's something about her that makes me think she needs to be in the world, not in the woods. You may make for quite the pair, but I'm sure you've already considered that you'll outlive her . . ."

Henelce paused, his tone having turned sympathetic as he trailed off. Darian nodded slightly, unhappy to hear someone else acknowledge something that constantly sat in the back of his mind.

"Well, did you ever consider that Bane might *outgrow* you? Or that there might be another calling for her in this life other than just loving you? She may stay in these woods because it's where you are, but what if she were faced with another choice?"

Darian recalled his words to her about going back to Corengale, but the thought of Kiera suddenly seemed like a dream from a hundred years ago. *Yesterday. That was only yesterday.*

"She has already told me *this* is where she wants to be. She doesn't want to leave this forest or the home she has with me, and I don't want her to leave—"

"Then why aren't *you* anywhere near where she is?" Henelce felt the prickle of energy as Darian's temper flared. "Something come between you?"

"She's . . . *distracted*." Darian let out a defeated sigh. There was no use in trying to hide what was on his mind.

"With another male, I suppose . . ."

"She crossed paths with some hunter roaming the forest while she was hunting yesterday. I wasn't there when they met, but I saw how she *reacted* to him. I wanted to kill him, and she wanted to *talk* to him, and now . . ."

"Now I don't know what to think. There was a change in her when she met Alyk, but I thought it had to do with something else. The interest she shows in this hunter confuses me. I can't tell if she's just curious or if I'm losing her."

"Come now, Darian, are you really that surprised?"

"*Yes!*"

"Then you have quite the challenge ahead of you if you choose to continue to live in denial. She's only human, after all."

Darian had to keep from grinding his teeth as he waved the Shephard away when he tried to put his hand on the Aeroyn's forearm. Henelce's expression was almost sympathetic, but Darian looked like he wanted to rip something apart.

"Now, don't go getting all huffy!" Henelce wagged his index finger at the bigger being. "Think about it—who follows *who*, Darian? You might protect her, care for her, *love* her, but *Bane* calls the shots, whether or not you see it or like it. You've learned her language. You'll kill to defend her. Would you die for her too?"

Darian bit his lip, crossing his arms as he studied the ground and let that idea filter though his brain.

"Yes. Yes, I think I would."

"Fair enough. But if she *asked*, would you walk away? Would you let her follow a path of her choosing if that was what she wanted?" He pointed at the arm band on Darian's bicep that divided his tattoo. "And what of your old mate? Does Bane *know* why you wear that?"

Silence.

"*That's* what I thought." Henelce shook his head and kept walking. He picked up a pinecone and tossed it up in the air, only to catch it again, heading back in the direction of the campfire.

"What the *hell* is that supposed to mean, Shephard?" Darian yelled as he stomped after the enigmatic little man, wishing to Tirath he had run into *anyone* else.

Thirty-Two

The sun spilled over the edge of the hood of her cloak, and Kiera made a face as she pulled it farther over her head to block the offending light. She nuzzled against the warm body next to her, throwing her arm over the broad chest and breathing in the smell of dry earth, cool forest air, cedar and mint . . .

"You know, you're kind of *cute* when you do that."

Her eyes popped open to find Connor on his back, propped up against his pack with his hands behind his head and smirking at her. Apparently he had been watching her sleep.

Kiera suddenly realized she was just about as close as she could get without being completely on top of him.

Wonderful.

"Ugh! *You*! Go away!" Kiera rolled away from him and curled up on the hard ground, hiding her face in the crook of her arm, wishing simultaneously that *she* was in a tree, *he* was Darian, and she hadn't moved because now she was *cold.*

I'd rather deal with being cold than face him after last night . . . So much for sleeping! Her guilty thoughts were keeping her wide awake.

"Is that any way to talk to the man you just *spent the night* with?" Connor poked her in the ribs, his voice rife with sarcastic insinuation.

Kiera sat up and glared at him.

"Sleeping *next* to you—"

"On *top* of me—"

"—does *not* constitute *spending the night*!"

"—makes me wish we hadn't been wearing *clothes*."

"Argh! What is *wrong* with you?" Kiera stood up and hastily dusted herself off. "Tirath must have put your brain in that cock of yours because it seems to be the *only* thing you think with!"

The words were out of her mouth before her hands could get to her lips to stop them, her face immediately turning crimson. Connor's eyes crinkled around the edges, and he put his fist to his mouth, his body shaking with silent laughter.

"*Oh?* Is *that* my problem?" Connor could barely articulate the words as he laughed so hard he snorted. *She's so fun to toy with . . .*

"Look!" Kiera snapped as she bent down and grabbed the front of his shirt, lifting him up bodily toward her. His giggling inflamed her further, and she started yelling in his face. "*None* of this is a *joke* to me, Connor! Darian's *gone*! *You* are driving me *crazy,* and— Ack!"

Kiera didn't get to finish her rant because she was suddenly falling forward; Connor had kicked her feet out from under her. But Kiera didn't let go of his shirt and ended up breaking her fall on top of him, knocking the air out of his lungs before he could catch her.

"Okay . . ." Connor wheezed, coughing, ". . . that didn't . . . go as planned . . ."

"Serves you right, *Dirtbag,*" Kiera giggled.

"*Sure . . . now* you . . . laugh." Connor was trying to breathe, but all he could think about was how to do that without moving Bane off him. She still had a grip on his shirt, her face just above his, the scent of honey faintly discernable. His breathing slowly came easier, and Connor reached up to pushed the hair out of her face, tucking it behind her ear.

"You know, if this goes much further, Darian's going to kill us both," Connor whispered as he ran his thumb over her cheek. *Stop touching her, idiot!*

"I'm not sure that will even matter. He's already going to smell *you* all over me." Kiera's words held some combination of guilt and dismay as she frowned at the thought.

"But not like *that,*" he sighed, frustrated. "Bane, I told you I wouldn't come between you two, and that's why I didn't take advantage of the situation last night. *You* weren't exactly trying to stop me, and I certainly don't have a death wish—otherwise, I would have let you leave me tied to that *tree.*"

Kiera bit her lip to stifle a laugh, and he envied her teeth.

"Woman, I'm *really* trying to be on my best behavior here. You aren't making that . . . *easy,*" Connor said gently as he shifted slightly under her, and Kiera was suddenly *very* aware of the contours of his body. She was surprised at how much she could feel even with a few layers of clothing between them.

Kiera knew she was pushing it when she still didn't budge, and she felt his hand creep up slowly against her hip, the warmth of his fingers filtering through her thin leggings making her skin tingle. When she didn't push his hand away or try to get up, Connor took a chance and pushed up her tunic to rest his hand on the small of her back. He licked his lips, watching her, and she could feel his heart racing under her fingertips when she finally let go of his shirt and laid her palm flat against his chest.

He's nervous! Kiera was fighting the urge to smile. He had been the one trying to seduce *her,* and now *he* was nervous. *What a funny thought.*

"I guess we had better get a move on before something *happens.*" Kiera patted his chest and tried to get up, but Connor tightened his hold, keeping her pressed against him. His other hand went under her hair, and he pulled her closer.

"Your *best behavior* is pretty terrible, you know that, *Dirtbag*?" Kiera breathed against his mouth.

"I said I was *trying*."

"Not very *hard*, apparently."

"Really? And here I thought I was actually doing pretty well, considering we're both still fully dressed." Connor winced and shifted uncomfortably. "You realize that's not the handle of a *knife* you're lying on, *right*?"

Kiera started to open her mouth, but Connor pulled her all the way to him, kissing her gently and shutting her up before she could ruin the moment.

Her heart picked up, and she stopped breathing.

He dropped his hand and let her go.

"Now get *off* me before I do something *really* stupid."

Thirty-Three

Alyk took his anger out on the stump with his sword, hacking left and right and parrying the inanimate object like it had a one-track mind to kill him. Sweat ran down his face, his hair was matted to his forehead, and his was shirt soaked through as he slammed the blade into the bark over and over, chunks of dead wood flying in all directions, the ground around him covered with small shavings.

Tance was still on his mind, and he was still livid. Alyk was almost panting, his muscular body thrilling at each impact, his reflexes sharp and focused. With each move, he yelled and grunted as he went through the exercises he had done religiously for the past decade.

He caught a sudden movement out of the corner of his eye and swung around, the tip of his sword aimed at the throat of a very big man with very black . . .

Wings? Alyk blinked in surprise.

"*Darian?*"

Thirty-Four

"And here I thought summer was finally *ending*," Connor grumbled. The pair had been walking for nearly two hours in the ever-increasing heat; they were both sweating and tired, the canopy seeming to hold in the heat of the early afternoon sun that was already baking the earth they were treading upon. There seemed to be no escape, and heat came at them from all sides. Even the trees felt warm to the touch.

They were headed east, trying to get as far as they could, but the relentless sun was making their progress feel painfully slow.

"Bane, I think we should stop and wait this out."

"I'm *fine*," Kiera scoffed, but she was lying, and badly.

Connor rolled his eyes.

"Oh, good grief, woman! Just admit that you're as *miserable* as I am in this," he huffed as he pulled his black linen shirt over his head, using it to wipe the sweat off his face before draping it over his shoulder.

"I'm *used* to this heat. And besides, *I'm* not the *idiot* wearing *leather* pants," Kiera smirked as she looked down at his legs as they walked, the highly oiled black calfskin stretched tight, making the pants look painted on. "How the *hell* do you get into those, anyway?"

Connor grinned wickedly in response, and Kiera punched him hard in the arm.

"Ow! I didn't even say anything!" His smile faltered as he rubbed his bicep, the spot already sore.

"You were *thinking* it."

"Then *you* were *too*!" Connor smirked as he punched her back, making her stumble.

"Ugh . . . *Why* am I putting up with *you*?" Kiera complained, trying not to laugh, but her smile wasn't so easily stopped.

"Because, dear lady, life without me would be *boring*." Connor realized he was only half joking; he was still wrestling with that notion when he noticed that Bane was no longer keeping step with him. He turned around to find her several feet behind him, staring up at a large oak with thick foliage and sprawling branches, some reaching almost to the ground.

Kiera smiled inwardly as she dropped her pack and jumped up, catching one of the nearest limbs, pulling herself up easily and clambering through the branch, disappearing into the clouds of leaves that rained down in her wake. Connor started back toward the tree when she left his view and was about to come up after her when he was hit in the face with something small and hard.

"Ow! Damn it, woman! That *hurt*!" Connor rubbed his forehead as he bent down to pick up the projectile. *She threw an acorn at me!*

He scanned the tree, but he couldn't see her though he could certainly *hear* her as her quiet laughter filtered through the air. Another acorn pelted him in the chest, and this time, he caught the direction. Connor dropped his pack and his shirt next to hers and followed her into the upper limbs, but she was nowhere to be seen. An acorn dropped from above, but the leaves were denser, and he couldn't see through them, so he climbed up a few more branches.

"Bane?" Connor called as he stopped and listened.

The sound of running feet below him told him he'd been had; Bane had dropped down and taken off south at a dead run.

"Yeah, go ahead, *run* in this heat!" he yelled after her. Connor shook his head as he started his descent, grumbling under his breath the whole way. He hit the ground and went to pick up his pack . . .

Which was gone.

"Of *course*," Connor sighed and rolled his eyes.

Bane was suddenly such a *perfect* name for her.

* * *

Kiera headed straight for the river. It wasn't far from where they had been trudging along, and she needed the break even if she wouldn't admit it to *Dirtbag*. She slowed when she heard the rushing water ahead and picked her way gingerly through the thorny bushes, trying to keep from getting caught up in the ravensthorn, which would be nearly impossible to get out of once it started to tangle. Kiera wondered if Connor knew about that particular weed.

She hoped not.

Darian hates this shit almost as much as he hates water. The thought of Darian made her mouth go dry. Kiera hadn't spent more than a day or two away from him in the past six years, and she missed him less than she thought she would now that Connor was keeping her company, but that felt like a flimsy justification.

I must still be mad at him for leaving me. He just ran when he hadn't liked what he was seeing. Well, flown really, but the idea applies.

It dawned on her then that it wasn't the first time either, and Kiera couldn't help but feel disappointment when she thought of the Aeroyn who had protected her for so long and his apparent inability to hold his temper.

And now I'm stuck babysitting Dirtbag. Kiera suddenly smiled. Connor wasn't so bad, and he was keeping his word, so she couldn't really fault him. *She* had wanted the idiot to live, and Darian was granting her wish, just not the way she had expected.

Connor wasn't turning out to be what she had expected either. She replayed the kiss from the night before in her mind, the way he had tasted and his mouth had fit to hers without the threat of sharp fangs; for the first time, Kiera felt like she might be on a level playing field, at least physically.

Darian adored her, protected her, loved her . . .

But he also overpowered her and kept the world at bay, and she was starting to think it wasn't always a good thing. Connor was following behind her without trying to guide or push, and he seemed just as curious about *her* as she was about *him*. But he was refusing to help make a bad situation worse by allowing either of them to take it further, and Kiera found she respected him for that.

If there's any blame to be placed for this mess, it rests squarely on my own shoulders. Only a fortnight ago, I let someone else out of these woods without killing him, and I thought he was beautiful too. But Alyk only kissed my hand. I certainly didn't stop Connor from kissing me.

Kiera could admit that Connor was physically appealing, but it hadn't been all that long ago that Alyk had almost had the same effect. She just hadn't let Alyk get that far. She frowned at the thoughts about the only other man she had spoken with at any sort of length in the past six years as she set the packs at the river's edge and picked up Connor's dusty black shirt. She fingered the finely woven linen, the scent of mint and cedar all over the fabric . . .

Kiera plunged it into the water, letting the article of clothing swirl in the mild current. Her dark-brown tunic was next into the chilly stream, the dirt and sweat of the past few days washed away by the slow-flowing water.

Once she had laid their shirts out side by side to dry in the sun, Kiera removed her boots and thigh strap and waded slowly into the water, trying to keep her leather bodice from getting wet. She would have simply taken it off if she had been alone, but with nothing underneath, she wasn't so keen on being half naked as Connor seemed to like to be. Kiera smiled to herself as she bent forward and splashed cold water on her face, bringing it to her lips in her cupped hands, the ends of her hair dangling down, brushing the glittering liquid that swirled around her. She stood and ran her wet hands through her hair, depositing cool droplets on her scalp.

Little did she know that Connor was watching her in stunned silence from the shade of a willow at the water's edge. Retrieving the woman before him was turning out to be so much harder than Connor had ever expected, the idea of giving her up becoming more and more foreign as time went on.

Especially seeing her as he did now.

The sun above and the reflection off the surface of the water gave her pale skin and hair an enchanted glow. When she turned back toward the shore, her features were etched with the innocent look of being at peace with the world, making her appear soft and warm instead of hard and guarded. He followed her with his gaze as she wandered farther from the shore, and Connor found himself memorizing her movements and the way her body shifted as she carefully navigated the rocky riverbed. She looked almost *unspoiled* to him, a faint smile on her lips as she watched something move in the river, her fingers working to twist the water out of the ends of her hair over one shoulder.

If I could paint, this is how I would want her immortalized on canvas. Just like this. She's . . . perfect. Connor suddenly realized he could have told her he loved her at that moment and meant it . . .

Whoa, whoa, whoa! What? This is getting out of hand. Wanting to strip her down and do every imaginable deviant act I can think of is one thing, but love *her? No, not this one. I have to remember what she* is.

Connor sighed and covered his face with his hands. He reminded himself again that he still had a job to do, and at the end of that, Bane would hate him anyways, so he might as well kill whatever was trying to build in his brain before he did something else terribly stupid.

Like kiss her.

Again.

This is getting too complicated. I should just drag her screaming to Eryce . . . That particular train of thought made his stomach try to crawl up his throat. *Okay, so I'm not a* total *bastard.*

The mark of royalty intrigued him, making him incredibly curious as to which kingdom Bane was from and if anyone was looking for her. He hadn't heard anything recently, but she had been out in the woods for Tirath knew how long.

She could be from outside this kingdom. That mark is pretty rare. Maybe someone would keep her safe . . .

That idea was cut short when he noticed that Bane was heading back in his direction. Watching her legs emerge from the water, tan leggings clinging to her skin, was doing bad things to Connor's brain. He was having a hard time concentrating on anything else. Except how *uncomfortable* he was getting.

These leather pants have got to go.

Connor shook his head, trying to clear his conflicting thoughts. The movement caught her eye; Kiera had either known he was there or wasn't terribly surprised because she simply smiled and started toward him.

Kiera stopped just outside of the branches of the willow where they dipped into the water, creating a cool, shady umbrella around him.

"Are you coming out? Or am I going to have to come in there and *drag* you out?" Kiera asked sarcastically as she pushed the branches aside, peering in at him.

"What's a day without a challenge?" Connor grinned, but it felt heavy. It felt *fake*.

No, not yet. Don't do that just yet. Connor tried to look casual, like he hadn't just been undressing her with his eyes. He leaned against the tree and was immediately set upon by ants. Ones that bit. She giggled as he swatted at them, cursing loudly and swiping at his bare arm and shoulder.

"You don't do well in the *wild*, do you, *Dirtbag*?" Kiera laughed and shook her head as she turned away from him and went back into the water, leaving Connor behind to watch every inch of her backside as she waded further out.

He was hot and tired, and sweat was running down his back even in the shade. It didn't take long for him to decide he'd had quite enough of the heat.

And his pants.

Connor pulled off his boots and untied the sides of his pants, stripping them off and tossing them on the grass. He waited until Bane's back was turned and she bent forward for another drink of water before quietly wading out, keeping the massive willow between them.

Once the shallows came up to his knees, he dove under. The water was icy but a welcome change to the heat, and Connor tried to remember the last time he had gone swimming in a river, figuring it must have been sometime in his early teens. He broke the surface to find Bane looking around for him, her expression crestfallen when she found he was in the deeper water without her.

"*Well*? Are you just going to *stand there*, or am I going to have to *drag you in*?" Connor mocked her before he dropped back under the shimmering surface and swam toward her, stopping to stand at a point he hoped was deep enough to cover him from the waist down.

It was.

Just barely.

That's all I need. Cold water makes for bad first impressions . . .

"I can't get my armor wet," Kiera pouted a few feet away, the water coming up to her hips as she crossed her arms and shifted her weight.

"*So*? Take it *off*!" Connor's smirk was bordering on lewd, but he didn't care. "You can keep you *pants* on, at least."

"Turn around, *Dirtbag*."

So she's not such a chicken after all.

"Oh *fine*," Connor huffed dramatically as he rolled his eyes and turned in a complete circle to face her again.

"Damn it, Connor! Turn *away*!" Bane was red faced and giggling, the way she was covering her eyes with her hand making Connor grin. He was really starting to love the sound of her laugh . . .

Rein it in, moron! Connor finally stopped laughing long enough to comply with her exasperated command and stood with his back to her, listening to Bane get out of the water and back in, followed by a splash as she dove. He turned back just in time to catch a streak of white moving away from him under the river's surface; Connor waited until he knew where she would probably come up before dropping back under the water, pushing off from the bottom and heading in her direction.

Kiera's head popped up, and she was just deep enough that she couldn't touch the bottom. A moment or two later, Connor broke the surface right in front of her, his feet firmly planted on the rocky bed.

"Well, well. Fancy meeting *you* here," he purred quietly. They faced each other for a moment before he tentatively reached for her, and she smacked the top of the water, splashing him in the face. Connor was coughing and laughing as he went to splash her right back, but Bane dove under and tried to take off downstream.

Good try, woman! He caught her ankle before she could get too far. Bane sputtered up, swearing and laughing and trying to kick away from him, but Connor wasn't going to let go. His face was a mask of determination as he pulled her toward him roughly then pushed her up against one of the large boulders that dotted the middle of the river, pinning her against it with his weight so she faced him with no hope of escape.

All at once, they were only chest deep in water, and Kiera knew what every inch of his body felt like. Connor found out that she didn't leave her pants on after all.

"You really don't believe in playing *fair*, do you?" Connor's voice was husky in her ear as his hands found her waist, and he ran his fingers up her sides, tracing the indentations of her tight fitting armor lingering on her wet skin. He couldn't see much standing that way, but he could certainly feel it.

None of it was making him less inclined to stop touching her, either. There was no need to tell Bane that he wanted her. She could come to that conclusion all on her own.

Goddess above, I want to kiss her . . .

"I'm not the one that jumped in *naked*, Sir *Best Behavior*," she chided sarcastically even though her hands were on his chest, her eyes closed as she quietly memorized the feel of his skin against hers. But when she opened them and looked up at him accusingly, Connor smirked and trailed his fingers down her right side, all the way to her knee. He pulled her leg up and around his hip, unable to help himself.

"Fully *clothed*, just as I suspected . . ." Connor half expected her to squirm and try to get away from him, but she used the new leverage to pull him harder against her, making him groan. He let go of her knee and caught her face in his hands, his expression serious as he searched her eyes with his.

"What are we *doing*, Bane?" he whispered as he leaned in closer so his mouth hovered just above hers. "Tell me to *stop*."

Don't do it, idiot. Don't you dare. He knew this was a terrible idea, and he wasn't about to take all the credit for it when she was playing into it too. Connor needed to hear her say it because he was beginning to not care if it was. Voluntarily naked, pressed against him, standing in a river, he needed Bane to tell him *no*.

"*Why*? We both know that you can't come any further between Darian and I than you already *have*," Kiera breathed as she wrapped her other leg around him, and Connor sucked in an involuntary breath, his cock trapped against his abdomen by the hot folds of her sex.

Okay. She has a point. Connor had never allowed a woman to make him this miserable. It was getting very hard to say *no* in their dangerous *game*, and now he was the only one resisting; it was usually the other way around. Connor was well aware that Darian would hunt him to the ends of the earth if he gave in, but Bane was the threat of death made *welcome*. In his current position, Connor was having a difficult time simply thinking straight at all, much less make a life and death decision.

"Because we can't keep this up . . . *I* can't keep this up. That *bird* of yours will eat me if this goes too far."

"Only if you intend to hurt me, Connor. Otherwise, the choice is mine as to who lives and dies, and I don't want to kill you *just* yet."

Connor smiled at that, chuckling softly. He ran his thumb over her bottom lip, wanting to taste her, wanting that honeyed scent all around him. He didn't want to stop touching her, and his hands were doing the exact opposite of the words coming out of his mouth as they worked their way into her wet hair.

"As nice as that sounds, there are lines we shouldn't cross . . ." Connor was having trouble focusing on what he needed to say and why it was important to leave those boundaries untouched. Bane didn't help matters when she leaned back, exposing her throat to him, deliberately daring him to take it further, putting herself in that vulnerable position to see what he would do.

"And what if those lines didn't *exist*, Connor? What *then*?"

Point taken. So much for rule number one. Connor stopped giving a damn just long enough to take the bait, kissing under her jaw and down her neck, crushing her against the boulder at her back as her arms went up around his shoulders. The soft gasps and moans coming from Bane were making his body react without conscious command, his hands roaming her pale skin under the water's surface, her legs wrapped tightly around his hips causing a tremendous amount of friction between them.

Torture didn't even begin to cover it.

Their lips found each other, and Connor almost lost total control when Bane pushed her tongue into his mouth . . .

The sound of flapping wings startled them out of their passionate embrace as a large heron took off from upstream. It was all the reminder Connor needed that they had no idea where Darian actually was, and getting *caught* would put both of them in much higher peril, no matter if Bane thought she could stave off the aggressive and territorial creature she had already shared a bed with.

As attracted as he was to Bane, he still valued the idea of his body remaining intact. Connor rested his forehead against hers, trying to calm his breathing and slow his heart, his whole body trembling. Kiera nuzzled her nose against his, trying to kiss him.

"I'm going to regret this, aren't I?" he panted.

"Regret *what?*" she breathed. Bane opened her eyes and peered up at him coyly through her lashes.

Connor didn't respond as he took a deep breath and forced himself to let her go.

"*Oh.*" Bane looked so disappointed that Connor had to fight the urge to just slide inside her and be done with the whole damned thing. Instead he pushed against her hips gently until she unwound her legs from around his waist, but she kept her arms circled around his neck, holding him close.

"Yeah, *oh*. This has to *stop*, Bane." Connor ran his hands up her arms, pulling at her wrists, trying to get her to untangle herself completely without having to use force. "Not what I want either, but we're treading on dangerous ground here, and I can't let this happen. Darian may forgive you, but I won't be the one to give him a reason not to."

Connor pulled away from her, shivering as her hands slid off his shoulders and down his chest, backing up until the only thing touching both of them was water. He ran his hands back through his hair, trying to catch his breath.

What the hell am I doing?! That was too close.

"Connor?"

"*What?*" He looked up to find her watching him, a ghost of a smile on her mouth.

Oh, please, say anything other than for me to keep touching you, he thought, though the rest of him wanted the exact opposite.

"I think . . . I think I *trust* you," she replied quietly.

Except that.

Thirty-Five

"Yield?"

"No!"

"Are you certain? I can fight *harder*," the beast breathed in his face. "Although, at this point, you may just end up missing a limb or two. You certainly are putting in a lot of effort for *sparring*."

Darian had Alyk pinned to the ground and the edge of Alyk's sword pressed against its owner's throat. The man could feel his muscles trembling as he tried to keep the Aeroyn at bay.

Finally, he had to give.

"Well done . . . beast," Alyk stammered.

"Those are brave words for a man stuck *under* one and at the wrong end of a sharp object." Darian chuckled and cocked an eyebrow at the defeated man, waiting for the words.

"I yield."

Darian relented and helped Alyk to his feet, and the sound of metal on metal filled the air as Alyk sheathed his sword. They had been sparring for at least an hour in the heat. Darian wasn't even sweating, but he *was* covered in dust; he shook off, sending a cloud of tan mist into the air. Alyk was considerably dirtier and muddy from the dust they had kicked up clinging to the moisture all over his exposed skin. His tan shirt was soaked through and dark brown, and his bracers left large white bands on his wrists of clean flesh when he finally removed them to pour water from a pouch over his hands and arms.

"Tell me, what did that tree ever do to you?" Darian was eyeing Alyk's previous partner—the poor, defenseless stump looking like it had been attacked by a wild woodcutter with terrible aim.

"I almost killed my brother." Alyk's expression registered somewhere between anger and disappointment, and Darian couldn't help but know what the man was feeling.

"And whose fault was that? *Yours*? Or *his*?"

"You sound just like Henelce with a question like that," Alyk said as he looked up in surprise

"You forget that I've *met* Tance. I remember a skinny, angry youth with too much to prove and not enough brains or brawn working in his favor."

Alyk smiled and shook his head at the Aeroyn's assessment as he went back to cleaning the dirt from his skin. It was pretty accurate, now that he thought about it, especially when he replayed Tance's stupidity in trying to take on Bane when they had first crossed paths.

Just one more incident where I had to let him learn . . .

The thought of Bane made Alyk realize that she hadn't appeared, and he felt the need to be on guard all of a sudden, his hand going to the pommel of his sword expectantly as the trees rustled above in the breeze. Their last encounter had been enough to tell Alyk that crossing her was probably a bad idea and she would keep her promise. They weren't quite in Baneswood, but Alyk wasn't sure that mattered to her.

Darian didn't seem like much of a threat, but Bane was another story.

"Relax, Alyk. She's not here."

Surprise number two. Darian's arrival had been a bit of a shock, but the absence of *her* seemed downright *unfathomable*.

"You *sure*, bird? I thought you two were *inseparable*."

"I would *like* to blame *you*, but apparently we both have *competition*," Darian growled as a dark look crossed his features, and the hair on the back of Alyk's neck stood straight up. The Aeroyn thumbed at the band on his arm, not so much focused on Alyk but looking through him.

Surprise number three. It's turning into quite the day.

"*Me*? What do *I* have to do with . . . *what*? Bane *hates* me!" Alyk was totally confused; maybe *disliked* was a better term for how Bane felt about him, but she definitely hadn't been *attracted* to him. *Had she*?

Alyk had certainly liked *her* at first, but somewhere between knowing too much and a healthy fear of a woman who had been trained by a creature from a warrior race made him backpedal fairly quickly. That pretty exterior was a deceptive mask, and Bane no longer resembled the girl he had seen running wild in Corengale.

Actually, now that I think about it, she's exactly the same: untamed, demanding, roaming the woods in boy's clothes . . . Her subjects may have dwindled to single digits, but they still followed her innately and loyally because of her royal blood. That idea was far less foreign than the one that said she had *liked* him.

"Am I *missing* something here? There is no way I had anything to do with whatever's going on with Bane, and I'm surprised you even think I would have been *competition* to begin with!" Alyk was watching Darian in open disbelief, but the Aeroyn looked like he might be ready for another sparring match.

Without the option to yield.

"You absolutely *did*. She *changed* . . . when *you* touched her."

Alyk had to wrack his brain to recall what Darian was referring to, suddenly scowling and rubbing absently at his collarbone as the memory of the mark Bane had left on him took precedent.

"Now wait a minute, Darian. I met a woman in the woods, and I showed her a sign of *respect*. Whatever happened on her end was beyond my control, and I certainly didn't *know*! She hid that well enough behind the bruise that took a week to heal."

"Then she might as well have kissed you." Darian's expression softened, and he suddenly laughed.

"There is no possible . . . What? I thought she was going to *kill* me!"

"Not likely. Bane was concerned about what you knew, but she liked you. I could smell it on her. We spoke about it, and I thought the matter was done with. But when *Dirtbag* showed up . . ." Darain sighed. "Well, apparently the door was still *open*."

"*Who*?" The surprises just kept coming, and Alyk couldn't tell if he was amused or a little jealous.

"Some hunter in the woods that brought down a boar she was stalking yesterday. He knew more than he should have, not unlike *you*, but not the same information you possess. Although with the way Bane was looking at him, it probably won't be long before she tells him. She certainly wasn't going to let me *kill* him." The look on Darian's face said the Aeroyn was still struggling with the thought of Kiera with another male, but he stubbornly resolved to not go looking for her just yet. Darian crossed his arms and leaned back against the mangled stump, lost in thought, staring at the ground.

"Whoa, whoa, whoa, wait a second. *Yesterday...*? You *left her with him*?" Alyk was stunned. Not only had Darian *not* killed the intruder but he had given the woman he loved over to the care of a total *stranger*. That idea would have seemed far more absurd if he hadn't already witnessed the bird leave her in the care and company of other outsiders, but he also remembered Darian *tolerating* the company of the group. That Darian was referring to this intruder as *Dirtbag* piqued Alyk's curiosity and told him that whatever Bane had shown in regard to feelings toward *him* was far different than what the Aeroyn seemed to suspect with this other man.

Darian thought back on his conversation with Henelce as he stared at the ground. His voice was full of defeat when he finally answered.

"In a way, she sort of *asked* me to."

Thirty-Six

Neither moon had hung in the sky that night. The stars were giving off just enough of their own luminescence that the surrounding forest, finally devoid of winter snow, wasn't completely pitch black, but very nearly enough that it would have been very difficult to navigate without an alternative source of light. An enemy darker than that moonless night was waiting impatiently just on the rim of those trees, but the girl peering out the window from the second story of the castle she called home couldn't have known that. Even her father, Garegan the Second, had little worry of any threat, though there had been some quiet rumors around the castle of villagers seeing blue smoke rise from the surrounding hill as the night would shoo the day to bed.

"I don't like it, Spero. It makes me nervous that you're dismissing this out of hand."

The use of their surname made Kiera cringe; she knew her father hated being called that name instead of Garegan. Her mother was doing it on purpose to make her point, and his annoyed answer certainly reflected that she had hit her mark.

"Just hunters or woodsmen trying to get warm, I am sure of it. I will send out riders if it would make you feel better, but I doubt there is need of such action. A few small fires cannot warm many, and the villagers say they have not seen any more smoke in the past two days."

Queen Serra, Kiera's mother, brought those rumors to Garegan's attention again while he was in his library where he had been spending much of the winter, teaching all three of their children to read. There was no real need for Garegan to do this himself as they could well afford tutors for the children, but it was a family tradition that Garegan felt was very much one he wanted to instill into his offspring.

The King of Corengale loved his children, though Kiera, now fourteen summers old, sometimes wondered how he felt about her mother. Kiera didn't know the details regarding the events that led up to their marriage or what transpired after; she only knew that her mother usually looked like she loathed her husband, and had Kiera known that her own fate would soon be similarly sealed as Garegan prepped to announce the wedding between her and the man she had been betrothed to once the weather was warm enough, she might have found herself hating Garegan too.

Kiera thought she could probably count the number of times she had seen her parents carry on a conversation of more than ten words in the past year on one hand since they usually avoided each other like one of them was diseased, but the blue smoke seemed to worry her mother enough that she approached Garegan without hesitation and spoke her concerns. There had been bandits and thieves in the woods for as long as Kiera could remember, and probably well before she was born, so the news of the smoke hadn't bothered her in the least. The fact that the smoke was blue seemed to alarm her mother, and she heard the word Sukolai fall from her mother's lips as she watched them over her book on the far side of the library.

The color drained from Garegan's face, and he looked away from Serra, turning his attention to all three of his children as they read then to the fireplace with its bright, hot flames dancing gaily, ignorant to the sudden chill in the room. Kiera saw the tear sparkle as it trailed down his cheek from his closed eyes.

When he finally looked at his wife again, Garegan's face was full of open fear.

"If you are right, then it's already too late."

As if cued by his very words, the doors of the main hall below them slammed open, and the muffled screams of the other people in the castle began a morbid choir's song under their feet.

* * *

The only flesh she had ever smell burning was that of whatever animal had been slaughtered for their dinner. Human flesh, however, did not make her mouth water; the oily, black scent of bodies covered with clothing and hair set ablaze left her mouth dry and her stomach threatening to claw its way up and out of her throat. Everything—and everyone—in the castle was being incinerated from within, and Kiera could hear the frighteningly calm voices of the Sukolai as they goaded their enormous cobalt dogs onto the fleeing servants and any remaining guests who happened to still be in the castle that night.

Her father's guards, some in heavy battle gear, were ripped to shreds; their leather-and-plate armor, effectively able to deflect arrows and even some heavier battle weapons, were torn and punctured under the teeth and claws of the cobalt hounds as though it were made of cloth and tin. Flesh ripped like silk under a dull blade, and screams ended with a sickening gurgle, only to be picked up in a different timbre as the next victim fell under the claws of the dogs and the blades of the Sukolai.

Kiera watched the animals in rapt terror from the top of the stairs that descended into the main hall. Its pristine appearance was being ravaged by the men in midnight blue robes with the help of swords, torches of green fire, and the cobalt blue dogs at their command. It was like watching the slaughter of pigs in a yard: it was disgusting, brutal, bloody, and repulsive, yet you couldn't look away until the carnage was over.

The princess was spellbound.

One of the dogs spotted Kiera and needed no coaxing from his master to come for her. Her flesh crawled as it stalked toward her, its muzzle dripping with blood and bits of flesh, its massive paws leaving red prints the size of her hand in its wake as it climbed the stairs. It bared its teeth at her, its yellow eyes boring into hers, seeming to see the bones through the flesh, its ears flattened against the lush fur on its neck. Kiera could remember wondering abstractly if that fur was soft when it wasn't covered in bits of meat and singed from the fires spreading through the room below.

As the dog approached, she realized its golden eyes weren't focused on her but past her.

Movement out of the corner of her eyes made her turn her attention away from the threat of death at her feet, and Kiera was surprised to see her brother Gary standing beside her, his arrow pointing straight at the face of the monster on the steps. His hands weren't shaking, and he had one eyes closed as he held the arrow sighted on one of the huge yellow orbs in the monster's head. The dog felt the threat and leapt straight at Gary, opening its jaws as it lunged, and he released the arrow just a little too late. The projectile pierced through the top of the dog's skull from inside its mouth, and the yellow eyes rolled back as it landed on top of him full force, now dead weight, crushing him under its useless paws. Gary gasped, unable to move or breath, staring at Kiera with eyes that pleaded for help.

But Kiera was frozen in place, and she gazed at him in the same detached way she had been watching the poor excuse for a battle downstairs as her brother suffocated under the weight of the dead beast. When his eyes closed and the life went out of him, she turned her attention back to the mêlée raging below.

Within seconds, her hand was pulled so hard that Kiera thought her arm would rip from its socket, and she was suddenly being dragged by her mother. Emilie's small hand clutched tightly in one hand and Kiera's in the other, Serra ran slightly ahead of both girls, urging them back past the library and toward the rear stairs that would lead them out of the back of the castle and into the open field to the north that was rimmed with the same woods the Sukolai and their dogs had come from. Her mother's black wool cloak was tied to her shoulders, and it flapped behind her, blinding both girls when they tried to look at each other as they ran. Down the wooden stairs they went, their feet sounding horribly loud as they descended, and Kiera suddenly heard her father's voice on the other side of the wall as he cried out in pain. She almost stopped, but her mother had no intention of letting that happen; Kiera was nearly dragged off her feet as Serra swept onward, ignoring the sounds in the rooms beyond.

They reached the door to the outside, and Emilie rushed forward to open it and to get out of the castle. Kiera smelled urine, and she felt pity for her terrified little sister when she realized that Emilie had wet herself as they ran, her skirt drenched. Emilie hurried outside, and she was immediately snatched up by a cobalt dog that had been prowling the perimeter of the castle. Kiera heard a tiny squeak of surprise that was quickly followed by silence as the dog was already dragging her away, distracted with ripping her young body to pieces. Serra was no longer running, the shock of seeing her littlest child suddenly slaughtered causing her to come to a dead stop. Kiera pushed past her mother, grabbing her hand, and pulled Serra after her.

Serra stumbled stupidly behind her, staring at the spot where her favorite child, one born from a single night of passion with a nameless guard, was quickly becoming a red smear in the black night. Kiera raced on, refusing to look back, and the sound of hooves thundering toward them called her attention to a dark rider as he came at them from the right side.

He was on a black horse, seeming to come out of the night itself, leaning over expectantly with his arm extended, one of his eyes glowing faintly with purple light. He was slightly ahead of Kiera as he approached where their paths would cross, and she tried to stop from running right into his outstretched hand . . .

Kiera succeeded in stopping just inches short of his grasp, but her mother, still staring behind them, wasn't so lucky. She continued to run forward, and the rider caught the front of her dress with ease, immediately hauling her upward as he rode past. Kiera grabbed for her mother, trying to save her, but she could only catch the cloak, and there was a sickening ripping noise as it tore away from Serra's neck. The rider didn't even seem to notice, her mother now sprawled over his lap, and he kicked his horse to spur it on.

The princess stood wide eyed in the inky night, the grass of the field touching her legs under her dark-purple dress, her feet bare, her heart racing . . .

And completely alone.

Run, you fool! *her brain was screaming.*

Kiera needed no other urging. She ran toward the woods and disappeared into the night.

Thirty-Seven

"Bane? What is it?"

Her scream had startled both of them awake, and Connor was crouched over her protectively, looking for danger. Kiera was sweating, even in the cooler shade of the willow where they had fallen asleep on the warm sand once their clothes had dried, the heat simply too oppressive to do anything else. The sun was well on its way to setting, and the forest was starting to drop in temperature, especially near the river.

Kiera shivered as she pushed him aside and sat up, breathing hard, her hands trembling as she brought them to her face. Connor had only seen Bane scared of one thing—*him*—and that wasn't even real fear. It paled in comparison to what he was seeing in her now; this was obvious terror, and he could feel it radiate from her like heat. Connor wanted to touch her, to pull her close to him and tell her she was safe, but after last time, he wasn't taking any chances.

So he waited.

She just sat there with her head in her hands.

"Bane? Are you all right?" he asked softly, reaching out tentatively to touch her shoulder. Kiera let out a ragged breath, shying from his hand.

"Stop calling me that. I *hate* that name."

"What else am I supposed to call you?"

"You weren't far off with *princess*," she whispered, her answer so quiet he almost didn't hear her.

Fuck. And now it gets harder. Connor fidgeted, debating of he should say anything at all or just wait and see if she filled the silence, but impatience won out.

"Yeah . . . I, uh, I already knew that." He heard the words before he realized he was speaking them, and he immediately wished he could reel them back in. Kiera's head whipped up, and she stared at him with red-rimmed eyes. Emotions lined up to flicker across her face—fear, anger, hurt, disbelief—she couldn't tell if he was being facetious or serious. Connor reached out warily and touched the back of her neck.

"I'm not an *idiot*, Bane. *Anyone* who saw that birthmark would know what it meant. I just can't figure out where you're from—"

"*When* did you see the back of my neck?" Her hand went under her hair protectively to cover her mark as she pulled away from him. Kiera couldn't think of a single instance where her hair had been up or out of the way . . .

"You don't always see with your eyes," Connor replied without looking at her, his mouth forming a thin line as he turned his attention to the ground and started drawing in the sand; Kiera stared down at the outline of an ivy leaf etched in the grains under their feet when he moved his hand. Connor raised his gaze to study her reaction, a little confused that her features relayed neither surprise nor dismay.

"As far as I know, no one has been looking for a royal at any point in the past few years, and I would *definitely* know. I tend to . . . *mingle*." Connor raised his eyebrows at her, daring her to make a comment, but Kiera wasn't looking at him just then. Her eyes were still locked on the ground.

"That would be because no one knows I even exist. *My* family is *dead*."

* * *

Her memories of that night spilled out of her mouth as they sat next to the fire.

Connor listened quietly.

Kiera told him everything.

They had moved back from the river, the night chilling considerably, and if they had stayed close to the water, even the fire wouldn't have kept it at bay. Kiera and Connor were sitting next to each other against an outcropping of rocks, the leftover heat of the day seeping out of the earth and the granite, making it a warm place to rest against as she let her past pour out of her. She told him about her family, about the siege of Corengale, about Darian. About how she had woken up after the incident at the cabin to find her hair had gone completely white . . .

She's Serra's daughter? As in Eryce's *wife? That would make her Eryce's niece* and *daughter by marriage . . .*

On the outside, Connor was composed and thoughtful; inside, he was at a total loss as he considered *who* the girl sitting next to him really was. As far as he knew, Serra and Eryce were somehow related—half siblings or something—and they hailed from the same castle in Falyyn.

The logistics of that family tree made his head hurt.

Connor did the math and realized Kiera was older than he had originally thought, nearly twenty-one instead of the seventeen he had pegged her for. He had been around her age when the news spread that Garegan was dead, the royal family murdered and most of Corengale burned to the ground. He even remembered hearing stories around the lands he had traveled about Eryce's bride and how they had some sort of past history, but he had never paid much attention.

He hadn't realized how convoluted the story really was.

And then there's Darian . . . That smug bastard took her under his literal wing and made her into this, *hiding her out here and using her as his companion. He took her virginity* and *gave her blood that she should never have been exposed to, which has had Tirath-knows-what effect on her . . . And she loves him! I can't believe Darian actually got her to love him!*

Connor felt himself bristle when he thought of the Aeroyn. He knew enough about that particular race to be certain that bloodsharing was forbidden outside their kind, it was for good reason. Darian didn't seem to care, and if he knew what Kiera was, then he was setting her up for a lifetime of trouble by keeping it from her.

She should have been trained! She doesn't even seem to know! Connor had never wanted to defend someone in his whole life; people made their own choices, usually poor ones, and they paid for them. This was different. The choices here were not her own, and Connor suddenly wanted to kill something.

Preferably with *feathers*.

Instead he found himself gritting his teeth while trying to keep his exterior calm. Connor didn't want her to see how her story was affecting him, not trusting himself to open his mouth and not let something out he was going to regret as soon as it hit the air. Kiera couldn't see what Connor was doing from where she was sitting, but he was breaking small rocks apart with his fingers as he stared at the fire, the old habit was creating a little pile of dust next to his leg, just out of her view.

Do your job, idiot. Listen. Retain. Repeat.

It was what he was good at.

What he was paid to do, and do well.

But Connor was finding that he hated the idea of letting any of the words he was hearing come out of his own mouth. *If* he ever returned to Eryce, however, he would have to tell the king everything. There wouldn't be a choice in the matter. It hadn't been an issue before because Connor had readily handed Eryce the information he had acquired, but if he had something to hide, Eryce would find out, no matter what . . .

Connor's mind raced, searching for a solution, his expression grim as each one eventually involved *him* protecting her; as far as he was concerned, he wouldn't let her out of his sight if he had his way. He still had a few weeks before Eryce came looking for her. He could get her away from Baneswood and hide her, but then he would be doing just what Darian had done, and Connor didn't like that thought.

I could kill Eryce, and that would solve all sorts of problems, but she would still be stuck out here when she had a rightful place on a throne somewhere. But... does she even want that *life?* Connor wasn't sure he was up to the task of helping her get it back, but she would have to ask first . . .

He was watching her out of the corner of his eye as she talked on, but he had lost track of what she was saying as his own thoughts took over and drowned her out. He wished he had just kept her tuned out when he realized where the conversation was suddenly headed.

". . . and then there's *you*. I have no idea what to do about *you*."

Uh-oh.

"What about *me*?" he asked defensively.

Kiera turned bright red and kept her eyes on the fire ahead of her, keenly aware of the narrowed green eyes that were focused intensely on her. She could *feel* his gaze on her skin, and she suddenly regretted bringing up a subject she wasn't really ready to admit to.

You already opened your mouth, silly girl. You have nothing to lose. You can always just kill him if he doesn't feel the same.

"You . . . you scare the hell out of me." The silence that followed was deafening, and Kiera felt the red intensifying when she started to think she had read the entire situation wrong. *Maybe this is all a game to him . . .*

She jumped when he snorted a laugh, his voice rife with sarcasm when he finally stopped shaking his head long enough to respond.

"*Yes*, that's *exactly* what I do. That's why you were *terrified* to be in the river with me earlier, bare assed and ready to do *whatever* I would let you get away with." Connor raised an eyebrow, dangerously close to smiling, and Kiera jabbed him in the shoulder with her index finger, her expression full of open indignation.

"*You* started it, *you* stopped it, and you didn't even *finish* it. Besides, it isn't the *sexual* part that scares me—"

"Woman, do you have any idea how hard it is to tell you *no*?" Connor had turned serious and was watching her thoughtfully. Kiera gave him a look that said she probably had an inkling. Connor averted his gaze and picked up another rock, squeezing it with his fingertips until the pebble began to crumble apart.

"In case you hadn't *noticed*, *I* have been the one afraid to take anything too far. *You* trust me, and I don't even trust *myself*. So when you talk about fear, know that your actions haven't said you were scared of me at all. Nervous, *maybe*, but *I* have been the one saying *stop*, mostly because that Aeroyn of yours won't stand for you to be anything other than *his*."

One more rock turned into fine grains of sand. Connor suddenly realized just how jealous of that *bird* he really was.

He could feel her watching him.

"Kiera . . ." That name felt weird in his mouth. He almost preferred *Bane*. ". . . I am definitely not the *safest* choice for you. I'm certainly not a good one, and I don't even think I know how to *be* a choice if that's what you're worried about.

"I mean, honestly, after everything I've done in my life, having someone like you around is a huge conflict for me. You are a *job* that I can no longer see that way, and doing anything other than what I'm being paid to do puts us *both* in danger, especially considering *who* you are. Titles aside, you *belong* to Darian, which is why we're even stuck out here together to begin with, and the *last* think I want to be is a simple *distraction*. I really hope you're not just bored or curious because I'm starting to want what I can't have, and I don't like that I can't seem to control it. I've already changed having met you; I can feel it…

"*But* I don't know if I could change enough if it meant *keeping* you, and I'm not even sure that's what you would want anyway."

Just keep digging that hole, idiot. Connor was past the point of caring what his filter wanted him to say. He just let the words pour out like she had, returning the favor of honesty even if it felt like he was fighting for air in letting those particular sentences form where someone else could hear and understand them.

"Kiera, I need you to know that I won't give you willingly to Eryce, but if I see him, he *can and will* make me give you up. *That* scares me more than anything. If he kills me in the process, I won't be there to warn you or *protect* you."

Oh goddess above, I am so screwed. Connor felt a pang in his chest when he thought of her in danger. He felt his resolve shaping and taking hold: he would never let that happen if he could help it, and he fought the urge to suddenly take her hand to show her that he meant what he said.

"As far as letting you go back to Darian, well, he's probably about as good for you as I am, but at least with *me* you would have a chance at a life closer to *normal*, whatever *that* means. I won't walk away unless you tell me to, and I hope you never do because when I touch you, I-I mean . . .."

Connor was stuttering nervously as the thoughts that raced recklessly through his head hit the air. His brain was screaming that he should shut his damned mouth, but the words just kept coming.

"How . . . how do you fear losing something that isn't *yours* to begin with?"

Fuck! He immediately wished he could eat his words because he had a horrible feeling they were going to bite him in the ass. Connor could feel the heat spread up from his neck, darkening his tanned skin all the way up to the roots of his blond hair. He brought his hand to his forehead, shading his eyes, afraid to look at her.

The most obnoxious, arrogant, and dangerous woman I have ever met is making me blush. She must think I am a real jackass for even thinking like this . . .

"You're kind of *cute* when you do that."

Kiera's soft voice was right in his ear, startling Connor into involuntarily turning toward her.

Kiera grabbed his face and kissed him.

Hard.

Game. Over.

Thirty-Eight

"I still can't believe you just *left* her in the middle of the woods, Darian. You know absolutely nothing about him! What if he *hurts* her? You said you saw how she *reacted* to him, but what if something *happens* between them?"

Darian sighed, trying to ignore Alyk's questions, choosing not to think about it as he stared at the fire that would keep Alyk and Henelce warm for the night. Kiera could certainly handle herself, but the second question struck a chord because it had been kicking around in his own brain for a day and a half, and he was still trying to make it go away.

"Then it does, and there's nothing I can do." It wasn't a nonchalant answer, simply the truth. Things had changed so rapidly, and the Aeroyn wondered again if leaving her *had* been the right move. He had sworn to protect her, to keep her from harm . . .

But Kiera was a grown adult of her ilk. She would make her own decisions, and if *he* was what she wanted, there was no way for Darian to stop her. He had witnessed that look on her face, the way she had touched *Dirtbag* far too intimate to ignore. He felt he had given her permission by leaving the two of them alone as it was, and now Darian didn't know what he would feel when he finally saw her, and he knew he would have to at some point even if it was just to let her go.

What had my options really been? If I had just killed the man, she would have probably have been angry about it.

It might have changed things between them.

It might still . . .

Thirty-Nine

"You realize that Darian will kill me after this, don't you?" Connor whispered in her ear. He was curled up behind Kiera, his arm draped over her waist, their naked bodies nestled together in between the fire and the warm rock wall. He kissed the back of her neck, sucking lightly at her soft skin, and he smiled when he felt the rest of her instantly prickle with gooseflesh, the scent of honey faint but discernable.

How weird that she smells like that to me . . .

"You realize that doing things like *that* and bringing up serious subjects at the same time doesn't make either one easy to focus on, *right*?" Kiera rolled onto her stomach and propped herself up on her elbows so she could look at him as she spoke. Green eyes darker than her own stared intently back at her, and she wondered what else Connor was thinking. If she could have seen inside his head, she would have found him trying to memorize how the firelight played off the curves of her body and illuminated her skin.

If I have to eventually give her up, then I at least want these memories to stick. Connor reached out and pushed her hair back behind her ear, running his thumb over her cheek; Kiera realized she was actually starting to *like* that intimate gesture.

"I don't know, Connor. I think he knew this would happen eventually. If it wasn't you, it was probably going to be with someone else . . ." Alyk unexpectedly surfaced in her mind, and Kiera frowned at the thought as she stared off into the darkness.

Connor knew *that* look. Normally he would have felt relieved, but a pang of unexpected jealousy struck so deep it made him slightly nauseous. Darian was one thing; Connor was the one encroaching on something that belonged to the Aeroyn, whether or not he wanted to admit it, but someone *else*? That was a really unpleasant thought. *You've done it now, idiot. Good job.*

"Bane . . ." Connor smirked when Kiera gave him a disgusted look, but he didn't try to correct himself, ". . . I can't even begin to describe how strange *you* feel to *me*."

"*Really*? Why was I under the impression that you thought I felt pretty *good*?" Kiera smiled wryly as she pushed his shoulder playfully, and he caught her wrist, bringing her hand to his mouth. Connor kissed her palm, and Kiera closed her eyes, the feel of his rough, two-day beard a totally new sensation under her sensitive fingers.

"I think I'm falling in love with your skin."

Connor was surprised that those words had come from *her* as something similar skittered through his own mind. Kiera opened her eyes and rolled onto her side so that she was facing him, her gaze wandering down his body . . .

"Woman, you make me feel *naked* when you look at me like *that*." Kiera laughed as Connor pulled her toward him, and he kissed her deeply. He wanted her again as their limbs moved on their own and her hands wandered down his back. He felt her nails dig into his skin as he breathed her in, and the kiss intensified when he let her pull him on top of her and wrap her legs around his hips.

"Someone once said this might be fun without the *inconvenience* of clothing . . ." Kiera smiled against his mouth as Connor simultaneously laughed at her remark and continued to kiss her. He pressed his hard cock against her, savoring the warmth and wetness he knew he was only going to crave the longer they were together as he slid inside her, silently loving the way her breath caught as she arched her back under him and the way her nails dug into his hips . . .

Kiera was simply concentrating on trying to breathe while she ran her nails lightly up his back, making Connor shiver as he momentarily closed his eyes, lost in her touch. She shifted her hips, allowing him deeper access, and he lost all train of thought.

Connor lifted himself up on his hands, watching as her body moved under him, soaking in the view of her from that vantage point as the firelight played off her skin . . .

Little did he know, someone *else* was watching her, too.

Forty

The birds of the forest were incredibly loud as the light of the morning sun crept over Kiera, spilling onto her face and waking her to the fact that she was alone. Kiera abruptly sat up, her muscles painfully stiff from the combination of sleeping on the ground and their long night together . . .

"Connor...?" She felt instant panic when he didn't immediately answer, but a wave of relief washed over her when she spotted him, fully dressed and standing at the edge of the river with his back to her about twenty feet away.

Kiera wondered how long he had been awake as she threw off the cloak she had used for a blanket and dragged herself up, looking around for the clothing she had haphazardly shed the night before. She picked up her tunic and slipped it over her head, leaving the rest of her ensemble strewn about their makeshift camp.

The grass around their little corner of the world was dewy and cool, the droplets leaving her feet wet and cold, the sand sticking to them once she was on the beach. Connor didn't turn around as Kiera came up behind him and slipped her hands around his waist; he simply shifted his weight to lean back into her embrace, his hands finding hers and intertwining their fingers like it was the most natural thing in the world. Kiera rested her cheek against his shoulder, inhaling his scent, feeling her body react to him in ways that reminded her that her muscles were already sore enough.

"Kiera, I have to leave. Not now, but soon," Connor blurted out before he could stop himself. He cringed at his crassness, his words sounding far more nonchalant than he had intended.

Smooth, idiot.

"'Good morning' was the phrase I think you were looking for," Kiera retorted as she tried to pull away, but Connor wasn't about to let her go. He wanted to hold on to that moment as long as he could even if he had just ruined it for both of them.

"Look, I have some things to take care of that I cannot avoid, one of which will require a journey I'm not looking forward to making, but it has to be done. The other . . . If I get caught, I won't be coming back." Connor untangled himself from her embrace and turned to face her, his hands finding her upper arms, his expression serious. "Kiera, this isn't a *game* anymore."

Had it ever been? Connor studied her for a moment as he let his thoughts come together. He had promised himself that he would be straight with her, and he intended to see that through.

Mostly.

"Kiera, I-I've gotten myself into some very hot water between Eryce and Darian, and while I've always come out unscathed in the past, this time I'm not so sure. Darian may or may not be an issue, but that will probably depend on *you*, but I really don't know what to expect. I've never dealt with an Aeroyn before, and frankly, I'm sort of hoping you'll save me from him, but that will come down to what *you* really want. If that's not *me*—" Connor abruptly stopped talking and cleared his throat, changing the subject before Kiera could respond.

"What I *do* know is that *Eryce* is going to come looking for you if I don't bring you back. That was the agreement—if I don't show by the double full moon with you in tow, he is going to come find you himself, and he is absolutely capable of burning this whole damned forest down around you just to flush you out."

Kiera stared at him, her expression unreadable at first, and when she moved to cover her eyes with her hand, Connor was suddenly worried she might hit him again. The response that decided to come out of her mouth made Kiera realize just how tired she was of hiding in the trees, her voice some combination of irritated and defeated when she finally broke her silence on the subject.

"And you're suggesting that I do *what*, exactly? That I *run*? That I *hide*? Yes, I'll do that because it's worked *so well* for me so far. Darian did his best to keep me away from a world that wants to hurt me, but to what end? *You* found me. *Alyk* stumbled across me . . ." Kiera looked up just in time to see the dark look of jealousy contort Connor's features when Alyk's name passed her lips, and she rolled her eyes, refusing to even explain who or what Alyk was as she went on.

"*My point is*, I walked away from the world, and it found me anyway. Even Darian realized that. He questioned how honest I was being with myself about going back to Corengale, but it wouldn't be that easy. I can't just show up, anoint myself queen, and expect things to simply fall into place. You have to understand that the Corengale I knew doesn't even *exist* anymore—"

"So you *have* thought about this."

Kiera didn't respond at first to Connor's interjection, looking past him with her mouth set in a grim line. She would never admit to Darian how many times she had sat contemplating what her life would have been like if that night had never come to pass, mostly because she didn't think he would understand.

But Connor was completely different story.

"More so lately than I care to admit, I think. I *could* make the same arguments to you that I made to Darian, but I don't even believe them anymore."

Kiera sighed and shifted her weight, and Connor suddenly looked obnoxiously please with himself when she winced, her legs apparently unhappy with the movement.

"Sore?"

"Shut up."

"Good to know I can give an *Aeroyn* some competition."

"Connor?"

"Hmm?"

"You're an *idiot*."

I know, Connor thought as he pulled her to him and felt her laughing in his arms. He kissed the top of her head, relieved at the break in the tension; he knew things were going to get complicated very shortly, but they were simple for the moment if they put everything else aside.

"Come. If I have caused you pain, it would only be gentlemanly of me to relieve you of that *ache*."

Kiera giggled as Connor let her go and took her hand, pulling her back toward the remains of the fire. She hid behind her veil of hair when she realized her clothes were still strewn all over the hard ground, but Connor didn't seem to notice or care.

"Sit," Connor commanded as he turned his back on her to grab his pack and rummage for something at the bottom. He was grinning wickedly when he found what he was after and pulled out a silver glass bottle with a cork stopper. Tossing his pack aside, he turned his attention back to Kiera and her bare legs that he was very much in the mood to allow to distract him of the things he still had to the fore.

"Why do I feel like I'm going to regret asking what *that* is?"

"Woman, don't ask questions when a man has an idea in his head as to what he want to do to you. Just shut up and lie back." Connor was all seriousness as he knelt in front of her, and Kiera complied warily, propping herself up on her elbows, watching as he pulled the stopper to pour a small amount of a golden liquid in his hands that smelled strongly of mint. The strong scent overpowered the air around them, and she took a deep breath, wondering if that was what coated his skin and made him smell so damned delicious to her.

"What is it with your attraction to mint?"

Connor shrugged, rubbing his hands together before smoothing the warmed liquid onto her calves. Her skin immediately started to tingle, and the soreness began to dissipate. He rubbed the liquid in slowly, using pressure against the stiff muscles, and Kiera felt her entire body start to relax under his touch. She lay back and closed her eyes, getting lost in the feel of his hands as they moved up to her thighs, his touch warm, comforting, and incredibly sensual.

"Tirath's grace, Connor. *Where* have you been all my life?" she breathed as his touch melted the stiff muscles under her skin. She laughed quietly at her little joke, but she felt Connor's hands hesitate, and he didn't respond. She opened her eyes and sat up enough to look him in the eye, surprised when he turned bright red.

"*What?*" she demanded.

"I . . . uh . . . just realized that you aren't wearing any *pants*."

"Oh," she smirked as she lay back, willing him to continue. "Here I thought it was something I *said*."

Forty-One

"Quit lagging, *Dirtbag*! If we can keep this pace, we'll reach the edge of the forest in an hour!" Kiera sounded almost excited as she called back to him over her shoulder, and Connor felt his heart sink.

It was already late afternoon, the air still very warm but nowhere near as insufferably hot as it had been the previous day. They were moving quickly and quietly along the trail, their quiet little camp already several miles behind them. Connor was silently kicking himself for using his muscle balm on her, knowing it was his own fault they were moving as fast as they were toward where she thought Darian might go.

Connor was quietly praying that the Aeroyn had already headed back to the castle and was waiting for her there; then she would be stuck with him for a few more days.

"Time goes by too fast…"

"Yes, it certainly *does*," she replied solemnly.

His head jerked toward her response to the words Connor hadn't realized weren't just in his head. Kiera gave him a half-hearted smile and kept walking.

He stopped in his tracks.

Do not *open your mouth . . .*

"Kiera . . . Come with me?"

Why do I bother?

"You and I both know that's a bad idea, Connor." Kiera stood frozen a few paces ahead of him but she didn't turn around.

Why the hell are you even asking that? You know she'll choose the Aeroyn. Hopes up equals hearts broken, moron. Connor approached her slowly, knowing he had verbally cornered her, asking her to make a choice he wasn't sure he wanted to know the answer to and that she probably wasn't ready to make.

"Letting you *kiss* me was a *bad* idea, *princess*. This is a *terrible* one. But . . . I—"

"Are we back on this subject *again*? Placing blame as to *who* started *what*?" Kiera snapped defensively, crossing her arms and shifting her weight as she looked back over her shoulder. "I have to see Darian before I can even think about making a decision like that. Which, by the by, I was starting to look *forward* to before you opened your *mouth*!"

156

I told you so, idiot.

The look on Connor's face when she finally turned toward him made her soften a little, but not much. She had bigger issues pinging around in her brain, and they trumped any stupid *errands* he might have on his plate, hands down, but she had expected him to simply *leave* once they found Darian because they both knew the Aeroyn would *never* tolerate his presence otherwise. It hadn't ever crossed her mind that he might have other ideas . . .

"I wish I had an easy answer in all this," Kiera sighed, feeling incredibly conflicted.

"Woman, you have the scent of *me* all over you, and you *know* he's going to be angry. *You* may be off limits for those teeth, but that race is extremely protective of their *mates*, and neither of us knows what he's going to do." *Especially if you make a choice he doesn't like.* Connor realized that particular thought might be wishful thinking when he reached out to touch her shoulder and Kiera stiffened under his fingertips as they brushed her shirt. She was putting up walls, and it surprised him when it *hurt*.

"*Don't*. Don't you do *that*, Kiera. You must know you're running toward his wrath, and I'm the only one who will stand *between* you two if necessary. Don't try to hold me out now when you've already let me in."

"Did *I*?" Kiera suddenly had her defenses up, an angry expression contorting her features as she jabbed him in the chest with her index finger. "Did I *let* you in, or did you *force* your way in? Didn't you tell me that I was just an *assignment*? Isn't *this*"—she gestured between the two of them—"what you *do?*"

"Hey!" That accusation made Connor's temper flare unexpectedly, and Kiera felt a weird sensation of panic course through her. He reached for her, grabbing her more roughly than he meant to, and Kiera slammed the butt of her hand into his chest out of reflex, forcing him to let her go.

"Ow! *Seriously*, Kiera? Do you think this is an *act*? Even *I* am not this good." Connor narrowed his eyes at her, rubbing his sternum reflexively, considering his next words carefully before he let them loose. One misstep would probably end with him tied to a tree and *left* for the wolves this time, and he wasn't about to let that happen if he could help it.

"You have every reason to not trust me, Kiera, but what I *do* usually leaves me free and *someone else* broken. *Not* the other way around."

Oh, for the love of Tirath . . . Don't do it.

"I don't feel all that *broken*, Connor." Her words may have been full of sarcasm, but her demeanor had changed slightly; just when Kiera thought she knew what she was doing, Connor threw her another challenge, and he did it again as he shifted the subject, trying to get her to listen.

"Do you even *know* what that mark on the back of your neck means? Has anyone ever told you?"

"You're not even going to try to defend yourself, are you?"

Connor ignored her when she tried to talk over him. Even Darian wasn't going to be able to help her if she didn't learn just what she was capable of.

"For the love of Tirath, woman, quit running that mouth of yours for a minute and *listen!* It's not just a mark of royalty! It means that people will innately *love* you—they will congregate around you and even follow you to their *deaths* if you ask. It's probably a *good* thing you're out here on your own because you are like a *siren*, and you pull at the strings of hope. Anyone who doesn't know what you are and can't defend themselves emotionally against your call will fall at your feet.

"Let me put it this way. All you have to do is walk down the street of a village with intention, and you could amass an army that would follow you to the ends of the earth. *If* you learn to control it."

"Shut up, Connor! It's just a birthma—" She was cut short as he put his hand gently over her mouth, watching her unsmilingly. Connor really didn't like the next words he had to say, but she was loose and untrained. He didn't want to think about what might happen if she ever tried to rejoin society . . .

Or if the King of Rhonendar got his greedy hands on her.

"You are a *unifier*, Kiera, just like your father, and his before him. Some have used that mark for peace, and some for war, and it's exactly *why* your ancestors became royalty. It's why you *could* rule, if you chose to take it that far, and a big part of why I can't give you to Eryce. You could be a very powerful *weapon*, Kiera, and I won't let someone abuse you for their own gain, and that is *exactly* what Eryce will do with you if he finds out what you *are*.

"I *won't* let that happen. Not to *you*. Not if you'll let me help."

Kiera felt her anger dissipating as curiosity mixed with a little fear took its place. She had no idea what he was even talking about, but the notion of being used against her will was not one that sat well with her. It finally dawned on her that Connor wasn't telling her these things just so she would *know;* the man that had been *hunting* her was making a serious effort in trying to *protect* her.

"Is that why you want me to come with you?" she asked quietly, wondering what other *motives* he might have in wanting her to follow in his wake.

"Maybe . . ." Connor shifted uncomfortably, knowing full well he had already said too much. Kiera waited, watching him intently while Connor was looking at anything but her, his arms crossed defensively. She stepped up close to him, their bodies nearly touching, and put her hand on his chest; Connor's heart was racing, and he swallowed hard.

He's nervous! He had every right to be. If he answered the wrong way after everything that had already been said, she was going to let Darian take his anger out on Connor instead of coming to his defense. Kiera slid her hand up to his neck and around the back of his head, running her fingers through his hair. Connor stiffened, trying not to lean into her touch.

"Connor? Are you . . . are you afraid that you might *love* me?"

"What gave you *that* impression? I risked my neck to get into these woods to take you to the man that is paying me for your pretty hide. Do you *really* think I am going to risk my safety further by admitting that I *feel* something for you?" Connor's defensive training kicked into high gear, and sarcasm poured from his mouth as he tried to keep hidden what was plainly written all over his face.

"You are the *worst* liar I have ever met," Kiera whispered. "Answer me straight, *Dirtbag*—*a*re you asking me to come with you because you feel *obligated* to keep me safe, because this birthmark is having an effect on you . . . or because you want *me* to go?"

Might as well jump into that hole with both feet, idiot. No point screwing this up halfway.

"That depends on whether this is one-sided or not. If it is, then it's just the *influence* of your *mark* over me. If it isn't . . ." Connor finally met her gaze, the words serious, his expression bordering on terrified. ". . . then I am in *much* deeper water than I originally thought."

Kiera was quiet for a moment, taking that in. The whole idea that she could somehow *make* him love her against his will seemed absurd, but now that she had to consider that as a possibility, she realized that she hoped it wasn't true.

"Well, *Dirtbag*, I have to say I'm glad *that's* out in the open."

"What's is?"

"That you feel it *too*."

* * *

How long he had been kissing her with her back pressed against that tree, he didn't know. Connor only knew the moment it was cut short because his shoulder was suddenly being devoured by searing pain, and he couldn't breathe.

He heard Kiera scream his name before darkness and the forest floor slammed into him, and the pain suddenly stopped.

Forty-Two

Alyk and Henelce were riding slowly through the forest, keeping to the border path. Darian was on foot beside them, and he suddenly stopped in his tracks when he heard *her*.

Not just her voice.

Her shrill scream.

Darian felt all of the hair on his body stand straight up as adrenaline dumped into his veins, and he beat his wings hard to take off from the forest floor. He emerged from the canopy into the blindingly bright afternoon, gaining height and flying fast in the direction of startled birds taking flight and her panicked cries. Kiera wasn't far, less than a mile to the south of them, and she was yelling for someone named Connor.

His companions had heard her too, and once Alyk had his startled horse under some sort of control, he kicked her hard in the sides; the mare almost dismounted him, she took off so fast.

Henelce was right behind him.

All three of them raced toward the sound of Kiera's screams, and Darian felt a horrible pain in the pit of his stomach when the forest suddenly rang with silence.

Please let her be okay . . . I don't care what's happened—just let her be okay. Darian flew fast over the tops of the trees, trying to catch her scent. When he finally spotted her, he was momentarily confused; he saw a flash of white, a flash of black, and the body of a man sprawled out on the ground.

Darian suddenly realized she was fighting someone, and he dove straight for them.

* * *

"Back off, Darian! This one is *mine!*"

Blood was running down her face from her nose, and Kiera was dual wielding with her black glass dagger and a throwing knife, barely keeping her attacker at bay. Her scent was so strong it was making Darian's head hurt, the air rank with a sweet smell and a low hum that threatened to draw him to her.

The sensation was so overwhelming that it took Darian a moment to realize just *who* she was fighting. The attacker wasn't a Sukolai or even some forest thief; it was *Jaçon*, and the elf was just as bloody as she was. Kiera had already gotten in one or two good hits, his dark-blue blood streaming down his chin from his split lip, but it was going to take a hell of a lot more to bring him down...

Alyk and Henelce rode in at a gallop, making an incredible amount of noise as they came crashing through the underbrush as fast as their mounts could maneuver through the obstacles in their path. Alyk reined his horse up short in surprise and Henelce's mount almost ran right into his as both of them tried desperately to comprehend the scene before them.

"*Jaçon?* What the *hell* are you doing?" Henelce yelled while Alyk jumped down and drew his sword, the sound of unsheathed metal ringing through the clearing as he tried to come to Kiera's defense, but Darian held him back.

Neither combatant looked away from the other. Distractions weren't going to do either of them any favors, but Jaçon knew now that he wasn't going to win. He'd had a good chance if it had been only her with the other man out of the way, but now there were odds he couldn't compete with and survive.

"I knew this was a waste of time!" the elf shouted as he lunged at Kiera, his mythril blade shattering her glass dagger, the shards spraying back at her, ripping through the thin material of the neck and shoulder of her tunic, spattering it with blood. She ignored the pain and caught him in the face with the butt of her useless weapon; all three bystanders winced when they heard the bone in his jaw crack. The blow sent Jaçon reeling, and he was starting to wonder if he might have miscalculated . . .

Kiera didn't give him time to think about it as she threw her other knife, and he ducked it, just barely. She was suddenly weaponless, and now all she had to defend herself with was her strength, her bracers, and her armor.

Against mythril, Kiera might as well have been wearing paper.

"Bane! Here!" Alyk tossed her his sword, and Kiera caught it by the pommel, swinging it deftly in a tight arc, testing its weight and balance. She seemed awkward with it for a moment while she dodged the elf, but the blade came to life in her hand as she swung it hard and sent the blade whistling through the air.

Alyk watched her with a deep respect as she moved so fast that Jaçon didn't have time to properly parry her attack, and the broadsword bit into the back of his arm as he tried to deflect it. The elf reflexively covered the wound with his other hand, and Kiera immediately used the opportunity to her advantage; she kicked Jaçon hard in the chest, sending him into a backward somersault, but he was right back up on his feet, her boot print visible on his tan shirt.

"Yield, elf!" Kiera wasn't going to back down, and she came at him again, countering his attempts to keep her at bay with angry, destructive blows. "I *will* kill you!"

Never show your cards. Darian cringed at her outburst, the sign of *weakness* considered a mistake. First rule of training: Don't let the enemy know whether or not you will kill them. Let them assume that you always will. Period.

That she was also breaking the second rule made him grit his teeth when he realized that she was *emotional* in her defense of the man on the ground behind her.

"Don't think killing me will change *anything*!" Jaçon laughed at her as he spun away from a blow aimed for his shoulder, the blade coming a little too close for comfort. "Sorveign will just send someone in my place! He wants you badly enough to spare *me*, and he will spare others if I fall! I told him you wouldn't listen!"

He knows I'm alive? What could he possibly want with me? Sorveign and her father had been friendly, but Connor's words suddenly rang through her head.

"Amass an army just by walking down a village street . . ."

That is not going to happen! Kiera felt a renewed determination as those implications hit her full force, and she parried a feint from Jaçon's blade as his fist came right at her face. Kiera leaned backward as she went to her knees, his knuckle grazing her cheek but doing little damage. She tried to control her fall, her momentum allowing her to swing her blade with both hands as she went down, straight across his stomach . . .

If Jaçon hadn't been wearing mythril chain, the blow would have cut him in half; instead it just sent him to the ground, coughing blood. Both were breathing hard, but Kiera was back on her feet within seconds, stalking toward her opponent and ready to finish what *he* had started.

"You don't know what you've done, elf! How *dare* you hurt someone to get to *me!*" she seethed as she swung the blade in a tight arc, threatening to behead him with her next blow . . .

Jaçon's eyes were wide as he hastily pulled something out from under the neck of his shirt before the tip of her blade could reach him. She felt the void when he was suddenly gone, and the blade cut through the still air unimpeded.

"Kiera! Are you *all right?*" Darian sounded panicked as he came toward her, Alyk and Henelce on guard in case the elf reappeared, but Kiera's concern wasn't for *herself*. She dropped the sword in her hand, breathing hard and still bleeding from her nose, but she ignored Darian and went straight for Connor.

He was on his side and had an arrow sticking out of his right shoulder. Kiera's heart was beating fast as she knelt beside him and put her hand under his nose, feeling for breath; she felt a wave of relief when she realized he was only unconscious. The arrow struck her as faintly familiar, but she didn't have time to try and remember from where.

Kiera looked up at Darian with determination in her eyes, and she said something he wasn't expecting. The look on her face made Darian blanch when he realized that she *cared* about *him* . . .

"I won't even ask because I know you well enough that you will refuse. Just help me get him to a healer! I can't let him die!"

The Aeroyn was dumbfounded; he simply stood there as the Shephard hurried past him to help.

"Let me, Bane," Henelce said as calmly as he could as he pushed her aside and Connor onto his stomach, using his knife to strip away the wounded man's shirt. Blood was oozing slowly out from the entry wound, and Henelce pressed hard on Connor's back as he removed the arrow. Connor moaned, and the blood started flowing *much* more freely . . .

Kiera's vision blurred as tears welled up in her eyes, the thought of losing this man slamming into her so forcefully she felt instantly breathless. She was fighting against an overwhelming sense of panic as Henelce pressed his hands against the wound in Connor's shoulder and closed his eyes, muttering under his breath. It was an eerie feeling to watch the blood flow in reverse, back into Connor's body, the ragged gap in the skin sealing shut and leaving no trace of a scar.

Together, Kiera and Henelce rolled Connor onto his back, and Kiera stayed crouched protectively over him. She counted the seconds as his breathing rapidly becoming much more regular, and he coughed as he came around.

"Connor...?" Kiera ran her hand back through his hair as he opened his eyes. The first thing he saw was her face covered in blood, and he panicked.

"Kiera? What the hell happened? Why are you bleeding?" Connor reached up for her, pulling her close.

All Kiera could do was laugh as tears flowed down her face.

Forty-Three

"*W*e need to *talk*."

Understatement of the century, Kiera thought indignantly in silent reply. She could feel Darian's worried stare as she scrubbed the blood from her face with a dampened piece of Connor's ruined shirt and took stock of the damage. Her nose was a little tender but unbroken, her shoulder was sore but bearable, and she did not want to talk *at all*.

"*About?*" she hissed over her shoulder, her fury bubbling just below the surface.

You left me in the middle of the woods to fend for myself, and now *you want to* chat *like we are the same as we ever were? Snowball's chance in hell, bird.*

Her angry thoughts only fueled the flame, and she was quietly debating which of those exact words she wanted to say next as she glanced toward the rest of the group.

Henelce and Alyk were sitting well away from them with Connor, filling him in with the details of what had transpired as they were setting up a ring of stones for a fire. The more familiar duo was chattering away and filling the silence with their voices, but Connor was barely paying attention, his gaze flitting again and again to the large gray Aeroyn and the woman he was getting to be more than a little fond of. It was taking everything he had to remain seated and let her fight the inevitable verbal battle she was going to end up having with the creature she had allowed to call her *mate*, even if it didn't end in his favor.

Alyk had given Connor a white shirt to replace the second one he had ruined so far, and Kiera found she preferred it over the black as she caught his gaze. She went back to cleaning up and ignored the *beast* next to her as Darian leaned against a tree, purposely blocking her view with his wings. He was silently marking his *territory* with that gesture, and his protectiveness of her felt far too late to make Kiera anything other than angry.

Darian was watching her attentively as she gingerly removed her ruined tunic and took stock of the spattering of little rips in her flesh from the glass shards. She could see him wince out of the corner of her eye as she picked out a few embedded pieces and rinsed the rest clean with water, continuing to act like he wasn't there as she dabbed at the small cuts and pulled her tattered shirt back over her head. The wounds would heal and leave a constellation of scars across her chest and shoulder, but they were superficial.

Nothing she couldn't deal with.

"You should take from me, Ki—"

"*Absolutely not!*" Kiera yelled, cutting him off as she narrowed her eyes at Darian. Her vehement response caught him off guard; she had never refused him before.

"Kiera—"

"*What*? What could you possibly want from me, Darian? How *dare* you offer your blood to me when you would have let him *die*!" Kiera had never reacted with true hostility to Darian before, and she was suddenly in his face, her scent totally different as the fragrance of honey soured into a pungent and rancid vanilla. The other three looked up, surprised by the outburst; Connor's expression said he might come after Darian, but Alyk laid a hand on his arm, telling him quietly to wait.

Kiera was in no mood for an audience, and she threw the blood-soaked cloth she had been unconsciously strangling the life out of at Darian's chest and stomped off.

The Aeroyn stood there with his back to the others, stunned.

"Are you going to go after her this time? Or should I?" The words were out of Connor's mouth before he could stop himself.

Okay, idiot, you're not talking to her anymore, so tread carefully. When Darian turned slowly, the look on his face made Connor's mouth go dry and the hair stand up on the back of his neck. *Too late . . .*

"*You—!*" Darian stalked angrily toward the group, his steely gaze focused on the blonde hunter, trying to stare him down, debating which limb he wanted to remove from the man's body *first*.

Oh, here we go... Connor folded his arms over his chest and sat back against the rock behind him, crossing his legs in front of him at the ankles. He would have looked casual had it not been for the arrogant directed at Darian, inflaming the Aeroyn further, but those green eyes were serious; Connor wasn't in the mood to play. And neither was Henelce as he moved closer to Connor, ready to intervene.

"What about *me*?" Connor demanded.

"*You* did *this*!" Darian bellowed, seething.

"*Did I*? Because I seem to remember *you* taking off like a spoiled child who didn't want to share his *toy*!" Connor's outburst stopped the Aeroyn in his tracks. Connor eyed Darian threateningly, lowering his voice. "Go *after* her, Darian. She's upset, and probably a little fragile. It's been a rough couple of days. Keep that in mind, or *you* might end up on the receiving end of *Dirtbag*. And be *nice*, otherwise you'll have to answer to *me*, and you have *no idea* what I'm *capable* of."

Darian towered over Connor, anger radiating from him, but the man didn't look away. It wasn't until Darian turned and took off into the air to find Kiera that Connor let out the breath he had been unconsciously holding.

So this *is Dirtbag,* Alyk thought as he glanced nervously back and forth between the two males, suddenly wanted to know the whole story.

"Well done. Darian's not an easy one to stand up to." Alyk looked relieved and a little amused. "I know—I've already been up against those claws. Now that I think about it, Henelce is the only one who hasn't been on the receiving end from one or both of them."

"Oh, give it time," Henelce chuckled and went back to setting up the fire, but Connor wasn't listening; he was still staring at the spot where Darian had disappeared.

That overinflated bird and I need to have a conversation at some point. Might as well start by showing I have a back bone. Maybe he'll actually take me seriously.

Forty-Four

Kiera was a good fifteen feet up in a tree, leaning against the trunk with one foot flat on the branch she sat upon, the other dangling freely beneath her as she tore leaves into confetti.

"Go away, Darian. I have nothing to say to you right now." Her tone was no longer angry, but she was certainly exasperated. She wanted time to cool down, to think, and the familiar *beast* was already *pestering* her.

He knows better . . .

Darian watched Kiera from the ground, trying to remember who had that silly habit first; one of them had definitely picked it up from the other. He shifted his focus just enough to figure out which limb he wanted to use as a perch before he crouched down and jumped up to catch hold of the branch below and to the left of her, pulling himself up and settling so that he was almost facing her.

"Henelce thought you should know about this," Darian said quietly, caressing the band on his arm with his thumb and trying not to look at her as she glanced down at him.

"I'm not in the mood for *stories*, Darian," she retorted. No emotion, walls up, one more leaf torn to tiny pieces.

"You know that I can smell *him* on you." His tone was accusatory as he shifted subjects, and she could feel the hurt radiating from him.

"And you're not even surprised," she countered flatly, trying to stay calm as she plucked and decimated another defenseless piece of vegetation.

"Kiera—"

"Darian, you *left* me!" she shrieked as she looked down at him coldly. *Now* she was angry. "You saw something you *didn't like*, and you were just *gone*! What am I supposed to *say* to you?"

Kiera pulled her dangling leg up, balancing cross-legged on the branch. She blinked back frustrated tears as she took a deep breath, trying to keep her next words decidedly less aggressive. And hurt.

"At least you had the *decency* to come back and *talk* to me about it the first time you let jealousy get the better of you, and *here* you are, in the company of the very same *man* you didn't want me to let live in the *first* place."

Darian stared at the ground, letting the birds and squirrels fill the silence for a few moments while he let Kiera get back under some sort of control. He was trying very hard to not fight with her, but the *scent* of another male on her skin was bringing back old memories that he would rather forget . . .

"What . . . *happened*?" Darian finally asked quietly when Kiera went back to ripping leaves to shreds. She sighed heavily and leaned her head back against the trunk as she considered how to respond, her hair getting caught in the bark mildly annoying while her anger and her recent blood loss made her tired. Her limbs felt a little heavy, and she sighed deeply as she realized, for the first time in a *long* time, how hard being human really was without the help of Darian's blood. It *hurt*, but she had earned the pain defending Connor's life, and that gave her at least *some* comfort.

"*Why* are you even asking me that? What do you need to know that your senses don't already tell you?" Kiera was still angry, but her voice was losing some of its edge as her rhetorical questions hit the air. They both knew *exactly* what had happened, and Darian hadn't even needed to be there.

"You neither want nor need gory details, Darian, and I will spare you at least that. But . . . whatever is between he and I . . . Connor is . . . *different*." Kiera paused, taking a deep breath, trying to get her jumbled thoughts into some sort of order before she let them hit the air and wasn't able to reel them back in.

"Sometimes I feel like I have spent far too long out here in these woods, and other times I think I would rather watch them burn than go back to a world that I no longer know how to survive in. These men suddenly appearing in my life are wrecking havoc with my brain: Alyk knew who I *was*, but Connor knows who I *am*, and you have helped me grow from one to the other. I am struggling to decide what *I* really want...

"But I didn't stop loving *you*, if that's what you're after. I don't think that's even possible. You have watched over me for a long time now, but *Connor*, he . . . he's willing to help me walk my own path, while you've directed me along yours," she glanced at the Aeroyn, "and I don't know that I'm *okay* with that anymore."

Kiera hesitated before asking the next question, hoping she was wrong; if Darian had known and *kept* it from her, he had knowingly put her in danger, and that was not an idea that settled well for her.

"Darian, do you know what a *unifier* is?"

There are several curse words in the Aeroyn dialect; every one of them lined up and repeated loudly in Darian's mind before he answered her soberly.

"Yes, I do. You are not the first of your kind that I have crossed paths with," he admitted guiltily.

"Uh-huh . . . and is there a *reason* you've never told me what *I am*? Did you ever, for even a moment, think that I *knew* what I am capable of?" She waited for him to respond, but he was so quiet Kiera felt the need to look down and make sure he was still there when no answer came after several seconds of silence.

Darian was staring hard at the branch she sat upon, slowly digesting that Kiera knew what she was and what that meant.

It means she will leave. Darian gritted his teeth. *That dirtbag is going to end up missing crucial pieces of himself very soon . . .*

Kiera was silently furious, the air tinged with fetid vanilla as she shifted on the branch. She had trusted Darian with her life, and he had knowingly put hers in jeopardy. He couldn't even tell her *why*. It suddenly dawned on her that he had trained her to be like *him*—ruthless, uncompromising, a killer of men. Darian had given her the skills to be *exactly* what would make her an effective weapon. Kiera's mouth went dry, her green eyes hard as she stared at him, her voice deathly quiet.

"Darian, did you . . . did you train me for *war*?"

That got a response: a hurt and subdued one.

"*No*, Kiera. I trained you so you could keep yourself safe in case I wasn't able to." Darian finally looked up at her, eyes narrowed. Kiera could feel the hairs rise on the back of her neck, and she could smell that thunderstorm scent. "That *dirtbag* better not have been putting ideas in your head! I will *shred* him if that's the case!"

"Don't you threaten *him*, Darian! I'll—"

He winced at her protectiveness of Connor, and Kiera had to stop herself before she said something awful that she wasn't going to be able to take back once she cooled down. Frustrated, angry, and hurt, Kiera threw the pieces of the leaves still in her hand that were staining her fingers green to the forest floor, finding it harder and harder to stay calm. She had tried to keep her voice level, but it came out angry anyway. Exasperated and completely *done* with their conversation, Kiera scooted forward and swung back off the branch, holding onto it so that she was dangling right in Darian's face.

"The *only* thing Connor did was tell me *what I am* and how I could be *used*, and that *alone* is good enough reason for *me* not to kill him. If Sorveign wants me, he's going to have to get in line because I have *bigger* things to deal with first . . ."

Kiera let go and dropped to the forest floor to walk back to the group, calling back to him over her shoulder as she left Darian to consider his next move.

". . . and *you* will either help me or *get out of my way!*"

* * *

"Are you all right?"

"*Fine*," Kiera snapped at the man who had approached her. She was hungry, tired, and sore, and she didn't want to talk about anything just then, not with *him* or anyone.

Connor took his cue and handed her an apple and a piece of bread and let her be. He wanted to look her over, but he wasn't about to push it, hoping she would come to him on her own when she was ready. He sat down on a flat rock on the other side of the ring of stones, his elbows on his knees, watching Alyk set up the fire; the last thing he wanted was for her to go back to calling him *Dirtbag* and meaning it.

He was a little relieved that she had returned alone, and Connor refused to let impatience ruin whatever chance he had of Kiera choosing him over the *bird*. He was still debating how bright of an idea it actually was to take her with him but was quickly finding he cared less and less if the notion was good or bad. He just wanted her there every step of the way, and he probably wasn't going to take *no* for an answer.

At least he's *smart enough to give me time to cool*. Kiera frowned, already making comparisons between Connor and Darian that were putting Connor in a better light . . .

Henelce suddenly plunked down next to her, and Kiera couldn't help but smile wryly at the odd little bearded man who seemed somehow outside them all.

"Can I ask a favor?" he chirped brightly.

"*Now*?" she sighed, her smile faltering as she looked away and picked at the bread.

"Of course, *now!*" Henelce retorted, looking at her like she might be crazy when she met his gaze.

"What do you want, Shephard?"

"May I see your mark?"

"Oh . . . *that*." Kiera wondered why Henelce was even curious, and he caught her suspicion, offering up an explanation before she could formulate the question.

"My dear, I *train* your kind, and I *know* the call of the *marked* when I feel it. I thought I had smelled it on you weeks ago, but I wasn't sure until you had your defenses up. I want to see its shape since there are three different ones, and I'm curious as to know which line you are from."

"It's an ivy leaf."

"May I see?" Henelce didn't seem all that surprised, and Kiera watched him warily for a moment, wondering *what* he actually knew about her.

"Knock yourself out," she shrugged as she set the bread on her knee and bit into the skin of the apple just enough that she could hold it with her teeth as she pulled her hair up with both hands. Her ridiculous pose brought forth raucous laughter from Connor, and Alyk couldn't help it either but all she could do was glare at them while she held her hair out of the way. Henelce ignored them completely as he got up to stand behind her, touching the mark gingerly as he inspected it.

Kiera waited only long enough for Henelce to finish that when she no longer felt him making contact with her skin, she dropped her hair, removed the apple from between her teeth, and threw a pebble at Connor. There was a loud *smack* when it connected with his chest.

"Ow! Damn it, woman! Stop throwing things at me!" Connor gave her a hurt look as he rubbed the spot she had pelted, and Alyk laughed like he hadn't been so amused in quite a while. Kiera finally joined the better mood and smiled.

"Serves you right, *Dirtbag*." She retorted through a mouthful of apple when it suddenly dawned on her that they were one short. "Alyk, where's your brother?"

Alyk stopped laughing and exchanged a look with Henelce, who was still standing just behind Kiera. She jumped when the Shephard answered her instead; she hadn't felt his presence still so close to her.

"Tance has gone on to bigger and better things, hopefully far, far away."

"Well, *that's* a relief. Little bastard would have probably tried to kill me in my sleep!" She was immediately sorry as soon as the words passed her lips, and Alyk's only response was a hostile look. "I'm sorry, Alyk. I didn't—"

"Just let it *go*." His sharp dismissal was all he had to say on the matter, and if Alyk didn't want to give up details, she wasn't going to ask. Maybe Darian would tell her if she ever started speaking to *him* again, but Kiera decided it wasn't important just then. She was simply glad the little booger wasn't around to cause more problems.

Sudden movement distracted her, and Kiera turned her attention to Connor, who was closely examining the arrow that Henelce had pulled out of his back less than an hour earlier. Kiera realized that something was still nagging at her as she chewed, that the projectile in his hands looked familiar . . .

She took one last bite of her apple and threw the core into the bushes as she stood and crossed the short distance between them, holding her hand out expectantly.

"Can I see that for a moment?"

Connor, not forgetting the sting of the pebble Kiera had volleyed at him, held it possessively against his chest, looking up at her through his lashes.

"*No*." He smiled inwardly at her annoyed sigh, but he kept his face serious.

"Connor, stop playing around. This is important." Kiera's hand was still out, waiting for him to hand her the arrow willingly before she *took* it from him.

"And what if I *don't*?" he said innocently, but a smile was tugging at his mouth, and it was getting harder to keep a straight face. Kiera moved closer, and Connor could sense her studying his movements, looking for an opening to snatch the projectile away from him.

He was ready for that.

Two can play at this game . . . Connor acted like he was inspecting the fletching, holding it close to his face with his head down, and she took the bait.

"Give me tha— Ack!" Kiera had lunged for the arrow, and Connor swept his foot out to catch her weight bearing leg to knock her off balance, her momentum sending her tumbling into him. He dropped the arrow and caught her, using her forward motion to roll her over so Kiera was on her back and draped across his lap with his face just above hers.

"I am getting *really* tired of falling on you, *Dirtbag*," Kiera snapped, trying not to laugh.

"Well, *that's* too bad. I was just starting to *like* it . . ." Connor wanted to kiss her, and he pulled her closer; the heady scent of mint and cedar flood her senses, her body involuntarily reacting to him as Kiera brought her hand up to his face, getting lost in his warmth and his eyes . . .

The sound of a throat clearing startled them both, making them look up in surprise. Alyk and Henelce were staring at them with wide eyes, and Kiera turned a bright shade of red as she dropped her hand. After a few days totally alone, she had briefly forgotten that no one else knew what had gone on between them.

Connor hadn't. He had used the moment to his advantage, and it wasn't lost on Alyk. Or Darian, who had been approaching quietly, now stopped not far behind them.

Let them challenge me. See what happens.

"Can I have the arrow, *please*?" Her voice was quiet and embarrassed, and she wouldn't look at him. Kiera was in an awkward position, and the way Connor was holding her meant he would either dump her on the floor or help her up.

"What part of *no* don't you understand?" he asked sarcastically. Kiera stifled a laugh as she smacked him in the chest, and Connor turned up the drama, acting wounded. "Look, Crazy Lady of the Forest, I don't need to take this kind of abuse from yo—"

Fuck it. They're going to find out anyway, Kiera thought just before she grabbed Connor's face and kissed him. *That* shut him up.

"*Now* can I have the damned *arrow*?"

"Oh, *fine*." Connor sat back and let her up, handing the arrow to her disinterestedly as though she had only just asked him nicely. Kiera made a face at him as she sat down next to him, studying the weapon, trying not to look at anyone else.

"If you're done with the show of *dominance*, *Dirtbag*, I would appreciate you keeping your hands to *yourself*." Darian's voice was cold, and Kiera cringed; she could feel the tell-tale thunderstorm being barely held at bay.

Connor looked over his shoulder at Darian with a smirk and raised eyebrows, *challenge me* written all over his face. Kiera smacked Connor in the arm with the arrow, trying to save his stupid hide from angering the Aeroyn further, but to everyone's surprise, Darian sighed and broke eye contact first.

Kiera couldn't help but feel a little relieved. At least there wasn't going to be a fight.

This time.

FORTY-FIVE

"You were right—it *is* her. Are you going to tell her?" Henelce asked softly as he pulled the saddle off his palomino. He glanced at Alyk to find the younger man chewing his lip, obviously debating what he should do as he checked his own horse's hooves.

"Not now. I *would*, but—"

"Two is enough for her to deal with?"

Alyk's head jerked up, and he met the Shephard's curious gaze.

"I wasn't in *love* with her, Henelce. I had never really met her, and had only gotten to see her as a child from afar. That doesn't really make me *competition* as far as I'm concerned, whether she liked me two weeks ago or not."

"So you're not going to tell her you were betrothed to her?"

"What the hell difference does it make *now*?" Alyk hissed in a loud whisper, starting to get irritated as he dropped the mare's back hoof back into the dirt and ran his hand over her withers so he could follow the line of her leg and check the front.

"It was a royal decree, Alyk," Henelce reached over and poked Alyk in the arm, startling the younger man, wanting his full attention. "You're both alive, so it technically still stands as valid. She's not the only one that's *marked*, and she *will* need to be trained—it's obvious she hasn't been. I *know* you felt her pull when she was defending Connor. Imagine if they had been in a tavern and she couldn't control it."

Henelce went back to adjusting the stallion's bridle, making sure it wasn't too tight. He patted his horse's neck and fed him a cookie from his pack, rubbing the palomino's nose as it chewed.

"She's in much more danger with *him* than she will be if she stays with Darian. You saw that interaction between them . . ." Henelce said grimly. "At least promise me you'll talk to her at some point. She has a right to know."

He shot Alyk a knowing look, and the younger man went back to his task, shaking his head.

"All right, Henelce. I'll think about it."

Forty-Six

The arrow in her hand was made of ash, the fletching white and yellow, the tip barbed iron. The sun glanced off the light colored wood and the sharp tip that had been cleaned of Connor's blood . . .

Where have I seen this before? she mused.

"That looks just like the one that I pulled out of your leg," Darian said, leaning against a tree with his arms crossed over his chest, watching Kiera fiddle with the projectile from the other side of the unlit fire. Alyk and Henelce were still gone, tending to their horses, but Connor was right beside her as she sat cross-legged on the ground, lounging against the rock at his back with his hands behind his head, focused on the arrow as she turned it in her hands.

"It *does*, doesn't it?" Kiera was quiet, a phantom pain in her calf reminding her of the injury that no longer existed. *Was that really less than a week ago?*

"That makes me wonder how long he's been tracking you," Darian answered, watching her thoughtfully. "But it doesn't explain the scent on the message. Elves don't have a scent marker."

"What about indigo berry? Ink from it will smell like that which a person most loves or fears, depending on what state they're in when they touch the parchment." Connor had opened his mouth, and Darian immediately bristled.

"No one asked *you*, *Dirtbag*," Darian snapped, but Kiera ignored the jealous *bird* and gave Connor a curious look instead.

"Do I even want to know what that is used *for*?" she asked, somewhere between curious and suspicious.

"*What*? It *was* useful in my world," Connor replied, looking a little sheepish as he shrugged.

"*Was*?" Kiera didn't really believe he could leave his life behind, and part of her didn't want him to.

"Maybe . . ." Connor reached out and tucked a strand of hair behind her ear, his thumb brushing her cheek. *Don't make promises you can't keep, idiot.*

"Can we *focus*, please?" The angry outburst from Aeroyn on the opposite side of the fire made them both look up, but Kiera had nothing to say to him as she gave him a dark glare and went back to playing with the arrow. He was already irritated, and watching the exchange between them made him want

175

to drag Connor out of sight and bleed him dry. Darian couldn't stomach that Kiera was acting like he wasn't even there, her focus solely on the man at her side. Angry or not, she was being incredibly disrespectful, and the Aeroyn knew she was better than that.

Then again, the current set of circumstances had never come up, and it dawned on him that he might just be *hoping* she wasn't really that *cruel*.

Kiera was getting tired of the display and felt keenly aware that, at some point, the male bravado was going to have to stop, and she was going to have to make it clear that she wasn't going to stand for it. Connor was pushing, and Darian was reacting; it was like watching two dogs with a stick, and she half expected them to start barking at each other and baring their teeth. Kiera refused to be the stick, and she wasn't going to let them break her either, but she knew she was going to have to choose sooner or later, and someone was going to be hurt.

She felt guilty knowing that *someone* was going to be Darian.

Kiera sighed as her focus fell back on the arrow in her hands, unsure if she could walk away from both males if they didn't try to figure it out between them, not really ready to give up either one if they couldn't.

She was silently grateful when Alyk and Henelce broke the building tension with their return.

"Focus on *what*?" Alyk addressed Darian, and it struck Kiera as odd that they seemed comfortable with each other. Alyk had been the first to pique her interest, knew things about her that made him dangerous, and Darian was acting like none of it wasn't an issue.

Darian let go of something? Did hell freeze over, and no one told me? That thought put a wry smile on her face.

"Why your friend Jaçon was tracking me and for how long," Kiera piped up as she looked back and forth from Henelce to Alyk. "When was the last time you saw him?"

"Close to ten days at this point. We were almost to Chirk when his signet ring called him home. We hadn't seen him again until today." Alyk's answer sounded a little distracted because he was focused on the arrow in her hands. "*That* is definitely one of *his*. Or, at least, it's standard issue from what I've seen."

Henelce kept quiet, his hand in his pocket, fingering the crystal still safely tucked away. Jaçon hadn't used the porting crystal to return because he hadn't needed to, but he would certainly be back for it with the double moons approaching. Henelce knew that particular elf rather well, and he couldn't really fault Jaçon if he had simply been following orders, but he couldn't believe that Sorveign would have sent someone to *kill* Kiera…

"Shephard?" Connor was watching him carefully, the tell-tale signs of someone *hiding* something written all over his face. "Care to share *your* thoughts on this?"

"Wait . . . Do you still have that *crystal*?" Alyk turned at Henelce expectantly.

"What *crystal*?" Connor perked up, butting in before the Shephard had a chance to even open his mouth. "Did he give you a porting crystal?"

"My goodness, you two are quick. Questions, questions everywhere . . . Which to answer first?" Henelce chuckled and shook his head as he pulled a small, clear crystal out of his pocket and handed it to Alyk. "I was debating if I wanted to even admit to having this. I can just see one of you having Darian put it high in a tree or throw it into a deep pool." He watched Alyk play with the crystal for a moment before turning to Connor. "What do *you* know about porting crystals?"

Instead of answering, Connor reached behind Kiera and picked up his pack from the other side of her. He rummaged around for a moment and pulled a small black bag out of it.

"Quite a bit actually, since I have a set of my *own*," he chirped proudly as he dropped a six-sided, luminescent blue gem into his hand.

The jewel was flat on the top and bottom, the edges faceted, and the entire stone no more than an inch wide; Kiera was mesmerized as the interior pulsated with a faint blue light when she leaned in to study it. She put her hand on Connor's wrist to keep him from moving so she could see it better and felt his pulse pick up under her touch. To her surprise, the gem beat faster too, and she suddenly realized it was mimicking Connor's heartbeat.

She had never seen anything like it.

"They're not exactly a common item, but I know of at least five other sets. These were passed to me by my *mentor*."

Kiera tore her gaze away from the pulsating stone in time to see Connor exchange an odd look with the Shephard, and she eyed him suspiciously. He stared back at her with mock innocence, making her laugh, and she let it slide, reminding herself that there was a whole lifetime of mischief behind Connor that she didn't know about yet, no matter how familiar he felt to her.

"I know they are nearly impossible to find, and they have to be renewed during the double full moon," he went on. "Apparently there used to be dozens of sets of them, but so many have been lost over the years that the number of them still in use is unknown. Mine isn't even a full set. I have six including the homing crystal, but I never had the seventh, and neither did the man who gave them to me. They still sync with each other without an issue, but the *ritual* has to be modified every time one is lost."

Kiera was totally fascinated, and she felt keenly aware that she had been out of the world for far too long. She knew none of what the other three seemed to take as common knowledge, and Connor was talking about these stones like he was teaching a child; she gritted her teeth when she realized he was doing it for her benefit. She counted it as one more strike against Darian for keeping her hidden for so long, and Kiera found herself trying to annoy the Aeroyn on purpose by leaning against Connor while she pushed the gem around on his palm, caressing his skin as she examined it more closely.

"You had better stop doing that," Connor whispered huskily in her ear. "Your *bird* is getting mad, and I'm rather *fond* of this hand."

Kiera snorted a laugh and sat back, letting him put the stone away and avoiding the intense gaze of the Aeroyn ten feet away. Darian was glaring at them, trying to ignore the sidelong glances he was getting from Alyk and Henelce.

He didn't want their pity.

He wanted her to *stop*.

"What do you know about cross porting?" Henelce kept up his questioning, simultaneously trying to diffuse the situation and test Connor's depth of knowledge.

Connor was only too happy to oblige because porting crystals were one of the few things he found truly *interesting*. "Only that it's possible, but you have to have at least three sets and two other heartbeats. It won't work otherwise."

"That isn't necessarily true. You *can* do it with two sets, but only two gems will cross port."

"Wouldn't that depend on which points were touching—?"

"Okay, whoa! I'm getting lost." Kiera finally put up her hands in defeat when the ensuing debate started to sound like another language. "How do these even *work*?"

She looked to Connor to explain, but it was Alyk who started talking, the clear crystal in his palm glittering as the late afternoon sunlight filtered through both the trees and the stone.

"What Connor has in his hand is a *homing* crystal, and what Jaçon left behind is called a point stone. A full set of porting crystals consists of seven gems, all carved from a single stone—a homing crystal and six point gems."

Alyk paused to pick up a nearby stick and clear away the pine needles and random debris from the forest floor at his feet. Using the end of the stick, he drew a circle in the dirt with a much smaller hexagon in the middle, radiating lines away from each point of the hexagon until they touched the outer circle's edge.

"When they're all together, they look like this, and only the stones cut from the same set will work with each other. The owner of the gems has to *claim* them for them to work, and they have to have all or most of their set for the crystals to properly respond. In order for them to work, the stones have to communicate and sync with the energy of the owner's soul—all it takes a drop of blood smeared on each crystal by the person who plans to use them, and that can be done at any part of the year. That bond won't be broken unless the owner dies, or they are assumed by another individual.

"But the stones don't work forever. Every double full moon, the set needs to be gathered and reignited in a ritual, usually by someone who has natural magic or in a magic heavy area—"

"I take mine to the Runes of Obilio. That's how I know there are at least five other working sets, because I am not the only one who uses it."

Alyk looked up with a scowl on half his face, annoyed at Connor's interjection, and Kiera slapped her hand over Connor's mouth, motioning for Alyk to continue. Alyk looked back and forth between them, thoughts and emotions he wasn't expecting creeping quietly into his mind as he dusted off his hands and went back to his explanation.

"Okay, so, to use the crystals, the owner must carry the homing crystal with them at all times. Point crystals can be set anywhere, but they must already be synced with the homing crystal and be given a specific command for each place they are set. If you left one at, say, a tavern, you have to give both the homing crystal *and* the point crystal a specific command to be able to return to your point crystal.

"You don't happen to have a point crystal with you, do you? The visual is easier."

This time Alyk turned to Connor expectantly, and Kiera dropped her hand, wiping it disgustedly on Connor's borrowed shirt; he had been licking her palm, trying to get her to voluntarily remove it.

"Not with me, no, but I can explain." Connor picked up another stick and moved into a cross-legged position as he wiped his mouth on the back of his sleeve. He drew two *X*s on the ground in front of them, about a foot apart, labeling them *P* and *H*.

"Now, if you have the homing crystal in your hand," Connor pointed to the *X* labeled *H*, "and you want to go back to the tavern where you left your point crystal," he dragged the stick toward the *X* labeled *P*, "you tell the homing crystal *tavern*, and you are suddenly *there*. They're pretty damned useful. *I've certainly avoided some very sticky situations because of them.*"

Kiera ignored the last sentence and his wide grin as that information settled into her brain, and she started to have questions of her own.

"You're telling me that this is what Jaçon used when he disappeared?"

Connor and Alyk both nodded.

"And the one he gave to Henelce . . . he can just show up wherever Henelce is at any point and time, am I right?" Kiera was *very* uncomfortable with this idea, and she suddenly understood why Henelce had been hesitant to give the crystal up. If Sorveign was after her and they had an access point that allowed Jaçon to appear among them, what was keeping him from grabbing her and disappearing?

"Yes, that's exactly right. There is, however, a catch—you will appear in the vicinity of the crystal, but if it's moved, you will still port to that crystal, you just may not like where you end up." Connor answered before Alyk could, focused on the clear gem in Alyk's hand. "I like the bottom of a lake idea, personally."

It bothered him immensely that someone else was after her. Eryce was one thing because he'd had the opportunity to intervene, but the *Elves* wanted her too? Connor wasn't sure he even wanted to know why, and he had serious doubts about keeping Kiera away from them if they decided they wanted *her* alive more than *him*. The porting crystal in their midst made him that much more nervous.

Guess I won't be sleeping any time soon . . .

"Okay, I understand so far, but what is *cross* porting?" Kiera's question hit the air, shifting the thoughts of everyone who was staring at the clear crystal as though Jaçon might suddenly appear. Henelce reached out and gently took the stick from Connor and knelt to rub his hand over the dirt to clear away the previous drawings. He drew two six pointed stars side by side with two of their points touching, continuing the lesson.

"This is where it gets complicated, so stop me if you can't keep up. When you do the reignition ritual, you have to set your stones in a six-point star pattern so that they are equidistant from the homing crystal or, in Connor's case, a five-point star. The set becomes useless if there are fewer than three-point crystals, but you can take two incomplete sets and make a bigger set by *cross* syncing. The blood from both people have to be on the point crystals you wish to sync, and that can *only* be done during reignition. Otherwise, the stone will simply go dormant until it's cleansed and reconnected to the owner of its homing crystal.

"When you do this, two homing crystals or more, if you do it right, can port to the same destination, and only one person has to give the command for both homing stones to react—the point stone itself will hear the command and reach out to *both* homing crystals and draw them to it.

"*That*, however, also has a catch—if person A needs to port to that particular spot without person B showing at the same time, they have to set an additional crystal set only to themselves, or they are both ported to that point no matter where they are or what they're doing. It doesn't help either if person B has forgotten completely about the previously set up meeting . . .

"It's led to some very *awkward* situations when used improperly, some of which I'm *still* trying to *forget*."

Even Darian cracked a smile at that comment. Alyk shook his head, chuckling as he took up the lesson, continuing with the last bits of pertinent information.

"When the stones are cleansed and passed to another soul, all previous commands assigned to the stones are broken and reset. Even if the owner does not change, those commands will no longer work after the double full moon if they are reignited properly, and the stones will fade and stop working if they are not reignited every year and a half."

"So can two people use the same homing crystal to port *together*?" Kiera voiced one last question; Connor shifted uncomfortably because that was *exactly* what he had planned to do with her to deposit her on Eryce's doorstep, and she caught the guilty look on his face. "I'll take that as a *yes*."

Forty-Seven

The day was finally ending, and the last rays of the sun were turning the wisps of clouds overhead a brilliant pink and orange that darkened slowly to a deep amethyst as the daylight was chased away by the dusk, the night following close behind. The stars were out in full force before darkness had wrapped itself around their corner of the world while the forest came alive with the sounds of the crickets and frogs as the daytime fauna quieted and settled to rest.

Kiera couldn't remember the last time she had felt that *tired*. She was lying lengthwise on her stomach across a low branch of a live oak, her hands under her chin and her ankles crossed over the limb to help keep her balance. Connor was facing her, leaning against the same thick branch that cradled Kiera, trying to talk to her, but she wasn't really listening. Her nose and shoulder were still sore, and while it was a minor inconvenience, Kiera couldn't help but think of Darian's gift of healing . . .

But she had made a pact with herself that she wouldn't take any more from him. She felt like it gave him *ownership* over her, and that idea had been turning her into something she really didn't want to be.

". . . you look like a big cat."

Kiera closed her eyes momentarily when Connor's words finally filtered through as he reached up to stroke her hair out of her face. His fingers trailed gently across her forehead, and she smiled faintly, knowing he was *memorizing* her.

Kiera felt comforted by Connor's touch, by his nearness, but now that she was around Darian again, she also felt a confusing sense of loss: twice now Darian had left her behind, and she felt like she was losing her best friend. Darian had been her only companion for so long, and being surrounded by other people willing to help fill the void somehow made her sad. Kiera had driven the wedge between herself and the Aeroyn that much further by making damned sure he knew that she and Connor had been together; apparently she had gotten her point across since he hadn't tried to talk to her at all for the past couple of hours, and she wondered if she wasn't being a little mean.

Kiera sighed, shifting on the branch so her cheek rested on her hands, opening her eyes to stare at the fire and Darian, fifteen feet away.

"What's going on behind those pretty eyes?" Connor sounded genuinely concerned about her, but Kiera didn't even know how to answer. She glanced down at him and furrowed her brows, thinking.

"Truthfully, I don't really even know. The things I thought were true suddenly *aren't*. My whole world has changed in three days, and I have a horrible feeling it's about to change even more."

"I can see that, and on the subject of change, I was serious earlier—I want you to come with me, Kiera. I cannot stay, and I need to know that you're *safe*. This is the first place Eryce will look for you, and with Alyk and Henelce in possession of that crystal, Jaçon will be back to finish what he started before too long."

"Keep *me* safe? You ought to worry about your own hide, *Dirtbag*, since being around me almost got *you* killed. You're lucky Henelce was there—"

"I don't even remember that, so it doesn't count." Connor continued to stroke her hair, and she was getting lost in the sensation, sleep getting harder to keep at bay.

She was so exhausted . . .

"Connor . . . ?" Kiera sounded far away.

"I'm an *idiot*?"

"That's not what I was going to say . . ." she whispered. Her eyes were closed, her breathing getting deeper. Connor watched over her as she fell asleep, his hand still in her hair, wondering how long it was going to be before the words that rang in his head would come out of his mouth.

I love you too, Kiera.

Forty-Eight

Connor volunteered to take the first watch of the night as everyone settled down, promising to wake Henelce and Alyk when the moons were high. Darian had agreed to stick around for a bit since he wasn't going to want to sleep for a while yet though he was rethinking that once he realized he would have to be up with the closest thing to a *rival* he had encountered in his entire time at Kiera's side.

Connor was sitting cross-legged on the ground as he inspected Kiera's throwing knives, checking them for burs and testing their edges for sharpness to keep himself both busy and *armed*. Even though he still felt energized from the healing of the wound from the arrow, the next few hours had the potential to be dangerous, and he wasn't about to fall asleep with Kiera's *bird* anywhere near him. Not until he had said what he needed to say.

Darian was perched on a rock on the other side of the fire, his arms resting on his knees, staring off into the darkness, quietly contemplating ways to torture Connor that would be slow and painful.

Connor, however, already *knew* how to torment Darian; all he had to do was open his mouth.

"Don't look so miserable, Darian. I'm not happy about this *either*."

"*Don't* talk to me," Darian hissed in return. The scent of a thunderstorm filled the air, and the hair rose on the back of Connor's neck as he fought his instinct to react *badly*.

"She missed you, you know," Connor continued as though he hadn't heard the Aeroyn's temperamental answer.

"*Yes*, I can see that in the way she looks at *you*." Darian couldn't keep the sarcasm and the barely contained fury out of his words, and he didn't bother to try.

"Whatever is between her and I has *nothing* to do with the two of *you*, so don't blame *me* for *your* actions," Connor sighed, trying not to get exasperated. "*She* knows you screwed up, *you* know you screwed up, and you haven't even *bothered* to apologize." He continued, waving the tip of one of her throwing knives at Darian like he was wagging his finger at a small child.

"*She* is in a lot of danger, and *my* goal is to keep her safe. I would appreciate that becoming *your* focus too. This isn't the first time I've been in a situation like this, but it *is* the first time I've actually *cared*, so keep that in mind. Plus I have my own neck on the line, so don't think this is some easy decision on my part; protecting her means I can die, too. But I know what to expect out there in the real world, and she is no safer here than she is hiding in plain sight. Honestly, Kiera is safer with *me*, and I refuse to let you or anyone keep me from protecting her.

"Thing is, I also know *women*. Right now, I'm new and shiny to her, and she's using me as an excuse to stay mad at you, but at some point, she'll cool down, and she'll want you around. If you don't want to alienate her, at least *try* to be interested in making life for *her* a little more comfortable even if it's not pleasant for either of *us*." Connor went back to focusing on which knives needed sharpening, ignoring Darian's wrathful gaze.

"You have quite the ego, *boy*, acting like you care more about her than I do. I have *protected* that girl since she was still a child and—"

"*I* didn't leave her alone in the forest with some strange *man, Darian*." Connor looked the Aeroyn right in the eye, challenging the *bird* to refute him.

"How long will the two of you *repeat* that?" Darian growled as his frustration got the better of him.

"Until you tell her you're *sorry* for it," Connor shrugged, his gaze falling back on the blade in his hands. "Otherwise she'll continue to remind you, and I'll continue to support her in that endeavor." He finally put the knives aside and adopted Darian's pose, taking the opportunity to study the bigger being.

"This whole *protecting* thing is all relatively new to me. I actually find this whole situation rather funny, considering I was *hunting* her."

"You had *better* be joking, *Dirtbag*. I have no qualms with killing you," the Aeroyn hissed as his wings twitched.

"While I don't doubt that, I'm dead serious. Eryce paid me to find her, and she knows it—"

"*What?*" Darian's expression might have been amusing if the conversation hadn't been so dangerous; the Aeroyn's features couldn't seem to decide if he was going to kill Connor or if he didn't believe the words coming out of the man's mouth.

"Shhhh! Let them sleep," Connor whispered loudly as he picked up a small rock and started to break it apart.

"Kiera was a *job*, Darian, which is why I was even in these goddess-forsaken woods to begin with. It's what I *do*. I gather information on people, seek them out, and then I track them down so I can ruin their lives. Once in a while, when the money's right, I bring someone back and don't ask questions. So in a way, this is sort of *your* fault—if I hadn't let you tie me to that tree, I would have taken her to Eryce and walked away richer, never knowing who or what she was. Now that I know, I would rather do everything I can to keep her away from him."

He paused to turn his attention to the tree Kiera was sleeping in, Henelce and Alyk curled up on the ground below her. None of them had stirred. Connor dusted his hands off, searching the ground for another victim before he moved to the next thing on his mind.

"Don't forget that she's *human*, Darian."

"What is *that* supposed to mean, *Dirtbag*? That I shouldn't love her? Protect her? *Want* her? What does it matter to me that she's *human*?"

"It means that you have no idea how to be anything other than what *you* are, and *she* won't ever be strong enough to take that on. Not fully, no matter how much of your blood you give her." He glanced up at the Aeroyn, half expecting the beast to be coming toward him, but Darian had his head in his hands.

"Is that why you're banished?" Connor asked quietly. Darian didn't answer at first, but by the way he stiffened, Connor knew he had struck a vein. "Does she know?"

"No . . ." Darian's answer was muffled, and Connor suddenly had to fight to keep his own voice down.

"Oh, for the love of Tirath, Darian, you're not even being *honest* with her! You hid what she *is* from her, you abandoned her, and now you want to challenge me for *protecting* her? I turned *traitor* because of what she is, not because she *happened* to cross my path—" Connor suddenly shut his mouth and took a deep breath, trying to get himself back under control before he said too much.

He actually felt a little sorry for Darian because the Aeroyn was getting more and more likely to end up the loser in this, no matter what. If Kiera chose to follow *him*, Darian was going to be by himself once more, and that thought felt heavy and depressing. *This is too serious. I can't keep this up.*

"Darian, can I ask you a question and have you answer me honestly?"

The Aeroyn sighed and dropped his hands, looking at Connor for the first time without the threat of death present in his gaze. "*What?*" he snapped.

"Did you *know* that there were *ants* on that damned tree when you tied me to it? Those little bastards itch like hell."

Darian just stared at him for a moment, but once he started shaking with quiet laughter, Connor couldn't keep a straight face anymore. He had hated Darian so much at that moment, but it was funny now that he looked back. It was something *he* would have done.

"I can see why she likes you," Darian chuckled, the break in the tension coming as sort of a relief.

"She doesn't. She thinks I'm an idiot," Connor sighed, smiling reverently. *And I hope she never stops.*

* * *

Kiera woke briefly to a warm kiss on her forehead and a familiar large hand in her hair.

"I'm sorry, *Princess*," Darian whispered.

"I *know, beast*," she sighed and shifted slightly on the branch. "Darian?"

"Yes?"

"Don't kill him."

He smiled sadly once her eyes were closed again, knowing she was already lost to him.

"I'll try."

Forty-Nine

"Thank Tirath *that's* over and done with!" Eryce bellowed as he angrily threw his gloves onto his bed, his valet following close behind and trying in vain to help the enraged King of Rhonendar out of his ceremonial robes. Eryce wasn't interested in the man's idea of proper removal; he pushed Calvin away and yanked his robes over his head, flinging them at his hired help.

"There! Now stop pestering me and *leave*!"

"Yes . . . yes, sire . . ." The valet stammered quietly, bolting from the room and letting the door slam in his frightened wake. Calvin knew better than to be in the way when Eryce was in one of his moods. Tirath only knew how many bodies he had dragged out of his sovereign's rooms at this late hour. Calvin wasn't at all interested in becoming one of them.

Eryce slammed his fist into the heavy post of his mahogany bed, making the entire piece of furniture complain loudly against the marble floor as it shifted. The king was seething, had been for over an hour, and now that he was in his rooms, he let his anger out on the inanimate objects in his path. His blood pressure was too high, his thin, white cotton shirt soaked with sweat, and the eye was burning in his skull.

"That *bitch*! In front of my entire court!" Eryce roared as he kicked one of the chairs in front of his fireplace, and it collided with the table next to it that held a crystal decanter. The sound of shattering glass filled the air, and the room suddenly stank of rum, the table tottering noisily as it regained its balance and settled back into place two feet from its original location.

No matter what Eryce destroyed in the room, it would pale in comparison to the damage that had been done by his wife that evening; Eryce's forty-third birthday celebration had been in the works for over a month, and Serra had ruined it in less than thirty seconds flat.

He might have understood *why* if he had been able to see it from *her* side . . .

* * *

Serra sat next to her husband at the elevated table in the center of the main hall of the Arx, looking mildly vacant. She had bled so heavily over the past few days that she knew she had lost another child, and she hadn't even bothered to tell him. She was too fragile now to carry anymore, and Serra knew her body was trying to tell her to stop. She thought back to Corengale and the man who had given her two of her three dead children, and she couldn't remember a good reason for hating Garegan.

Maybe she never really had.

Eryce, however . . .

Serra reflected on how little she cared for him anymore. His fight to keep her in his life had come fifteen years too late, and the past six in his presence had bordered on torture. She still felt the keen loss of all of the people who had suffered because of his love for her; Eryce had taken away everyone who mattered to her and tried to fill the void with just himself. Her whole world had been left to the whims of other people, and Eryce's name was on the list of those without her best interest in mind more than once.

Serra wondered again how she had ever loved him at all.

He treated her well enough, but whatever had been between them over two decades ago had started fading for her after Kiera was born. It was obliterated completely when Eryce buried both her parents and her children, and Serra had never forgiven him for taking her out of the life she found herself trying desperately to replicate. She never would.

Eryce has the perfect symbol for himself in that arrogant golden lion, she thought to herself, and not for the first time. Serra hated the animal he had adopted as his crest, the one that was splayed over his chest and that adorned every banner and servant in the room. Eryce had taken over her life like a male takes over a pride: fighting for the right to the females and killing the cubs of his predecessor to bring the females back into heat so only their heirs would live on. Serra felt that analogy hit far too close to home. She was his trophy, his "pride," and she shouldered the burden of being loved by the man at her side every time he turned her way.

Maybe that's why I'm being such a bitch to him on his birthday. She almost laughed outright, quietly enjoying Eryce's reaction as she ignored him on every count, including his demand that she stop drinking the heavy red wine after he noticed she was already on her third glass and hadn't touched her food.

She liked the feeling of control over him that feeding into his annoyance was giving her, and Serra wanted to push it as far as she could before he took that away too and send her out of the room like a servant or a child. She had long ago ceased to care who was watching them since they all knew anyway, and Serra hated the faces around them that were starting to blur too. They all tried to be respectful, but she could always see the pity in their eyes as they let her avoided talking about her past, Corengale fading into oblivion like it had never existed . . .

Eryce reached out and grabbed her wrist when she went for her glass again, startling her out of her heavy thoughts. Serra felt something in her finally snap, the navy velvet dress Eryce had ordered made for her rustling slightly as she turned bodily toward him, fire in her drunken eyes.

"What are you going to do, Eryce? You can't take any more away from me than you already have. Just kill me and be done with it. You know you've thought about it. I see it in your face when you look at me," Serra hissed maliciously as she leaned toward him, not bothering to try to cover that she was inebriated as the dignitaries and councilmen within earshot looked on uncomfortably.

"Go to bed, Serra. You're tired. I'll excuse this poor display . . . for now." Eryce hadn't wanted to threaten her, but she was very good at getting under his skin in just the right way as she purposely embarrassed him. Serra tried to shake Eryce's hand off her arm, and when he didn't let go, she suddenly stood and knocked over her chair, letting it bang loudly against the raised wooden floor.

The entire room of four hundred guests went quiet.

"You should have just left me there!" she shrieked, startling her husband and everyone in the hall. Serra yanked her arm from Eryce's grip and stormed out of the room, leaving every set of eyes trying to look anywhere but at him...

* * *

Eryce was leaning back against the heavy mahogany desk in his room, his knuckles white as he griped the edge of the sturdy piece of furniture, finally able to calm down and think straight as the minutes had turned into nearly an hour and midnight approached.

When his thoughts turned to his wife this time, he couldn't help the guilt that crept in alongside the images of her that he had carried in the back of his mind for a good three quarters of his life. He had loved Serra enough to take her away from Garegan, but the damage inflicted by him had shaken her mental foundations until they started to crumble. Eryce was well aware that Serra blamed him most of all for the turns her life had taken; Tirath knew she told him enough. She blamed him for not fighting for her when their father had married her off, for killing her entire family, and now because she couldn't seem to bear any more children after their twins.

Deep down, he knew she wasn't wrong.

Serra had told Eryce once that she fought with him more than she ever had with Garegan because she hated Garegan *less*, and she was no longer the woman he had known and loved all those years ago. Since her arrival at the Arx, she had taken to drinking heavily, a habit she probably still thought he didn't know about, and over the past *year*, almost every conversation between them had ended with her screaming at him, and he had avoided her more and more.

Why dwell on these depressing thoughts, great king? Go to Serra, Eryce. End her pain. Let her go. The eye burned brightly in the socket, heat and light making it more than uncomfortable, and it was whispering in the back of his brain that it was hungry. It wasn't the first time that particular thought had surfaced, but this time, he was seriously considering giving in. His head and heart were pounding, and Eryce felt to pull of its will, urging his feet toward the door, trying to gain control . . .

Screams from down the hall took precedent over the persistence of the eye as they distracted him back into the present.

"Sire, we tried to stop her!" Calvin cried as he burst through the door, his voice and eyes wild with panic, but Eryce was already past the valet and headed for Serra's rooms thirty feet down the hall.

Her door stood open, her maid was sobbing on the floor, and the drapes were fluttering in the late summer air. Eryce held onto the frame of the door, trying to stay steady on his feet.

He didn't have to enter the room.

He knew it was over.

From four floors up, Serra had made the decision to end her life.

The eye was suddenly very quiet.

Fifty

"Arveneg, come *on!*" Alyk whispered as he yanked on the reins to no avail; he was having a hard time getting the horse away from the tree Kiera was perched in, worried that either the mare or his quiet swearing at the big animal might wake her. The white-haired woman was apparently still asleep even though the morning was well under way, and he was trying to get the stubborn black mare the leave quietly.

Arveneg was having none of it.

As it so happened, Kiera *was* awake, and she had been for a while; she was just taking stock of her aches and pains from the previous day without moving or opening her eyes. She shifted slightly, turning her head so she could see what Alyk was doing, and was met with the soft nose of a large horse sniffing curiously at her. It had been a long time since Kiera had been around horses, but she had loved riding when she was younger. Memories of racing her brother across an open field brought with them a feeling of joy, and she remembered her own beast rather fondly . . .

Kiera reached out and patted the nose with the white lip, thinking she recognized those big, black eyes.

"Come *away*, you stupid horse! I'm sorry if she's bothering you, Bane. She just won't *listen*." Alyk tugged on the reins again, and the horse ignored him completely.

"I'm not surprised. *Listening* was never her forte."

Alyk stopped trying to get the horse's attention, staring instead at the woman above him with a confused expression, wondering if he had heard her right. Kiera ran her hand up the horse's face and scratched behind her ears, and Arveneg responded by rubbing her head against the branch Kiera suddenly had to cling tightly to so she wouldn't fall.

Both of the humans started laughing as the horse shook the entire tree until the scent of honey filled the air and flooded his senses. Alyk held his breath, trying to fight against her call . . .

"Stop that, you silly beast! Shh, I missed you too." Kiera was whispering in the horse's ear, nuzzling her face against the Arveneg's soft nose as the honey scent slowly dissipated. She smiled warmly and patted the thick neck before she pushed the beast away and rolled off the branch.

"Bane?"

"*Kiera*," she corrected disgustedly. "Please call me by my real name, Alyk. I hate Bane."

"I, uh, sorry . . . *Kiera*, do you *know* this horse?"

"I *should*. She was mine. I never thought I would see this menace again." Arveneg was calming as Kiera stroked the horse's neck and withers, ignoring the man who still had the reins in his hand that stood just a foot or two away.

"You know, I kept thinking you were going to fall out of that tree last night. How do you even sleep like that?"

Kiera smiled to herself, the question striking her as funny considering she had been sleeping in the forest since well before she had ever ended up having to survive in it.

"You said you were from Corengale. Did you ever see me running around in boy's clothes? My hair was darker then." Kiera turned her attention from the beast before her to address the man that would have been one of her subjects. Part of her was glad that class distinction no longer existed when he answered her with a question of his own.

"You mean, like you do *now*?"

"I—" She looked down at her dirty tunic and boots in embarrassment, making Alyk laugh and Kiera smile sheepishly. "I suppose I do still run around like a *boy*, don't I?"

"Yes, I saw you like that on several occasions. I remember being envious that you were able to run off and go play in the river on hot days when I had to help Deidric with his armor, and clean up after the horses, and sharpen swords—"

"My mother would be furious!" Kiera interjected, snorting a laugh at the memory. "Oh, I used to come home with leaves in my hair and scrapes up my arms on days when we were entertaining, and I was supposed to already be in a dress and ignoring everyone at the dinner table. And my father, he didn't care *what* I did with my free time. I was already betrothed, so as long as I came home in one piece, he was happy to just let me do whatever made me happy . . ."

Kiera grew quiet, suddenly looking at the ground to hide how saddened she was that the family she spoke of no longer existed, even if it felt oddly good to talk about them with someone who knew. She missed the surprised expression on Alyk's face when she mentioned the betrothal, but he recovered before she looked at him again, blinking back her tears.

"Thank you for that, Alyk. It has been too long since I had good memories of my family brought back to me. I hadn't realized how much I *miss* them." Kiera felt a lump in her throat trying to form as she leaned against Arveneg and stroked the horse's withers, her white hair a stark contrast against the black coat of the mare. Kiera found it comforting to have something so familiar near her, even if it no longer belonged to her.

"I remember them well, and I think your father would be rather proud that you've made it this far, Kiera." Alyk put a hand on her shoulder and gave it a gentle squeeze.

"I just wish I could ask him what all of you have been asking me in your own way." She smiled sadly, and Alyk dropped his hand back to his side.

"And what is that?"

"What do I do next?"

Fifty-One

"Good morning," Connor whispered.

"I see you've learned the right phrase for this time of day, *Dirtbag*."

"You better be well rested, woman, because I'm going to run you *ragged* later," Connor threatened huskily as he wrapped his arms around Kiera from behind. He hadn't slept much, but he wasn't going to let being *tired* get in the way of teasing her.

She leaned back into his arms and intertwined her fingers with his, no longer caring if the others saw the affection, not that anyone was nearby to see anyway. Alyk and Henelce were tending to their horses, and Darian wasn't anywhere close either; he had left when the moons were high to hunt and sleep higher up, and Kiera knew him well enough that he probably wasn't even awake yet. It didn't matter. They were all well aware by now where things stood between her and Connor, and now she was ready to defend it.

The scent of mint and cedar flooded the air around her, and Kiera inhaled deeply, enjoying the scent she was starting to associate with *him* before bursting his bubble.

"I swear to Tirath that cock is the only thing you think with," she chided. "You realize we're not *alone* anymore, *right*?"

"Yeah, about that. I had a *thought*, and I wanted to see if you might be interested." Connor kissed her temple, and she felt the pull of her healing chest as the skin stretched when she leaned her head back against his shoulder. Kiera winced and started to tremble.

"Are you all right?" Connor's voice was full of concern, and Kiera started to shake harder. When the odd trembling turned from silent laughter into giggling, Connor sighed and shook his head.

"A *thought*? Was that a *new* sensation for you?" she sputtered, trying to keep her voice down.

"Woman, you're going to *regret* teasing me," he growled.

"You started it, *idiot* . . ."

Connor held her tighter, thoroughly enjoying the moment, even if he was about to ruin it. He was glad that she felt good enough to laugh, but there were serious things on his mind, and he needed her to pay attention. He waited until she stopped shaking and settled against him once more.

"I know I asked you to go with me, but I didn't tell you where I was headed. If you *are* interested in following me, you may not be so inclined once you know, but listen for a moment before you say *no*. I need to gather my porting crystals, which in reality should only take three minutes, but there's one that I haven't used in months, and I'm worried it won't be easy to get to. That's the journey I was talking about when we were at the river. I need to retrieve that crystal, and I want you to go with me."

"Where, *exactly*, is that crystal?" The way Connor shifted made Kiera wonder if she really wanted to know.

"A, uh, graveyard . . . in the mountains . . ."

"Why in the *world* would you ever need to go to a graveyard?"

"*I* didn't. My mentor had it on him, and . . . well . . . that's where he was buried last winter. I haven't had the chance to get it back."

Kiera suddenly untangled herself from Connor's embrace and stood back to face him, a look of disbelief etched on her face. Connor's hand went to the back of his neck as he smiled sheepishly at her.

"So, wait, let me see if I have this right . . ." Kiera held up her hand and started counting her next words off with her fingers. "*First*, you want me to go with you to a graveyard, *then* desecrate a grave, and *then* help you get a crystal off a *dead man*?" Kiera asked incredulously, crossing her arms, shifting her weight. She didn't like this idea at *all*.

Connor simply nodded.

"Are you *joking*? Please tell me you're joking." She studied him, looking for cracks in his mask of honesty.

"Dead serious."

"Connor!" Kiera smacked his arm, and he laughed at his own bad pun, putting his hands up in defense.

"I *am* serious, I promise. Joseph died, and he wanted to be buried in the mountains. I didn't know until it was too late that he was gone, and his wife buried him with several of his items from our work because she didn't want others to get to them. That, unfortunately, included one of my crystals.

"I need that crystal, Kiera. It's the only one I can't port to, and I want to make sure you stay safe. I won't beg you to come along, but it could be pretty *fun* if you did . . ." Connor grinned, raising his eyebrows suggestively.

"I get the feeling there's more to this. What's the catch?" Kiera stared unwaveringly at him, and his smile faltered.

Damn it. She can already read me.

"No catch, but there *is* something else, and it's something I have to do *alone*. Digging up a friend is creepy, don't get me wrong, but I have to be very, very careful retrieving one other crystal—"

"Do I even want to know *where* you left that one?"

"Eryce's library," Connor blurted out before he could stop himself. Kiera visibly paled, that answer one she had been expecting even less than the first.

"Connor, there is something *seriously* wrong with you."

"*And*? You had already figured that out before you had sex with me. Several times, I might add. I was sort of hoping we could *continue* that trend," Connor purred as he reached out for her and pulled her against his chest. He lifted her chin and kissed her just gently enough for it to feel unfinished, and Kiera wrapped her arms around his neck, pulling him back down to her so she could kiss him properly.

"Is that a *yes*?" he breathed against her mouth.

"You can't just *leave* the one in the library?" Kiera replied quietly, looked up at Connor through her lashes, willing him to be reasonable or at least reasonably less interested in doing something very stupid and exceedingly dangerous.

"I *could*, but then I would be down another stone, and I happen to like them. I want to pass them to my kids someday."

"*You* want *children*?" She had not been expecting *that* to come out of his mouth. The idea of Connor dealing with little versions of himself struck Kiera as incredibly funny, and she rested her forehead against his chest as she started shaking again with silent laugher. It was Connor's turn to pale as he sighed and shook his head, worried that he was even talking like that.

"*Maybe*. One step at a time. I never thought I would find someone I wanted in my life. Might as well totally complicate things and add a couple of screaming brats to the mix. If I can find someone *stupid* enough to deal with me, then I see no point in screwing it up *halfway*." Connor's words may have been tinged with sarcasm, but his expression softened as he reached up and tucked a strand of hair behind her ear, touching her cheek with his thumb.

Kiera suddenly realized that he meant *her*.

"As *flattering* as you wondering if I am *dumb* enough to take on that responsibility might be, I thought you didn't know if you could change if it meant *keeping* me?"

"Now wait one second, woman. Who said I was talking about *you*?" Connor laughed quietly, loving that she was playing right along.

"Okay, *fine*. Then the answer is *no*." Kiera made a face at him as she pushed against his chest, trying to back away, but Connor wasn't about to let her go that easily. His face was suddenly serious, and he held her closer.

"What if it *is* you?" he whispered, almost afraid of her answer.

"*Still* not going . . ." Kiera looked up at him defiantly, but he could tell she was trying not to smile. Connor laughed, knowing he was winning.

"We'll see about *that*," he teased. "And while I'd like to stay here and fool around with you all day, my available time is getting short, and I need a serious answer. If you *are* interested in coming with me, I have a plan that I've been kicking around in my head for a couple of days now, so hear me out.

"As far as my crystals go, I can get to the first two easily. One is at home, and I would like to go there first. The other is at the Inn-land Starfish at the Breach, and my room is paid up for at least three more days. It's also the closest crystal to the graveyard, so that helps us. One is in Joseph's coffin, and *that* will take the longest to get to because we'll actually have to land travel so it will take maybe a week, but that makes three. The last is already at the Runes, and I have to head there anyway for the reignition, so once I have the once from Joseph's coffin, we can port directly to the Obilio and be done with the whole damned thing."

"That's only *four* stones, *Dirtbag*. I *can* count. When were you thinking of getting the one from Eryce's library?"

"*That* is an excellent question. I have no idea." Connor chewed his lip, thinking. "I'm trying to find a way to leave that one for last, and you will *not* be going with me. Eryce is unpredictable, so I won't know if he's is in the library or not when I port. That will be the hardest part because if he *is* there . . ." Connor felt his chest tighten when he thought of the possibility of leaving her for good.

Kiera was quiet as that sunk in. She hoped Connor knew what he was doing. *Well, he* has *gotten this far in life without killing himself.*

"Assuming I *am* dumb enough to follow you, when would we leave?"

"Is that a *yes*?" Connor almost choked on the words as he regarded her with genuine surprise. He had expected her to simply say *no*.

"That depends if I like the answer to my question."

"Oh, well, I would love to take you to see my home today *if* you're interested. I don't know that we'll see much more than the bedroom, but at least I can change clothes and get a hot bath."

"You don't do well in the wild, do you, *Dirtbag*?"

"Goddess *no*! I *hate* being dirty!"

"Only on the outside, apparently," Kiera giggled as Connor's hand went from her waist to her rear as he leaned down to kiss her. "You're *terrible!*"

"Fair is fair. I answered your question. Is that a *yes*?" he asked coyly, his mouth hovering just above hers.

"You're not going to give up, are you?"

"Not if you'll go. I'll pester you until you're so tired of me you say *okay* out of exasperation. Or maybe I'll just tie you to a tree and let the ants get you. See how *you* like it," he growled.

"You're far more annoying than ants could ever be, but threatening me won't get you a straight answer, considering you've already called me *stupid*. I hope I don't have to remind you that there is a *very* upset Aeroyn who will want to know my whereabouts. I can't just *leave* and not know if and when I'll be coming back. May I suggest a compromise?"

Kiera felt the pang of her own betrayal, knowing she was going to say *yes* once she told Darian. There was nothing he could do, but he was going to be hurt. She wasn't looking forward to that.

"No, Darian can't go." Connor's expression was so serious Kiera couldn't help but snort a laugh at the idea, finding it incredibly absurd.

"*That* wasn't what I was thinking, and I can assure you he wouldn't want to go anyway. You said you had been staying at the Starfish. Can we be back at the tavern by the time your room needs to be paid again?"

"Oh! Of *course*. Why?"

"Well, Henelce and Alyk said they were headed to the Runes, and I would want Darian to go with us into the Montes if he's willing. Can we ask if they would be willing to meet us at Grant's Perch and accompany us to the graveyard? It will take them a couple of days to get to the Breach anyway if they stick together, and I would feel better having more than just one *arrow attractor* at my side, traveling into a place I've never been."

Connor thought over the logistics of travelling as a group instead of just a pair into the Monte's Gelu and Aeroyn territory. Darian might have a problem with heading into his people's land when they got back; rather, his people might have something to say, probably with something pointy, but Alyk and Henelce as added protection was a welcome thought . . .

It was feasible if they all agreed. Connor had to admit it wasn't a bad idea, *and* it would give them a chance to spend a day or two at his home, far, far away from Baneswood. No one would find Kiera where they were going.

"I guess we can ask. This is a good plan. I like this plan. I never thought I would say this, but I like that it's *we* in this plan."

"I like it too." Kiera smiled up at him. "You seem to be making all sorts of changes since you met me."

"I *know*," Connor's face was suddenly grim. "And I'm terrified to see what *else* you'll get me to do."

Fifty-Two

"It's not my choice, Kiera. It's yours, and I can't make it for you."

No temper tantrum. No "absolutely not!" bellowed to the heavens. Kiera had been expecting an entirely different reaction. *Who is this Aeroyn, and what has he done with Darian?*

"That's it?" Kiera couldn't tell if she was surprised or worried when Darian simply shrugged and looked away. She had never seen him so nonchalant. Not when it came to *her*. "You realize that I would be gone for two days, and I have no clue *where*."

"As long as you come back in one piece, it's not a bad idea. I'm okay with it if this is what you want."

"You're *serious*." Kiera narrowed her eyes at Darian, waiting for the argument that never came. She hadn't expected this to be *easy*.

"I could have *sworn* I *just* said that." Darian heaved and exasperated sigh and finally looked up at her, the vivid green eyes trained on him a little unnerving in their intensity. "*What*, Kiera?"

"*You*. Something's *different*. I don't like it." Kiera looked him right in the eye, willing him to be straight with her. "What happened between yesterday and today?"

Darian pursed his dusky lips together, thinking. Kiera crossed her arms over her chest and shifted her weight, obvious impatience showing through loud and clear on her features as she waited. Darian finally let out a defeated breath and adopted her annoyed pose, mimicking her on purpose.

"What choice do I really have in the matter? You've already made a decision. I can see it written all over your face. Don't make this harder for me, *Princess*. I knew this was coming when I spoke to that *Dirtbag*, and he made his point . . ." Darian suddenly looked uncomfortable. "I can't even *argue* with it. I think I might . . . actually . . . *respect* him for it."

Kiera was wide eyed, her face contorted with complete disbelief at the words coming out of the Aeroyn she had known for too long and never seen act so *strangely*.

"Did Connor *threaten* you? Are you *feeling* all right?" She reached out to put her palm on his forehead. "I don't have to go you know—"

"Kiera, stop. I'm *fine*." Darian finally laughed as he peeled her hand off his face, holding it in his. "The fact that I'm even *part* of this plan and that you're *asking* this of me helps to make it at least somewhat bearable, but don't think I won't hunt him down and rip him to pieces if you end up hurt. It's not an easy thing to let you go, but if this is what you want to do, I'm not going to try to stop you.

"However, if you *are* going to follow that *idiot*, just you remind Connor to keep his hands to himself when you get back here. Watching him molest you was *not* what I wanted to wake up to this morning."

Kiera turned bright red as she hurried to close the gap between them. She wrapped her arms around him, hugging him tightly so he wouldn't see her threatening tears.

"I love you, *beast*," she whispered against his chest.

Darian held her for a moment, breathing her in, already feeling like she was totally gone.

"I love you too, *brat*. Now go, before you change your mind."

Fifty-Three

"Connor? What is that *noise*?"

Kiera thought the roaring in her ears was from the porting itself, but it continued when she opened her eyes. A strange crashing sound that was muffled by solid walls filled the air, and it came and went with an odd repetition, almost like a slow, stuttering heartbeat.

"That, my dear, is the *ocean*."

Part Two

Fifty-Four

A sky that should have been blue was gray in the late morning light with the fog still hugging the eastern coast of Rhonendar, the moisture in the air clinging to every surface it could find. It was cooler there, several hundred miles away from her home, and Kiera pulled Connor's heavy cloak tighter around her as she stood alone on the second floor balcony, taking it all in.

Sea air was so completely different than that in the forest, the sound of the gulls piercing the late morning gloom the only birdsong Kiera could hear over the concussive noise of the waves crashing below her as something called a *tide* came in. The salt spray created a mist outside the three story stone villa that belonged to Connor, the sea ceaselessly throwing itself against the cliff the house was built upon a little unnerving as its power made the floor under her feet tremble.

The small *palace* where she was now a guest was large enough to house at least ten people in separate rooms, and it seemed like a sprawling waste of space for just one man. Then again, she had a whole forest for a bedroom, and the only other home she had known was a much larger castle full of people, so it was hard for her to gauge.

Kiera had forgotten how good it could feel to be in a *home*, and Connor had nice taste. The rooms were big but well furnished, if not a little masculine with dark wood furniture and neutral colors throughout, but it definitely felt like *his*, and she had liked it immediately.

The crystal was situated in Connor's office on the first floor of the house, and the only time he was ever in that room was when he was working or when he ported home. The room was the same mess he usually liked it to be with piles of paper and random items stacked haphazardly on the big oak desk and the shelves that lined one white wall half empty. The office was his private sanctuary, and while his staff knew better than to try and clean, he suddenly wished he didn't have that standing order in place as they both nearly tripped over the piles of books he had left strewn about.

Kiera didn't seem to notice the mess like he did as she inhaled deeply and took in her new surroundings, the room smelling of parchment and ink and faintly of cloves. She turned around to find that only half the room was cluttered; the other half was completely bare, save for a small weapons rack that held a fairly plain broadsword, a staff, and a small dagger, a woven mat covering that portion of the marble floor.

Connor wasn't about to let Kiera stay in there. It was full of things she wasn't going to like if she started doing anything other than glancing around, and he would rather show her the world outside of a room that Connor wasn't sure he wanted to set foot in ever again. His office was sort of an oxmoron for him as he had never needed the money but had enjoyed the work, but he had made a pact with himself that it was all going to come to a stop if it meant keeping this woman in his life. Connor grinned at Kiera and took her hand, dragging her behind him out of the room that was all too familiar to him and completely foreign to her.

He opened the office door and pulled Kiera into a short hallway, wanting to show her the rest of the much cleaner space he called home.

"Anybody home?" Connor's voice echoed throughout the house, his loud words reverberating off the marble floors and the stark walls of the lower level.

"Boy, stop yelling! I'm old, not dead!" came the reply from the other end of the hall.

Both of them jumped as they were immediately accosted by Peter, Connor's valet and groundskeeper. Kiera hadn't expected anyone to even answer, much less be only a few steps away from where they had appeared, and Peter seemed just as surprised by her presence; his eyes went wide when he saw that Connor had a woman in tow.

"So that is why you've been gone." Peter pushed his silver spectacles up his narrow nose until they were back in place in front of his faded blue eyes, looking Kiera over like he would rather take her outside and scrub her down with a horse brush and a bucket of cold water than let her roam the house in what she had on.

"Peter, you be nice to her. This is Kiera, and she will be—"

"Yes, yes, all well and good, but that girl needs a bath and some new clothes." Peter waved Connor aside and circled Kiera, looking her over. "Where on earth did you find her? Does she even speak Common? Well, girl, speak up! Do you?"

Kiera was trying to decide if she was offended or if she wanted to laugh. She already felt like a bedraggled mess in her bloodied tunic and dirty boots, the old man now in her face making her back up instinctively.

"You leave her alone, you old grouch! You'll get your way soon enough, but behave." Connor stepped between them, and the old man's eyes went right to the shirt that Alyk had given Connor the day before.

"Bringing home some mess of a girl, dressed in these rags . . . Do I even want to know what you have been up to?" Peter looked up fearlessly at Connor with his hands on his hips, reminding Kiera of Henelce. Connor towered over the man, knowing Peter was totally flustered and trying not to show it.

"I'm sorry, you would think I work for you! I need a hot bath and something decent to eat, and I haven't slept much in the past few days, so don't go pushing your luck. Go do your job and leave me be, Peter. If I need you further, I will call for you."

Peter puffed up his thin chest, looking thoroughly offended as he turned on his heel and stomped off. Connor shook his head as he reached for Kiera's hand, grinning broadly.

"Sorry about that, and yes, he's always like that. Has been since I was a child, so don't take him personally. He's just glad I'm home. Now, let me show you the rest of it."

Connor led Kiera quickly through the first floor of the house, letting her get a glimpse the big expanse of the sparsely furnished main hall, the dining room that sat at least sixteen, and the library. None of the rooms felt as lived in as the office had, making it seem a little more like a museum than a place of residence, but Connor wasn't interested in really showing her the lower floor. They would have to climb the stairs if they were ever going to make it to the room he really wanted her in . . .

Their tour was interrupted halfway through as Connor's housekeeper, Viola, entered the library with a feather duster and squealed in delight to see him.

"You're home! With a girl! It's about time! This castle needs a princess!" Viola pushed past Connor as though he didn't exist, curtsying quickly before taking Kiera's hands in hers and beaming up at her with a welcoming smile. Viola was a petite, middle-aged brunette with kind brown eyes, and she was absolutely thrilled that Kiera was in the house, no matter what she had on.

"Now, Viola . . . don't start . . ." Connor tried in vain to stop her, but the bubbly woman paid him absolutely no mind as she overwhelmed Kiera completely with her attention, making Kiera want to hide behind the man she suspected had known this, too, was coming by the exasperated way he rolled his eyes.

"Oh, Connor! Shush! What is your name, my dear? You are so very welcome in this house, and I hope you like something other than cured meat and cheese because this brute only eats that junk even though he knows I am a perfectly capable cook. What do you like to eat? Such pretty green eyes! How did you meet Connor—?"

"Viola, you will have plenty of time to bother Kiera later. Go help Peter. I think he's in the kitchen." Connor played the one card he knew would shut her up, and it worked like it always did when he wanted her to leave him the hell alone.

"He had better not be! He knows better! Kiera . . . What a lovely name! I must say it's nice to have a pretty face in the house, but please excuse me, as I have to go get a rat out of my pantry." Viola winked at Connor before she hurried away from them, yelling for Peter. Kiera let out a breath she had been holding, wondering if this had been such a good idea after all.

"You knew that was coming, didn't you?" Kiera looked up at him accusingly. Connor didn't say anything as he grabbed her hand and pulled her upstairs into his room where he was safe to flop backward onto his bed and start laughing hysterically. He had never brought a girl home, and now he knew why he had avoided it.

"Thanks for the warning, Dirtbag." Kiera kicked him in the leg, which only made him laugh harder; she huffed in annoyance and walked to the window to look outside, only to be met by a wall of gray, so she turned her focus onto the room itself.

There was a large, white porcelain tub next to the fire on one side of the room while the heavily carved four-poster bed made of dark wood dominated the other, covered with white sheets and a green-and-gold damask comforter and piled with about a dozen pillows. A desk, a vanity with a mirror, and a plush brown chair rounded out the furnishings, and a thick, circular white rug in the middle of the room covered most of the dark wooden floor that ran throughout the second story.

It was simple, clean, and comfortable, and it had Connor written all over it.

The walls of the castle Kiera had grown up in had always had tapestries and portraits adorning the walls, but there was only one piece of art in the room: a large mural of a blue dragon covered the wall over the fireplace, its flaming breath seeming to be the source of the fire already burning in the grate.

Kiera was still studying it closely when Connor finally gained control of himself. She barely heard him when he sat up to pull off his boots and yank Alyk's borrowed shirt over his head, promptly throwing it on the floor. He climbed off the bed and came after her in just his torturous leather pants, wanting to welcome her properly to his own, private world.

"Fancy meeting you here . . ." Connor purred in her ear. Kiera turned bodily toward him, and he immediately pulled her into his arms. When she leaned back in his embrace and reached up to run her hand over his chin, Connor's expression morphed to one of disgust. "Ugh, I know. This cactus on my face is such a menace."

"I kind of like it. You would fit right in with me in Baneswood now. It's very 'forest ruffian.'"

"You take that back!"

Kiera giggled as he pulled her closer, leaning in to kiss her . . .

They didn't get that far. Kiera's face turned bright red when Peter pushed his way grumpily into the room with a tray of sandwiches and found them wrapped up in each other. Peter ignored them completely as he set the tray on the desk and crossed the room to start the water for the tub as though Connor wasn't glaring at him.

"Bath and a shave for you first, boy. That poor girl is going to need a good soak to get all that dirt off her." Peter continued to ignore them as he busied himself with opening drawers to the vanity and removing the things Connor would need to clean up. The man took a moment to look over his handiwork, double checking that everything was where it should be before he turned his attention onto Connor.

Kiera thought Peter was going to have a heart attack when he took a good look at the man he had obviously taken care of for a very long time.

"Boy, get out of those ridiculous pants! I am throwing those away!"

Connor rolled his eyes, the argument an old one.

"Peter, get out. I can do all this myself. And the pants stay . . ."

Kiera smiled to herself, her first memories of Connor's home already good ones. It felt odd, really, to be there, but she was glad it wasn't a small, cramped house; Kiera wasn't sure she could trade acres of trees and running water for something that made her feel claustrophobic, even if it was only temporary. Connor's home felt open and airy with its high ceilings, white plaster walls, and the large arched windows that faced the bay.

Kiera's eyes wandered along the barely visible coastline, and she could just make out a few of the homes and businesses of Siren's Bay that stood three or four miles to the north while the fog obscured a majority of the city. The house was close to civilization but far enough away that it still felt secluded, even without a dense forest surrounding it like she was used to. There was a copse of very tall trees that Kiera didn't know were eucalyptus a little further down the cliff in the other direction, but most of the land flanked either side of the house seemed to be rolling hills of green grass punctuated by the occasional shrub. It was a dramatic change to the scenery she was used to but beautiful to her nonetheless.

Kiera took a deep breath of the salty air and caught a whiff of mint and cedar.

"Your bath is ready, *Princess*."

She could hear the smirk in his voice he approached her from behind, rubbing his hair with a thick towel. Clean shaven and redressed in a white long-sleeved silk shirt that was untied at the neck and tucked into fitted black wool pants, Connor looked far more natural in that setting than he had out in the woods. Kiera noticed that his boots had been polished, all of his clothing obviously expensive . . .

And incredibly sexy.

"What, *exactly*, am I supposed to wear once I'm out? I don't have anything clean, and Peter will throw a tantrum if I show up anywhere in this house in these same clothes."

"Oh, I have something you can *wear*, all right." Connor's mouth erupted into a wicked grin. "*Me*."

"Then I'll just need another *bath* . . ." Kiera sighed dramatically and rolled her eyes.

"I'll wrap you in a sheet if I have to, but Peter wants your measurements so he can go to town and find you something *appropriate*." Connor reached into the cloak and found her hand, dragging Kiera back into the house, but she held her ground and raised her eyebrows.

"*A-ppropriate?*"

"Woman, I'm happy to have you naked the whole time, but Viola and Peter may *frown* on that when we go downstairs for dinner." Connor tugged her almost off her feet and pulled her into the house, closing the leaded glass door behind them so the roaring and the cold suddenly diminished. The water in the tub was invitingly warm when Kiera crossed the room to put her hand into it. The steam that rose off it smelled sweet and soft like honeysuckle.

"*That* is going to have to wait for a moment." He pulled her away from the tub, stopping her short in the middle of the room. "Stand here . . ." Connor lifted her chin and locked eyes with her, his expression bordering on mischievous. ". . . and *trust* me."

Connor's eyes never left hers as he untied the cloak and pushed it off her shoulders, letting it hit the floor and puddle around her feet. Only once he lifted her hands so that she held them palm up as he undid the buckles of her right bracer did he shift his focusthe left, tossing the dark brown hide pieces behind her once they had been stripped from her wrists.

"Lift your arms."

Kiera complied, and he pulled her tunic over her head and dropped it on the rug. His gaze wandered over the still fresh spattering of nicks on her chest, silently relieved that they were almost healed by whatever amount of Aeroyn blood was still running through her veins. He ran his fingers lightly over her collarbone, careful to avoid the tiny wounds that marred her pale skin.

He moved closer as though he intended to kiss her but crouched down and lifted her foot instead, pulling off one boot then the other until Kiera was barefoot on the soft rug. Standing and moving behind her, Connor ran his hands over her shoulders to gather her hair and push it over her left shoulder, enjoying the slight shiver that resulted in gooseflesh under his touch.

He traced her mark lightly for a moment before allowing his hands to wander between her shoulder blades in search of the ends of the ties that kept her fitted leather bodice in place. Connor undid the knot and started unlacing it slowly, deliberately pulling each crossing of string with one finger completely from the battered and worn piece of armor, watching what his hand was doing while she held her hair out of the way.

Connor realized he wasn't just *enjoying* this; he was *savoring* it as he slipped his hands under the heavy leather piece, peeling it off the woman he would rather feel under his hands. The bodice, too, found the floor, and Connor let his fingers trail down the indentations where the boning and layers of leather had left marks on her back, Kiera's breathing changing as he touched her. Connor wrapped one hand forward around her waist and pulled her naked back against his silk shirt as he leaned forward and ran his right hand down over her hip . . .

Connor kissed her shoulder, sucking lightly at her skin as his fingers undid the buckle that held her thigh strap in place. Kiera barely noticed as the familiar piece fell away, her eyes closed as she concentrated on what every touch from Connor felt like. The warmth from his hand on her stomach cooled rapidly when he removed it, making her shiver and her nipples harden.

Kiera actually *liked* being naked, but it had never felt this *good*. Being undressed by Connor was incredibly erotic, and she was reveling in every second of it. She felt Connor back away slightly so he could push her leggings off her hips, his hands following the contours of her legs as he removed the finally piece of offending clothing and she stepped out of it, quietly watching Connor pick up her tunic and the leggings . . .

. . . and then walk right up to the fire to throw them in.

So much for erotic!

"Hey!" Kiera put her hands on her hips, suddenly annoyed. *Naked* and annoyed. "Those were *mine*!"

"*Relax*, woman. I didn't get rid of your boots or your armor. Just the things I won't ever have to see on you again. Now hold still." Connor had a lopsided smile on his mouth picked up a cloth measuring tape, a pencil and a piece of paper from the desk. He stood in front of her and dropped the pencil and paper at her feet.

"Arms out," he commanded, and Kiera sighed, stubbornly keeping her hands on her hips, thoroughly irritated over her clothes that were rapidly becoming ash a few feet away. Connor crossed his arms over his chest, his expression stern.

"You do realize that you are in no position to argue, *right*? You're naked, hundreds of miles from home, and under *my* roof. I would think carefully before you decide to get all high and mighty over a few *rags* that I'm going to replace with something that does you *justice*."

Kiera debated inwardly if she wanted to refute him, but she finally caved and lifted her arms to hold them straight out.

"Thank you. Now quit fooling around so I can continue *torturing* us both," Connor whispered huskily in her ear as he started his measurements.

Kiera smiled and closed her eyes as he wrapped the tape forward around her bust, his fingers purposely grazing her nipples as he brought it together between her breasts and read the numbers. He wrapped his arms around her waist, running his fingertips over her skin as he brought the tape together, trying to concentrate on the numbers instead of the woman under his hands. She could feel his breath on her stomach as Connor read the tape and made his notes. He repeated the motion on her hips, and Kiera felt her heart pick up speed, the anticipation of his touch making her hypersensitive, every caress magnified.

"Arms down."

Connor's voice was soft, and Kiera let her arms relax slowly. Her skin broke out in gooseflesh again as Connor touched the end of the tape to the top of her shoulder and ran it down her arm. He moved to the nape of her neck and pressed the tape down the length of her back, off her hips and all the way to the floor. He knelt there, pushing Kiera's feet slightly apart, bringing the tape up to the very top of the inside of her thigh, his fingers just barely brushing her, making her shiver.

Connor let his hand linger . . .

Kiera could feel his hesitation, both of them wanting to take it further, but Connor broke the spell by trailing his fingers up and around her hip as he stood back up. Kiera was mildly disappointed, but the last measurement Connor took was around her neck, and he faced her for that one, using the tape to pull Kiera forward so he could kiss her deeply.

"Okay," he breathed against her mouth when he finally broke the kiss. "Now get in the tub so I can go give that crabby old man downstairs a *purpose* in life."

After all the torture she had just undergone, Kiera wasn't going to let him out of the room that easily; she wrapped her arms around his neck and pressed her naked form against him, trying to get Connor to bend and take her right there on the rug.

Connor was breathing hard when he eventually pulled back and tried to untangle himself from Kiera's embrace. He had dropped the measuring tape on the floor in favor of touching Kiera instead, and she laughed when he groaned as he bent to pick it back up. He folded it neatly, collecting the paper and the rest of her gear, trying to put space between them and catch his breath.

"I'll see what I have lying around that you can wear for a while, but I wasn't kidding when I said it's probably just going to be *me*."

"Connor, wait—"

"Why? Are you going to call me an *idiot*?"

"*No*," Kiera smiled as she approached him cautiously. "You could have done a lot of things over the past few days, but you chose to give me a reason to trust you instead. So I want to thank you for already making this feel so . . . *good*."

"Don't thank me yet, Kiera. Give it time. It may get *better*. You can thank me *then*." Connor winked at her and left without another word though the ones that rang through his brain made him smile as he descended the stairs.

I may just try to top this every day for the rest of my life.

Fifty-Five

The only time Kiera ever took a hot bath was in the winter, and then it was a chore, and the water never stayed warm for long. She could feel the tension seeping out of her as she sat there, neck deep in warmth, her hair wet from submersing herself completely, watching the fire dance in the hearth. Taking a bath had been something she had hated as a child, begrudgingly accepted as a teenager, and missed thoroughly now that she was an adult.

That had changed now that it was a luxury instead of a necessity, and she wondered how she had ever hated the smell of the soap, how soft her skin felt once it was thoroughly cleaned, the way her scalp tingled since she had scrubbed away the dirt and sweat . . .

Goddess Tirath, I have missed this. Two days of civilization is going to be too short. I can already feel it.

Connor opened the door quietly, smiling when he heard her sigh contentedly as he entered the room, purposely making a noise so Kiera would know he was behind her. He already liked the idea of her sharing this space with him, and he had been thinking of ways to keep her there as he gave instructions to both Peter and Viola, including those to leave them the hell alone until dinner was on the table.

"Peter left for town and should be back in a few hours. Until then, it's just you and me."

"*And* Viola . . ."

"Thankfully, she's at the other end of the house, cooking like I have a dinner party scheduled instead of just one beautiful *princess* as my guest." Connor laughed quietly when Kiera threw him an irritated glance over her shoulder. He leaned against the high footboard of his bed, directly behind her, waiting for her to get out of the tub. "I didn't tell her who you were though I've certainly had to evade enough questions about you. But it wouldn't matter if you were a housemaid or the Queen of the Moons—that woman *always* overreacts."

"Hand me that towel, would you?" Kiera leaned her head back against the rim of the tub, looking up at him through her lashes, giving him a warm smile.

As soon as he moved to do what she had asked, Kiera stood up, letting the water pour off her, reaching for the towel in his outstretched hand, smiling faintly to herself when she heard Connor's breath catch.

"Woman, you are going to *kill* me if you keep that up . . ."

She had turned her back on him to wrap herself in the soft cloth, and she glanced over her shoulder with an innocent look. Kiera knew *exactly* what she was doing, and after the torture of getting measured, Connor could wait until she was *dry*.

Kiera stepped out onto the rug, turning her profile to him as she slowly wiped away the droplets still clinging to her, starting with her arms and working her way down. She heard his breathing change as Connor watched the towel touching her curves from a little more than a foot away, and by the time she bent to dry her legs, he'd had enough.

"I don't care if you're still *wet*," Connor declared as he yanked the towel away, throwing it aside. "I've been doing things to you in my brain for almost an entire day, and now that I have you to myself, it's time to let them *out*." Connor picked her up and walked her over to the bed, and Kiera laughed when he unceremoniously dropped her on top of the down comforter, which puffed up around her like a cloud.

"Is that any way to treat a *lady*?" Kiera cried with feigned indignation.

"Of course not, but you won't be a *lady* until I see you in a *dress*. Until then, you're still a forest ruffian, and I will treat you any way I *please*."

Kiera laughed harder as he pulled his shirt over his head and kicked off his boots. Connor crawled onto the bed, supporting himself on all fours, straddling her thigh and pinning her down.

"Hey! Why am I the only one totally naked?" She poked him in the chest, still giggling.

"I want to take my time . . . and if I take my pants off now . . . it won't last very long," he replied between kisses.

"Funny, I don't . . . remember *any* of the other night . . . being terribly *short*," Kiera retorted, her words punctuated by Connor's attempts to shut her up.

"You *must* be joking . . ." Connor brushed the damp hair away from her neck so he could kiss his way down her collar bone. "Just *trust* me."

"I do, Connor. If I didn't, I wouldn't be here." Kiera caught his face in her hands before he could move further. The way her chest tightened before the words in her head escaped her mouth told her they were true.

"Connor . . . I-I think I love you."

"Oh, thank Tirath! And here I thought I was the only one!" Connor was being obnoxious, and Kiera smacked his cheek playfully, suppressing a giggle.

"I mean it, Connor. I love you." Kiera felt her heart pick up when she said it, and Connor's expression softened.

"Kiera, you loved me the first time you *touched* me. You just didn't know it yet." Connor caressed her face, running his thumb across her cheek, and Kiera closed her eyes, leaning into his palm.

It's amazing how things can change in just a few short days.

Kiera let go of Connor's face and wrapped her fingers around his wrist, bringing his palm to her mouth, kissing the center. She kissed her way to the end of his index finger, biting the tip gently, slightly opening her eyes to find him staring at her, barely breathing. Connor groaned when she took his entire finger into her mouth, sucking lightly, pulling it out slowly . . .

"Okay, Crazy Lady of the Forest, that's just about enough of *that*." Connor sounded like he was having a hard time concentrating on even getting the words out of his mouth. Kiera smiled and went for his thumb instead. She felt him shift his weight, pressing his hips against her thigh. She knew what *she* liked, and apparently, they had similar tastes. Foreplay with Darian had always been all about *her*, and it was exciting to turn the tables.

Connor was going to regret staying half-dressed if she had anything to say about it.

"What's the matter, *Connor?* Are your pants *too tight?*" Kiera slowly scraped her teeth across the pad of his thumb, holding him still when he tried to pull away, taking his thumb into her mouth, making Connor hiss through his teeth and his skin break out into gooseflesh.

"Oh, that is *not* fair," he breathed.

Kiera released his thumb from between her lips and interlaced their fingers, wrapping her other hand around the back of his neck and bringing his mouth to hers. She squeezed her thighs together around his leg, using all her force to catch Connor off guard and roll him onto his back, pinning one hand above his head. He was startled at the quick move, but she wasn't about to give him time to react. Kiera kissed him hard, pushing her tongue into his mouth, breathing him in while Connor just tried to remember to breathe at all.

"*Stay.*" Kiera let go of his hand, and Connor did what he was told, letting her move down his body, kissing her way down his chest and stomach, running her hands along his sides until both her fingers and her lips reached fabric. Her hands found the ties on each side, and she deftly undid them one at a time, pulling Connor's pants lower until his cock was free. She wrapped her hand around the shaft and licked the tip, and he arched his back, his hands twisting the sheets . . .

And just like his fingers, Kiera took his cock into her mouth, sucking lightly, pressing her tongue against the underside of his hard sex, lifting her head slowly and looking up at him.

"Kiera . . . you had better stop . . ." Connor's voice sounded barely controlled; he was breathing hard, his eyes closed, his heart racing. But Kiera ignored him completely, pushing her mouth down around him again as his hands found her hair. Doing that to Connor was making her wet, and she ached to have him inside her, but it was too much fun to ignore. Kiera was slow with it, exploring every inch of him with her tongue, her hand wrapped around the base of his cock.

"Kiera, I'm not kidding . . . You have to stop . . ."

"*Why?*" She brought her mouth off him slowly, but she didn't remove her hand. Kiera licked him lightly, making him gasp.

"Because I won't be held responsible for what I am going to do to you if you finish me off this way."

Kiera laughed at that.

"Were they things you were going to do *anyway?*" She asked innocently before she licked him again, this time with more pressure.

"Maybe." Connor suddenly smirked.

"Then shut *up.*"

Fifty-Six

Darian sat with his new travel companions not long after the sun had started its afternoon descent. Alyk and Henelce had been riding through the forest with Darian walking beside them for the past few hours, discussing the upcoming journey into the mountains and stopping to take a break in the midday heat.

"Darian, are you sure you can even go up there?" Alyk was concerned, not only for Darian but also for the rest of them if his tribe caught wind of him back in their territory without an invitation.

"I shouldn't, but if it keeps all of you safer, I will. None of you speak our language, and even if you did, I know them in ways that you do not. I know their customs, their rites, and their weak points. I have been respectful of the borders until now, and I do not go to cause trouble or try to rejoin their society, so they shouldn't see me as a threat, just an intruder with no business there."

"But why were you banished to begin with?" Alyk asked.

Darian sighed and ran his hand back through his auburn braids before answering the question he knew would be coming sooner or later; he had been avoiding that subject for at least a dozen years, and had never told Kiera *at all*. But the old memories surfaced easily enough, and he could almost feel the blood on his hands again . . .

"About twelve or thirteen summers ago, I killed an elder and another member of our people without presenting a challenge."

"Was it in self-defense?" Henelce piped up. "I know those customs as well as you do, Darian –"

"*No*. I caught him with my mate," Darian cut him off before assumptions could be made about his innocence. The Aeroyn had knowingly committed a crime against his people, and he refused to take anything other than full credit for his actions.

"I had tried to ignore the rumors, but there came a day when I no longer could, and I brought my own justice down upon them. Leci and I hadn't been sanctioned as a couple for very long, but we had grown together as younglings, so it was an easy enough match. I thought I loved her, and she liked me, but it wasn't until after we were paired that I realized something was missing between us. Leci had agreed to be my mate, but I don't think she ever took our vows seriously. Not like I did. She just wanted a strong male, and I think she saw me as weak after I made decisions without asking what she thought.

"I found out afterword, when they decided to banish me, that there were *several* strong males Leci had been 'interested' in, and had I killed any of *them*, I would have been justified. There were even a few that had been keen on ending *my* life because our bonds are unbreakable unless one of us dies, or both agree that we no longer wish to follow the same path.

"Had I known where her head, and the rest of her, was really at, I would have walked away. The elder was no friend to me or our people, and I *knew* what *he* was capable of, but I hadn't realized *she* was so power-hungry that she would throw me to the wolves just to gain a higher standing.

"We were still mated, and I was refusing to give up on us when I caught them. In my rage, I killed her too." Darian sighed and gritted his teeth, the memories of Leci's tricks replaying in his mind as he thumbed the band on his arm, staring at the ground.

"It left the rest of the council with an odd dilemma—I should have been put into the elder's place for besting him, but because I killed without presenting a challenge, that technicality meant I was to be thrown out. I took the life of a leader, and *that* was unacceptable, whether or not he was with a mated female."

Leci still haunted his dreams on occasion, and he could picture her in his mind's eye. With raven skin, hair, and feathers, Leci had been darkly beautiful, but those deep-grey eyes of hers had been cold to him when he had followed her scent and caught her red-handed. They hadn't even let him stay for her pyre though he had seen the smoke billowing up from the double funeral the day after he was escorted to the edge of their lands and left on the human side to fend for himself.

The Merides River that snaked along the edge of the Montes Gelu created the tribe's easternmost border. It was also the river that fed into and flowed south from Breech Lake in his own back yard, creating the western border to Baneswood; Kiera had always wanted to cross it, and he would never tell her anything other than *no*.

Darian was glad now that he had never told Kiera that story; he wasn't proud of his reaction, and he had certainly never wanted her to fear his wrath. She was already well aware of how capable he was of causing an unpleasant death to those that threatened the ones he loved. Darian never wanted her to think he was capable of doing it to *her*.

Connor, however, will be fair game if he hurts Kiera. Darian had already made that very clear to the man before he and Kiera had left that morning. His begrudging respect for Connor had deepened when he had asked that Darian never let him forget it. Connor had told Darian of his plan to take her to his home on the far eastern edge of Eryce's kingdom, and with both Eryce and Sorveign threatening her, it didn't sound like a bad idea.

He couldn't argue with Connor's insistence that Kiera would be safe, even if only for a day or two, and that had been the only reason he had agreed to let Connor take her out of his sight. The last thing he wanted was to put her in further danger, and with the current threats on their doorstep, keeping her safe from the outside word was no longer an option, even if she wouldn't re-enter it willingly.

Ready or not, the world had decided it was going to come after *her*.

Fifty-Seven

"I thought you were sending Peter to get me something *appropriate?* There is no way I can wear this! Do you have any idea how long it's been since I last put something like *this* on?" Kiera was holding the piece of clothing he had handed her as far away from herself as she could, her expression mildly horrified.

Connor took the dress from her and laid it out on the bed over the disaster of rearranged pillows and rumpled bed linens that had been their sanctuary for the past several hours.

"I'm going to guess the answer to that is *never* since that's a newer style and you've been playing in boys' clothes for at least six years. What's wrong with it? I thought Peter did an excellent job in picking this out."

The dress in question was a deep, warm shade of eggplant and made of finely spun wool blended with silk. It would fit high on the chest, but the back was low, and it would hug her in the right places because it was cut on the bias. He had instructed Peter to find a dress in a dark green or purple, and he had brought back three; Connor had liked this one best. It would have been a little severe against her skin if it had been any darker, but the sheen from the silk mixed with the deep plum dye would contrast with her hair and eyes to bring them out instead of compete with them.

Connor *knew* how to dress a woman. Unfortunately, that wasn't helpful when the woman didn't know how to dress *herself*. He thought Kiera would look best in something simple, and this was perfect.

Kiera, however, wasn't happy about the option that had been presented to her. She had on one of his long-sleeved black shirts, which felt cool and smooth against her skin, and Connor certainly didn't mind the length since it barely covered to her thighs, but she couldn't wear it out of the room.

Well, technically she *could.*

Connor just wasn't going to *let* her.

Kiera crossed her arms and shifted her weight, and Connor wanted to take that shirt right back off her. Watching her move, even when she was annoyed, was like putting a candle in a room full of moths; all of Connor's thoughts gravitated toward her. More specifically, they gravitated toward things he wanted to *do* to her. Kiera was terribly distracting, and Connor was enjoying every second he had her alone.

Now, to get her into this dress . . .

"Oh quit pouting. I'll *compromise* with you." Connor had brought a parcel wrapped in paper with the dress, and he bent to retrieve it from the floor where he had dropped it. He set the parcel next to the dress, trying to keep a good poker face.

"I wasn't going to give you these until tomorrow, but I also had Peter find you some suitable clothing for when we go back, as well as a new set of bracers and boots. If you don't like the dress, you can change into these."

"*Fine*, I'll put the stupid thing on." Kiera rolled her eyes.

"Good." Connor lifted her chin and kissed her lightly. "I'll see you downstairs."

"I sort of hate you for this, you know," Kiera growled through her irritated expression.

Not as much as you're about to, Connor thought as he smiled brightly and left the room, laughing quietly to himself as he descended the stairs.

Dinner was going to be *fun*.

* * *

Kiera stared at the dress as though it was made of slugs for a minute or two, debating if she would rather just open the parcel and come down in whatever he had left for her to change into otherwise. She reached out and fingered the garment again, the silk and wool smooth and warm under her hand. She didn't hate the *material*, just the fact that it had been shaped into a *dress*. Kiera picked the abhorrent piece of clothing and walked it over to the mirror, holding it up against her chest.

"I can't tell what this stupid *thing* would even look like," she growled at her reflection. Kiera finally gave up and pulled Connor's shirt off then the dress over her head, feeling it skim her curves as she smoothed it into place. It needed a little tailoring, but it fit well enough . . .

Kiera studied herself in the vanity mirror, completely unused to seeing herself clean and dressed like woman. Her eyes, even without the usual rim of black, shone a brilliant green, and her hair made a stark contrast as stray strands of white clung to the shoulders. The purple *monstrosity* had three quarter sleeves, a high neck that cut straight across her collar bone that hid the new scabs and forming scars from the shattered dagger dotting her chest, and a hem that just brushed the floor.

Okay, I like the color, and I'll admit that it's flattering . . . until I turn around. Kiera pursed her lips as she turned her back to the mirror and looked over her shoulder at the reflection of her exposed skin. The dress was cut so low it almost showed the muscular dimples above her backside, the skirt flaring away from the lowest point and creating a short train . . .

"I am *not* wearing this!" Kiera declared as she stomped back across the room to the bed and reached for the wrapped parcel. She hastily tore the paper, but once she saw the contents, she stopped short.

Beneath the simple wrapping were at least twenty large white roses and a short note:

Wear the damned dress and come downstairs.
I'm starving. – C

"Why you *little*—" Kiera's annoyance dissolved into exasperated laughter, and she reflexively held the roses up to her nose to breathe them in before setting them down gently on the desk alongside the note. Connor had left her trapped, and unless she wanted to eat naked or go hungry, Kiera was stuck wearing the *thing* he had given her.

"I am going to get you for this, *Dirtbag*."

* * *

"You took long enough," Connor huffed. He had only been downstairs for about five minutes before Kiera wandered down after him, and he heard the padding of bare feet before he saw her.

He froze when he did. *I thought I liked her naked . . .*

"It needs tailoring," Kiera complained, sounding grumpy. She was ignoring Connor as she brushed at the material, trying to get it to sit the way she wanted, still debating if his trick made her angry or if she loved him more for it.

Connor approached her a little warily, walking around her slowly, taking her in now that Kiera looked like a *woman* instead of an *outlaw*. He was struck with the image of the way she had looked when they had been at the river and wanting to paint her image in that soft, unguarded moment; this was the first of hopefully many that would certainly rival that, even if she was irritated.

She looks so different.

"I like it, but it . . . *needs* something," he mused.

"*Yes*, to not be on *me*," Kiera grumbled, crossing her arms and shifting her weight to glare over her shoulder at him since he was behind her now. Her hair swept aside and exposed the long strip of her pale skin to him, and Connor fought the urge to drag her back upstairs and grant her wish, but food was first. Viola had been busy and would be hurt if they didn't eat. Connor wasn't keen to suffer her wrath; housekeeper or not, Viola would *never* let him live it down, and Connor was quite a fan of his peaceful existence.

But his mind wasn't on his housekeeper. Connor had a shiny object in his hand as he closed the gap between them and slipped something over Kiera's head, pulling her hair gently through the delicate silver chain so the pendant dropped into place on her chest, just over her heart.

"No, it needed an addition. I want you to have this."

Kiera immediately picked the simple piece of jewelry and studied it closely. The pendant was circular and set with a six-sided blue stone that pulsated with a faint light as it sparkled in her hand. It dawned on her suddenly that she had seen that particular stone before.

"Connor, is this your homing crystal? I can't wear this!"

"It's not *mine*, though I am free to give it to you. It was my grandmother's homing crystal, but the points have all been lost, so it doesn't work in the traditional sense. It does, however, sync to *my* heartbeat, and always will."

Kiera was a little stunned, the implications of the jewel not lost on her as Connor wrapped his arms around her from behind and kissed her exposed shoulder, silently loving that Kiera was dressed but naked at the same time. The scent of honey flooded his senses, and Connor breathed her in, still amazed that he affected her so strongly . . .

. . . and that *he* could *sense* it.

"Now let's go eat before Viola comes looking for us. She'll never let me be if I don't bring you into the dining room and give you a proper *meal*."

"You could have at least gotten me a *proper dress* . . ." Kiera laughed as Connor took her hand and led her toward the dining room, and he flashed her a lopsided grin.

"Now *where* would be the fun in *that*?"

Fifty-Eight

The utensils felt a bit awkward in Kiera's hand since she had gotten so used to eating with just her fingers and sharp blade, but her mother's voice kept sounding in her head, memories of being corrected every time she held her fork or her knife or her cup the wrong way making her feel like she was eight years old again. She was determined to keep Serra's sharp words at bay without adding her own as she fought to remember how to eat like a civilized being instead of a forest animal.

Connor had watched her struggle at first, but the glare Kiera had directed at him when he tried to help kept his mouth firmly shut unless he was taking a bite of food.

Now that dinner was over and she was simply picking at the apple tart on her plate, Kiera actually *wanted* the awkward silence to end.

"Connor, tell me about Joseph."

"*That*," he pointed the tines of his fork at her, still chewing, "is a very long story."

Kiera put her utensils down and folded her hands under her chin, staring at him.

"Can I *at least* finish eating first?" Connor was greeted with silence. Just bright green eyes trained on him expectantly as Kiera waited for the *very long story* to begin. "Woman, you are going to drive me *insane*."

Connor threw his napkin on the table with a dramatic huff, but he was finished anyway, and he knew it. After a few days in the forest, he was ravenous, and Viola had outdone herself with a roasted duck and simple root vegetables braised with garlic and oil. He was thankful she had chosen to make something just rustic enough that it wasn't foreign to Kiera, and they had both cleared their plates.

I cannot remember the last time I sat at this table. Connor took a sip of white wine, which he had been drinking slowly throughout dinner, thinking now that it paired better with the apples than it had with the fowl. Kiera had barely touched hers, unaccustomed to the strong smell or its overpowering sweetness, a reminder to both of them that there was just one more item to add to the list of things she had been missing out on. However, Connor wasn't going to fault her if she didn't like it; it wasn't his favorite either.

"Where to begin . . ." He leaned back in his chair.

This was going to be very interesting, indeed.

* * *

"The funny thing about the story of Joseph is it actually starts with *me*. I was born in Glory Run, which is about forty or so miles almost directly west of here, and when I was four, I was taken from my home and ransomed. My family never paid, and I was left on this very doorstep."

"Connor, *please*. Just the *truth*." Kiera made a face at him that said she didn't believe him, but he didn't crack.

"That part *is* true," he countered.

Kiera held his gaze with a hard stare, waiting for him to smile and tell her he was only kidding, but he just regarded her seriously until she finally adopted his pose and sat back, accepting his odd answer as fact.

"All right. Was this Joseph's house, then?"

"No, this house belonged to my grandmother. I was left here by my uncle Godwin when he didn't get any money for *kidnapping* me, silly bastard." Connor broke into a bright smile when Kiera rolled her eyes, but it faded as he went on.

"I am the only child to parents that don't want each other, much less me, so when my favorite uncle showed up one day and led me out of the house, it took my parents almost an entire day to even realize that I was gone. It took Godwin almost that long to sober up and write a ransom note, which got him laughed at and me deposited here for *safekeeping*. My mother had no siblings, and her parents were dead by the time I was born, but on my father's side are my uncle Godwin, who was a drunk, and an aunt that ended up in a royal court somewhere, but I haven't ever seen or heard from her.

"Then there was my grandmother Celeste, who was my father's mother, though they couldn't have been more different. My grandfather was someone I never knew, but I have been told that he and my father walked similar paths; believe me when I tell you it was not a surprise to find out he died at the end of a blade a year or two after I was born.

"After her husband died, Grandmere took over this estate, and she threw wonderful parties and had this house filled with people much of the time, so it feels a bit empty now with just me, and I am gone too much to consider bringing Delámer back to its previous social status. Celeste was sweet, kind, generous, and the most cunning woman I have ever met; I miss her on occasion, but she's been gone for several years now, and she left me this house when she passed. There's a portrait of her in one of the rooms upstairs if you want to see it later, but those are all the people I'll admit to being related to.

"Back to me: now, when I showed up on that front stoop, I was cold and wet because it had been raining, and I stank of rum because my uncle had deemed it prudent to make sure I stayed *quiet*. It was Joseph that stumbled across me when he came outside, heading for the stables, and apparently I grabbed his leg and wouldn't let go.

"Once they figured out *who* I was, Grandmere Celeste wrote to my father, Markus, to let him know that I had been found and asked if I shouldn't simply stay with her since he seemed to be having trouble keeping track of me. The reply she got was a short note that said 'Fine, but only until he's old enough to be useful,' which makes me think he missed me *terribly*. Honestly, I doubt they even noticed I was gone. My father and I do *not* get along, my mother is a coward, and I refuse to acknowledge them *either*."

Kiera caught a hint of bitterness creeping into his words, but it was gone as he continued, sweeping his hand out to indicate the house.

"So my childhood was spent here, and my grandmother was thrilled to have me. Grandmere used this place as a sort of sanctuary when she wasn't busy having a social life, and when I showed up she had several other people living here with her. They have all gone on to live other lives and follow other dreams since I took control of the property, but none were ever asked to leave. I think they had come here specifically for *her*, but I was never as friendly with any of them as I was with my *mentor*, and *he* left to follow his own path quite some time ago, too. But this place . . . *This* is where Joseph's real role in my life began.

"Joseph was not the type of man who liked children, and he wasn't very good with me at first, but I took to *him* immediately. I was always following him around and asking him questions and mimicking him, probably driving him crazy, but he eventually came to accept my presence. He came and went pretty frequently but always remembered to bring me something small from his journeys, even if he was gone for six months or more.

"There were several others that took a keen interest in me, but it was Joseph that offered to take me with him see the kingdoms when I turned ten, and to *train* me, even though we were so *different*."

"You mean like Darian trained *me*? Was Joseph not *human?*"

Connor paused and leaned forward with his elbows on the table and rested his chin in his hands, gazing at her with a mild and unreadable expression. He had been waiting for this to come up, and he was surprised she had never caught on.

Henelce and Alyk certainly had.

"Joseph was just as human as you and I, Kiera. He offered to train me to use my *gifts*, just as I'm sure Henelce would like to train *you*." Connor continued to watch her placidly, and Kiera was starting to get annoyed.

Very annoyed.

"You are driving me insane! Stop talking in circles and just get to the poi—"

"You never did notice my *mark*, did you?"

If he comes up with any more surprises, I'm going to hit him.

"What *mark*? I've seen every inch of your body, and you don't have any marks. Scars here and there, but nothing like *mine*—"

"*Oh*? What's *this*, then?" Connor turned away from her and pulled his ear forward.

Behind his right ear was a definite birthmark, but one that she would have easily missed, the curving § shape mistakable for a lock of hair. If his hair had been any shorter, she would have had a plain view of it, but Kiera was starting to realize it wouldn't have mattered if she *had* noticed; she knew so little about their *kind* that she would have simply dismissed the damned thing out of hand.

"Is *that* why we're so attracted to each other?" Her eyes were wide as she reached out to touch the shape Tirath had tattooed on him before he was born. Kiera had had no idea he knew what *she* was because they were one and the same.

Connor seemed to think her question was terribly amusing and gave her a wry smile.

"Funny thing, we shouldn't be able to stand the sight of each other. The *marked* don't like one another for one very simple reason—we have an inherent distrust for *influence*, no matter the type or the sex of the other person. We can *smell* it, and it stinks to us, and I'm interested to see how *you* react to someone else of our ilk.

"Only . . . you *don't* smell like something awful or rancid to me. I have no idea *why* we can be near each other, but your scent of honey is pretty damned delicious, so I'm certainly not complaining. I wasn't entirely sure as to *what* you were when I met you, and it wasn't until I touched your neck that I realized I was in for an enormous amount of *trouble* . . ."

Kiera was studying him, and his scent suddenly flooded the room; she closed her eyes and smiled as she breathed him in. The mint and cedar smell vanished, and she opened her eyes to find Connor watching her intently, his chin in his palm, a slight smirk on his lips.

"It's still so *weird* to see you react like that, and the fact that we can catch each other's scent is strange indeed. I have been around enough of us to know that *influence always* smells awful to me, and I can peg one of us in a crowd easily because the closer we get to each other, the stronger the smell. I have yet to meet anyone else that I can be around for more than a few minutes without getting a headache and wanting to vomit.

"The *marked* don't mix well, and it's worse when we end up having to share space with one of our own. Not only does the scent create a sort of an oil and water situation, but *we* tend to end up in betrothed marriages with people we despise because some believe that keeping up the bloodline is important. My parents were forced together, and *they* certainly hate each other. I can only imagine yours were probably like that too, since I know they were both *marked*."

Connor went quiet for a moment, letting Kiera think before opening her mouth to answer him. Knowing *that* particular piece of information put a few things into perspective when she thought back on her parents; she had always just assumed they hadn't even liked one another. It had never dawned on her that there could have been another reason for their uncivil tongues or their unwillingness to be near each other.

"My parents weren't exactly *happy* to be in the same room with each other, no, but I don't remember either of them smelling weird to *me*. On that note, I *have* been thinking about my family more as of late. I think my father may have been hiding my heritage from me, and I *do* remember him forbidding me to read certain books. We fought about it just before Corengale was ruined . . ."

Kiera paused as the memories attempted to resurface, and she pushed them back down, trying to keep her dinner and her tears inside her body where they belonged. The *last* thing she wanted at that moment was to be overwhelmed by horrific images and incredible sadness; Kiera took a deep breath, blowing it out slowly, calming enough that she could ask her next question.

"But what makes *us* so different? The rule should still apply, but it doesn't seem to make any difference on my end. You're just, well, *you*."

"I have been *trying* to figure that out. As far as your family not smelling odd to you, well, that doesn't change for girls until they start their cycle, and boys take a bit longer, usually after they turn sixteen or so. The fact that we're from different lines could be a possible explanation, but I've *never* heard of it happening before.

"Maybe it's because we're such polar opposites." Connor reached for her hand, squeezing it gently, his expression turning thoughtful.

"Or maybe it's because you have really bad taste, and I'm just willing to play along. I don't have the slightest clue as to why we fit like we do, Kiera, and I'm not going to pick it apart to see how it works and risk the pieces not fitting back together again."

Connor stood from the table, pulling Kiera after him.

"Come. If I'm going to continue this story, I can tell you right now, I'm going to need a drink. Let's find somewhere else for me to embarrass myself more comfortably."

And let's just hope you still love me when I'm done.

Fifty-Nine

Connor led her out of the dining room and into the main hall, waiting until they were seated on a large brown velvet divan near one of the big windows that looked out over the grounds at the back of the house before continuing his story. Kiera curled up on one end with her feet under her dress while Connor poured a glass of rum from a nearby decanter and sat at the other, his glass in his hands as he leaned forward with his elbows on his knees.

"Now, I heard Henelce tell you that there are three marks, and I'll give you what I know without boring you completely. There's yours, mine, and a ϒ shape. All three have their own significance, unique rules, and boundaries, and they are passed on by the male side of the line at random unless he has children with a woman also bearing a *mark*, as their offspring are guaranteed to carry forth one mark or the other.

"*I*, dear lady, am a *Lure*, and was guaranteed to be because both of my parents carry the same symbol on their skin. I cause people to see what they want to see in me, to *trust* the words coming out of my mouth without a second thought, and I can charm the pants off just about anyone when I put my mind to it. I may as well have *talk to me* tattooed on my forehead, and in my line of work, it's incredibly helpful.

"Of course, I don't have to use it *that* often since I'm *good-looking* too." Connor had a quirky smile contorting his mouth, suddenly looking very self-important. He winked at her, his bright white smile turned on full blast; Kiera was giggling, struggling to take him seriously and failing miserably.

"Connor, there is not enough space for me, you, *and* your ego in this room, and you already know you can't affect me, so quit while you're ahead and tell me about the other *mark*. I know I'm a *Unifier* and what it means, but what's the third?"

Connor's bright smile faltered a bit. He'd had enough experience with the *Raze* to know that they were not to be crossed and that they were almost *never* to be trusted.

Even *if* Joseph carried it on the inside of his left wrist . . .

"That is the mark of the *Raze*, and they are arguably the most dangerous of us if they are bent on destruction. King Hærrion carried that particular *mark*, and we are all *very* lucky that Eryce didn't inherit it, though your mother did. The *marked* throughout the kingdoms were sort of stunned when your father and mother were announced as wed. Those lines had crossed before but never on a royal level since *Unifiers* tend to seek out their own kind to keep the line *pure* when they hold a position that high, and Serra was the first *Raze* queen these lands had ever known.

"Joseph was a *Raze*, and he could implant thoughts and mold them to what he wanted people to think, playing on their fears. He had the ability to ruin marriages, business relationships, friendships . . . I didn't realize until a few years ago that my mark was *exactly* why Joseph had been willing to train me—I lured people into trusting me and telling me their dirty little secrets, and Joseph used that information to turn people against each other. We made one *hell* of a team."

That particular admission made Connor feel surprisingly self-conscious. He was a little worried Kiera would think differently about him once she knew his story, suddenly not so sure he was ready to divulge some of the uglier truths that pertained to his past.

"Joseph decided that I should start training young, and that is actually pretty common for us because we need to have boundaries and structure before we hit puberty and the *influence* gains strength. I hated the lessons that had to do with the families and who had used their *influence* to what end. History is *not* my strongest subject, but learning to control my abilities was fairly easy once I got the idea. It might be a little harder for you because you're going to start sort of backward, but I have a funny feeling you'll figure it out."

Connor took a sip of rum as he turned to Kiera, eyeing her curiously, tapping his fingers against his glass.

"I can't help but wonder *why* Garegan hid what you *are* from you especially with the *mark* you carry. You're by far the most dangerous of us because you can affect an enormous number of people, not just a limited few. Darian certainly didn't help either . . ."

Connor was talking more to himself at that point, but Kiera's darkening expression at the mention of the Aeroyn that had protected her for so long was enough to remind him to tread lightly.

"Don't look at me like *that*! Even though Darian knew *what* you are, he probably didn't know how to help, and it likely didn't make matters easier with your *influence* around him, especially if you were in the middle of becoming an adult. Your energy was almost certainly all over the place without either of you even realizing it, and I would be willing to bet some of the dulled edges on him are because of your abilities. Aeroyn are *not* that friendly or trusting otherwise, and they certainly don't back down.

"I will, however, give him credit for teaching you what *he* knew, like ripping apart your enemies with your bare hands." Connor paused to tilt his glass at Kiera as he pointed at her dress.

"Seeing you like this is much more deceptive, and if I didn't know what I do about you, I would think you were defenseless and timid. Not some crazy lady of the forest who could beat me senseless if she actually bothered to really try . . . which, by the way, you never have. Even that first time you hit me, you pulled it a bit. I know that because Alyk told me you almost shattered Jaçon's jaw when I was *indisposed,* and an elf is a much more resilient fighter than I am."

"Any time you want to spar, I'm game."

"As far as I am concerned, the only *sparing* I'll be doing with *you* will be in that bed in about ten minutes when I'm finished with this story and this glass and I drag you upstairs."

"Don't want to hit a *girl?*" Kiera gave him a wicked grin, unwilling to let him out of *playing* with her that easily.

"I would say *no,* but I actually *have* hit a girl, and she absolutely deserved it."

"When was that?"

"When I was nine, but *that* is another story for another time. Back to *my* story—Joseph dragged me with him around the kingdoms after I turned thirteen, teaching me how to use my gifts for monetary gain."

Kiera's grin soured into a disgusted look, and it was his turn to laugh.

"Hey now, I *never* said we all use our gifts for *good,* and many of us tend to hide from the rest of the world because there are those that would *use* us for their own gain. As a matter of fact, I *know* I told you I am a devious bastard, and the combination of Joseph's *gift* and mine was a pretty potent mix. I was *good* at it, too, but now that you're suddenly part of the equation I can't help but feel like maybe I was just trying to stay occupied . . ."

Connor was studying the floor as he took another sip of rum, savoring the warmth as it trickled down the back of his throat and spread through his chest, contemplating where to go next with his tale.

Kiera took the opportunity to reach forward and lift the glass from his hand, bringing it up to her nose. She breathed in the spicy vanilla aroma of the amber-colored liquor and took a tentative sip. Connor watched her curiously as she sat back out of his reach, holding the glass in her lap.

It somehow didn't surprise him when he realized she wasn't going to give it back.

"Woman, you should have kept the name *Bane.* It was so much more *appropriate.*" He sighed dramatically as he got up to get another glass. Kiera smiled, taking deeper swallow as Connor sat back down and gave her a pointed look.

"Be careful with that. It's smooth, but it's strong, and it *will* knock you on your ass faster than I can. I'm only warning you because you're not used to it—"

"Yes, oh, *Master Lure*." Her sarcasm brought that lopsided smile back as she took another sip, and Connor put up a hand in defeat, willing to simply let her learn on her own.

"Go ahead, drink away. *I* won't stop you. Just know that I also won't hold your hair if you drink too much and your stomach no longer wants to be friends with it when the morning comes."

"Are you going to chide me or finish this story?" Kiera retorted, growing impatient.

"You really are something, you know that? I am actually starting to wonder how I ever survived without you." Connor gave her a bemused look, and Kiera heaved an exasperated sigh.

"Connor—"

"Let me guess—I'm an *idiot*."

"And *then* what happened?"

"Okay, okay. Let's see, where was I . . . Oh yes, *training*. For the most part, *we* are well educated. We sort of *have* to be because I can tell you we're far more dangerous when we can't control our abilities . . . or if we don't know about them. Garegan put both you and a lot of people in danger by hiding what you are, but you're not the first that I've seen that has had to backpedal and start training late—you're just the *oldest*. You should have been well trained by the time you were twelve, and I had already been under Joseph's tutelage for about seven years by the time the next part of my story comes into play.

"Just after I turned fifteen, Joseph met his wife, Dianna, and things . . . *changed*. We were about thirty miles north of here in Yaga Bay, tracking down information on an insufferably talkative woman that was causing all sorts of problems for one of the rich men in the area by spreading gossip about his fathering several children in the village. It isn't even an uncommon rumor, but the man's new wife had caught wind of it, and *she* was furious, threatening to *remove* that which allowed him to get into the debacle to begin with if it turned out to be true.

"Joseph's presence was quietly requested, and he dragged me along for some real-world experience—up until that point, I had only observed, and to this day, I swear the man pitted me against that woman on *purpose*. Not the wife, mind you, but the town gossip, and I didn't even have to charm her to get her to talk to me. I stupidly offered an ear to bend, and she *wouldn't shut up!* I suddenly had this obnoxious, pompous, self-indulgent middle-aged know-it-all of a woman following me *everywhere* for an entire day, and then the next when I was unlucky enough to cross her path again. I nicknamed her Quicksand because once you were sucked in, you were *never* getting out of talking to her unless you died.

"Once I finally untangled myself from her and Joseph had stopped *laughing* long enough to listen to what she knew, he started digging into who had which children, using his *influence* to make the women deny the claim. Now that brings me to something you'll have to learn—our *influence* has varying degrees of effectiveness once you can control it, and the more you use, the quicker you'll wear out. Depending on how strongly he chose to affect someone, Joseph could make implanted thoughts permanent, though he didn't always like to be that forceful, and the changes would simply fade with time.

"It was also a brilliant business tactic on his end—once he collected his fee, Joseph would usually warn our *clients* that his powers only lasted so long, so he would need to be paid to return and *maintain* those changes. Otherwise, his work was done, and they would part ways with the understanding that his services would no longer be needed. Some never asked him to come back, but most usually had enough to either fear or gain to make it worthwhile to them to agree to his methods. Extortion was that man's *forte*, and he played the game *very* well . . .

"Now, in that particular instance, there were six women in total that needed to be silenced, and using that much energy left Joseph so tired he slept for an entire day and a half after he finished with the last one. When he felt good enough and went to collect our fee, the man who was supposed to pay us laughed in his face. Crossing Joseph was never a good idea, and while he wasn't a mean man, per se, he liked to be *creative*—he threatened to not only undo what he had done, but he would add to the mix by making Quicksand think *she* had given birth to a child by the man and influence the man's wife to think *he* was not her husband and throw him from the house. That jackass doubled our fee and paid up front to shut Quicksand up so the problem would go away entirely, and so would we.

"Joseph pocketed that money and *influenced* Quicksand as promised, but he made the change only temporary. I remember how hard we both laughed when he told me what he had done—Joseph had given her a phobia of *cats*, and she wouldn't leave her house because one sat at her door, crying to come in. I felt a little sorry for the beast because it was *her* cat, but he said the affects would wear off in less than a week and the cat would be fine. We were still in Yaga Bay for a few days after that, and I used to stand outside the window and wave."

Connor smiled at that memory, still finding it tremendously funny. Kiera seemed to agree as she almost choked on her drink, trying not to laugh and swallow at the same time.

"During that time, we had been staying at the Grey Stallion Inn, and Dianna was a barmaid in the tavern. She was maybe six or seven years older than me at the time when Joseph caught sight of her while we were eating dinner, and he sent me back to our room early to study and get some sleep. He told me later that he had ordered anything he could just to talk to her, and when she finally agreed to see him the next day outside the bar, he was a different man entirely. Joseph was in love with Dianna from the first time he saw her, and I remember feeling jealous that he was suddenly spending all his free time with her, but that changed once we got to know each other. She moved here shortly after we returned, they were married within a month, and Dianna was a member of our team after that.

"That is until she got pregnant with their daughter, Zoë, less than a year into their marriage, then she wasn't allowed to travel with us anymore. Joseph was a braver man than I because Dianna wasn't going to let her husband go traipsing all over the three kingdoms without giving one hell of a fight, and she's *scary* when she's mad. Dianna is maybe five-foot-even, couldn't have weighed more than 120 pounds when she was almost nine months pregnant, and she *still* terrifies me to this day.

"Joseph was just about six-foot-tall, heavily built, and fairly intimidating in his own right, but against Dianna's temper, he might as well have been a small child he was so cowed. There were several times that I thought he was going to quit our business outright because she hated his prolonged absence, but Joseph wasn't about to give up an income that kept his wife and child well situated, so he came up with a compromise—he put some of the money he made to good use and bought her a small *mansion* in the Southern Estates, porting home every two weeks to see his family. Depending on what we were up to, sometimes he would take me too.

"I actually feel pretty guilty because I haven't seen them in almost a year, and they are the closest thing to a real family I have ever had. Zoë is coming up on twelve by now and is sort of a surrogate little sister. Dianna is warm, funny, very bright, and she taught me a lot about women in general. You can credit her with my ability to charm a girl without using my influence because I can tell you that Joseph was about as smooth as gravel.

"In fact, she would be really proud of me with those roses . . ."

I forgot about those. Kiera turned a shade of embarrassed pink when it struck her that Connor was being sweet to her in ways she would have never expected from Darian, or *anyone*, for that matter. Kiera fingered the pendant with her free hand, realizing it was the only piece of jewelry she had ever worn; the idea of taking it off felt almost foreign.

Connor watched her fiddle with the gem for a moment before he continued his tale, his sheepish smile fading as the next part of his story developed in his mind.

"Anyway, once Dianna was squared away, we continued to port all over hell and back. I was maybe a little younger than you when I finally got caught doing something very, very *stupid*."

Connor suddenly emptied his glass with one swallow, not really wanting to open his mouth further. He got up from the divan and retrieved another few ounces of rum, taking his time while contemplating how to make himself out to be less of an ass than he suddenly felt.

Just jump in with both feet, moron. You're already this far, and it's not like you can take it back. No point screwing it up halfway. Don't think about it, just talk. He could feel Kiera watching him, but he couldn't look at her as he came back to perch himself on the edge of the seat, uncomfortable with admitting the part of the story that came next. Connor glanced at Kiera briefly but found his glass to be less likely to be judgmental so he stared at it instead. *Yeah, I see no way this could end badly . . .*

"I would like to think I'm a quick study, and when I learn a lesson, it usually only takes once, but more often than not, it's learned the *hard way*. I have absolutely no defense for what I'm about to admit to, and I'll just get it out there and hope you don't hit me. Believe me when I tell you it was a *huge* fiasco and a decision I regret to this day. It's not a mistake I was willing to make twice, I'll tell you that much, and have not been foolish enough to make since.

"Shortly after I turned twenty-one, I slept with a client's eldest daughter. I was *very* in control of my *influence* by that point, and I know I had nothing to do with how that girl thought she felt about me. Joseph had accepted an assignment in Glory Run to help one merchant drive a rival out of the same street in the trade district, and it was then that I met Talia.

"Raven hair, big brown eyes, and too smart for her own good at the ripe old age of sixteen, she immediately pinned me as *the one*, and I had no idea. She flirted with me, asked me questions about my life and what I enjoyed, invited me along for walks through the Trade District, sought me out and asked my opinion on all sorts of things . . .

"I, being young and dumb but believing otherwise, was flattered that she seemed to like me for *who* I was, having no idea that she was just looking for a rich, good-looking husband. I hadn't been very interested in women up to that point because people were just *jobs* to me, but Joseph saw what she was doing; he warned me that her intentions were different and to tread carefully.

"Being the brilliant man that I am, I ignored him completely. I took Talia's virginity, avoided her for a few days after the fact, and then broke it off completely because I realized that I didn't actually *like* her. I didn't think anything of it because I didn't know I was being set up to begin with, but she had other ideas—she ran to her father to tell him she was pregnant, and I was going to be the newest addition to their family. Joseph said 'I told you so,' her father almost killed me, and *I* almost had to marry her. I probably would have ported her to a distant location, gathered up my crystal, and left her there because after that, Talia drove me absolutely crazy.

"I was grateful when Joseph took pity on us both and helped me out on that one by using his *influence* on both the girl and her father and finding some other village idiot to take my place. And Talia didn't end up pregnant until *much* later, thank Tirath. After the wedding, Joseph made me purchase a piece of land for the happy couple just to make the point that stupid mistakes get expensive quickly and to remind me to turn on my brain *before* I took off my clothes."

"You *still* haven't learned that lesson, have you?" Kiera grinned and poked him in the arm.

"Of course not! If I had, *you* would already be at the Arx—" Connor stopped talking, wishing he could eat his words when Kiera visibly paled.

I trusted him not to lie to me, and he could have ported me right to Eryce. He still could. The idea that Connor was supposed to have simply handed her over to Eryce seemed unreal, and Kiera avoided his gaze; she toyed with the pendant instead, watching the pulsating light beat faster. *He had* better *be nervous. I won't be pulling any more punches if he tries anything stupid.*

He wanted to apologize, but the words rang too true, and he would only be saying "I'm sorry" to make himself feel like less of a jerk. Connor took a deep drink from his glass, turning his attention out the window directly in front of them, refusing to look at her either as he cleared his throat and went back to telling his story, breaking the awkward silence.

"That whole mess bit me squarely in the backside, and I thought I had learned my lesson until I found myself seeking out *other* assignments less than six months later. Joseph didn't want any part of what I was getting into, and with his family to look out for I can't say I blamed him."

"I hesitate to ask *what* you were doing, but if it's anything like what you were up to with me, then I probably don't need to, do I?" Kiera's question was quiet and rhetorical, and Connor could hear just how much his careless words had hurt her.

I'm trying to be honest with her, to give her an idea of what she's falling in love with, and I don't like the words coming out of my mouth any more than she does.

He stood up and closed the gap between them, settling next to her, pushing her hair back and tucking it behind her ear, trying to get her to look at him. Kiera stubbornly kept her profile to him, not ready to give in yet. Connor sighed and let her be.

"Yes and *no*, and this story doesn't get any better," Connor said softly, knowing he had already reminded Kiera that she had several reasons not to trust him.

He was about to give her one more.

Please don't hate me when I finally close my mouth.

"I-I took up *seducing*. There is a *lot* of money to be made by helping rich men get rid of their wives by acting as an interested lover and giving the husband grounds for divorce. It wasn't exactly a big leap with my *gifts* to take that on, and that's why I knew about the indigo berry ink. I've used it and my *influence* in tandem on several occasions to get my way, usually to the benefit of the highest bidder."

He stared at his nearly empty glass as he went on, a little afraid of the critical gaze that was certainly directed at him by the woman at his side. Connor went quiet as he counted backward in his head, trying to place a certain memory along the timeline of his *career* of the past few years.

Was it really that long ago?

"I apparently very much enjoy tempting fate because I took up a job that I knew right away was going to end badly for everyone involved and did it anyway. Almost two years ago, one of my *affairs* turned into a dramatic production that almost took my life—the husband hired me, poisoned his wife once he knew I was in the picture, and *then* the smug bastard actually tried to implicate *me* in her death. I ended up in chains and sitting with my head in my hands for three days before Joseph came to my rescue, and I *dealt* with the bastard on his wife's behalf.

"That . . . was the only time I have ever taken a life, and I cannot say I regret it. However, it was also the *last* time Joseph helped me out of a sticky situation, and he told me not to contact him anymore unless I wanted to see the family that missed me and was ready to change my ways. Before he left me to my own devices, he gave me his set of porting stones, saying he was tired of trying to keep track of them and figured I needed them more than he did since I wasn't learning from my mistakes, only repeating them. He showed me how to use them, had me set one with the command *home*, and pocketed the damned thing before I could say anything else.

"Joseph told me then was that I was following a foolish path and to quit, but I just buried myself deeper, thinking I could prove him wrong. Not long after we parted ways, I started answering requests to track down and bring back wives or mistresses that had run off. Once he caught wind of *that*, Joseph refused to talk to me about my work altogether, and one of the last times I saw him was for the reignition ritual that winter. We didn't speak much after that, but Dianna would send me letters on occasion to keep me apprised of their lives and ask me to visit, which I stubbornly refused to do.

"I was always too 'busy' and kept telling myself that I had good reasons not to port *home*, but for the life of me, I cannot remember what they were. My work took up much of my time, and the money in bounty hunting is excellent *if* you're good. Considering I've almost doubled what my grandmother left to me, let's just say I'm not terrible.

"But once I heard about *you*, I took the assignment as a personal challenge—I saw the body count and decided I had a better shot than anyone who had tried so far, considering they were no longer competition, and none of them were *marked*. I wanted to prove to myself that I was *that* good, and I certainly wasn't discouraged when I found out that Eryce wants you alive *and* has a high price on your head. *I* approached *him* because I thought I knew what I was getting into.

"I never imagined it would lead to *this* . . ."

Connor trailed off as he finished the last of his second drink, his gaze focused on the setting sun over the rolling hills behind the house, feeling incredibly stupid. He had always been able to justify his actions in his own mind.

Until he had to explain them to someone else.

Especially to someone who *cared*.

"So what happened last year? How did Joseph . . . die?" Kiera was watching him quietly, his green eyes flicking back and forth over the landscape as he drummed his fingers against his empty glass. Connor swallowed and took a deep breath, and Kiera suddenly realized that he was trying very hard not to cry.

"It's actually tragically boring—Joseph went to bed one night, not feeling well, and didn't wake up the next day." Connor shrugged, his answer sounding a little deflated. He didn't want to admit that his friend and mentor was really gone. It hurt every time he did.

"Joseph was a few weeks shy of sixty-two. Dianna had him taken up into the Montes Gelu and buried in a graveyard that very few people even know about. She sent me a letter about his passing, asking me to come to the funeral, but I wasn't home at the time, and I didn't even read it until two months after he was already gone." Connor went quiet, willing the tears he had yet to shed to cease before they ever started. He took a deep breath and forced it out his mouth, trying to keep calm . . .

He almost lost his composure when he felt her warm hand on his forearm, squeezing gently, the scent of honey flooding the room. Connor stared straight ahead, pushing the words past the lump in his throat as he ended his story.

"Joseph was the closest thing to a father I ever had, and I missed his funeral. That bothers me just about every day."

Sixty

"At least you can finally ride her. She's been a bit antsy since Kiera left, hmm?" Henelce reached up and patted Arveneg's snout once she was tethered to the tree.

"You can say *that* again," Alyk growled as he gave the black mare a dark look. "I'm getting *rid* of her once we get to Grant's Perch, *if* she makes it *that* far."

He and Alyk were finally making camp for the night as the evening light started to fade, still many miles and another day's slow ride through the brush from where they would be meeting Kiera and Connor. Darian had taken off once they found a spot to settle, heading well away from them to hunt and keep the wolves at bay.

"Have you considered giving her back to Kiera? I'm sure *she* won't mind having this beast back under her control." Henelce fed Arveneg a handful of grass, checking the water bucket between the horses to make sure they had enough for the night.

"Yeah. Then she'll have *two*—"

Henelce turned sharply, wagging his finger angrily in Alyk's face, the comment made under the young man's breath not able to escape the Shephard's sharp ears.

"*Don't* you say things like that! I *know* I taught you better, and Darian is *not* a target for your annoyance any more than this horse is. What has gotten into you, anyhow? You've been nothing but surly since we ran into Kiera again."

Alyk turned bright red, and Henelce's eyes went wide with surprise.

"*Oh*." Henelce cocked his head, watching Alyk suddenly study the ground. "When?"

"I-I don't know."

"You are going to have to tell her, you know."

"*Why?* I cannot see any way for that conversation to end well, Henelce. In fact, I can't see any way for that conversation to end with me still *breathing*," Alyk huffed as he tossed a piece of wood on top of the stack he had set up for a fire, feeling defeated.

"As if *that* wasn't enough, I'm worried about Tance being out of my sight. I feel like I've loosed him upon unsuspecting people, and with no one around to *correct* him, how long do you think it will take for him to get himself into a situation that he won't survive?"

"One can only hope it doesn't take too long, boy. Otherwise, he and everyone around him are going to be in for one bumpy ride. Personally, I hope he learns how to keep his mouth *shut* and his hands to *himself*. No one is going to put up with that shit for very long."

Alyk sighed, silently agreeing with Henelce. Crouching down and trying to avoid further conversation altogether, he went to work with a flint and tinder to get the fire started.

"Move back. I'll do that. And stop grinding your teeth." Henelce nudged Alyk's leg with the edge of his boot, waiting until Alyk got to his feet and brushed himself off before snapping his fingers, the dried branches suddenly bursting into flame. Alyk threw the flint aside and stood, everything about the situation he was now finding himself in and unable to avoid for much longer starting to truly seep under his skin.

"Well, since I'm of no use *here*, I'm going to see about hunting something down for dinner." Alyk cast an irritated glance at the black horse that was far more of a pain than a convenience as he picked up Henelce's crossbow and a few extra bolts. "I suddenly have the urge to *shoot* something."

Sixty-One

The fire had dwindled low, the room getting darker and cooler. Kiera lay awake with her head on Connor's naked chest, his breathing slow and regular as he slept peacefully. She was tired, but the crashing of the waves outside and the stillness throughout the house were unfamiliar, and sleep was out of the question.

This feels too weird. It's too easy to be behind these walls, in this bed, to feel safe and warm with this man. I feel like I'm forgetting who I am. She couldn't help but wonder if that was such a terrible thing. *Did I even* like *who I was?*

Her heavy thoughts wouldn't let her rest. She finally decided to get up, pulling away from Connor quietly, picking up the shirt he had let her wear earlier from the floor and pulling it over her head. She approached the fire and quietly added another piece of wood, the warmth and light increasing almost immediately, illuminating the mural of the blue dragon that seemed to stare her in the face . . .

Kiera suddenly very much felt the need to breathe fresh air, the warm room feeling cloying and close as she headed toward the balcony door. Connor's cloak was still draped over the chair by the desk, and Kiera pulled it tight over her shoulders, bringing the hood up before stepping out onto the balcony and closing the door gently behind her.

The night would have been quiet except for the incessant waves thundering off the rocks below. The stone floor under her bare feet was cold and damp, and Kiera could feel the whole house tremble slightly when she closed her eyes, the relentless pounding of the raging ocean making her heart pick up speed.

She hadn't decided yet whether she loved or hated that sound. Kiera reached up absently and fiddled with the pendant, finding comfort in the solid stone that rested warm against her skin. She felt totally overwhelmed, the options before her daunting; while Kiera wanted to help Connor and very much wanted to *love* him, the idea of leaving Darian completely alone made her sad. With Darian she had found a *home*, but here, in this new and beautiful place, she could probably find another if she let herself.

How do I choose one life over the other? Do I even have that choice to make? Either way, I'll be putting one of them in danger, and neither of them deserves to be under fire because of me. Kiera was grateful that Connor was trying to protect her, and while Darian had always done the same, she felt that *she* had to take some sort of responsibility on her own safety and do the right thing for all of them. She knew Eryce wasn't going to let her continue to haunt Baneswood without a fight, and now Sorveign wanted her for Tirath-knew-what reason. . .

All of it felt like far too much for her to shoulder, but her choices would shape her future from that point forward. Kiera wasn't convinced she would be able to do it *alone.*

Maybe that's why I agreed to come here. Connor took me out of all that to give me time to think. I have to be smart about this. She thought back to a few hours before and how his story had left her unsure of her feelings at first; she had wondered if telling him she loved him had been the right choice. When he had finally kissed her and taken her back upstairs, those doubts had seemed far less important.

Kiera rubbed her fingers over the stone, the flat surfaces getting more and more familiar the longer she played with the new and foreign piece of jewelry. She knew Connor had meant for it to be a token of endearment, but she was starting to wonder if it was a mark of *possession*—that she was *his.*

Would that be so awful? If he loves me too, then wouldn't that be the goal? To be his? Kiera sighed and leaned forward against the railing, the few fires still burning in the city just to the north seeming like a continuation of the starry sky overhead, making the night seem endless. Connor had promised to take her into Siren's Bay in the morning, and Kiera was looking forward to being among people again as long as he had actually gotten her decent clothing like he said he had. She already felt naked without her armor or her boots, and experiencing that level of exposure made her feel too vulnerable. *I better not have to wear that dress. I would rather* be *naked . . .*

"*Hey.* What are you doing out *here*?" Connor sounded sleepy as he came up beside her and leaned against the railing to her left. Kiera hadn't heard the door open or his footsteps, but she was glad she was no longer alone, even if she had just been wondering if she was really okay with all of this.

"Kiera, are you all right? You've been very quiet since after dinner." Connor turned around so he could face her and leaned back, letting the railing support him as he crossed his arms, studying her. It was chilly with the cool breeze and the moisture from the ocean, but Connor didn't seem to mind as he stood out there with her in just his wool pants.

Kiera barely noticed.

"Do you have any idea what it's like to have your world change so dramatically you start to forget who you thought you were?" Kiera asked, looking up at the stars overhead as though they might have the answers she sought. The hood of the cloak slid back and pooled around her shoulders, the light of the rising moons reflecting off her pale skin and hair made her look spectral. Connor felt like he was staring at an apparition.

If I ever have to come back here without her, she will haunt this place until I no longer breathe.

"Was I *wrong* to bring you here?" Connor sounded like he really didn't want an answer to that question. "I'll admit to being selfish in wanting to have you to myself, but I did it to be closer to you, not drive a wedge between us."

"Honestly, Connor, at this point, I'm just trying to keep my head above water. I've had a lot of information thrown at me in a very short time, and I'm still unsure how I want to deal with everything, especially since I no longer have just myself to consider.

"But *you* are not the only change I face, Connor. I love that you brought me here, more so than I thought I would, but this world makes me nervous because I haven't been in it for so long. I'm not sure how I will fit if I decide to come back to it or if you'll even allow that to be an option . . ." Kiera turned her head to find him watching her, and she couldn't tell if he looked disappointed with her or himself. She parted the cloak so he could see the pendant.

"Connor, why did you give me this?"

Connor pulled her toward him, wrapping his arms around her under the heavy mantle, leaning forward to rest his forehead against hers. *You might as well tell her, idiot. She already knows.*

"I know Baneswood is where you think you belong, but I want you to consider thinking of *me* as your home."

"If this was a week ago, I would have laughed at you if you told me that I would fall for you and actually *want* that sentiment to be true. In fact, I would have *punched* you and left you tied to a *tree* . . ."

Connor laughed quietly at her joke, and Kiera smiled wryly for a moment, but it faded as her tone turned serious.

". . . but having something like this homing crystal makes me feel like what's building between us is incredibly fragile. It makes *me* feel fragile, and I'm struggling to stand on shaky ground."

"What if you didn't have to do it *alone*, Kiera? What if you belong *here*, not out in some forest—"

"I wasn't *alone*, in case you've forgotten, and it's not up to *you* where I *belong*." Kiera could feel her defenses going up, and so could he. She tried to pull away, but Connor wouldn't let her go, one hand on her lower back keeping her pressed against him as he lifted her chin with the other.

"*Don't*, Kiera. I'm sorry if this is coming across possessively because I'm not trying to force you to stay with me. Part of the reason that I gave you that pendant was so that you'll always have a piece of *me* with you, even if you ultimately go back to playing in the woods . . ."

Connor reached up and tucked a strand of hair behind her ear, holding her gaze with his, suddenly wondering why it had taken so long for him to let the words come out of his mouth as he held her gaze. The idea of being without her made him feel like he couldn't breathe.

"And don't think I won't follow you there. *You* are where *I* belong, Kiera. I love you."

The look on her face said everything he needed to know: she had already said it and had been just waiting to hear Connor admit he felt the same.

"Well, I'm glad *that's* finally out in the open," she breathed against his mouth as she moved to kiss him.

Where have I heard those words before?

"What? That I *love* you?"

"No, Connor. That you love me *too*."

Sixty-Two

The voice of a single bell rang through the halls of the castle, striking witching the hour. If the man in the great hall had heard it at all, it didn't outwardly register. He sat alone with his thoughts, staring vacantly at the table in front of him. Only yesterday it had held food for guests, all of whom had been there to celebrate the passing of another year.

Today, it held his wife.

Eryce had avoided coming into the hall during the day as the servants cleaned her body and dressed her all in white, laying Serra out on the monstrous table, covering her from head to toe with a sheer white sheet to hide the damage from her fall. But once the darkness had chased away the light of day, Eryce had found he was unable to justify staying away any longer; he had been a one-man army when he had stormed the hall by taking up a chair and ordering everyone *out*. His staff had crowded jasmine and lavender all around her body in preparation for the next two days when the entire kingdom could walk past her and pay their respects before she was laid to rest in the tomb he'd had built just for her.

He had heard everyone whispering that Serra looked like she was asleep. With the dozens of candles in the room, Eryce thought she looked like she was made of wax.

How do the words go? "We are in death as we were in life"? The irony that Serra was now just an empty shell of the woman he had loved wasn't lost on Eryce; she had already been that way before she was taken from him for the second time. He ran his hands back through his hair, unable to take his eyes off the ghostly figure that had haunted him since his early twenties.

They had been brother and sister in a household of five children, and Eryce was the oldest, the heir to the kingdom Falyyn and Castle Pearla, though he had claimed them by force instead of by rite. His mother, Jessandra, had died giving birth to him, and Eryce was almost three when his father remarried. Isabelle had been kind to him, but her four daughters had always come first, and he had never felt like a brother so much so as a *guardian* to his sisters. Serra was the second to last to be born, and she had been their father's favorite with big green eyes and wavy black hair . . .

His sisters had arrived in quick succession, and Eryce had been seven when *she* was brought into his world. Being the third of four girls meant she would be one of the last to marry, and in her he had found an unlikely friend even at a young age. Serra had followed him everywhere she could once she could walk on her own, and she was given the freedom to go with Eryce on errands in the townships around the Pearla when she finally turned five.

He smiled slightly when he remembered Serra at that age; she had been a sweet, kind, quiet little girl, her favorite pastime to pick flowers and give them to Eryce, telling him she loved him best. When he was lost in his studies, she would crawl up into his lap and sleep against his chest while he tried to read and not wake her. She wouldn't eat a new food unless he did first, and when she was eight, Serra took a pair of shears to her hair and cut it short so she could look more like *him*.

Eryce loved her and protected her, and he was rarely seen without her when he was home. As he got older and his studies increased, he was gone for longer and longer periods of time, but Serra was always the first person he sought out as soon as he set foot back in his father's castle, usually with some small present for her.

She was always happy to see him return.

That innocent dynamic changed dramatically just after Serra turned fourteen. Eryce had been home for about a week and was planning to leave again in less than two, but he would forever remember what time it was, the name of the book he had been after, the smell of the room when he had walked into their father's library . . .

Serra was sitting at the window, her knees drawn up under her skirts and her book as she read in the late morning light, the sun illuminating her white dress and her fair skin. She looked angelic with her profile to him, her graceful neck with the ϒ *mark exposed on her bared shoulder, her dark tresses spilling over one shoulder, her fingers delicately turning the page before retreating toward her face to absently play with a curl.*

Eryce thought his heart had stopped as he stood there, dumbfounded.

Serra must have felt his intense gaze because she suddenly looked up. When she realized who was standing there, those green eyes sparkled as she smiled and patted the window seat, inviting Eryce to sit with her, the familiar scent of fresh green apples flooding the room . . .

He almost walked away from her, he was so nervous.

"I have something to tell you," Serra said quietly as she set her book aside, bringing her arms around her knees and locking her hands together as he sat as close as he dared, trying not to touch her. The look on her face said she didn't like the news any more than he was about to. "Father has chosen someone for me."

Serra could not have uttered more devastating words; Eryce was stunned. Hærrion hadn't mentioned even entertaining the thought of suitor for her yet, but Eryce hadn't been home for over three months. The king could have been up to anything in that time, and he certainly didn't need his son's permission to find husbands for his daughters.

"Who told you that? I would think it's a bit soon, considering Katelyn and Andraea have yet to be betrothed—"

"That was my argument when he told me an hour ago, but Father is insisting that it be me. He wants a treaty with Corengale, and I'm to leave in a week to marry Prince Garegan. I tried to find you to tell you, but you were still out riding, so I waited for you here, knowing you would turn up eventually . . ." Serra's smile was bitter as she reached out and took his hand, and his skin thrilled under her gentle touch. He didn't know it then, but it would be the last time he would touch her for fifteen years.

"I know I don't have a say in this, but if I did, I wouldn't leave. I don't care about treaties or politics or what's 'for the best of our people' if those things take me from my home and put me somewhere I do not choose to be.

"I would stay here . . . with you, Eryce. I wish you had chosen me first." Serra hadn't been so blind as to how she felt about him and had loved Eryce quietly for over a year. A marriage between them wasn't forbidden, but it hadn't been likely since Eryce hadn't seemed inclined to marry anyone.

At twenty-one, he should have already been married and should be working on having a son to continue the line, but he had been more interested in politics and his freedom than dealing with women who wanted to be stuck with him for the rest of their lives. His father couldn't make him choose, though Hærrion certainly pushed enough pretty girls into his path and sent him on every errand throughout the kingdom that involved high-ranking families with eligible daughters that he could.

Eryce suddenly wondered how much of that had been his father's way of keeping them apart while Hærrion made other arrangements for his daughter. "Duty over happiness" was one of the king's favorite sayings, and Eryce could already hear those particular words in his head as his anger rose, and the room started to feel like it was closing in on him.

He stood and walked out without an explanation, leaving her there, confused and calling after him. His heart broke a little more every time he heard his name echo along the halls until he went down a flight of stairs and heard it no more.

Goddess Tirath, anyone but her. Why her? Why now? His thoughts were a mess as he wandered the castle, ending up at his father's bedroom when he didn't find the current ruler on his throne or in the dining hall. He could hear Hærrion with either Isabelle or one of the maids on the other side of the door, and he walked away without bothering to knock, not particularly interested in trying to talk to his father while he was busy being a man *instead of a* king.

"What do I even do? What can *I* do?"

The only answer he could come up with was nothing.

Eryce had never felt so helpless or so stupid. Serra had been right in front of him the whole time, and now she was already gone...

He had never loved anyone else.

Eryce got from his seat next to the table, barely noticing when the muscles of his lower back protested to the movement. He approached the table cautiously, gently pulling back the thin veil, totally unaware that his hand was shaking slightly as he stripped the cloth away to reveal her face.

He winced when he saw the woman he had loved so marred by what he had hoped was at least a quick death because it would not have been painless. The servants had done a good job cleaning her wounds, but there were dark marks now where the blood had settled under the lacerations in the left side of her face, the bones of the cheek and brow on that side slightly misshapen. Her arm had been broken, but that was hidden beneath the long sleeves of the white gown he vaguely remembered as one she had worn the previous spring.

Serra looked thinner than he remembered, more wasted than he had ever realized, and much older than thirty-six.

She was too young for life to have been so hard on her. Eryce felt his temper flare, the old hatred for a man long dead still fresh and vibrant in his heart when he thought about the way both his life and hers had been altered by their father. Eryce had tried to talk to him about Serra's betrothal the next day, but Hærrion evaded him every time he approached, eventually demanding that Eryce leave him in peace.

It didn't matter to Hærrion if his son was distraught or that his daughter had remained locked in her rooms and refused to come out because decisions had been made and fates sealed. Everyone else was excited, and it wasn't long before the entire family was packed up and ready to see Serra wed.

He still remembered that day, too. Serra had been stoic and silent when she had left her rooms and went down to the waiting carriage on her own. She had drifted past him as though she were lost in a dream, but when she stumbled slightly on the cobblestones in the courtyard and the scent of wine floated to him as he followed not far behind, he realized she was drunk, and his heart broke that much more.

There was simply no turning back.

Eryce hadn't even tried to kiss her goodbye.

Once the caravan passed the castle gates, Eryce felt the need to be destructive, and he took his pain out on those around him. He was surly and aggressive to the staff, bedded half the girls in the kitchen so roughly that they scattered like roaches every time he came into the room, and spent countless hours sitting alone in the library, drinking rum and ignoring his obligations. When the train of horses and guards and covered carriages had come back through the gates three weeks later missing one pretty face, Eryce felt like his heart was no longer in the kingdom he would one day rule.

Hærrion refused to watch his son mourn the loss of a love he hadn't wanted to encourage between his children. The king hadn't been blind to how Serra acted around Eryce, and the idea that his plans could be unwittingly thwarted by two people in his own household was more than Hærrion was willing to tolerate. It was with that in mind when he approached his son and tossed a sealed envelope on the table in front of him the day he returned from seeing his favorite daughter wed.

"Eryce, stop moping about like some love-drunk fool. You *will* forget *her.* Serra was marked and always intended for someone of the same, and Garegan was as perfect a match as I could have wished for. You would be wise to never let any feelings you might have to grow in the first place—in your position, you cannot afford to feel too much, or your subjects will always consider you weak.

"This marriage was always about strategy, and I do *not* care *if either of you were happy about it.* We strengthen our alliance against those outside this realm, and now that all three of the reigning castles have a familial tie, we shall profit far greater than we ever have. Duty above happiness, boy. I say it for a reason."

Hærrion leaned forward and jabbed the letter with his index finger, pinning it to the table.

"This is from her. I asked her to tell you goodbye since you didn't seem inclined to do so before we left, but if I were you, I would simply burn it. Nothing in this will give you peace of mind."

His father had left him without another word.

But Hærrion had been right; that letter had been heartbreaking, and Eryce could still remember every word. All it had done was fuel a fire that was starting to rage out of control, and it had been later that same day that Eryce had screamed at his father in front of their entire family while dinner was being served.

Hærrion kept chiding Eryce for slamming his utensils and sloshing his wine, and Eryce's sudden outburst at the King of Falyyn caught everyone by surprise. No one else had known that Eryce had loved Serra, and the argument that ensued was heated on several sides. Eryce threatened to pay his father back for taking her from him, and Hærrion had ended the entire fight by bellowing for Eryce to get out or he would be dragged out.

The prince had sought refuge in the lower halls of the castle among some of the cooks and the maids, two of whom took pity on Eryce and lifted their skirts for him just as they did on a regular basis for his father and half the guards. After that, he drank until dawn, trying to forget *her* with the help of a glass and naked flesh, neither of them distracting him from the pain in his chest.

The words of her letter kept playing in his head.

All he saw was Serra.

Hærrion sought him out the next morning where he slept on a wooden bench in the servants dining hall. Eryce didn't even get the chance to fight back: Hærrion had ripped Eryce off the bench by the front of his shirt and beaten him into unconsciousness, inadvertently blinding the prince in his right eye . . .

Eryce didn't wake again until the next day, and by then, he was already inside a moving carriage with an armed escort and a physician to tend his wounds. He was handed a letter once he could see well enough that said he was being sent to live with his uncle Phelix at the Arx Luna, his father deeming it prudent to remove his son from the Pearla for the time being, though he was willing to forgive him and wait for Eryce's temper to cool.

That day never came. Eryce continued to threaten Hærrion from afar, replying to letters with a cold and unforgiving hand, and he never once wrote to Serra. He had sworn to repay the man who had ruined the woman he loved if he ever got the chance, and Eryce bided his time, using it as wisely as he could.

After Eryce had been at the Arx for five years, he unexpectedly got his way when his uncle was killed in a skirmish with a dignitary over a game of chess. No one questioned Eryce's right to that particular throne since he was already running the show by the time the drunken fight erupted and Phelix paid the ultimate price. It still made the current ruler chuckle to think of the stupid man he had taken over for, especially when the rest of the staff, upon any mention of Phelix, replied "King *who*?"

Once he had free reign, Eryce had used his newly acquired money and his power to quietly started building an army, recruiting all the way to Glory Run in the Valley of Storms, right on Hærrion's doorstep. It took Eryce almost seven years to amass his legion, stealing men from all parts of the map, paying those that were willing well to serve him and paying those that weren't so willing with pain and enslavement. The Sukolai had already been interested in his money for over a year at that point, and he was more than happy to use all forty of them and their dogs as part of his raid on the Pearla.

It was a day he would always look back on with *pride.*

Ten-thousand men had marched on his family's castle, and like soldier ants on a carcass, his forces overran his father's lands and overwhelmed the Pearla's dwindling forces, taking them under Eryce's control within a matter of hours. Eryce had led the poor excuse for a battle himself, taking the lives of his father, his stepmother, and anyone who tried to stand in his way as he went after them both. Eryce would never forget that surprised look of recognition as he approached Hærrion fearlessly, and his sword found a home in his father's chest.

"*For Serra,*" Eryce whispered…

He had never felt so righteous as he did pulling his blade from the king's stilled heart.

Once Falyyn was under his control, Eryce had turned his enchanted gaze southward. Corengale was next to be destroyed, and they never saw it coming, mostly because Eryce didn't do anything right away. He continued to trade openly with Garegan, allowed the people of Corengale passage into his lands without question, and replied to letters with a friendly hand.

It took four years.

But Eryce was patient, and once he knew Garegan no longer feared his wrath, he made his move. The King of Rhonendar had savored the burning of *that* castle and the surrounding city like no other.

He had been there with his small band of Sukolai and had watched the men and the hounds cut through the inhabitants of the castle, making them scatter like roaches in sudden torchlight. Garegan's forces had been caught completely by surprise, and even the knights who still called Corengale home were ripped apart as they tried to defend their king and castle; forces Kiera had never seen stormed the front gates once the Sukolai had started the blaze, and several thousand men tore Corengale to pieces as the night dragged on. Eryce and his forces were unstoppable, and the Sukolai didn't lose a single man, just one dog, while Corengale lost over three thousand and the residents scattered to the four winds when the castle had been lit by dragonsfire and surrounding structures had been burned to the ground.

Eryce had been the one to capture Serra as she raced across the field with her daughter, and he remembered almost mistaking one for the other as he hunted her down by that sweet apple scent that was heavy on the wind. He knew the exit she would be flushed from, and there were strict orders in place that she was not to be harmed.

Everyone else could simply be destroyed.

He had taken Serra away from the carnage as quickly as possible, his horse finally foundering after several miles. She had hugged him close when she had realized who had rescued her, and Serra thought he had saved her at first, but when he rejoined the Sukolai the next morning, she had just stared at him incredulously when she realized *why* Eryce was there.

Serra was never the same after that.

Riding through the gates of the Arx was hard for her, and she didn't leave his rooms for two days once she was able to lock the door behind her. Serra clung to him when darkness fell every night for a week, and Eryce could still remember waking in the night to her absence, finding Serra staring out the window to the south as though she could see Corengale if she looked hard enough. She would fight him when he tried to touch her if she didn't instigate the contact, insisting finally on having her own rooms, and Eryce had let her be, giving her space and time.

A month later, he had approached her about marriage, and Serra hadn't answered him. Eryce left her alone, and she had sought him out after two nights had passed, drunk and wanting to be near him, telling him *yes*.

She had cried the entire first time they were together. It didn't dawn on him until much later that those tears were never shed in joy.

All for the love of a woman . . . he sighed.

Serra seemed like a bad dream now, the beautiful demon before him who had already been a ghost when he finally had her back. He found himself hoping that they were both free of each other at last and that he could close that chapter of his life.

Serra had slammed the book shut on her own story.

Eryce was simply ready to turn the page.

Sixty-Three

"*Damn it, woman! Slow down!*" Connor yelled, but his voice was getting farther away...

Kiera kicked her horse harder, loving the thrill of the swiftly moving stallion under her as he ran at breakneck speed toward Siren's Bay in the early morning mist. They weren't traveling far, only a couple of miles, but the thought of being able to *fly* across the ground was too tempting. Kiera had picked the better horse on purpose, leaving Connor with the older gelding, which was apparently in no mood to go faster than a slow canter.

It was Connor's own fault; he had said, "Pick one," and she did. He never asked if Kiera actually *knew* anything about horses. The stallion would have looked less appealing to an inexperienced rider with his slimmer frame and plain brown coat when compared with Santine, the sleek black gelding Connor was following her on, but Kiera saw that fire in Kruzeb's eyes and knew he wanted to *run*.

She was only too happy to let him.

An earsplitting whistle rang through the air, and Kiera's horse slowed immediately.

"You take away all my fun!" she yelled over her shoulder. Kiera was laughing hysterically as Connor came up beside her, all seriousness.

"*You*, young lady, need to wait for your *elders*, or next time I'll make you wear that *dress* and ride side saddle like you *should*."

Kiera tried to give him a disgusted look as her horse matched his in step, but her smile kept getting in the way as they rode side by side for the last few hundred yards into town.

The pair was well into the city limits before they dismounted and walked with their horses in tow into the middle of the square, which was bustling with activity. Both the animals and Connor seemed used to the noise and the mixture of smells from both the people and the sea, but for Kiera, it was overwhelming. Memories of Corengale flooded her mind, and Kiera felt out of place and right at home all at once, the sensation making her a little unsteady on her feet. Connor took her hand and led her on, the warm smile directed at her his way of silently promising to protect her in such a strange and crowded place.

Once she was actually *in* it, Kiera realized that Siren's Bay was a *much* bigger city than she had originally thought. It followed the rolling hills along the ocean's edge for quite a distance, and she wanted desperately to explore, though Connor had told her that they were only going toward the port where the weapons and foreign trade districts were. The buildings that lined the gravel paved streets were built of light gray, tan, and red granite blocks with slate roofs, and there were colorful banners for the shops that hung into the street from awnings and balconies. People, animals, Elves, and a few other races that Kiera had never seen and didn't know the proper names for were absolutely *everywhere* going about their business and ignoring them completely, the buzz in the air making her heart pick up under her new shirt.

Connor hadn't been at all surprised that morning when Kiera had asked after the other clothes Peter had supposedly purchased, and he had almost told her they didn't exist just to annoy her. He still hadn't decided if he was glad he had given in or if he had only made things worse for himself now that Kiera wore a set of black wool pants not unlike his own. With ties at the side and fitted to her legs, the pants hugged her curves in a way that Connor found startling. The leggings he had burned had been skin tight, but the way these molded to her seemed somehow obscene, and Connor knew he had an uncomfortable day ahead of him as soon as she had put them on. Her cream silk shirt was punctuated by a black corseted vest that cut under her breasts and fit snugly over her armor, both pieces equally maddening in their feminine curve and sharp contrast. The highly oiled black riding boots that covered her calves and laced up the back completed a look that made Connor want to strip Kiera bare every time he glanced at her.

Kiera had asked if there was any way to get kohl to cut the glare while they were in town, and she was thoroughly floored when he produced some from the vanity. She certainly hadn't been expecting that, and Connor didn't bother to explain, just watched quietly her as she rimmed her brilliant green eyes with it.

She was absolutely striking, and every man in the immediate vicinity was craning their necks to look at *her* while Kiera was busy looking at everything *else*.

"Dolmeneigh!"

They both turned when a loud, excited male voice called from across the square, and the owner of the outburst fought his way through the crowd as he came trotting up to them. Connor smiled broadly as he stepped forward and shook the hand of a short, fat, balding man, who was sweating profusely despite the cool morning air.

Kiera barely noticed, busy staring at Connor, the surname he apparently answered to catching her by surprise.

Why have I heard that name before?

"Jack! Good to see you! What news?"

The squat little man was out of breath, and he didn't answer right away as he bent down to put his hands on his knees, trying to gulp air.

"Ugh, I have *got* . . . to stop . . . doing that! I'm going to drop dead from *exhaustion* one of these days! Whew!" Jack exclaimed dramatically as he wiped at his brow with the back of his tan sleeve, which simultaneously left a brown smear across his forehead from whatever was stuck on the grimy fabric and smoothed the wisps of hair on his mostly bald head back into place.

Kiera was trying not to smile.

Jack had only run about a hundred feet.

When Jack had finally caught his breath enough to open his mouth for something other than breathing, he glanced at the woman to his left, almost annoyed that she was eavesdropping so blatantly. All at once he realized that Kiera was standing there *with* Connor, and he looked back and forth between the two of them with confusion evident in his expression.

"Dolmeneigh, is this gorgeous *beast* of a woman with *you*?"

I suppose there are worse compliments in the world. Kiera was trying not to laugh at the odd attempt at flattery while Connor smiled proudly and nodded.

"Jack, this is Kiera. She's from the other side of the kingdom, and this is her first time in Siren's Cove. I can *see* that look in your eye old man, and just between you and me, she's taken, so quit while you're ahead."

"My dear, please excuse me. I have never seen Connor anything other than alone, so you are *quite* the surprise! My name is Jack Liberon, and I welcome you to our city." He winked at Connor as he reached for her hand.

Kiera saw what was coming and tried in vain to simply shake his when he grasped her fingers, but Jack forced his sweaty mouth onto the back of her hand, making Kiera grimace when his head was down. Connor was turning a different color trying to suppress his amusement.

I'll get you for this, she mouthed.

"Kiera, Jack is sort of my information headquarters for the Cove. He's the owner of the best book store in a hundred miles, and he knows just about everyone."

Jack let go of Kiera's hand and bowed quickly to Connor, giving her the chance to wipe her hand on the back of her pants without him noticing.

"Thank you for the praise, my boy! You know *flattery* will get you *everywhere* with me." Jack nudged Connor in the ribs with his elbow as he smiled brightly, showing his yellowing teeth and his brown eyes crinkling at the edges. "Do me the honor of coming to my shop? Then we can talk where it's less crowded, and I can fill you in and get you two some tea. There has been *much* news!"

Jack didn't wait for an answer because it wasn't really a question, and Connor rolled his eyes, knowing Jack would simply come find them if they didn't follow willingly. Mr. Liberon waddled back toward his shop, which was much farther than Kiera had thought it would be as they trailed behind him, and she was thoroughly lost by the time they reached his storefront and had the horses tied up behind one of the larger buildings she had seen so far.

A bright red banner embroidered in brilliant yellow stretched across the façade proclaimed the store's name to be the "Bay Book Emporium," while long, triangular banners of the same color fluttered from the edge of the roof, images of open books and rolled parchments adorning the pennants and repeating the theme. There were four fluted pillars that held up the front of the gray building with purple and white wisteria covering each about halfway up to the second floor windows, the vines buzzing with bees that seemed oblivious to their presence as they went about their day.

A pair of large wooden doors studded with brass stood open to the city, inviting people in.

The sight that greeted her upon entering the rather austere building was startling. Garegan had been an avid reader and had possessed quite a library, but it paled when compared to the wealth of books, scrolls, manuscripts, and maps strewn about the two floors of the building. The second story was visible from the first because the ceiling in the middle of the lower room had been cut away, leaving only the outer walls and a wide path around the top of the room in which they now stood. A grand spiral staircase with a wrought-iron rail dominated the middle of the store, every step holding a book or scroll or sheaf of paper at its edge, the entire place illuminated by the leaded glass skylights that made up most of the ceiling and the stained glass windows that lined the south facing wall.

The store smelled sweet and musty at the same time from new print and old books, and Kiera breathed deeply, loving the scent of *knowledge* that tinged the still air. The haphazard way the inordinate amount of paper and parchment was strewn about made the store seem it was a huge mess at first, but the more she looked around, the more Kiera realized that things were organized in distinguishable areas; it only looked messy because scrolls rested on top of every flat surface they could be set upon, including the random tables and chairs set out for patrons.

Kiera felt the urge to explore, but Jack ushered them toward the back and through a heavy blue velvet curtain where his own quarters were hidden. Once Connor allowed the drape to fall back into place behind them, Jack started yelling for a woman named Gayle, swearing loudly when she didn't immediately show herself. The back rooms of the shop were no less cluttered than the store itself; the only difference being that the items upon which scrolls were perched were personal pieces of furniture instead of rows of books for sale.

"Quiet down, you grumpy thing! You would think this place had caught fire! What do you *want*?" A young woman appeared, grumbling to herself and carrying an armload of books that she nearly dropped when she saw *who* was in tow.

Gayle's face lit up in a bright smile, and Kiera felt Connor squeeze her hand. She was roughly the same age as Kiera, maybe a year or two older, and pretty with curly blonde hair and playful blue eyes. Petite, slender, and wearing a flattering yellow dress, Kiera thought Gayle looked like sunshine.

It took her a moment to notice that all that *light* was directed right at *Connor*.

The protective jealous hit her like a wave, and Kiera suddenly understood how Darian had felt; she couldn't help but wonder if maybe she hadn't been a little cold. Darian had been defending his *territory* the only way he knew how, and Kiera had ignored him for a rival male. Then again, she had never had the opportunity to see Darian take interest in another female either.

Now that the tables were turned, Kiera regretted how flippant she had been. Seeing the way Gayle devoured Connor with her eyes made Kiera realize that Connor had done the very same thing to *her*.

Connor is mine! Kiera truly knew the depth of the words when they rang in her head as she debated how much of a threat the blonde beauty really was.

Connor had known what was coming, and he kept his influence strictly to himself. Gayle had loved him since she was a little girl, and she had followed him around like a puppy whenever she found out that he had come home to see Grandmere for most of his life. Connor had never had even the *slightest* interest in her, but Gayle just kept trying. Now that he had the opportunity to really draw the line between them, Connor was quick to make sure Gayle knew *exactly* where he and Kiera stood. Kiera was silently grateful when he put his hand around her waist with obvious affection and introduced her to the pretty little blonde, both of them quietly enjoying watching that bright smile falter.

"Gayle, this is Kiera. She is my . . . *guest*, and is visiting from the other side of the kingdom for a few days. I expect you to be *nice* to her." *Maybe now she'll take me seriously. Tirath sometimes grants miracles . . .*

"Nice to meet you, *Kiera*. Connor, this is *quite* the surprise . . . I always thought you would come home with a woman who at least *dresses* like one." Gayle giggled coyly at her own little joke, the glint in her eye openly mean.

Pretty face, ugly mouth. Kiera bristled at the comment, and Connor was immediately irritated and angry. Connor eyed Gayle darkly, feeling like he was twelve again and having to peel her off him. He tightened his hold around Kiera's waist before he came to her defense, and his own.

"Careful with what you say, *Gayle. I* may not be able to hit you now that we're no longer children, but Kiera *can*, and she probably *will* if you push it. I certainly won't stop her—"

"*Girl, get your fool head out of the clouds and get us some tea!*" Jack yelled, turning purple from the exchange.

Gayle's smile fled her mouth, and she unceremoniously dropped the books at her feet as she left, looking back over her shoulder and still trying to catch Connor's eye with her pretty pout. He totally ignored her.

"I'm sorry. I should have warned you about that," Connor whispered in her ear. He was so used to travelling alone that he hadn't even thought about how other people might react to an *addition* in his life. Kiera was feeling better about the whole thing once Connor put his foot down, even though she was fairly certain the blonde was going to spit in her cup. It suddenly struck her as funny that he was almost hiding behind her, trying to keep this Gayle at bay. Kiera smiled wryly as she wondered who *else* she was going to have to *shield* him from.

Poor, sad, beautiful Connor . . . Chasing the girls away with a stick.

"Don't listen to her, Kiera. She's probably just as surprised as I am that Dolmeneigh showed up with a woman at his side. You don't look like a *man*, my dear. Any woman who can pull off *that* look like you can, well . . . I think you look *decadent*." Jack winked up at her, and Kiera thought Jack needed to learn to keep his compliments in his mouth.

Connor moved toward the table he knew they would end up at, and Jack cleared a mound of papers from the surface with a sweep of his arm, scattering it like down out of a ripped pillow. Their host pulled out a chair and dusted it off for Kiera as Connor took the one to her left as he normally would. Jack sat his pudgy frame to her right, immediately turning his attention behind him after Gayle.

"Now, *where* did that girl *go*? She had better not be pouting in the kitchen. Dolmeneigh, I am *mortified*, but *you* know how she is," Jack apologized as he turned back around. They exchanged an exasperated look, and Connor laughed.

"Yes, I certainly do, but Gayle is still young and pretty. One day, someone else will catch her eye, and she'll forget all about me. Eventually I'll be able to come here without the threat of death by *flirtation*."

"Oh, Dolmeneigh, I hope so. She needs something better to do with her time than spend it here with her grouchy old father." Jack chuckled, and Connor sat back in his chair to cross one ankle over the other knee, folding his arms across his chest, the discussion one they had had too many times to be anything but funny.

Kiera was mildly surprised to hear the two were related, and she assumed that Gayle took after her mother. There were no portraits of anyone as she glanced around, but Connor picked up the conversation before she could think on it any further.

"Jack, you said there had been much news. I haven't been home in several weeks, so I am afraid I'm a bit out of the loop."

"Oh! Yes, and thank you for reminding me! I get so forgetful in my old age . . . Anyway, Eryce's queen is all the talk! You know the story about how she ended up at the Arx after Corengale fell. It's been, what, six years now? I can't even say that I blame her, jumping from her bedroom window like that—"

"What?" Connor and Kiera were both surprised, and Connor was the first to recover.

"Jack . . . wait . . . before you continue..." Connor started to panic. He had forgotten completely that her mother was still living, and Kiera probably had no idea; Serra was about to die all over again, but Jack was already on a tangent and wasn't listening to Connor's attempts to shut him up.

"—his birthday was yesterday, and he had a roomful of guests—"

"*Jack*—"

"—and she was drunk! That poor woman was drunk and angry—"

"*Jack! Stop talking*!" Connor yelled so forcefully he startled Gayle as she was bringing in the tray of tea. Kiera jumped too, and Jack just looked at Connor in confusion, his mouth open to articulate the next words that never came.

"Kiera. Outside. *Now*." Connor stood quickly and took her by the arm, trying to keep his hand steady as the adrenaline rushed through his veins and he almost upended his chair. She didn't fight him as he pulled her out of her own and followed him through the maze of books and papers, several falling to the floor in their wake as they stirred the air with their retreat. He walked around the outside of the building, back to where their horses were tied, still dragging a startled and concerned Kiera behind him.

Once they were close to their waiting mounts, Kiera tried to yank her arm away, but Connor tightened his grip, making her wince.

"Connor, wait . . . Ow! What the hell is *wrong* with you?"

He didn't seem to hear her, his breathing shallow as he tried to figure out how to tell her that the one person still alive in her family was gone. He wasn't even looking at her, his eyes focused on the ground when he stopped and stood in front of her, not realizing he still had a death grip on her bicep.

"Connor?" She spoke quietly when he finally stopped pulling her. "Connor, you have to let go. This *hurts*."

Kiera laid her hand over his, trying to get him to calm down and at least ease off. Connor looked at his own hand in surprise, not realizing he had been squeezing so hard, abruptly letting her go. He ran both hands back through his hair and forced out a frustrated breath.

"I am so sorry, Kiera. I-I just couldn't let him keep talking. I should be the one to tell you . . . This is not going to be easy to say—"

"That my mother is dead?"

"You *knew*?" Connor stared at her with wide eyes, shocked. Kiera was rubbing her arm where Connor's fingers had wrinkled her shirt, and she shrugged in response. Connor suddenly felt like an idiot.

"I knew she was *alive*. I knew she was married to *Eryce*. I saw the decree when it happened. I had gone to Grant's Perch for candles, and it was nailed to a post. Corengale was still smoldering, and she had moved on. Please don't ask me to feel any *sympathy* for her."

"Are you . . . *okay*? She was your *mother*, after all."

Kiera gave him a funny look and crossed her arms over her chest.

"Serra stopped being my *mother* in my mind when she *chose* to marry the man that killed our family. She had other paths she could have taken, and yet she wed the bastard that slaughtered our family and took our *home*. I stopped grieving for *her* a long time ago.

"Now, can we *please* go back in? I want to hear what happened."

"I-I'm sorry for all that. I didn't mean to hurt you." Connor wanted to touch her, but he wasn't sure how she would react. Kiera saw his hesitation and closed the gap, knowing Connor had been more concerned about how she would take the news. The bruise would heal.

"Connor, *don't*. You forget who you're talking to. Trying to protect me is not a bad thing, but *think* before you do it next time. I admitted to loving you, but that doesn't mean I will be held responsible for beating you until you can't see straight if you catch me off guard like that again." Kiera ran her hand up his arm and squeezed gently, trying to reassure him that she was all right. When her mouth tugged up at the corner, Connor relaxed a little;

he still felt awful, but he knew what she meant. He pulled her against him, wrapping his arms around her shoulders and hugging her tightly.

"Don't worry, *Dirtbag*. You can make it up to me by buying me something *sharp* before we leave." Kiera snuggled into his neck, the scent of cedar and mint strong, his body warm against her. All he could do was laugh.

"*Deal.*"

Sixty-Four

Alyk and Henelce rode alone, heading westward on the final leg of their trek through Baneswood toward the old castle and Grant's Perch. The day was warm, and their progress shaded from the afternoon sun by the thick canopy, the forest floor dappled with sunlight filtering through the leaves and illuminating the particles of dust that floated in the air.

Alyk took a deep breath, the smells of the forest clean and sweet and comforting. The sound of birds fluttering and chirping in the trees and along the ground were almost musical, the whole forest feeling aglow with *life*. Knowing her like he had when they were younger, he could see why Kiera had chosen to hide there instead of in some city.

Although her bird probably hadn't given her much of a choice . . . Darian had flown ahead over an hour ago since they were only half a day's ride from the Breech, and the Aeroyn had felt like he was slowing them down by walking alongside. Kiera and Connor would be returning the next morning, and they wanted to be in Grant's Perch before the sun set and the ferrymen stopped crossing the Oriens for the night.

Connor had told them he was lodged at the Inn-land Starfish and would meet them in the downstairs tavern by midmorning.

Now they just had to get there.

Alyk's thoughts turned to the blonde *hunter*, unsure how he felt about *Connor* and his exuberant display of affection for Kiera. She had been so *rigid* when he had first met her, but Alyk couldn't deny the changes he could plainly see now that she was *accepting* someone's attention. He had been thinking about *her* since their exchange, and she was starting to seep into his brain in ways he was growing more and more uncomfortable with. Alyk knew far more about her than she probably realized, and while he was mildly worried about it being her *influence*, he had been able to stave it off so far. Considering he hadn't seen her in several days, he *knew* it had nothing to do with her *mark* or the power it possessed.

He simply couldn't help thinking about the warm smile she had given him, or the sound of her laugh . . .

"I *told* you so. You need to talk to her," Henelce chided as he broke the silence. He had been watching Alyk *think* as they rode, letting his horse pick his own way through the underbrush as he warily studied the younger man's expression and the inner turmoil written plainly on Alyk's face. The Shephard could only guess at what was on Alyk's mind, and it was either *her* or Tance.

He went for the obvious first.

Alyk snapped out of his thoughts to look at his pudgy companion with an expression of surprise that morphed into one that was some cross between embarrassed and defeated.

"Henelce, I *can't*. You *know* I can't. Kiera's gotten herself wrapped up in Connor, and I doubt he'll even let me anywhere near her when they get back. There is no way she'll listen to me anyway, and it's not like anything I have to say will make the slightest bit of difference to either of us."

"You never know until you try, and you're going to have to *try*, Alyk. That betrothal isn't going to go away just because you feel like it isn't worth the paper it's written on. Connor certainly seems to be intensely interested in her, and she in him, so there's no telling how quickly things will progress between them.

"Let me put this into perspective to you, boy. If he asks her to marry him, you'll *have* to tell her because she won't be able to accept, and it would give Connor all that much more reason to dislike you when the two of you should be working together to *protect* that girl. Kiera is a threat to Eryce on several levels, and he will stop at nothing to get to her if he finds out who she really is... Or *you*, for that matter."

Henelce was trying to be gentle, but the reality was a harsh one: Alyk couldn't go to Eryce, and neither could Kiera, and the betrothal was legally binding enough that nothing could be done *without* him. Once the king knew Kiera was still alive and that his wife's daughter was still a contender for his throne, *none* of them would be safe.

"I can't argue with you on that count, but I don't think I would try to enforce the decree." Alyk was watching Arveneg's mane bounce as she trod on. It still struck him as strange that he had Kiera's horse from so long ago, the beast under him a direct reflection of its previous owner.

"Now, that response worries me, boy, because that means you've *thought* about it, and you're right—it's *not* a good idea. You *know* it's not up to you. Just because Garegan is gone doesn't mean that decision died with him, and if Kiera marries outside of it, she will be going against a royal command and subsequent to punishment by the law, no matter who she is. Even *if* she agreed to marry *you*, she would be exposed. Eryce is already breathing down her neck, and that would just be fuel to the fire if he caught wind of it."

"Henelce, that piece of *paper* applies to two people, one of whom *no longer exists*. We may still answer to the same names, but her *title* is gone. *Corengale* is gone, and Kiera is *not* the kind of woman to give a damn about anything signed by her father that isn't what *she* wants." Alyk was starting to get irritated. He was *not* in the mood to talk about his thoughts and feelings on the matter, but Henelce would just hound him if he didn't.

Henelce, however, *was* in the mood to talk about that particular subject, and he waited quietly for Alyk to get the rest of what was in his head out of his mouth. Henelce didn't consider Alyk as just his *pupil*; he was his *friend*, and the Shephard cared about the boy. Now that Alyk was over twenty-one, Henelce could choose another assignment, but he wasn't interested in abandoning the Man just yet.

It wasn't often that a Shephard actually *liked* the charge they were responsible for, and to see Alyk so conflicted made him worry.

"I was there when they talked about this, and I cannot tell you how off-putting it is to have two men decide your fate in front of you like you don't exist. Garegan had summoned us from the estates because he had been considering a possible betrothal, and when he brought it up, my father refused at first because Kiera's *marked*, and there was the bloodline to consider.

"Turns out, Garegan wasn't interested in making sure it was extended. He told my father he wanted to 'stamp it out and let the line fade into oblivion' because all it did was cause turmoil and heartbreak. Garegan and Serra had been forced into their marriage, and they couldn't stand each other *because* of their shared heritage. He didn't want that for Kiera, knowing that if she ended up with someone *marked* that the marriage would be doomed before it ever started.

"Garegan wanted someone from a solid family that he trusted to keep her safe and happy and to keep her *influence* in check because he didn't want her to rule the way *his* father had either. That's why *you* were assigned to me—to help me help her to control it without her ever knowing what she was and to give me the tools to fight it if I needed to. Everyone in the kingdom was forbidden to speak to her about her abilities, and they all avoided her like a veritable plague wherever she went because of them.

"Honestly, I doubt she ever really noticed. Kiera was always caught up in her own little world, and Garegan wanted to keep her that way until she was married. I was supposed to be formally introduced to her on my sixteenth birthday, but we never got that far . . ." Alyk sighed and ground his teeth, drawing an annoyed look from the Shephard riding beside him.

"Spero was going to pass the throne to Kiera instead of his son because of the mark *she* carried. With the mark of the *Raze* on him from Serra's bloodline, Garegan didn't want to encourage the boy and was pushing Gary toward priesthood and celibacy since he had already secured me for Kiera, and our children wouldn't carry either mark forward like his son's could.

"I was training quietly at Corengale instead of at home because with the way Eryce was taking control of the map, Garegan wanted me to prepare for war, and if anything happened, he wanted me to take Kiera to the Southern Estates if Eryce looked like he might turn that blighted eye of his on Corengale." Alyk bit his lip, absently chewing on the side that didn't feel any pain. *So much went wrong . . .*

"You know, this is why I don't bother with politics. You humans are *idiots* sometimes. I mean, look at this logically, Alyk—*why* even put her in a position of power? If he was worried about the bloodline or her *influence*, why not just pass the throne directly to someone else? It was a naive decision on Garegan's part to put his daughter on the throne, especially considering her ignorance of her *influence*.

"He may have been able to keep her from being *trained*, but that only makes her more dangerous because *now* she cannot control it. Letting her assume the throne would have been like unleashing a wolf upon a herd of sheep—it does not know the destruction it causes because it's acting on instinct. Leaving her to figure it out on her own would have been *disastrous*—"

"I don't think Garegan thought that far ahead, Henelce, and then when the Pearla fell, he was too busy trying to protect his own hide from Eryce *and* work with Sorveign, and he didn't want her to feel the strain of that either.

"That's why Spero was always letting Kiera run free and act like a boy when he wasn't teaching her how to govern—he wanted her to know how being *happy* felt. He told me once that seeing her smile was the best part of his existence, and he thought it would help her rule with the heart of a woman but with the head of a man. I know that he hoped her ability to *influence* wouldn't affect her decisions or how she enforced them, and he felt confident that I could help to keep her level and fair."

Henelce wasn't really listening by the time Alyk finally closed his mouth because he was furiously stewing over the lack of training Kiera had received, reason be damned. She had the ability to be a very daunting foe to anyone who might threaten her or anyone she loved, and one wrong situation would be all it would take for her to become overwhelmed, draw people to her, and lose her life in the confusion.

He had seen it happen before.

"At the same point, Alyk, Kiera's ability is completely unchecked. No matter how capable she may be, unless she learns to get it under her own power, she's going to continue to put herself in danger. Take Darian for example—that Aeroyn has been *influenced* so much by her that it's changed his very *nature*. I didn't understand it at first because Kiera was on guard with all of us, but after seeing her with Connor and feeling the *influence* flare when she was defending him against Jaçon, I can now see how she could make an Aeroyn bend to her will, even if it wasn't intentional."

Henelce paused to pull at his beard, trying to think about the whole situation rationally. He had been training the *marked* for so long he couldn't even think of a time when he hadn't been involved in one line or another, but he had never seen one so *sheltered*.

Or so *oblivious*.

"Connor could be a very big problem for her. It's still hard to believe that they even like each other, considering they're both *marked*. I'm assuming that he *knows* what she is."

"I was thinking about that too. I know the stories, but there's one thing that is very different here—Kiera has been bloodsharing with Darian." Alyk was still on the fence as to whether he thought that was fascinating or disgusting, though his face said he was leaning toward the latter.

"Yes, I caught that much, and I can *see* that foreign blood move under her skin. Bloodsharing has been forbidden outside of their race since long before *I* was even on this earth, and that is still true. Their blood doesn't mix well with others, no matter how effectively it heals."

"Do you think it's changed her? The pallor is a little alarming, but it's how it may have affected her *abilities* that worries me. And her temperament—there's an aggressiveness about her that strikes me as an Aeroyn trait. Sort of *kill first, ask questions later*, and I don't know if that's from Darian or from his blood itself. She is obviously *changed* . . ." Alyk suddenly went pale.

"What if . . . what if Darian's blood made her *susceptible* to Connor? What if he's influencing her to get what he wants? Darian said he was *hunting* her… what if he never brings her *back*?"

Henelce mulled that over in his mind. It wasn't impossible, but with what he *knew*, it also wasn't likely, and Connor was too genuinely enamored with Kiera to take her to Eryce willingly. Aeroyn blood was potent, and it could cause issues when taken in large doses, but Kiera had most likely been sharing with Darian for several years now. There was no telling what it had done to her after long-term exposure.

However, there was an innate *dislike* between the *marked* and their own kind, which was why there were so few, and he couldn't see the bloodsharing as being the issue between Kiera and Connor. Connor should be immune to *her*, and even if Kiera was *stronger*, it still shouldn't have any effect on him.

Sometimes the pieces just fit where you don't expect them to.

"What if it has nothing to do with *influence* or Aeroyn blood, at all? Would you just accept that she loves him? She does, you know. You can see it." Henelce was blunt at this point, trying to gauge Alyk's reaction. He hated to see the boy so unsure and seemingly downtrodden, but Alyk wasn't making his own life any easier by hiding what he knew either.

"I'm not sure what to even say to that. Kiera is going to love whoever she's meant to, and if it's Connor, then so be it. If she finds what I have to say a challenge to her relationship with him, she'll probably get defensive, and I'm not really keen on being on the wrong side of her again."

No, not keen on that in the slightest, Alyk thought as he rubbed his collarbone reflexively. Henelce sighed, knowing Alyk was making a terrible mistake, but it was *his* to make if he chose. There was little the Shephard could do or say to change it.

"Well then, my boy, I guess it's just going to be a waiting game. But mark my words—if she agrees to marry him, you will absolutely *have* to tell her, and then you'll be stuck with whatever *reaction* you get."

Sixty-Five

"You want *that?*" Connor wasn't sure he was even surprised by her choice; after nearly two hours of wandering through the weapons section of the trade district, Kiera had finally found something that interested her. Connor had been under the impression that she had wanted a replacement for the glass dagger that had been rendered useless in her fight with Jaçon, and she had certainly settled on a blade.

But a dagger was *not* what had caught her eye.

In her hands was a broadsword with fine scroll work down the center of the blade, the grip covered with white leather, and the pommel was set with a green cabochon gem. It was perfect for *her*, but Connor was a little unnerved that she wanted a *sword*.

Kiera was focused on balancing it on the back of her hand, checking the center of gravity while Connor, and every man within ten feet of them, stared at her, waiting to see what she would do. She grasped the pommel, twisting her wrist to hold the blade parallel to the ground to check along the length of the weapon, making sure the tang was straight and true, oblivious to the attention directed at her.

"You know, I've trained with these, but I've never had access to one this nice . . . except when Alyk threw me his. It felt really good in my hand, and I want one." Kiera turned and looked at him pathetically, her eyes big and sad, her bottom lip almost pouting. "It's a pretty *big* bruise, Connor."

Oh, for the love of Tirath, you would *play the guilt card . . .*

"Done."

Her smile was worth it.

"On one condition . . ."

Her smile faded a little as Connor's got bigger.

". . . you have to wear that dress again later."

"*No.*" She set the sword back down, smile gone.

"Kiera, it's just a *dress!*" Connor teased as he came up behind her. "And I promise you won't be wearing it *that* long."

"Oh, *fine*. But only because you're willing to give me something big and pointy in exchange." Kiera giggled as Connor nuzzled his face into her neck, drawing jealous looks from the men around them.

"Woman, you are *terrible*..."

Neither of them noticed the uncomfortable look on the weapon's dealer's face as he tried to ignore the parts of their exchange that had nothing to do with the sale of his item.

"Actually, *you* already hold that title. I wouldn't want to take that away from you." Kiera grinned as she picked the sword back up, stepping forward out of his embrace to test the weapon without hitting him. Everyone around her gave her a wide berth when she started swinging it in a tight arc, then in an incredibly fast figure eight. With those clothes and that sword, she was the threat of death welcome all over again.

"Be careful with that, Kiera, or I might be forced to look for a *ring* for you too." Connor laughed when she almost dropped the sword midswing, but somewhere deep down, he knew that wasn't a threat.

It was a promise.

Sixty-Six

A letter had reached Eryce that surprised and confused him. It wasn't terribly long or detailed or even all that exciting, but it was the signature at the end that ended up pulling him from the mental haze of the processional and his focus to something that at least had the potential to be *interesting*. He had been in the hall for hours, watching the flood of false grief from his subjects as they passed his wife's lifeless form, the smell of lavender and jasmine cloying in the warm room as the day, and his subjects, marched on.

If the funeral had been for anyone else, Eryce wouldn't have been there for more than an hour, at best. Instead, the king had been staring vacantly at her body for half the day when someone had approached to give their condolences and pushed the folded parchment into his hand. He couldn't even remember if it had been a man or a woman.

Man King,

I write to formally request your assistance, as I have information that could be mutually beneficial.

If you refuse, I will be forced to take this project on alone, and you may not like the outcome.

I will send a porter to you within the week.

You may give your answer then.

My condolences,

- Sorveign -

Men and elves were naturally wary of each other, and Eryce had had very few encounters with their king by choice. For that elf to have sent him a note at all wasn't unlike the ruler hidden far to the west behind his wall of mountains, but to send one with a *porter* as part of the deal meant Sorveign wasn't going to take *no* as an answer to whatever question he wished to pose.

That idea made Eryce intensely curious, especially when he thought back to the closest thing to a face to face conversation Eryce had ever had with Sorveign . . .

Eryce marched down the narrow ledge of the upper wall on the south end of the Arx Luna, the boots of his contingent of guards that surrounded him loud in his ears as they headed toward the rampart. Six in front and four behind acted as a human shield of flesh should the threat Eryce was planning on throwing out of his lands decide he wished to annoy the newly crowned King of Rhonendar with anything sharp.

Rhonendar, the name he had bestowed on his melded empire just one week prior, meant "Endless Red" in old Common. Most of the subjects thought Eryce had picked it because of the amount of blood soaking the eastern and southern grounds of the decimated capitals he had waged war upon.

To Eryce, that word simply translated to home.

That the Elvin king from the other side of the Montes Gelu had shown up unannounced on his very doorstep irritated the new sovereign, the current intrusion that much more invasive since Elves had been banished from his lands for less than ten days. Their leader apparently felt that keenly enough to need to show up and demand an audience with the new king.

Eryce was happy to oblige.

From a distance.

Sorveign stood at the outer wall of the Arx Luna, his skin a livid dark blue, his eyes shining with angry magic. The group of two dozen Elvin archers that surrounded him aimed at anything that seemed like it could threaten their king, including the one that now watched from high above.

Eryce halted his company on the upper rampart, leaning forward fearlessly and studying the elf that was invading his personal space. Eryce was dressed enough like his troops that he was almost indistinguishable from his men, but that wasn't going to help him once he opened his mouth.

"Eryce!" Sorveign's voice rang out against the stone wall, his anger floating off him in waves, the air around him sparkling and popping with barely contained magic.

"Get off my land, elf! You have no business here!" Eryce willed the power he held toward the elf well beneath him, feeling the eye pull as it intermingled with the opposing ruler who had no rights on Rhonendar's soil.

Sorveign scanned the upper wall and spotted the source of the arrogant response, tempted to send his magic through the heart of the dark haired man, but the enchanted eye was already reaching for him, winding its way into his life force. If he struck now, they would both die.

"You would kill my people, and my allies, so easily? Man King, you would do well to take care with who *you anger in the future! You do not know what you ask when you invite my wrath—"*

"I'm assuming you refer to that pile of ash that used to be Corengale!" Eryce yelled back. "Those are my lands now, sprite, so keep to your side of the mountains! I will do as I damned well please with your kind that dare to trespass over the Merides! You can no longer trade here! Accept my generosity for what it is and do not make me start a war by killing you where you stand!"

Fifteen of the Sukolai had come forward through the ranks of soldiers surrounding the group of outsiders, gathering en force around Sorveign's small contingent, weapons drawn and their combined transference colliding with Sorveign's magic. The warring waves of exuded power crashing together created a hum in the air that made Eryce's teeth hurt.

"If I catch any of your people on this side of the Montes again, I will send them back to you in pieces!" Eryce crossed his arms over his chest, feeling far too high on power to deal with a being that lived too far away to be considered any real threat. Even if Sorveign could port his armies, they had no resources in his lands, and now they had no allies. Eryce had made damned sure of that.

"One day, Eryce, you will see reason, and you will know just how foolish working against me truly is! This is not the last you have seen of me, and I will return to this bloodied land when you have been removed from it! Mark my words, Eryce—you shall not rule for long! Rhonendar, indeed! My face will be the last one you ever see!"

Without warning, Sorveign and his troops suddenly vanished.

The elf king had never returned, though letters still arrived on occasion from both their ruler and others that wished to form an alliance, asking for an audience. Eryce had no patience for Elves, and he had simply never responded to any of them. When he had decreed their kind banished from his lands shortly after Corengale had been reduced to rubble, Eryce had done so with the intention to hurt Sorveign monetarily, knowing that their trade in his lands was a good portion of their income, and he wasn't about to give them any advantages.

However, there was no ignoring it this time. Sorveign was going to quite a lot of trouble to get his attention if he was going to send a porter, and the King of Rhonendar wouldn't be given a choice to go willingly.

Ironically, for as much as he hated his rival on the other side of the world, Eryce found himself grateful for the mental break from the fog of the funeral, even if it came in the form of a veiled threat from a being he didn't trust.

Maybe this isn't such a wasted day after all . . .

Sixty-Seven

The sun was well into its afternoon descent by the time they were headed back to L'eaumere, the brown stone villa coming into view as they crested a hill on the ride toward Connor's home. Kiera was struck again by the size of the house, the exterior far more detailed and ornate than the interior with its gabled roof and stone medallions above each of the arched windows of a lion's head in relief; the fleck in the brown stone that coated the outer walls sparkled in the bright afternoon light, giving the house an enchanted sort of feel.

Kiera suddenly hated the idea of leaving.

It was there that the *magic* between her and Connor had been allowed to run freely, her heart swelling with pride at the thought of having that particular man at her side. Connor had proven himself to be a far kinder and more understanding than she had ever imagined, and the idea of not having him in her life *hurt*.

Connor has certainly changed me too. I don't know that I will ever see myself, or Darian, the same way again . . .

Kiera realized then that she was a little nervous to see the Aeroyn again, and after her encounter with Gayle, Kiera knew she owed him an apology. She loved him still, but that deep ache she had once felt for Darian was lessened now, Connor's presence eclipsing the beast that had protected and loved her, her heart shifting focus to the man who had admitted to loving her, too.

She let the thoughts of her winged companion drift away as they rode quietly, Connor lost in his own reverie as they drew closer to the house. Kiera looked out over the expanse of grassy lands that seemed to emulate the waves of the sea they were approaching when the breeze rustled the knee-high fields of vegetation. Gulls circled en masse over the cliffs, their shrill cries getting louder as the gap between themselves and the edge of the ocean that ceaselessly pounded the rocks diminished and the sound of the thundering giant grew louder.

The sweet smell of the green grasses mingled with the salty tinge of the ocean air as the breeze wound around her, and Kiera breathed deeply, wanting to remember that scent.

I may never see this place again after tomorrow . . .

"Kiera, I've been thinking."

"Haven't I warned you about that? You're going to hurt yourself if you keep that up." Kiera smiled mischievously as she raised an eyebrow at him. He had been just as lost in thought as she had, but his mind was on an entirely different train than hers.

"I am going to remember all these times you insult me, woman. Just keep that in mind next time you want something else *pointy*." Connor smiled briefly, but it felt strained.

Kiera didn't seem to notice; she continued to grin as they rode slowly back toward the house, her new sword belted at her hip on her left side between them. The jewel flashed in the afternoon light, catching her eye and drawing her focus to the green cabochon that the dealer had identified as an emerald. Kiera could pick out the small flaws in the stone, the inclusions only adding to the beauty of the inset jewel, making it feel totally unique to her.

Connor had been watching it swing against her hip, too. Now that she had it, he wondered how she had ever seemed complete without it.

I just hope she doesn't feel inclined to use it after I close my mouth, Connor thought. *The longer I keep my mouth shut, the harder this will be. Now or never.*

"Kiera . . . I think I need to visit the Arx Luna. Soon."

"*What?*" Kiera's eyes and thoughts were wrenched from her sword to focus intensely on Connor, her tone full of surprise. Kiera reined her horse up, stopping Kruzeb short as she struggled to understand what he really meant since Connor's words had caught her completely off guard.

Connor halted Santine a few steps ahead and talked to her over his shoulder, not ready to face her just yet.

"Like I said—I've been *thinking*. I didn't mention it wasn't about anything *good*." Connor sighed, feeling guilty that he was not only ruining the mood, but this very much had the chance to ruin *him* if he got caught. "If Jack is right about the timeline, then your mother will have been gone for the first of the two days of royal mourning by the time the sun sets today. The notices say the funeral will be held on the twenty-first at high noon, which is in two days.

"Kiera, I *need* to retrieve my crystal, and with Eryce presiding over Serra's funeral, I should be able to get into the library and back out while Eryce is distracted. It's one of the only opportunities I'll have where I know for sure he'll be out and away from the castle entirely. I think... I think I need to take that chance."

Kiera was silent.

Connor might as well hit her in the chest.

"Kiera?" Connor turned Santine around and guided his horse to stand beside hers, his eyes searching her face, trying to read her.

"What if you don't come back? What *then*, Connor?" Kiera was trying to keep her voice level, but fear was creeping into her veins, making it hard to get the words out without them catching in her throat.

"Then Darian will be there to protect you like he always has, and I have no doubts that Alyk and Henelce will help to keep you out of Eryce's reach. But I won't go until we are back among friends and I know you are safe. Do not think I *want* to leave you, but I have to take this opportunity. I may not get another."

It struck him then that they hadn't been away from each other since they had met, and the idea of her absence made him keenly aware of exactly how fragile they both really were. Another thought that had been nagging at him kicked its way to the forefront of his mind, and he let it into the open air, trying to shift the conversation to something only slightly less serious.

"On a completely different and sort of parallel tangent— there is something I want to discuss with you after dinner. I'm not sure I'll have much of an appetite if we talk now—"

"Connor, stop. All this is doing right now is upsetting us both," Kiera cut him off, her chin trembling as she fought frustrated tears, her eyes cast down while she reached out her hand for his. "I *knew* this was coming, but I just didn't think it would be this soon. If this is all the time you're sure you can give me, I don't want to dwell on *what if*'s."

Kiera squeezed his fingers gently, regarding him seriously.

"Connor, take me *home*."

"Do you wish to leave so soon? I thought we would spend one more night here and go back to the forest in the morning, but if that is what you want, I will take you. I will not keep you somewhere you do not want to be." Connor sounded confused and disheartened, but he understood her choosing to leave him. He couldn't fault her for missing the comfort of a place she knew and the forest that kept her safe and hidden . . .

"Connor, you misunderstand. I don't *have* a home unless you are part of that world, whether that be in Baneswood, Siren's Cove, or anywhere I have yet to see. If *you* are not there, it will *never* be home."

Connor met her gaze, and the woman staring lovingly back at him who had fought him so hard just a few days prior seeming like a dream he had never wanted to think could be realized.

Five days. It took five damn days. I really am an idiot. He dropped her hand and dismounted, pushing Santine aside, reaching up for her and pulling Kiera down from the saddle so he could kiss her and hold her close. He took her face in his hands gently, feeling her pulse pick up under his touch.

"Crazy Lady of the Forest, I promise I will do whatever I can to come back safely to you," he whispered, his heart racing. "On one condition—"

"Connor, let go of the damned dress. I already said I would wear it *one* more time," Kiera whispered, suddenly annoyed.

"I don't give a *damn* about that dress." Connor smiled, but he couldn't laugh. He felt like he couldn't even breathe. For all the words that had tumbled out of his mouth, the next few were one's he would never regret.

"Marry me, Kiera."

Sixty-Eight

Darian was perched on top of the crumbling tower, looking out over the mountains that used to be his home while bits of unnoticed mortar rained down as he shifted. He was conflicted about setting foot and feather on the other side of the river, the journey one Connor needed to make, Kiera would surely follow to fruition, and one Darian wasn't sure he would survive.

The Aeroyn knew about the graveyard that Connor needed to travel to, *and* that it was right in the heart of his people's land. The cemetery itself was magically fortified, keeping those with no business there at bay, but Connor had seemed sure his necessity for entering was valid; Darian's reasons for treading that same patch of earth would not necessarily be seen in the same light. As long as Kiera wasn't risked in the process, he had no qualms with Connor taking his own life in his hands.

He knew full well that same decision would fall on his own dusky shoulders, and he had yet to decide if he was willing or able to take that task to heart. He remembered telling Henelce he would die for Kiera's sake, but that had been while he was still sure of her love and loyalty . . .

Darian's thoughts strayed to his charge, his lost *princess*, Kiera's face surfacing in his mind. It felt strange that she was gone, almost like she had never been there at all. He replayed memories of her in his head—her bright eyes, her smile, her determination when she wanted something and wasn't going to take *no* for an answer, how her skin felt against his—but something was shifting for him. He had always known he would outlive her, and in some strange way, it felt like he already had.

This must be what it will feel like when she's dead. Darian didn't like the thought of her passing into oblivion. Kiera was so strong, so vibrant, and the thought of a life like hers snuffed out made his heart hurt. He was trusting *Dirtbag* to take care of her while they were gone, and the Aeroyn knew he was going to have to take on a different role now with Connor in the picture.

But if the man hurt her or something went wrong, Darian wanted to be able to be there to help her pick up the pieces.

Tomorrow is on its way, and I will get to see her again. Darian closed his eyes, the wind rushing down from the mountains bringing the promise of rain and cooler weather now that the summer was waning.

Darian suddenly felt a chill.

Why am I not so sure I want to?

Sixty-Nine

Having sex with Kiera had been thrilling, and Connor had craved her constantly since the first time she had kissed him. Stripping her bare, tasting her mouth, feeling her skin under his hands, tangling his fingers in her hair, and getting lost in what it felt like to be *with* her so overwhelmingly good he had questioned whether he would ever want anyone else.

Making love to her, however, was so absolutely devastating that Connor couldn't even think straight enough to question how life without her might feel.

In that moment, all that existed was *her*.

He couldn't stop kissing her, touching her, and that honeyed scent coming from her skin was so strong it was euphoric.

Connor was never going to be the same . . .

Kiera terrified him when she didn't answer at first. Her face was unreadable as she looked back at Connor, gauging what his words really meant. What should have been a question she wanted to hear had come out as a command that she wasn't sure she wanted to obey, especially in the face of the promise to leave her and the uncertainty of his safe return.

She didn't even feel the tear fall until Connor was wiping it away. Kiera suddenly stood on tip toe and kissed him gently, refusing to answer. Connor felt her lip trembling against his, her mouth slightly salty as the tears ran down her cheeks and found their way between their lips.

"*Is that a yes?*" *He breathed cautiously.*

"Connor, I-I don't—"

"*Is that a no?*"

"*If you survive this stupid task and come back to me, I'll consider it.*"

"*And until then?*"

"*I love you, Connor, and that's all the answer I will give you for now. You're just going to have to continue to persuade me that you're worth the risk,*" *Kiera whispered against his mouth before she kissed him hard, clinging to him tightly, her arms wound around his neck as Connor struggled to catch his breath.* "*Now, if you don't mind, I think there is far too much clothing in the way to finish this conversation properly. Take me home before I take you here in this field and that grouchy old man you employ finds us.*"

Connor laughed softly against her mouth, the idea not unlike the ones in his own head. He took her hand and they walked the last bit of distance side by side with the horses trailing behind them, quiet the whole way, trying not to let reality break the spell as they tied the horses to the post outside the door.

The air was cool and the house quiet as they entered, Peter and Viola nowhere to be seen. Connor led Kiera upstairs, her boots clicking softly on the marble steps as they ascended and reached his room.

They were already locked to each other before the door was even completely shut.

* * *

Viola was thoroughly irritated that the pair was late to dinner until she saw the look on Connor's face. She had never seen him enamored with a woman, and this *Kiera* was different than just a passing fancy. She could feel intense joy radiating from both of them as they walked past her, oblivious to her presence . . .

Viola was suddenly just fine with reheating the soup.

Seventy

"I will forever thank Tirath if this is the *last* time I have to be in a saddle attached to this *beast*!"

Arveneg nipped at Alyk again when he tried to undo the girth strap under her chest for the third time, and he brought his hand up, threatening to smack the horse on the nose. Henelce chuckled softly and blocked his hand before he could complete the action, pushing the man aside and running his palm up the mare's face to quiet her.

"You have to be less aggressive with her, Alyk. She doesn't like *you* any more than you like *her* when you act like that. She's flesh and blood, and she feels pain the same way you and I do," Henelce chided quietly, running his hand over the horse's withers, calmly approaching her side to undo the saddle.

He waited until she took a deep breath, and when the horse exhaled, he pulled the strap taught to release it from the heavy brass buckle that kept the dark brown saddle in place on her back. Arveneg was several hands taller than his palomino, and Henelce moved aside to let Alyk could take the saddle down so the horse could rest comfortably for the night.

Henelce removed her bridle, and Alyk turned to follow him out of the stable stall, gritting his teeth when Arveneg nudged his back with her nose as he carried the heavy saddle, forcibly pushing him out of her rented room.

"Stupid horse," he grumbled under his breath. Henelce laughed as he closed the gate, and the two of them left their riding companions in the care of the stable boys to be fed and watered and brushed while they went in search of similar comforts for themselves.

They had reached Grant's Perch a few hours before sunset, both of them ready to sleep in a real bed, wash up with hot water, and get a decent meal that neither of them had to catch, cook, or clean up after. Now that the horses were settled, Alyk took a moment to really look over the little town that he had agreed to come to, the one that Kiera knew well and he didn't know at all.

The village consisted of small wooden cabins along the edge of the lake that housed less than two hundred people by Alyk's guess. There was a larger building with a blacksmith and boat repair areas nestled against the edge of the water and a few small shops with skins and cloth and local flora for those that might travel through, with the inn located at the center of town. The stables were located behind the Inn-land Starfish and on the side opposite the lake; Alyk could hear the gentle lapping of the water against the shore and the creaking of the boats as they swayed, knocking together and against the docks as he rounded the southern end of the building to follow Henelce inside.

The air was cool and clean as the wind rushed down off the mountains on the other side of the Breech, and Alyk caught sight of the ruined castle almost a mile away on the northern end of the lake, the decrepit fortress high above them on the cliffs that edged the upper half of the pool and created a natural defense to the ruined relic on one side. He half expected Darian to be circling the crumbling stone tower like some enormous falcon settling to roost, but the Aeroyn was nowhere to be seen. The sun was getting lower on the horizon, the Montes Gelu turning disorienting shades of orange and purple in the waning light of the day. Dark clouds were gathering to the south, a late-summer thunderstorm looming big and black on the edge of the peaks and getting darker as the day wound down.

Alyk adjusted his pack absently as he stood on the outer deck of the inn, watching the clouds rolling toward them, waiting to hear the roar of thunder or see the flash of the lightning he knew the storm would surely bring.

"It probably won't last the night. That storm looks like it'll dump a little rain, make a lot of noise, and be gone before the moons are high," Henelce predicted, his words startling Alyk out of his thoughts. The Shephard was watching the skies too, the darkening tempest that was headed their way a little disconcerting, but at least they would have a roof over their heads for it.

The autumn was fast approaching, and their impending journey could be delayed and altered if a storm like the one stealing over the Montes was any indicator of the weeks to come. Late August was known to get a bit wild with the weather, especially in the mountains, and Henelce expected the rolling storm to be the first of many that they would likely encounter as they traveled higher and the months changed names.

Henelce reached out and patted Alyk's upper arm, turning away from the younger man to head inside as the wind picked up a bit, rustling the oaks and ladder pines that ringed the lake. Alyk didn't acknowledge his companion as he continued to stare out over the water and the ridge of spiny mountains, his thoughts no longer on the storm above him but on the one that was threatening to grow in his mind.

I have to talk to her, and I simply don't want to. Alyk chewed his lip, thinking about Kiera, both as the girl he had watched from afar and known he was one day going to be stuck with and as the woman he had stumbled upon a few short weeks ago after having forgotten her completely. It had been jarring to find out she was alive, and to know he was still bound to her made him wish he actually *wanted* to be. Conflicting emotions warred in his head, one side wanting to claim her and the other telling him he was a fool for letting that thought even manifest and take shape.

"... *when* you *touched her* . . ." Darian's words fluttered through his mind once more. *What if* . . .

Alyk shook his head.

"Tirath help me. She might as well still be dead for all the good those thoughts will do me," he whispered out loud as he ran a hand over the back of his neck, his golden-brown eyes still trained on the darkening peaks they would soon be headed toward.

"Alyk? Are you coming inside or what?" Henelce popped his head out the door, his expression somewhere between exasperated and amused. "I thought you were behind me, and I was talking to you until I got halfway up the stairs—" His face suddenly turned serious. "You're not thinking about *Tance* again, are you?"

Alyk shook his head, his little brother the farthest thing from his mind.

"Just watching the storm is all."

"Well, get your butt in here and put your junk away so we can eat. They're making venison stew, and I'm *starving*." Henelce disappeared, and Alyk sighed. The Shephard's head poked out once more, his face a map of annoyance.

"And stop grinding your teeth!"

Seventy-One

I could get used to this, Kiera thought and not for the first time since she had set foot in L'eaumere. Having Connor to herself in this isolated palace of a home was a very appealing idea especially now that there was talk of a real future between them.

"You said you had things to discuss with me after dinner. If we're going to ruin this good mood with serious matters, then we had better get it over with," Kiera said, poking him gently in the ribs.

They had settled back on the velvet divan, watching the sun set, Kiera curled up next to Connor instead of on the other end. He had his arm around her shoulders, holding her close and breathing her in, wanting just a moment longer to enjoy their serenity before letting it all fall apart.

"Oh. Right. *That,*" Connor sighed. He wasn't sure how to even begin or broach the subject gently.

"Kiera, if something happens, I want to leave this house to you. Even if you never set foot in it again, I want to know that this place I love is in the hands of someone that I trust. Otherwise, it will go to my father, and that's the *last* thing my grandmother wanted."

"But . . . what if something happens to *me*?" Kiera was surprised and a little daunted by the idea of taking on the responsibility of the enormous space she had shared with him for just a few days. She liked the house and loved it because Connor was part of it and it was a part of him, but the idea of running it as her own? She didn't know if she was up for that particular challenge or if she ever would be.

"If Tirath takes you from me too soon, then I hope you will fight the light of death to haunt these halls. I won't be able to come back here without you." Connor's chest was tight. Thinking about *what if*'s was making his head hurt.

They sat there quietly, each trying to forget that the impending morning was going to bring an inordinate amount of uncertainty and change to both of them, but Kiera's thoughts strayed to something she hadn't really given much thought to. She hadn't had to when she was with Darian.

Now it was nagging at her.

While we're on subjects neither of us wants to discuss . . .

"Connor, there's something I want to talk to you about too, and it's sort of . . . *awkward*." Kiera stared at the glass in her hand; she hadn't realized this subject was going to make her *nervous*. "I-I don't know if I can have children."

"Why do you even bring that up?" Connor was stunned. It hadn't even dawned on him whether or not she could get pregnant. *Good job, idiot.*

"Because you should know before you get all wrapped up in the idea of marrying me. You said you wanted children, and I don't know if I can have them. Darian's blood may have made that impossible." The ensuing silence was deafening until Kiera could no longer stand it, and she poked him in the side.

"I *told* you this was *awkward*." She poked him again.

"Stop that. I'm thinking."

"I've *warned* you about that too, *Dirtbag*." Kiera smiled, but it was strained. "Connor, I haven't *bled* in a very long time, and I don't know if that means I'm infertile or if Darian's blood just put my body on hold. I didn't even realize why I had refused his offer after fighting with Jaçon until you said something about children.

"I thought I was just angry at the time, but looking back, I think my body wants to let his blood dissipate from my system and was telling me *no*. I couldn't bear children with him because our bloodlines don't cross that way, but with *you* . . . with you, I *could*."

Connor was quiet as he mulled that over, staring out the window. Darian had not won favor with Connor for his bloodsharing as it stood, but to find *that* out made him wonder if the Aeroyn knew just how deeply he had affected the woman he supposedly loved.

"When was the last time you received from him?"

"Two days before I met you. I'm pretty sure it was Jaçon that shot the arrow through my leg, and it probably took quite a bit of blood for me to heal, but I don't even know because I was unconscious." She quietly sorted through the memories of the past six years. Kiera couldn't think of a single week in any moon cycle going by without some sort of exchange between them. It had become a ritual, part of both intercourse and physical healing.

"Connor, what if I *can't*?"

He didn't even know how to answer her.

They were just going to have to wait and see.

Seventy-Two

Henelce lay awake, staring at the ceiling with his hands behind his head and listening to the storm as the rain pattered the slate roof and the wooden outer walls of the Starfish. He had been thinking about the coming day and Kiera's return . . .

. . . and how it might affect *Alyk*.

The man in the forefront of his mind had settled on the single bed to his left, sporting a similar pose but staring at the inside of his eyelids instead.

But Henelce knew the man was awake.

He could *hear* it.

"For the *last* time, Alyxander—*stop* grinding your teeth."

"I can't help it! The whole thing *bothers* me."

"Look, I don't know what's going on in that fool head of yours, but Kiera is coming back with *Connor*, whether or not you like it." Henelce turned his head to find Alyk's eyes open and his expression bordering on angry as though he would bore holes in the slate roof above their heads. "You don't have to go, you know. You could save yourself a lot of anguish by just heading *home*—"

"I *said* I would go. I gave my word. I'm *not* going to back out of it *now*," Alyk snapped, turning his annoyed gaze onto the Shephard in the single bed a few feet to his right. "Why are you pushing me so hard?"

Henelce sighed, Alyk's defensiveness showing his feelings more plainly than he probably intended to. "I just don't want you to start building a hope in that thick skull of yours that she's going to change her mind. It's just going to get you *hurt*."

Alyk let out a sarcastic and slightly bitter laugh. "Shephard, I seriously doubt there's any reason for her to choose someone that looks like *me* over someone that looks like *him*."

"Scars don't make a man," Henelce argued.

"No, but his *actions* do," Alyk yawned, the bitterness draining from his voice. "I'm not going to act on it because there's nothing to act upon. Kiera will choose what she wants and *who* she wants no matter what I—or any decree—have to say on the matter. So, please, for the sake of my sanity, drop it, Henelce. I have nothing more to say."

Henelce's only response was to roll onto his side and turn his back to his friend.

Alyk's eyes were getting heavier as the silence turned from seconds into minutes, the warmth of the fire lulling him to sleep.

"Just don't say I didn't warn you," Henelce whispered, more to himself than to the man he was trying to protect.

Alyk barely heard him as he drifted off.

Don't worry, Shephard. I haven't fallen in love with her yet.

Seventy-Three

The radiance from the morning sun shone through the windows, making the room almost unbearably bright. The sun had already been up for an hour, but Kiera was snuggled under the blankets and was refusing to acknowledge the beginning of the day. There were no clouds or fog that morning, and Connor didn't seem to believe in curtains; nothing filtered the strong light blazing in at them from the eastern sky.

Kiera woke to find Connor dressed and packing, the piece of dark-purple cloth he was rolling up suspiciously familiar. He jumped when she realized what he had in his hands and was immediately yelling.

"Connor, I am *not* bringing that *stupid* dress! *Leave it here*!"

He had rolled it tightly to shove into his pack, but Kiera was suddenly up and trying to take it away from him. He stepped back from the edge of the bed before she could get her hands on it, holding it well out of her reach, his expression serious.

"I know. *I'm* bringing it. Quit while you're ahead, or I'll find some really uncomfortable *shoes* to go with it."

"You *would*! Torturing me seems to be your new goal in life." Kiera made a face at him, thoroughly irritated, further annoyed that he was getting his way as she crawled off the other side of the bed to search out her own clothes. She smirked as she picked up Connor's black linen shirt from the floor and pulled it over her head after she adjusted her armor, followed by her new pants and boots and the fitted vest that hid two of four new throwing knives.

"Hey! That's my shirt! Where do you think you're going in *that*?"

Kiera kept the bed between them and the obnoxious twist to her mouth as she rolled up the sleeves and then turned her attention to the rest of the clothing strewn about on the floor. She folded up the shirt she had worn the previous day, ignoring his annoyed gaze.

The silk was nice on her skin, but it wasn't durable enough for their upcoming trek, and while he had given her two other shirts that were heavier cotton, Kiera found she genuinely wanted to wear *his*. If they were going to set foot back in the forest just so he could leave her again, she wanted something personal of Connor's in case she was left with Darian as her only company . . .

It suddenly struck her that it was going to drive the Aeroyn crazy to see her like this, the smell of Connor all over her and probably much stronger than it had ever been, but that was the least of her problems.

Time was running out.

"If you plan to drag me all over the map under the threat of that *dress*, I'm taking a hostage of my own. You keep that *thing* in the bag, and I'll let your *shirt* remain in one piece." Kiera brought the items she had prepped for her pack around the end of the bed, a sweet smile plastered to her face as she approached the man she was purposely trying to annoy.

Connor reached for the clothes and grabbed her wrist instead, making her drop the neatly folded pieces at her feet as he pulled her against him and kissed her deeply before she could protest.

Both knew they would have to leave shortly. Neither of them wanted to go. Connor had actually given quite a bit of thought to just leaving the stones altogether and asking her to stay at L'eaumere, get married, and live out the rest of their days quietly. To him, it sounded like more of an adventure than the one they were about to take on. He was not looking forward to any of it. *Maybe someday . . .*

"I think that's everything I need from here. My other gear is at the inn." Connor pulled back from Kiera to find she had tears in her eyes. "Kiera . . . *don't*. Let's do this and get it done so we can move forward."

He rested his forehead against hers, and she heaved a defeated sigh.

"They're just *rocks*, Connor. Is that really worth risking your life for?" He could hear the catch in her voice as she tried not to cry from frustration. Connor had known the argument was coming, and as much as he wanted to concede the point, he had a nagging suspicion that he would need his stones if she was going to become a permanent part of his life.

"I was thinking about that, and it *is* worth it if they end up keeping you *safe*. They can be very useful especially if we are able to return here and you want to go back to the forest at any point. If we try to make this work, I wanted to leave one of the crystals with Darian so you can go back whenever you want to." Connor put his hands on her shoulders and forced her to look at him, regarding her seriously.

"Kiera, I'm not going to pull punches here. Porting into the Arx is one of the more dangerous things I've ever had to do, and I would be lying if I said I wasn't worried too. If I don't come back tomorrow, you have to head south. Have Henelce take you to his homeland in the Southern Wood. You'll be out of both Sorveign and Eryce's reach there."

"If anything happens to you, I will track Eryce to the ends of the earth until one of us is dead—"

"No, Kiera, you *won't*, because I'll have Darian drag you all the way down there if I have to." Connor tucked a strand of hair behind her ear. "I need you to stop thinking about it, okay? There's a good chance that nothing will even happen. I will port in, grab the crystal, and leave. It takes seconds."

"Connor . . ."

"What?"

"Just . . . be careful."

He smiled at that.

At least she didn't call me an idiot.

Seventy-Four

"*W*_{*hoa . . .*}"

Alyk almost didn't recognize Kiera when she walked in, dressed head to toe in well-tailored and expensive black clothing that fit her in ways that made him realize she was so much more beautiful than he had ever thought. The tunic and leggings of her forest garb had made her look younger and more innocent than her outfit did, the mish-mash of clothing giving way to something far more sophisticated and surprisingly feminine. It didn't help that the new weapon she brazenly carried only added to the sex appeal as it dragged Alyk's focus to her hips.

She looks like a panther dressed like that, and that sword on isn't helping matters. As if she wasn't already creeping into my thoughts more than I want her to . . .

Henelce turned around in his chair, Alyk's openmouthed stare at Kiera suddenly justified. The pair had just walked in, Connor leading her after him, their matching black outfits a stark contrast to the greens, browns, and tans of the rest of the clothing in the room. Kiera was wary of the people in the little pub, knowing they probably all had an idea as to *who* she was, but no one seemed inclined to approach.

Probably because Connor looked like he would take someone's head off if they even tried to look at her wrong.

Alyk was suddenly aware that he was jealous of Connor, which actually struck him as mildly ironic because Kiera was always meant to marry *him*. He spotted the pendant on her neck as the shirt gapped when Kiera moved through the semicrowded room to join them. *He's giving her jewelry? Oh, that's not good.*

"Welcome back! Glad to see you both!" Henelce stood up and moved to the left of Alyk, giving up his chair so the two could sit beside each other. Henelce smacked Alyk in the arm, breaking his concentration.

"Quit staring at her," he whispered curtly. Connor was obviously already annoyed with coming back, and Alyk did *not* need to add to it, especially since they were probably going to be spending a lot of time together for the next few weeks.

"Hello, Henelce. Alyk." Kiera smiled and gave them a slight nod and took the chair across from Alyk, Connor taking the one to Alyk's right, turning his around and straddling the seat, folding his arms over the back. Kiera hadn't even noticed Alyk's expression before he was able to hide it.

Connor, however, *had*, and he smirked arrogantly at Alyk, knowing the man had been undressing her with his eyes. Connor wasn't the least bit worried; he was already well acquainted with what was underneath her clothes and that it was *his*. Alyk was only going to cause problems for himself if he didn't keep his eyes, or his hands, or any other part of him to himself.

"We shouldn't talk here, so we'll save the important stuff for when we meet up with Darian in an hour. He's expecting us to cross the river before the sun is high." Henelce turned his attention to Kiera, admiring her quietly for a moment. "You certainly know how to make an entrance, my dear."

"That's good to hear because yesterday, someone told me I looked like a *man*!" Kiera snorted a laugh as Connor clenched his jaw, thinking about Gayle. "Oh, Connor, let it go. I wouldn't have hit her. Why get my hands dirty when my boots would have sufficed?" Kiera teased as she punched him lightly in the arm.

Connor's only response was a wry smile and a shake of his head; he was trying to keep the woman he had always kept at arm's length out of his head without allowing Alyk to take her place.

"Anything happen while we were gone?" Kiera was directing the question at Alyk, but Henelce answered before he could open his mouth.

"Arveneg ran Alyk through some brush and almost dismounted him. That horse has been quite the stubborn beast since you left. Maybe you should take her back before one of them kills the other."

"That damned horse!" Kiera was laughing with her hand over her mouth, trying to keep quiet.

"Oh yes, *that* was fun. *Thank you* for bringing that up, *Henelce*." Alyk threw the Shephard a pointed look, getting upset over Henelce's attempt to lighten the mood by using *him* as fodder. Henelce grinned, but there was nervousness hiding in his eyes. He was playing a very touchy game with his charge, and Alyk wasn't going to forgive him if he pushed too far.

However, Henelce had seen the pendant too, and he knew what it meant. The simple piece of jewelry put them all in an awkward position, and Alyk was going to have to talk to one or both of them. *Soon.*

"I was going to purchase a horse for Kiera for this trek anyway since I already have one stabled here. Do you want to see if there's one you like and Kiera can take Arveneg?" Connor piped up, shifting the subject. It was a generous offer on Connor's part, and Alyk was surprised enough to allow it to distract him from being angry at the Shephard to his left.

"That's not a bad idea. I would rather walk than have to deal with that animal much longer, but I can afford a horse of my own." Alyk glanced at Kiera, trying not to focus too hard on her. "She's all yours."

Kiera's smile widened, excited to get her horse back. Her father had given Arveneg to her when she turned twelve, and Arveneg had never been keen on letting anyone else ride her after that . . .

The conversation ceased when food suddenly appeared at the table, brought by the barman. He was good-looking with dark hair and a cleanly shaven face, and he had blue eyes that danced over Kiera's body, ignoring that there were both men at the table and clothes on her skin. He reminded Kiera of Gayle when he directed a big, bright smile at her and stood directly between her and Connor.

"Well, *hello,* beautiful. I haven't seen *you* in here before."

If you were smart enough to know who I am, you wouldn't have even opened your mouth, Kiera thought as she stared at him for a moment, her expression blank while she decided how to handle the idiot. She started idly playing with the throwing knife that had suddenly appeared in her hands instead of tucked into the bracer at her wrist, using the tip of the blade to pick at her nails as her expression darkened.

"Go . . ." She flicked the small knife at the ground, embedding it in the floor between his boots, her eyes never leaving his. ". . . *away.*"

His smile crumbled, and she didn't have to say it twice. The barman disappeared, his sudden absence revealing the man she traveled with hunched over the back of his chair. Connor had his forehead resting on his arms, his whole body shaking.

"Connor?"

"*What*?" He wheezed, still laughing. He finally sat up, his face red, trying to breathe. Kiera threw a piece of potato at him.

"Shut up."

Seventy-Five

Eryce was impatiently drumming his fingers on the arm of his chair, clenching his jaw and reminding himself that he *shouldn't* grit his teeth, only to do it again. The days of mourning were getting to him, and he was silently thanking Tirath that those were the last few hours he was going to have to sit and watch his people walk past him to pay their respects. Tomorrow was the funeral, and he was just *waiting* for it to be over.

He had been done with the whole thing before it ever began.

Eryce was far more anxious to find out what Sorveign wanted, and the suspense was making the day go by too slowly. Waiting for the funeral to come and go had been bad enough, but now Eryce found himself getting very short with his staff while he *waited*, more so than usual. At least they had finally stopped asking him questions by the middle of the previous day, and for that small miracle, he was grateful.

But another *miracle* was causing far more havoc with the King of Rhonendar; his right eye was burning in the socket, and Eryce was ignoring it as much as he could. He had been dealing with it for so long that he couldn't remember what it felt like to not have heat or pain associated with that orb, and tuning it out was easier some days than others.

That day, however, it was testing the limits of his patience as the eye persisted to whisper in his mind that he needed to feed it. The living, breathing *thing* that resided in his eye gave him no peace, and he almost wished he had never agreed to accept it to begin with.

It wasn't often that Eryce had time to simply reflect on his life or some of the decisions that had affected where he now stood, but today was proving to be a good day to do just that since there was nothing else he could really do as people passed him in a blur, kneeling to pay their respects to their deceased queen. The myriad of colors kept blending together as his eyes stopped focusing on the moving shapes around him and his memories surfaced to block the images before him completely.

"Let me tell you the rules, *Eryce, son of Hærrion.*"

Eryce caught the scent of sage and something a little rotten as *her* voice sounded in his head. He could see the old woman in his mind's eyes, that single

293

encounter with the crone in the spring of his second year at the Arx still a vivid memory . . .

Eryce walked behind the jailor in the bowels of the Arx, his uncle Phelix too lazy to feel the need to see to prisoners himself. Eryce would have been annoyed that he was sent in his uncle's stead if he hadn't already been dealing with everything from taxes to doling out punishments for the past year; Eryce was just fine with the fact that his responsibilities seeming to grow every time Phelix was needed and didn't care to take the reins himself.

Eventually it wouldn't even matter what his uncle's title actually was; as far as the subjects of Onesta were concerned, Eryce had already risen to wearing the crown, and Phelix was only on the throne because the prince had real *work to do.*

A bony and gnarled hand shot out of one of the cells to his right as Eryce wandered too close to a seemingly empty cell, the dirty fingers leaving dark smears on his white sleeve. The scent of stale bodily fluids and musky sweat was overwhelmed suddenly by the smell of burning sage, and Eryce stopped in his tracks.

"How would you like to see out of that eye again, Great King?" she rasped, her face barely visible from under her shroud of tattered black.

"Let go of me, crone. I do not make deals with those behind bars."

"Who said I wasn't here by choice*?" Her laughter dissolved into a hacking cough, but her grip on Eryce's wrist remained steadfast. She smiled toothily up at him, her face coming into view as she pushed back her ruined hood with her free hand and moved into the torchlight. "Be kind, for I can* help *you move forward with both eyes open, Lionspride. You need only ask."*

"You know not to whom you speak, witch, and I will not tolerate your continuing to soil my arm. Let go before I remove that hand for *you." Eryce pulled his hunting knife from his belt, one of the last gifts Serra had ever given him, and the amethyst glinted in the firelight as he brought the blade to the underside of her wrist, promising to follow through with his threat.*

The crone released her grip on his wrist in favor of the bars on either side of her wrinkled face, and she focused her gray eyes on him with an intensity that was unnerving.

"Oh, I know who you are, Great King. I know what you will become. You are Eryce, son of Hærrion, from the kingdom of Falyyn and the line of the Raze. You were born to this world from a dead mother's womb and a disappointed father when he found that you didn't carry a mark. Not like that pretty sister of yours, the one you still carry such a brightly lit torch for—"

"Eryce? Who are you talking to?" Flynn had finally noticed that the prince was no longer following in his wake and had backtracked to find Eryce with his knife drawn and staring into an empty cell. Eryce felt his heart pick up under his shirt when he realized that the air around him was back to the fetid and rank odor that he always associated with the castle depths, the old woman gone as though she had never been, her words dissipating like smoke.

"No one. I thought I saw a rat." Eryce looked down as he sheathed his knife on his belt, the light of the torch on the wall illumination dark smears on his sleeve that were the only evidence she had been there at all.

It wasn't until the moons peaked that night that Eryce saw her again.

"Serra?"

"Hush, Eryce. Sleep, my love."

Eryce felt his chest tighten as her hand touched his brow, tracing the scars on the right side of his face, lightly grazing the marred lid of the ruined eye with pity in her own. He was on his back in bed, and Serra was straddling him, her hands caressing his chest as she sat up and exposed her naked breasts to the moonlight that poured in through his windows.

The only cloth touching either of them belonged solely to his bedding, her flesh warm against his in ways that had never been true.

"Why did you never tell me goodbye?" Serra's curls were tickling his shoulder and his face as she leaned forward and settled her weight on him, her fingers playing with the hair on his chest as she watched him intently with those big green eyes. "I waited for you to tell me goodbye, brother. I thought you loved me. Did you hate me so much for leaving?"

Eryce could smell her, the sweet perfume of green apples freshly cut haunting him every time he wandered past the fruit stands in the markets of Brigton. Her bright eyes were trained on his, the look on her face a cross of love and concern. He reached up and touched her face, the smooth skin of her cheek feeling so real . . .

"Serra, please stop coming to me in these dreams. I know that's all you are."

"Who said I wasn't here by choice, Lionspride?"

Eryce's eyes popped open, the room flooded with that burning sage scent, the woman draped over his naked chest the same old crone who had accosted him in the dungeon hours before.

"Get off me, witch!" Eryce fought against her, but she held his wrists down, the frail-looking woman far stronger than he. He cringed as she brought her face just inches from his, smiling toothily at him.

"My, my, Great King, you are quite the fighter. You will have to be if you want to achieve the greatness you are destined for." Eryce felt a crushing weight on his chest, the ability to breathe getting harder and harder. "That is the weight you carry, dear boy. It is the weight of lives you have yet to take, and that burden will only grow heavier as you forge ahead."

The crone was suddenly gone, the weight evaporated, and Eryce inhaled a ragged, gasping breath, coughing and tasting blood.

"Now, about that eye . . ."

Eryce sat up, still coughing and trying to breathe. The crone was replaced with Serra's naked form sitting at the end of the bed, her knees drawn up to her chest and her cheek resting atop her knees as she watched him thoughtfully.

"Don't you defile her image, witch! I would deal with you as you are. Bringing her into this will only goad me into killing you."

"As you wish, Great King." Serra disappeared, replaced by the dirty old woman in the ratty robes leaning against the bedpost where she stood at the end of the bed.

"Stop calling me that, crone."

"Why? You will be so if you choose to be, and that is why I am here—to offer you a choice. Before you lay two paths, Eryce, son of Hærrion; one leads to greatness, and the other toward darkness and oblivion, but they are not carved in stone or always easy to discern. Your choices will mold them into one twisting path, and your decisions to show mercy or bring death will shape the future you have yet to explore. You may become a source of light or a shadow that is cast over the lands around you, and accepting or refusing my offer will be the first footstep along whichever path you choose.

"Know now that you may refuse me, but I will not make this offer twice. I can help you with your blindness, but there are consequences to your decision. You have already dealt with the loss of that eye for over a year, so you know the disadvantages it holds. Accepting the gift I possess will bring its own difficulties, and it will create a relationship that cannot be broken without the loss of life."

Eryce stared at her in the dark, the moonlight flooding the room and illuminating his surroundings. The crone, clad in tattered black, made a weird void in the moonlight, as though her form sucked in and swallowed the light that dared to touch her.

"I offer you a companion, Eryce. It will see for you, help you look into the hearts and minds of those you choose to follow with your gaze and take the lives of your enemies. But beware that this is not a permanent fix to that lost eye, and it needs souls to survive. It will protect you, heed you, and share its power, but it will also keep those around you at bay. You will never know a love like the one you try so desperately to forget.

"It will need to be fed on a regular basis or the inhabitant will starve and start eating away at your own life force. If you do not die by sword or sickness, this will be your undoing, and maybe well before your time. Know that before you agree, Lionspride, for it cannot be undone . . ."

It was the best—and worst—choice Eryce had ever made, and the ritual had hurt like nothing else he had experienced thus far. Eryce remembered how he had thought the eye would burst through the back of his skull as the *inhabitant* forced itself into the dead flesh and took up residence. The cold tingling that had seeped out from the eye now burned hot and bright as it reached into his consciousness and focusing its energy on the outside world, watching life go by for, and with, Eryce.

It had been there for the raid on the Pearla, the fall of Corengale, the birth of the twins, and the death of his wife. It knew what he was thinking, feeling, and sensing, and it was greedy for flesh and spirit alike.

It hadn't been fed since before his birthday, and after three days, Eryce could feel the eye pull at his own energy reserves, but it would have to wait. It couldn't be reasoned with, couldn't be quieted; at that point, it could only be tuned out. Eryce knew he needed to get out of the castle and wander the streets of Lower Brigton to find a whore or two whom no one cared about and buy their lives, but it would have to wait until the moon was high . . .

Then he could have peace.

Seventy-Six

"Do you know what the best part about having this horse is?" Kiera's question was directed to the man she had her back to as she stroked Arveneg's nose, the sleek and stubborn black mare calm under her touch. She cooed to the horse like she had when she was young, and Arveneg responded by nudging Kiera with her nose, trying to rub affectionately against the woman that obviously still loved her.

Connor had seen people bond with animals, but this was a little more like Arveneg only wanted to serve Kiera. He wondered if it was because of her *influence* or if the horse just really liked her.

"What's that?" Connor asked as he put his foot into the stirrup of the saddle fixed to the brown gelding he had stabled nearly a week before. He swung himself up, settling for a moment before adjusting the bow across his back so it didn't hit the leather seat. Reagan was a bigger horse than Connor was used to since he usually rode Santine, but the gelding was also well kept and good-natured; the last thing Connor wanted was a steed that didn't heed him like Arveneg wouldn't for Alyk.

"She won't listen when *you* whistle." Kiera grinned as she mounted Arveneg, ready to ride out.

"You just remember that when your legs are sore from the first day's ride and I refuse to use my muscle balm on you."

She stuck her tongue out at him as she adjusted her own stirrups and settled onto her horses back for the first time in over six years. It felt familiar and weird all at once . . .

"Oh, you can use *that*," Connor pointed at her mouth, "on *me* anytime you please."

Kiera voiced no argument as she retracted her tongue and winked at him, enjoying the flirtation and the giddy moment. It didn't matter what Connor still had to do just then; for that moment, she was happy.

Both of them had forgotten that Alyk was behind them, and *he* was simply trying to ignore the exchange as he saddled the white-and-brown appaloosa mare Connor had purchased for him. Alyk couldn't help bristling against his will.

Stop it, stupid. You didn't love her, don't want to marry her, and she isn't keen on you either, Alyk mentally chided himself, but he was annoyed and jealous just the same. He looked up when Kiera clucked her tongue to get her horse moving, kicking Arveneg lightly in the sides; Alyk watched her long white hair bounce in waves as the horse sped to a trot and then to a canter . . .

"You better quit now, while you're ahead."

While you still have *a head.* Connor didn't have to voice the second half of what he desperately wanted to say, his condescending tone more than implying the threat he was only barely keeping from passing his own lips. He had been watching the man still fiddling with his tack while Kiera took off, and the longing on Alyk's face was coming through far too loud and clear for Connor to mistake it for anything else.

"I'm sorry, Connor. I don't know what my problem is," Alyk lied, looking sheepish, knowing *exactly* what his problem was and keeping his mouth deliberately shut.

"I *do*, and it had better *stop*, Alyk. I don't like the way you've been looking at her, and I can tell you right now, you won't like *me* if you can't control it," Connor snapped as he turned Reagan around and coaxed the horse into a trot, then a canter, taking Reagan through his paces as he went after Kiera.

Alyk simply stood there, watching the pair as Connor caught up to Kiera, knowing that coming between them was the last, and only, thing he wanted.

"Goddess, help me before I do something stupid."

* * *

"Darian!"

He heard the pounding of hooves before he caught sight of Kiera racing toward him on Alyk's horse as she broke the treeline, and the change in her was so obvious he felt a little stunned.

Kiera suddenly seemed so . . . *human.*

Darian had seen her in plenty of different outfits and naked more times than he could count, but *this* was different; seeing her in well-tailored, solid black was startling. This was Connor's version of Kiera, and Darian had to admit, it suited her.

It dawned on him then that he felt more like a guardian than a lover to her now. Kiera was no longer the teenager or even the young woman Darian had loved for so long. She had *matured* in some strange way over the past few days, and he felt oddly detached from her.

Kiera reined up and jumped off her horse without bothering to tie Arveneg up, running into his arms and hugging him hard. Darian wrapped his arms around her and buried his nose in her hair, breathing her in. She *felt* happy, her energy high and the smell of *her* mixed with Connor's mint and cedar sweet and strong.

"Kiera . . . You feel . . . *different*." Darian pushed her back, holding her at arm's length so he could look her over more closely. "You *look* different." *Maybe I'm just letting her go. She's no longer mine to protect.* He frowned at that thought.

"*What?*" Kiera was concerned for a moment, her head cocked to the side as she looked at him.

Darian shook his head and hugged her against him, simply glad she was there. He didn't let go as another horse approached, and a second dark rider came into view over Kiera's head.

"Woman, what have I told you about waiting for your *elders?*" Connor sounded like he was trying not to laugh as he approached them. He hadn't been far behind, but with Arveneg, Kiera had had a head start before they had even paid the ferryman. She had known right where she was headed, and she had taken off as soon as they were on hard ground, letting Arveneg find her own way on the trail, signaling only with gentle touches. Her horse didn't need a heavy hand, just a little guidance, and that was what other riders always failed to see; respect the animal, and it will respect you.

Kiera hadn't been the least bit surprised that Arveneg hadn't taken well to Alyk, and she had known right away that Alyk had wanted to *control* the beast instead of *trust* her. Arveneg was a smart horse, sometimes too smart, but she was also well trained and would protect her rider at all costs. Kiera could still remember when the mare used to escape from the stable and drive Gavin crazy, getting into the feed, the apples, springing other horses from their stalls and being a general pain in the ass . . .

"Darian," Connor nodded to the Aeroyn as he slowed Reagan to approach slowly, trying to gauge how Darian really felt about his presence and if he felt the need to *remove* it. Connor had already decided not to even bother to try to come between the Aeroyn and the woman he had basically stolen out from under him, and he greeted the Aeroyn with something akin to indifference as he waited for the other two to catch up. As far as he was concerned, Kiera was going to go where she wanted, and Connor could sense the change in Darian; the Aeroyn's expression said that he wasn't going to be an issue between them, and Connor was silently grateful.

Alyk and Henelce came into the clearing a few short minutes later, bringing up the rear on Spirit and Scotchy, their respective mounts.

Kiera backed out of Darian's embrace as they approached to hail them with a quick wave and walked up to Reagan, patting his snout before looking up at Connor.

"Okay, fearless leader, we're all here," she quipped, smiling up at him. Everyone was suddenly focused on Connor when the question passed Kiera's lips. This was *his* journey; they were just along for the ride. "What's the first move?"

"Kiera, we talked about this—I need to stay put for the day. Tomorrow will come soon enough, and around noon I'll to port to the Arx . . . and hope my *employer* isn't there," he responded quietly, leaning down so the words were less audible to the others.

It didn't help. Alyk and Henelce had not been expecting that answer, and even Darian showed concern, ruffling his wings reflexively.

"The Arx? I hope you know what you're doing, boy. Kiera has already lost too many of those she loves. If you do not return . . ." Darian didn't need to finish the thought

"Then you will keep her safe, *bird*. I have no choice in this unless I want to lose another stone to a man I refuse to serve while this woman lives and breathes. No matter what *my* plans may be, *she* will need to be kept at least three steps ahead of both kings that flank these mountains," Connor spoke seriously, leveling his gaze on the Aeroyn who had devoted his life to keeping her alive already.

Kiera cleared her throat, breaking the tension she could feel building among them all. An idea that made her suddenly smile popped into her head, and she decided they were *not* going to spend what was possibly their last day together worrying about the coming afternoon. They had almost twenty-four hours before she would lose sight of him for the first time and they wouldn't just be separated by walls and doors.

She wasn't going to let it go to waste.

"Then we stay put. If everyone else is fine with that, let's head to the castle and prep for the rest of the journey." Kiera didn't wait for a response from any of them and remounted Arveneg. She guided the horse to stand beside Connor's, leaning close so only he could hear her. "You and I have something important to attend to later this afternoon, *Dirtbag*."

"Oh? Should I be worried?"

Kiera smiled and kicked Arveneg, heading toward her derelict home without another word. Connor sighed and rolled his eyes, already expecting the worst.

He would just have to find out.

Seventy-Seven

Kiera stood at the edge of the cliff, naked except for her necklace. Connor was next to her, similarly dressed, the roar of the waterfall filling the air, the mist from the rushing water hitting rocks below swirling around them. She loved the way the sunlight filtered through the tiny droplets of moisture creating rainbows and the smell of the cool water as it filled her lungs. Kiera took a deep breath, feeling calm and at peace.

Connor knew what was coming; he wasn't even remotely excited. He had seen her do this once from the ground but had never climbed up to the top of the waterfall and looked over.

It was a *lot* farther down than he had realized.

"Are you *sure* about this?" Connor tried to keep his voice level as he looked down, the sun sparkling off the pool as it rippled, but the fear tinged it anyway.

"Connor, this is the *worst* possible time to start questioning my sanity. I'll push you if I have to." Kiera grinned at him. "Just don't hit the *rocks*. It's not that hard."

"The one time I saw you do this I thought you were going to sit at the edge. I guess I should have realized how Crazy Lady of the Forest you really were at that point. Could have saved myself a *lot* of trouble . . ." he grumbled.

"And I could have simply let Darian kill you and saved myself from your *mouth*," Kiera retorted. "Wait . . . you saw me do this? When was that?"

"About a week before I tracked you down and let you tie me to that tree."

Kiera grinned wickedly at him, remembering how he had squirmed when he was covered with ants and could do nothing about it.

"Is the big bad *man* scared of an itty bitty *waterfall*?" She pouted playfully at him.

"No . . . just the itty bitty thirty-foot drop."

"Oh *come on*, Connor. I have done this so many times I've lost count. Just *trust* me." She held out her hand for his, and he looked down at her outstretched fingers then into her eyes, still hoping she might be doing this only to test his resolve.

"Do I *really* have to do this?"

"Yes."

"Kiera?"

"What?"

"You're an idiot, and I sort of hate you for this."

Kiera threw her head back and laughed, but the look on Connor's face said he wasn't kidding. Her expression lost some of its mirth when she realized he was actually *scared*. Kiera softened a little and simply smiled at him, putting the strongest feeling of love she could express behind it, willing him to trust her. The honey scent on the breeze was overpowering.

"Connor, I will never ask you to do this again. I may not even be able to after tomorrow, but I wouldn't ask this of you if I thought it would put you in danger." Her hand was still out for his, and he finally took it. "Share this with me. *Fly* with me."

I must really love her . . . This is insane, Connor thought as he stood next to her, the cold mist making his bare skin break out in gooseflesh, his heart pounding in his ears.

"Just make sure you dive. It's deep." She squeezed his hand reassuringly. "You'll be fine."

Kiera let go of his hand and leaped off the cliff, a graceful swan dive keeping her clear of the rocks. Connor waited for her to resurface, and when she finally did, he took a deep breath and went after her.

The plummet took his breath away, the adrenaline kicking in as the water rushed up to meet him, and then . . .

He was under. All was silence except the low hum of the waterfall and his own loud heartbeat, the cold water enveloping him in a peaceful cocoon of weightlessness. The sun filtered through the water like rays through a dusty room, and he could feel the pull of the river as it continued on to the east. He suddenly understood why she loved that particular activity, and he reveled in the swirling water against his bare skin, the lack of oxygen the only thing keeping him from spending all day under the surface.

When Connor finally came up, Kiera was waiting for him in the shallows.

"Fancy meeting *you* here," she quipped quietly as she approached him in the chest deep water.

He reached for her, and she splashed him, and they went through the dance again of the first time they had been in the river together, this time with no intention of stopping, the adrenaline from the jump amplifying every touch.

As he pushed her up against the rocks, Connor couldn't help but wonder how he had ever found her.

The Bane of my existence actually turned out to be a good thing. What a funny thought.

Seventy-Eight

Henelce had Alyk cornered.

The Shephard moved to the left . . .

The man countered to the right . . .

They stared hard at the chess pieces in front of them, neither wanting to back down, both trying to anticipate the others next move.

They were in the ballroom of the ruined castle, cross-legged on the floor with the chessboard between them. A vast array of rusty and broken weapons lined the bottom edges of the walls around them, piles of moldering clothing and random leather boots, bags, and armor littering the stone floor in all directions. There was a clear-cut path in the mess from one side of the ballroom to the other and a large circular void around their game that Darian had allowed them to clear away. Large holes in the roof let in a patchwork of light that dotted the floor around them with random shapes, dust particles visible as they passed through the pillars of intermittent sunshine. Their chessboard was illuminated by one of the beams created by the late afternoon sun, making the ebony and ivory pieces Henelce always carried look enchanted.

"When are you going to talk to her?" Henelce was studying the board, running Alyk's possible moves through his mind as Alyk reached for his rook, moved to a pawn, finally deciding on his knight.

Just as Henelce knew he would.

"I have no idea, but I think I need to talk with just *her* though. Connor isn't happy with me right now," he replied distractedly, glancing up at Henelce as he waited for the Shephard to move the white bishop so Alyk could put him in check. He had moved his knight on purpose, hoping Henelce would take the bait.

But Henelce was no longer concentrating on the game as he suddenly focused on Alyk with a hard gaze.

"Any why is that, *do you think*? Could it *possibly* be because you're starting to watch her like you might *eat her*?"

"Do I?" Alyk was genuinely surprised by Henelce's assessment and his accusatory tone. He hadn't realized his actions could be interpreted that way.

"I would be careful if I were you, my boy. Connor is not someone you're going to want to take on. Kiera will side with him, and so will Darian. And then . . ." Henelce simultaneously moved a piece and made his point. ". . . checkmate."

"Ugh, I can never win at this game with you," Alyk huffed as he crossed his arms and flopped back against the wall behind him.

"Well, this board aside, you'll be playing a very dangerous one with the three of them if you decide that you are going to let the order stand, much less try to enforce it." Henelce studied Alyk, not liking the expression that was trying to surface on Alyk's face. "You're not *entertaining* that idea, *are you?*"

"What can I do, Henelce? I can't go to Eryce, and neither can she. All I can do is warn her and hope she doesn't do something *stupid*."

"You *should* have spoken to her sooner. She might not have accepted him."

"You think he's already asked? Connor has known her, what, less than a week?" Alyk scoffed.

"That pendant certainly makes me think so."

"I was wondering about that. It's a pretty piece but not exactly a ring. It certainly doesn't scream *proposal*." Alyk didn't look up as he started to reset the game and totally missed the Shephard's darkening expression.

Henelce smacked his hand flat onto the center of the board, startling Alyk and upsetting all of the pieces, several tumbling to the ground a foot below.

"A homing crystal is *not* something you give to someone you *like*, Alyk! You're giving your *heartbeat* to that person. It's one of the few truly romantic gestures left in this world, if you ask me." Henelce sat back and folded his arms over his chest, ignoring the chess pieces that were still rolling about on the board.

"People, most specifically you *humans*, are always finding ways to ruin romance and make it trite, like it's some passing fancy or unimportant. It's the exact *opposite*. This world would be terribly boring without love and ways to express it. Connor has the right idea, and Kiera is just sheltered enough to understand that it's not to be taken lightly, so don't mock something you very obviously do *not* understand."

Alyk sighed and gave up on the board, leaning back and looking up at the pockmarked ceiling. Small white clouds rolled by overhead, intermittently blocking out the sun. There was no easy answer, no matter how he approached it.

"What do you suggest I do?"

"Request a sanction for a marriage. Tell the courts you were betrothed, but she's no longer living. That would break the order, and if you are already married, Kiera would be free."

"Marriage to *whom*, exactly? *You?*"

"It's either that, or one of them can kill you." Henelce retorted seriously, his expression grave. "But do something *soon*, Alyxander. You've already waited too long as it is."

Seventy-Nine

"Kiera, can I ask you something?"

"That depends. If it's 'Can we jump off the cliff again?' I'll have to think about it."

"Woman, I'm trying to be serious here."

"Oh, *fine*. What do you want to know?"

They were lying out side by side on the rocks, letting the sun spill over them and dry their wet skin, and Connor knew he was about to ruin the tranquil moment.

"How do you feel about Alyk?"

"Where did *that* come from?" Kiera sat up and looked down at him, her expression somewhere between curious and concerned as she propped herself up on her hand.

"He's been staring at you since we got back, and I was wondering if you had noticed. His look seems to have . . . *intent*." Connor shifted and rolled onto his side, blinking away the sunspots.

"I haven't been paying any attention to him. I've been too busy watching *you* and trying to find ways to get you alone and *naked*," Kiera teased as she ran her hand back through his hair, a ghost of a smile on her mouth. "Like right now."

"I know that look too well to not know what it means; I've seen it on Gayle more times than I care to remember. But if he can't get control of himself, one of us is going to have to confront him, and he *really* won't be happy if it's *me*. I'm not wild about the idea of leaving you alone with him once we reach the cemetery as it is. The only hands that should be laid upon you are *mine*."

Connor reiterated the point by trailing his fingertips over her knee and up her thigh, and Kiera lay back on the rock, reveling in the warmth of the sun and the touch of his hand on her skin. "Speaking of alone and naked . . ."

Kiera could hear the smile in his voice as his hand went higher. Connor's fingers brushed against her gently, his touch turning firm as he parted the lips and found her clit, his mouth on her breast, and Kiera's hands in his hair. He slid two fingers inside her, pressing his thumb against her clit, using her own wetness to move his thumb in slow circles. He could feel her getting tighter around his fingers, her breath coming in short gasps, her hair splayed out on the rock.

"Connor, don't stop . . ." Kiera was shaking under his touch, her skin starting to flush a vibrant pink. He pressed harder on her clit and withdrew his fingers enough that he could add a third. She arched her back as he pushed them in, his fingers stretching her almost painfully tight, the added pressure taking her right over the edge. White-hot pleasure rippled through her, the combined stimulation making the orgasm incredibly intense. She felt lightweight as the heat spread throughout her body, and Kiera lay there panting, dizzy and trembling, unable to move as Connor withdrew his fingers and kissed her passionately.

"Okay . . ." Kiera broke the kiss and threw her arm over her eyes, trying to catch her breath. "You win."

"*Win*? Win *what*?" Connor grinned, looking obnoxiously pleased with himself.

"I'll *marry* you."

Eighty

*D*on't *show her you're nervous. Just talk to her. She'll understand.*

Kiera and Connor returned from the waterfall as the sun was getting low in the sky and had arrived back at the castle to find Alyk, Henelce, and Darian outside the walls, setting up a large fire. Alyk and Henelce had taken down a small deer in the woods not far from the crumbling exterior wall, and it was hanging in a tree, skinned and gutted, waiting to be cut into smaller pieces and put over a flame.

"Can we speak? *Alone*?" Alyk voiced the question to Kiera almost as soon as the couple had emerged from the forest, but he wasn't really asking. Kiera knew a command when she heard one, and she had to stop herself from lashing out at him. She narrowed her eyes at Alyk, suspicious as to what he wanted, especially after the conversation regarding him earlier.

Alyk was already irritating Connor, and he hadn't chosen a smart way to get back on his good side or stay on hers.

"If you feel we *must*," she replied coolly, hoping to get to the bottom of whatever was wrong with Alyk before things got heated and someone ended up bleeding. She nodded to Connor as Alyk took her arm and led her away from the castle, and Connor warily watched them go as he moved to help Henelce to keep himself distracted. He wasn't happy that Alyk was touching her or that Kiera was allowing it, but he figured she would let Alyk *know* if he made a wrong move. That didn't keep Connor from debating which of the man's legs he would break if Alyk did anything foolish.

Kiera almost led the way as they headed toward the edge of the grounds that were no longer easily defined as the forest continued its onslaught to overtake the man-made structure and absorb it back into the landscape. The vine covered castle that had been such a comfort loomed to her right, the darkening forest that continued to threaten to overtake it just a few feet to her left . . .

All of it was familiar, but none if it felt like *home* anymore.

Alyk waited until they were well out of earshot before stopping and turning toward her to adopt a defensive stance, looking her in the eye.

"Kiera, does the name Alyxander Fairaday mean anything to you?"

The question wasn't one she had been expecting, and she was quiet at first as she wracked her memories for any significance regarding that name.

"My father was friends with a *Charles* Fairaday. I know he was from one of the Southern Estates, and he had a couple of sons, but that particular name doesn't ring any bells. *Why?*"

"I was wondering if you had heard it before. It was my grandfather's name, the one given to me when I was born . . ." Alyk paused, licking his lips nervously.

Kiera waited for him to complete the sentence, but he hesitated a beat too long.

"What's your *point*, Alyk?" Kiera was getting irritated, crossing her arms and shifting her weight, her face a map of annoyance.

". . . and . . . it . . . it's also the name on a betrothal decree . . . along with *yours*."

It took her a moment to realize what he meant, but Alyk continued before she could respond.

"Even if the original order was burned at Corengale, copies still exist in every court from here to the coast. *Our* names are on that decree, Kiera. I was always meant for *you*. You can't legally marry Connor, or anyone else for that matter, unless you have it nullified first by *Eryce* . . . and *I* have to *agree*."

Kiera suddenly understood why Connor had been concerned: the look on Alyk's face said neither of those things was likely, and he was seriously entertaining the idea of separating her from the man she loved because she *legally* belonged to *him*. If Kiera had ever been that angry, she couldn't think straight enough in that moment to remember, and she hit Alyk before she even knew what she was doing, the fist that collided with his jaw knocking him to the ground.

She didn't draw her sword, but she really, *really* wanted to. Kiera stood over Alyk, looking coldly down at him where he lay sprawled out on his back in the dust. He was smart enough to stay there, the rank scent of rancid vanilla flooding his senses telling him it was *not* a good idea to test her limits further . . .

Things were about to get very ugly, very fast.

Connor was suddenly running toward them.

"Okay, whatever it is, it's not worth it, Kiera. Just walk away," Connor whispered hurriedly as he ushered her away from Alyk, taking her out of everyone's sight and into the forest where he could talk to her and help her level out. He figured Kiera wouldn't have hit Alyk if there hadn't been a reason, and probably a very good one. Of course, once he found out *why*, he was probably going to want to hit the man too.

Connor almost didn't even want to *know*.

* * *

Across the clearing, Henelce shook his head, his mouth set in a grim line. Darian was watching the other three, the movement from the little man to his left catching his eye, breaking his focus. Henelce tugged at his beard, watching Connor and Kiera fade into the trees as Alyk started to pick himself up from the dirt.

"Shit. I knew this would end in tears," the Shephard said aloud, mostly to himself.

"*What?* What just *happened?*"

"He told her . . ."

"Told her *what*, Shephard?"

"That she cannot marry Connor."

"Alyk's a brave man to try to get between the two of them. I didn't even think he was interested." Darian was thoroughly surprised.

"He wasn't. Not at first. Kiera and Alyk were betrothed when they were young. They're both still alive, and the courts will still see the betrothal as valid. Eryce would have to nullify it, and Alyk would have to let her out of it." Henelce's attention was fixed on Alyk, who was dusting himself off and flexing his jaw as he came toward them. Darian just stared at Henelce in disbelief, and the Shephard sighed.

"Judging by the way she hit him, I don't think he *will*."

Eighty-One

Jaçon could still taste blood in the back of his throat when he coughed, but the pain at least had lessened. Kiera had hit him so hard that the bruises on his stomach were in the shape of his mythril chainmail, leaving his abdomen covered with a patch of dark scales. It had been nearly a week since he had fought her, and this was the first day he had been able to get out of bed on his own. He would be fine in another day or two, but stretching still made him wince.

Pitting himself against her again wasn't on his to-do list any time soon.

Now that Henelce and Alyk are with her, I can't even risk porting . . . Jaçon was staring out the window of his home in Haven's Fall, looking up at the mountain range that divided them all, his mouth set in a grim line. He would have to find another way to get to her; otherwise, Sorveign would notice his *uselessness.* Then there would be no other chances, and someone would be sent in his place.

He had overheard the first private exchange between Alyk and Kiera, and when Alyk had whispered her name, Jaçon could easily put two and two together. He had visited Corengale himself on several occasions, and he recalled the name of the little girl that was forever making her nanny run after her while they were in the middle of a meeting with Garegan.

Elves have long memories, and that one had surfaced readily enough . . .

"She looks just like Serra, sire, with the exception of white hair where it was dark. I know *she's Garegan's daughter. I could* smell *it.*"

"Kiera? The older one? The one that *was* marked?" The Elvin king stopped walking and turned to his subject in surprise. Jaçon simply nodded as Sorveign turned thoughtful. "Well, that *is curious*. A marked *child running wild in the woods with an Aeroyn . . . What level of threat do you think she poses?*"

"I believe she has been bloodsharing, so I would imagine she's quite strong, but I couldn't get a gauge on her. Current threat level—minimal. The man king is after her already for another reason, but he wants her alive. If he gets his hands on her and realizes who and what *she is . . . we may be looking at war.*"

"Now there *is an unpleasant string of words, nephew. Do you think that little Spero would follow his orders?*"

"I'm sure she could be broken *enough to make that possible . . .*"

Now that he had seen her protecting the human male and had felt the pull of her *mark* and the blows from her sword, Jaçon knew Kiera could be quite the adversary, and against them, she could be incredibly dangerous.

If she were under Eryce's control . . .

Jaçon wasn't sure he even wanted to think about that scenario. There weren't many *marked* as it was, and most were well protected or hidden. Kiera was an open target, and a warrior on top of that, making her a much bigger prize than she probably realized. That she had made herself such an obvious enemy of the king on the other side of the mountains meant she was brazen; that she had survived after the fires of Corengale and in the darkness of Baneswood meat she was *not* some sniveling little girl who was afraid to do what it took to stay alive.

Combine fortitude and ruthlessness with the mark of the *Unifier,* and she could create a force that could win a war. Eryce was just the type to start looking outside his own realm to find new places to devastate now that he ruled all of Rhonendar, and if he was able to convince Kiera to do his bidding, there was no doubt in Jaçon's mind that Haven's Fall would be *next*.

Jaçon's fingers absently stroked the place on his arm that was almost completely healed where Kiera's borrowed blade had parted the flesh, his abdomen still a painful reminder that he had unwittingly bitten off more than he could chew. The act of chewing itself was still a little on the tough side, his jaw holding onto the low ache from the fracture that should be nearly gone by now.

Sorveign had not been pleased. The ruler of Haven's Fall had thought it best that Jaçon learn from his mistake and had only sent a healer to help with any internal bleeding so his nephew could at least live to benefit from the lesson.

"It's your own fault for provoking her. You should have just ported her here and let me speak to her . . ."

It still irritated Jaçon that those wounds had been inflicted by both a *human* and a *woman*.

He certainly wouldn't allow it again.

Eighty-Two

Kiera was already high up in a sprawling beech tree, furiously picking apart leaves and turning them into green rain. Connor had followed her up, leaning against the center of the same tree on the limb directly behind her, the two-foot diameter of the narrowing trunk separating them almost fifteen feet in the air. He was waiting for her to talk to him, and he could hear her muttering under her breath, but he was trying to let her cool a little before pestering her.

Connor almost got to the count of thirty before impatience reared its ugly head.

"Am I going to want kill him when you tell me why you hit Alyk?" He asked quietly over his shoulder, already tired of being left out of the conversation she was having only with herself.

The sound of ripping vegetation stopped, but Kiera didn't answer right away. Connor waited three heartbeats before he felt inclined to fill the silence.

"Look, I'm not sorry you clocked him. I told you what I thought was going on with him, and I think he needed that, personally. I was hoping it would be *me* to get to—"

"I'm betrothed to him, Connor. No shut up and let me think."

Connor narrowed his eyes, his mouth still open to finish the sentence as the implications of Kiera's words clicked into place. Now *he* wanted to hit something. It took him almost a full minute to respond.

"Do you . . . Do you know that for sure? I figured your father would have wanted you with someone who was *marked*." Connor was greeted with silence as green rain started falling again, albeit a little less aggressively.

"I *don't* know, but I don't see what he gains by *lying*," she answered quietly. "He *knows* he's poking a proverbial bear with a stick by even bringing that to me, and I can't decide if I would have rather have known sooner or had him wait until after you visited the Arx. That man has *awful* timing."

"Do you want *me* to talk to him?"

"And say *what*, Connor? I knew I was betrothed a long time ago, just not to *whom*, and I know the law when it comes to an arranged marriage—either my guardian has to let me out of it, or *he* does, and then it has to be formally requested and nullified by whoever is upon the throne . . ." The rain ceased as she momentarily paused, trying to remember the details to a law she had looked into long ago.

"Or he has to marry. Only if Alyk chooses a different bride would I be allowed to seek another engagement."

"Or if he *dies*?" The rhetorical question simply implied *I can make that happen*.

"Don't think that didn't cross my mind as soon as the words were out of his mouth. I had to *hit* him—otherwise I was going to *kill* him."

Connor was not happy with *any* of the answers she was giving him. He kept pushing, looking for a loophole. "What if you marry outside of Rhonendar? Surely if you were outside the kingdom—"

"Then Alyk can complain to the law, and I would be punished if I were caught. In this case, it's imprisonment, or if he requests it, my marriage would be void, and I would be immediately married to *him*. Eryce would make the final decision on that, and I'm pretty sure he wouldn't bother giving me to Alyk once he found out *who* I am."

"And if he says nothing?"

"I can't marry you in secret if you want it to be *valid*, Connor." Kiera turned halfway around, talking over her shoulder at him. "Do you even know what you have to *do* in order to be legally married?"

Connor was quiet. His one brush with matrimony thankfully hadn't gotten that far. Kiera sighed and explained.

"You have to publicly announce your intent to the courts with *both* names. If no one objects and there are no other claims found within three days of the announcement, you can marry. I can assure you that there are several people still in this world that would recognize *my* name and start digging immediately. A few would probably try to find me, Eryce being one of them."

"Are you sure I can't just kill him?" Connor wasn't convinced that simple solution wouldn't solve a lot of problems.

"Connor, it's not *Alyk's* fault, and probably wasn't even his *choice*. *I* certainly wasn't asked." Kiera let out a frustrated sigh, knowing her father had meant well, but it was hard to accept that she was tethered to someone who kept her from the man she loved.

"If anything, he told me and didn't have to. I don't know that he'll let me out of it, but at least I know where I stand. Honestly, I would rather know the terrain I'm treading upon."

Connor bit his lip, staring at the ground below.

There was *nothing* he could do.

"Well . . . Shit," he cursed.

"Yup. My thoughts, *exactly*."

Eighty-Three

Oh thank Tirath. It's finally quiet.

The sun was still just setting on the horizon though it hadn't been much higher when Eryce had paid for the first two whores over an hour ago...

All told, it had taken *five*. The first two he took one at a time on the street itself, leaving their bodies behind in the dim alleyways like the piles of trash that littered the space between the crumbling and closely set buildings of lower Brigton. The third and fourth were now a pair of corpses in another brothel a few doors down the unkempt street, and all of them had been well paid for with more gold than they were worth.

Eryce hadn't just paid for their services. He had paid for their *silence*.

He hadn't realized how much pent-up energy he had in him from the past three days of inactivity, but Eryce had certainly worn himself out with the last girl who now lay dead on the floor. She was young, late teens at best, and she had been hungry for him, wanting him to be brutal.

If the eye hadn't taken her life, his hold on her neck probably would have. Her eyes had been blue, bright, and sparkling, and Eryce had enjoyed watching the fear in them when she realized she was going to die, her struggling enflaming him further. Eryce had wished those bright eyes were green when he had her pinned against the wall as he finished, roaring as he flooded into her, the white light of the eye taking over the room for a split second as it took its share of his *prize*.

The King of Rhonendar was silently grateful that the *inhabitant* was finally sated, it's light dim and soft, and the burning in his skull has subsided from an unbearable ache to an almost pleasant warmth. That was all he really cared about as he leaned back against the crumbling and unpainted mudbrick wall, trying to catch his breath. Eryce felt like he could finally think straight, even now that he was exhausted. The funeral would commence two hours after the break of dawn, and he would have to be solemn and respectful for most of the day; if he hadn't escaped the confines of that damned hall and found his way here, to these back streets and dimly lit rooms, he would have probably killed anyone within arm's reach.

It had been quite a while since he had been in that area of Brigton, but he had found his way back without a problem, glad for once that the city around the Arx was big enough to support a healthy population of women no one else cared about. Now that Serra was gone, there was no one to notice his absence that mattered, no one to question what he was doing outside the castle at that odd hour, and that still felt bizarre. Eryce kept expecting to find Serra in her room, sewing quietly at her window or playing with the twins . . .

He had forgotten all about their boys, almost never seeing them because he found them tedious and annoying and his presence always far more disturbing to them than a comfort. Kaiden and Lodrier weren't much use to him as it was since neither showed the capacity to even speak in simple sentences at the age of four, nor did they carry Serra's *mark*. Then again, neither did Eryce. Serra and their sister Katelyn were the only siblings that had the Υ *mark* emblazoned on their skin, the *Raze* choosing at random and, in the case of his family, every other child.

Eryce bent down to pick up his shirt from the dusty floor, shaking it off before pulling it over his head. He had dressed all in plain black and walked out of the castle without a word to anyone, his staff too well acquainted with Eryce's moods to try and stop him or follow in his wake, and after Serra's tragic end, absolutely *no one* was going to try to stand in his way.

Down here, they couldn't find me if they wanted to. I might as well change my name to Bane.

His thoughts strayed back to the green-eyed woman he was waiting to get his hands on, realizing he hadn't given much thought to her in several days. He was still hoping that Delámer would show and bring her to him, but he expected him to fail like all his predecessors. Eryce hadn't wanted to incur the expense of a full-scale search party into Baneswood, but if he had to, he would.

Bane was still high on the list of priorities labeled "Things to Destroy." Eryce resolved that he would send forces out after her once the double full moons were come and gone and the Rains of Fall began. He would allow them to use whatever force necessary even if it meant burning down the whole damned forest and slaughtering every creature in it. She certainly couldn't hide behind a wall of ashes.

But Eryce still had something akin to *faith* in his hunter; Delámer still had a little more than a month to bring Bane to him.

Depending on what my council allows, I might not even wait that long.

Eighty-Four

I remember thinking he could have been beautiful if it weren't for those scars, Kiera thought as she stared at Alyk over the fire while he picked at his venison with his head down, avoiding her gaze and Connor's wrathful stare. Alyk had proved loyal and even a little helpful, but in opening his mouth regarding the betrothal, he had shown a side of himself that Kiera was definitely not a fan of. The more she was getting to know Alyk, the less she felt like they would ever have been good for each other.

Now that Kiera had to actually consider that as a *real* possibility, she found herself liking that prospect even less . . .

But what if Connor doesn't come back? Then what? He could be caught or killed, and I wouldn't even know. I wouldn't even be able to attend a funeral. Connor was still sitting next to her, warming her right side and silently threatening the man across the fire from them, but he might as well be a million miles away from her at that point. The suspense was driving her up a wall, and there was nothing to do but wait.

My mother's funeral is tomorrow, and I can't attend that either. While she had known her mother had lived, Kiera had never thought about the day Serra would die. She had never known if the rest of her family had been buried properly, and Serra may as well have died that same day for all the thought Kiera had ever given the woman since that day.

But now, her mother was about to receive a royal burial.

Why do I even care? She married Eryce. That should say it all. The fact that Serra had taken her own life didn't escape Kiera, but the details were a bit fuzzy because Jack had heard about her death from a ferryman, and Tirath only knew how many people had repeated the story before it found its way to his ear. She didn't trust the facts she had received. *There has to be more to it. No one kills themselves just because they're drunk.*

Kiera almost wished she could go with Connor even though he was risking his own life as it was. She wanted to be there to protect him, to help him if he needed it, but she knew it would just put them both in greater peril. She would never be able to forgive herself if something happened to him because *she* had been at his side.

And it certainly *would* if Eryce was anywhere nearby and caught Connor retrieving his stone. No matter what he said, Eryce's eye would see right through his lies, and Connor would probably be caught porting, which could have severe consequences if they were able to take his homing crystal away from him before he could use it. It wasn't illegal to use porting crystals, and they were so rare as it was that most people thought they were a myth as it was; but using them to get in and out of the king's residence was "a bit *frowned* upon."

Translation: They would kill him on sight.

I have to stop thinking about it. Connor will be fine. He said it would take seconds, Kiera thought worriedly, absently playing with the pendant at her breast, trying to let it go . . .

"If you don't stop *agonizing* and get your *influence* under control, you're going to have Darian all over you, trying to protect you. *Calm down*," Connor whispered to her, trying to be gentle. He was scared, too; he just knew how to hide it. "Take a deep breath. Think about something good. Think about . . . white roses."

Kiera smiled at that. She recalled the roses, the sound of waves breaking on the shore, the hot bath that smelled like honeysuckle, the way Viola had cooked dinner, the taste of rum on her tongue, watching the sunset . . .

The first time I kissed him . . .

Hearing him tell me he loves me . . .

Tears fell, not from worry, but from the magnificent memories Kiera would always share with him, no matter what happened to either of them.

A lot had changed in six days.

"I *will* take you back there, I promise. I refuse to fail at this, especially now, and if I get my way, we will spend the rest of our days with our only worry being who chooses what you wear to dinner." Connor kissed her temple and took her hand, squeezing it gently as he stood and pulled her after him. Without a word to anyone, they left the group behind and walked into the trees.

No one followed.

Kiera knew the area too well to not know where he was taking her; there was a clearing just south of the castle that overlooked Grant's Perch and Breach Lake, at least a hundred feet up off the water, and they were headed straight for it. That particular spot held many memories for her, and she had gone there often during the first year she had lived in her cold and forbidding ruined palace, hiding from the world. It had always brought her comfort to look out at the lives of people she didn't even know but somehow felt close to since they seemed to be trapped in the forest with her.

Kiera hadn't been to that spot in over a year.

The last rays of the sun were dying over the Montes Gelu, their lower peaks rimming the eastern side of the Breach, the lake itself reflecting the soft hues of the evening sky and the jagged black mountains that were cast into shadow as the sun set behind them. Kiera scanned the range as the forest they were picking their way through fell away and nothing blocked her view, knowing that was where they would be heading tomorrow as soon as Connor got back.

If *he comes back. I hope he knows what he's doing.*

The stars were just starting to appear in the night sky, and Connor walked to the edge of the cliffs, Kiera not far behind as she came to stand beside him. He was scanning the mountains too, *tomorrow* bringing too many changes and uncertainties to account for with any sort of confidence.

At least there is one thing I am certain about, Connor thought as he turned toward her and took her hands in his. Kiera could feel his heart racing, the pendant blinking rapidly under the cool linen of her borrowed shirt giving Connor's nervousness away.

"Kiera, I didn't do this right when we were hundreds of miles away from here, but I will now because I don't know that I'll have the chance to say it ever again . . .

"When I first saw you, I thought you were beautiful. The more I get to know you, the more you show me that warm heart under that tough skin, the more I *know* you were meant to be in my life. I have never met anyone like you, Kiera, and for *you* I want to be a better man. Tirath must have had you planned for me all along because I am *not* that lucky to have found you on my own."

He paused to brush the hair back from her face, tucking it behind her ear before running his thumb over her cheek. Kiera closed her eyes and leaned into his touch, the scent of mint and cedar flooding her senses and making her heart skip.

"I had you all figured out when I waltzed into your woods, Crazy Lady of the Forest. I had no idea how wrong I really was," Connor said softly, pulling her into his arms and kissing her gently. "I love you, Kiera, and I'll ask you one more time. I don't care who or what stands in my way."

Connor let her go and took a knee, holding her hands in his.

"Kiera Spero, I have never wanted anyone at my side more than I do you. I'll ask you from both knees if that's what it takes, and I'll pester you until you say *yes* out of exasperation if you don't give me a straight answer this time.

"Kiera . . . will you marry me?"

She felt the breeze cool the path of the tears already streaming down her face. Connor's expression was so determined she suddenly started to laugh as she nodded, unable to answer any other way. He had already known her response, but had asked again anyway.

I would ask her every day for the rest of my life just to remind her that I mean it. Instead of getting up, Connor pulled Kiera down to sit next to him. She nuzzled against his shoulder as he wrapped his arm around her, that single perfect moment in the chaos of both their lives one they would prolong forever if they could.

But the night kept coming, and soon the stars were bright enough to illuminate the rest of their corner of the world as they twinkled into life one by one . . .

And then, one by one, the stars began to fall.

Kiera had been so wrapped up in Connor and her changing world that she had forgotten about the star shower. It happened at the end of every summer, usually signaling the start of the autumn when the old stars died and new ones were born. The shower was one of those yearly occurrences that had lost its magic for her by the time she was ten and had become just another part of the cycle of life, but that night, it felt like the sky was putting on its show just for them.

Kiera continued to watch the stars as Connor lay back, and when she felt him reach for her hand, his was shaking. She looked away from the skies to find Connor staring straight up, tears streaming down the sides of his face toward the hard ground beneath his head as he swallowed hard.

"Connor . . . *don't*." She moved to lie beside him and rested her head on his chest, wrapping her arm around him and hugging him tightly. His heart was beating wildly in her ear, and Kiera could feel his fear as his energy changed. Connor pulled her as close to him as he could, his arms around her shoulders, watching the stars fall toward them with blurred vision.

"It was never supposed to be this *hard*, Kiera. It is killing me that I don't even know if I will be able to come back to you—"

"Connor, stop. I won't tell you goodbye tomorrow. I'll only tell you good luck."

"Well . . . you will know if I'm not coming back. The homing crystal will go dark. As long as it beats, I'm alive. That's part of why I gave it to you. So you will always know that I'm safe."

"You, sir, are going to be just fine, and I will be right here, waiting impatiently." Kiera looked back up at the stars glimmering through the atmosphere as they fell toward the earth. "You were right, you know."

"Right about *what*?" Connor's voice broke as the tears got the better of his words for a split second. He took a deep breath, trying to calm down, but he felt the tears well again as Kiera ran her hand down his arm and intertwined her fingers with his.

"Life would be boring without you."

Eighty-Five

Eryce peered over the edge of the intricately carved stone coffin that would hold Serra forever once the lid was sealed in place when the morning came and the casket was removed from the castle. He was the only one watching over it at that late hour, sleep still a long way off, even as tired as he was after his escapades in the lower part of his city.

He had asked that Serra be prepared simply for her final interment, and his staff had done well. Her body had been washed again and her gown changed to one of a vibrant green that would have matched her eyes. Her raven curls were splayed out on the red velvet pillow below her head, her hands resting on her chest, her fingers interlaced and her wedding ring fitting too loosely on her left hand.

The smell of flowers was strong in the hall, the casket itself full of wisteria, jasmine, and wild pink roses that had been gathered to fill the space around her. Eryce thought she looked like she was floating on a raft of blooms, the wildflowers reminding him of their childhood . . .

Eryce brushed the hair back from her temple, the curls falling back in place as they slipped through his fingers, her skin waxen under his gentle touch and almost as cold as the stone she was to be encased in. He smiled sadly as he plucked one of the roses from the bunch at her side and slid the stem under her hands.

The only tear he had yet shed fell on her cheek as he bent down and kissed her forehead one last time.

"I loved you *best*, little sister. One day, Serra, I will see you again."

Eighty-Six

The sun came up in complete ignorance of what its arrival meant to those under its ceaseless path. It never knew what emotions it stirred in the beings beneath its bright gaze as it roused the world from its slumber and chased away the night . . .

Eryce was prepping for the funeral in the early light, donning his ceremonial robes with a sense of calm that felt almost surreal.

Almost one hundred miles to the east, Darian coasted along the currents of the early morning, hunting for his own breakfast along the outer walls of the ruined castle while Alyk and Henelce busied themselves with a fire.

Connor and Kiera were nowhere to be seen. They were still lying naked in the room Kiera had once shared with her Aeroyn, locked in each other's arms and praying silently that this wouldn't be the last time they ever touched each other.

That day would be a turning point for all of them.

The sun simply didn't care.

Eighty-Seven

"Ready?"

"*No.*"

"Kiera, the sun is getting high, and the funeral should be well under way. I have to do this. Just wait here. I'll be back to annoy you before you know it." Connor regarded her seriously as he touched her face, tucking her hair behind her ear.

"You make it sound so *thrilling* when you put it like *that*," Kiera retorted as she rolled her eyes.

"Fine, then. I'll just *marry* you instead."

Kiera made a face at him, and Connor chuckled halfheartedly in response. Neither wanted this to happen, and he was having a hard time justifying risking his own hide when he could make do with only four of the little clear crystals like the one he held in his hand. Instead of dwelling on it, he pulled the homing crystal from his pocket and set it on the palm of his hand so that the two stones touched.

"*Kiera*," he whispered over them with closed eyes, picturing her in his head as he breathed the command over the glittering pieces of stone. The homing crystal and the point crystal began to glow, their energy intermingling and taking on the new *destination*, Kiera now impressed upon the clear stone that he handed back to her, closing her fingers over it.

"I think I will have to set one of these into a ring and always have you as a point to come back to."

"Connor . . . you're an *idiot*," Kiera laughed despite trying desperately not to cry.

"At least I'm a *romantic* idiot," he whispered playfully before he kissed her passionately, holding her firmly in place against his chest, neither of them wanting to let go as he broke the kiss and rested his forehead against hers.

"I love you, Bane."

"I love you too, *Dirtbag*. Now, go so you can return to me in one piece." Kiera stepped back out of his embrace, the point stone clutched tightly in her shaking hand.

Connor folded his fingers protectively over the homing crystal and closed his eyes.

"*Eryce . . .*"

She felt the void as Connor disappeared.

Kiera suddenly couldn't breathe.

Eighty-Eight

Eryce was nowhere near the Arx or his library, and he hadn't been all day. The moment Connor vanished, the King of Rhonendar found himself hundreds of miles away in the sanctum of Haven's Fall, Sorveign's palace on the other side of the Montes Gelu, wondering why he was being escorted down the hall in a wing of the Sanctum that felt more lived in than the rest of the ornate building he had been led through so far.

Elves stared at him as he passed them in the hallway, all of them wondering *who* he was. He ignored them completely and stared at the back of the willowy male he was following like an obedient dog. Eryce wasn't at all happy to be there, though the alternative wasn't much more appealing—being forced to mourn his wife's death with his people had been torture enough. He wasn't interested in celebrating her life with them too.

He had just finished the ceremony of laying Serra to rest in her tomb, and once people had started to disperse, an elf had appeared from behind one of the cemetery monuments, ready to take him. Tall and slender with long black hair and lavender eyes . . .

Eryce had almost walked away as the being that only barely resembled a human reached out to touch him, but Jaçon hadn't given the man king a choice.

Now they were headed toward Sorveign's private quarters, and Eryce was anxious to know why he was there alone.

Jaçon allowed Eryce to go first as they passed through a doorway at the end of the hallway. He stepped into what looked like an office with smooth white walls that held a desk and a few high-backed, dark-brown leather chairs scattered about. Books and scrolls were arranged neatly upon a row of shelves that took up an entire wall to the right, a silver tapestry with a willow embroidered in glittering silver thread centered on the wall to the left. The plush navy carpet muffled the sound of all footfall as they passed through the portico and stood before the Elvin ruler.

Sorveign was seated behind the enormous white ash desk that faced the door, situated in front of a wall of floor to ceiling windows that filtered the afternoon sunlight and threw Sorveign's face into shadow. The glassed wall made the room feel bright and open and Sorveign dark and ominous as Eryce approached, the Elvin king coming clear once he was close enough.

The King of Rhonendar had *never* forgotten that particular Elf.

Sorveign was taller than most of his subjects by a good three or four inches, putting him closer to seven feet in height and nearly a foot taller than Eryce himself. His hair was a deep blue-black with streaks of white at regular intervals that ran straight to his waist. His eyes weren't lavender like Jaçon's; they were a vivid, royal purple, and they were eerie to gaze into, reminding Eryce of his own enchanted eye.

Sorveign's smooth, pore-less skin was tinged with just enough blue to be noticeable, contrasting against the white robes he wore. If he had been human, Sorveign might have looked like he was in his late thirties instead of approaching 115. Like Eryce, the elf king didn't wear a crown, just a necklace that held a large glass pendant encasing a liquid metal that looked like it had a life of its own, and a platinum ring set with a red stone that glittered from its faceting. Sorveign had a playful temperament that could change instantaneously and, as ageless as he appeared, had been the supreme ruler of Haven's Fall since Eryce was still in diapers.

"Why am I here?" Eryce barked.

"Please, *sit*," Sorveign responded placidly.

No greeting.

No acknowledgement of title.

Just two kings on a level playing field and neither willing to give the other an inch.

Eryce was too interested as to why he was *summoned* to give a damn about formality as he took the chair to Sorveign's left, settling into it stiffly. His escort took the other, seating himself casually with one foot over the other knee, leaning back and slightly away from Eryce, looking bored.

"Eryce, I am glad you chose to come. Please accept my condolences. I hear you have finally laid Garegan's wife to rest," Sorveign continued with feigned sympathy once his *guest* was seated.

Eryce hadn't been expecting the insult. He narrowed his eyes angrily as he stood up and tried to walk from the room, but he was suddenly paralyzed by a prickling sensation of pins and needles when Sorveign reached out with his magic and stopped the man king in his tracks.

"Eryce, if you leave this room without either myself or my nephew to escort you, you will be killed as soon as you open that door. I will release you, but you will *sit down* and keep your *temper* and that goddess-forsaken *eye* to *yourself*."

Sorveign released his grip, and Eryce slumped into his chair. The Elvin king sat back in his own and brought his palms together, resting the tips of his fingers against his mouth and his elbows on the armrests at his sides.

"Now, *Man King*, I have information that I think you might find . . . *interesting*. I hear that you have quite the problem with a *woman* in one of your woods."

So that's *what this is about!* Eryce felt his temper flare further.

"That little bitch kills my men every chance she gets!"

"So I gather. Bane has also tried to kill one of mine. We may have a common enemy." Sorveign interlaced his fingers and rested them over his stomach, nodding to indicate the elf seated next to Eryce. Jaçon sat up and set his foot on the floor, leaning forward to rest his elbows on his knees so he could look at Eryce from a slightly lowered vantage point. *I don't bow to you, Man King, so don't get any ideas.*

"I have seen her, spoken to her, and fought her. Do you *know* what it is you seek when you go after this ghost in the trees?"

"I am after a *woman* that has been a thorn in my side for more than a *year*. Beyond that, she's just another notch on my belt." Eryce was getting increasingly annoyed. *Why are they even interested in her?* He neither liked nor trusted the elves as it was, and they were holding back information. Eryce could feel the eye start to warm. It could sense the hesitation in Sorveign.

"So you were *not* aware, then, that she is Serra's eldest *daughter*?"

Eryce sat straight up and slammed his fist on the desk, but Sorveign didn't flinch, the Elvin king enjoying the reaction from the volatile man more than he thought he would.

"No! That is *not* possible! *No one* escaped from that damned castle! I was *there...!*" But something tugged at the back of Eryce's brain, trying to get his attention. He paused and allowed the memories to surface, recalling that night.

Two women ran toward him, dark hair flying behind them as they rushed from the burning castle. The light of the green flames illuminated them weirdly, and it took a moment for him to figure out which was Serra as he leaned down to catch her, almost mistaking one for the other . . .

He had been so focused on Serra that he had ridden off before he made sure that the girl was taken care of. Eryce groaned as that realization hit him, knowing this mess was likely his own damned fault. Apparently, Sorveign knew it too. That was why Eryce was even there: the King of Rhonendar had wounds he didn't know about, and his Elvin counterpart had been kind enough to grind in a little salt.

"She's *marked*, Eryce. With Garegan's ivy leaf, if I remember correctly. She could be *very* useful to us both, and I would give you the opportunity to work peacefully with me. Let both of our kingdoms prosper . . ." Sorveign raised an eyebrow and nodded slightly toward Jaçon, ". . . since I just so *happen* to have a way to get to her."

Jaçon pulled the homing crystal up and out of the neck of his shirt, dangling it in front of Eryce.

"I would rather you catch her and kill her *if* you can. You didn't need to bring me here to ask my *permission*, as I would be glad to be rid of her, *marked* or otherwise. If she *is* Serra's daughter as you say, she won't work with me any more than she would get a pig to sing and play a lute."

Eryce was looking back and forth between them, furious that they had that kind of information and his own men had not survived to relay anything even close to him. He folded his arms and leaned back as he scanned them for mistruths, wary of taking their words as fact, but the eye was quiet.

"Ah well, you see, *that* is where I beg to differ. She carries *your* blood, even if only partially. I don't want to spill the *blood of a king* without his permission. Inciting a *war* has never been my intention, though considering the way you have treated my people and my *friends*, one could argue that it might be *yours*."

As soon as the word *war* was on the table, Eryce understood why he was in that room. He had stepped on Sorveign's toes repeatedly, and the elf was tired of losing men and money to the stubborn man king who refused to work with him. The threat of using the girl against the human side of the mountains was one that sent Eryce's blood pressure through the roof, the eye flashing brightly as it grew excited by the thought of killing the elves before it.

"First you insult me, and then you *threaten* me? I thought you were too *weak* of a ruler to provoke the proverbial bear with a stick, Sorveign. Tread lightly, or you will find out how good possessing a *Unifier* really does you when I invade your home and burn it to the ground with you inside." Eryce was seething as he narrowed his eyes at the willowy being; the implication of the ivy mark finally made Eryce connect the dots of the enigmatic puzzle Sorveign was setting up. He knew, and could certainly admit, that control of a *Unifier* could prove deadly against his own people if they were able to use her the right way . . .

A slight smile played across Sorveign's mouth as Eryce shifted angrily.

"Eryce, if I wanted to *threaten* you, I would simply do it. I am just making you aware of the circumstances. I'm *upping the ante*, as you humans like to say. I had hoped we could come to an agreement over her and use her toward mutual gain, but I can see that you're not interested in something that might be beneficial to both my people and yours.

"Bane is quite the fighter, and she would be a beautiful addition to my own armies. I warn you now, Eryce, that I *will* seek her out, with or without you."

"I wish you luck with that, Sorveign, as I already have a hunter on her, and he tracked her down weeks ago. She is to be brought to me by the double full moon," Eryce responded dismissively, his fingers drumming on the smooth leather of the arm of the chair.

Sorveign was suddenly having a hard time keeping a straight face.

"Yes . . . *about* that. Apparently, *he* is *marked* too, and quite enamored with her, from what I understand."

"Enamored with her *several* times, in fact. I grew tired of *watching*." Jaçon nodded in agreement, all seriousness.

Disgusting race, you elves. Lies and mistruths at every turn, Eryce thought, but the eye did not seem to agree, stubbornly remaining quiet. *I told him to get her to trust him, if he had no other way of bringing her to me in good condition . . . That arrogant bastard is being paid to retrieve her, not fuck her.*

"Now you are just trying to makes me wonder if you're telling the truth. The *marked* hate each other. I know as well as you do that they don't mix, and I can't see it happening now. If he *is marked*, then he's playing a deadly game by acting like he's *enamored with her*, as you put it."

"Something tells me otherwise, dear *king*. She's *full* of surprises." Sorveign wasn't about the tell Eryce that she was banded with a swordsman, a Shephard, and an Aeroyn along with her *marked* lover.

Go after her and see what happens, you stupid man. She's already collecting deadly allies . . . and I hope to be one of them.

Sorveign suddenly stood, and Jaçon followed suit. Eryce remained seated for a moment, deciding whether or not he trusted these *creatures*, knowing he was being dismissed. When he finally stood as well, Sorveign extended his hand across the desk.

"I would like to shake your hand, Eryce. It's such an odd human custom, but I think it is appropriate here when I wish you the best of luck in finding her first."

Eryce didn't bother as he gave Sorveign's hand an irritated glance, refusing to touch the *thing* that towered a good foot over him. He knew this was now a timed game, and the elves not only had a head start but also had more information than he ever did.

Sorveign dropped his hand after a few seconds when Eryce didn't take it, a placid smile spread across his mouth, the façade exuding benevolence and calm as he nodded to Jaçon.

"You may take this *king* back to his castle, Ja—"

"It's about *damned* time! I have my own kingdom to attend to, and you're simply *wasting* your breath. There was no need for me to come here or for us to speak in the future. Good *day*, elf."

Sorveign's smile fell away, and for the first time, Eryce truly understood the mistake he had made by giving this particular elf a cold shoulder. Eryce felt adrenaline dump into his veins as he involuntarily reacted to the frigid glare, and the magic that prickled his skin, his heart suddenly racing as he tried to keep his face and demeanor calm. Sorveign's purple eyes dances with malice and little pinpricks of light that told Eryce that the elf king was barely keeping his anger in check.

"Keep in mind, Eryce, *if* I gain her first, you won't live to regret the burning of Corengale for much longer. It was out of respect for your *wife* that I let you be, but I will *make sure* that warrior princess is instilled on the throne you stole from her when you destroyed her father's kingdom . . ." Sorveign leaned forward and rested his hands on the desk before him, his face a map of aggression and rage.

". . . with *your blood* for the *paint.*"

Sorveign had finally drawn a line in the sand, and Eryce had acquired one more enemy. One he had every right and reason to fear.

Jaçon touched Eryce's shoulder before he could respond, and they vanished.

Eighty-Nine

"How long are you going to stand there with your eyes closed?"

Sudden tears fell from her lashes as Kiera opened her eyes. Connor was right in front of her, the smell of mint and cedar overwhelming at first, and Kiera suddenly realized she hadn't been able to smell him at all for the few short minutes he had been gone.

"You had better be *real, Dirtbag* . . ." she whispered.

He smiled warmly as he reached up and cupped her face in his hands, wiping away both tears with his thumbs, leaning in to kiss her gently.

"Are you *kidding*? I am too delicious to be anything but a dream. You should know that by now, *Princess*."

"I told you never to call me *that*."

"I'm pretty sure I can defend myself this time if you try to beat me senseless, Crazy Lady of the Forest."

Connor pulled Kiera into his embrace, letting her relieved tears soak his shirt.

He held her that way for a long time.

Three down. Two to go . . .